Truth or Dare

By Aimee McNeil

Truth or Dare

Limitless Publishing, LLC
Kailua, HI 96734
www.limitlesspublishing.com

Formatting: Limitless Publishing

ISBN-13: 978-1-68058-333-5
ISBN-10: 1-68058-333-6

Dedication

To my husband, Ryan,
the man that owns my heart.

Chapter One

Sophie stared at the blank canvas in front of her, trying to still her shaking knee. She had been nervous when she arrived this morning. The impending art class had her anxious. It was to be her first nude model session. She had painted many people over her time as an artist, but this was the first time she would be staring at two naked people for a complete two-hour session, translating their exposed bodies onto her canvas with the experience of her hands—hands that currently moved restlessly over her supplies as the seconds ticked by. Everyone else in the class seemed to be in a state of boredom as they watched the clock on the wall.

The professor sat as his desk, loudly sipping his morning coffee. He kept checking his watch, and then confirming that the time correlated with the wall clock. "Hopefully it shouldn't be too much longer," he mumbled as his eyes traveled toward the door, his fingers tapping annoyingly on his desk. His round stomach threatened every button on his shirt as it stretched over his width. His hair was in desperate need of a trim and his beard was riddled with gray. Despite his unkempt appearance, he had grown on Sophie, his appearance quite suitable for the rough-edged professor who seemed to view the world in its own unique light.

Sophie followed his gaze toward the open door. Giggling erupted in the hallway before a young woman shuffled in. "Sorry, Professor." She smiled, her face flushing with color.

"So sorry." The entrancing male voice bordered on sarcasm as the man filled the doorframe. His large presence demanded the attention of everyone in the room because of his dangerous beauty. Sophie's eyes widened in panic and she ducked behind her canvas to avoid being recognized. She could feel the blood rush to her face. Ashton King was standing in her art class with a robe that he barely had tied. *What the hell was he doing here? Just breathe. Just breathe.*

Sophie remembered the first time she had met Ashton. It was her first day at her new school. Her mother had moved them halfway through her freshman year to start her new job. Sophie remembered how nervous she'd been when she walked into her new classroom.

Everyone looked up at Sophie as Mr. Walters, her teacher, introduced her to the class. She found it overwhelming with the sea of eyes on her. She found herself looking down at her worn red shoes to avoid her embarrassment.

Mr. Walters directed her toward the only empty

seat in the class. Ashton was the first person she locked eyes with, and he was the most beautiful boy she had ever seen. He had long blond hair that fell perfectly around his tanned face. His steel blue eyes looked back at her. A smile formed before she realized it, but he did not return the gesture. She let the smile fall as she slid into her desk and turned her attention toward the front of the class. She heard whispering around her, but she couldn't make out any of the words. She tried to make herself as small as possible in her seat, hoping no one would pay any mind to her.

She couldn't shake the feeling that Ashton's gaze was still on her, and it made her uncomfortable. She felt a gentle tug on her hair, causing her to turn around. Everyone seemed to avoiding making eye contact. She turned back with the notion that she might have imagined it, but again someone tugged on it. When she turned this time, the faces behind her were obviously suppressing their laughter. The next time someone pulled her hair, she couldn't help but cry out at the unexpected pain. The teacher spun around from the chalkboard to assess the interruption.

"Sophie?" Mr. Walters narrowed in on her. Sophie couldn't tell if he was angry at her or not because he seemed to have a permanently pained expression on his face.

"Sorry. It won't happen again." Sophie gave a polite smile to Mr. Walters, who gazed at her from over his glasses.

"Is there a problem?" he asked, studying her.

"No, sir."

"Good." He continued onward with the lesson. Sophie turned around in her seat. Ashton was the only one willing to meet her hot glare. She leaned forward in her seat and pulled her long hair up over her shoulder, twisting it tightly in her hands. When the bell rang, signalling the end of class, Sophie rose quickly to her feet. She turned back toward Ashton, leaning down toward him so he would see the meaning in her words. "I will not play your little game," she said angrily at him. His eyes were so beautiful she almost lost her nerve. "Leave me alone." She was ashamed how much he affected her. Sophie was so overwhelmed that she didn't notice that someone put their foot in her path. She tripped and fell between the rows of desks, landing on the floor. She looked up at a girl with a head full of perfectly curled blonde ringlets.

"Oops." She laughed at Sophie. "Nice dress, by the way. Where did you get it? A dumpster?" The girl's laugh was shrill. Sophie couldn't stop herself from looking down at her dress with new eyes. She had been excited to wear it on her first day. She had found the perfect material and made sure she paid special attention to the detail when she made it. She had learned to sew when she was a small girl. Her neighbor, Mrs. Martin, would watch her when her mother worked late. The first time Sophie was introduced to sewing was when Mrs. Martin sewed lace cuffs on her favorite T-shirt when it had grown too small. Now as she looked down at the material she had adored, she couldn't help but suddenly want it off. It felt too tight, too constricting, and tears threatened to fall.

When Mrs. Martin passed away, Sophie remembered crying herself to sleep for days. Mrs. Martin had treated her like family and her kindness would never be forgotten. She had shown Sophie everything she had known about sewing and she had told her beautiful stories about her life. Mrs. Martin had left her sewing machine to Sophie, and she had treasured it from that moment on. It was all she had left of her friend.

Sophie was so embarrassed she couldn't bring herself to speak. Instead, she left the laughter behind and stormed out of the class.

It was the first time that Sophie's anger at Ashton bloomed within her, along with many other confusing feelings that always pulled taut in the pit of her stomach. It was impossible to breathe when he was near, impossible to think—he was a force that pulled and pushed her past her limits. It was also her first experience with Lucinda Jones, the perfectly fashioned queen of the school who held sway over everyone. She was Ashton's girlfriend. Lucinda had made it her personal mission to make Sophie's life hell for the rest of their high school years. Sophie had quickly become a social pariah because Lucinda deemed her an outcast, leading to the loneliest years of her life.

Based on the lustful looks that Ashton was now giving the other model, thoughts of Lucinda were currently the furthest things from his mind. Lucinda had always claimed that she and Ashton were soulmates and would always be together. It was nice to think that for once something finally didn't go Lucinda's way, but the thought immediately made her feel guilty.

Sophie tried to hide herself behind her canvas as Ashton and the strawberry blonde positioned themselves in their suggested pose. She watched Ashton's confident demeanor and wondered how he could be so casual about stripping down in front of a room full of strangers.

Sophie's excitement began to build in the pit of her stomach with the thought of seeing Ashton naked. She completely loathed him for the years of hell he and his horrid girlfriend put her through, but was curious how far his perfection reached.

Ashton discarded his robe and Sophie took a sharp intake of breath before she could stop herself. Ashton's eyes met hers briefly before she slipped behind her canvas. Her face flamed so hot she thought it would melt off. The room became too hot, stifling. *Just breathe. Just breathe.* Taking a deep breath, she opened her eyes and noticed Sally watching her. They had become familiar over the weeks of their course, but that was the extent of their friendship. Outside the classroom their lives took two very different paths.

Sally smiled at her and mouthed, "I want to lick his entire body." Sally gave her a wink before diving into her paints. If only it were that easy for Sophie. She felt like a complete mess. *Please let me get through this.*

Sophie considered just leaving the class with the little dignity she had left. The only thing stopping her was the fact she *needed* the credit for this class. The sitting was important for her final mark. Her hands shook with embarrassment as she reached for her brush. It was amazing how many old emotions began to stir now that she was in Ashton's presence again. She had hoped with the passing of time those intense feelings would dissipate and be nothing more than some weird twisted high school attraction.

Sophie kept her body sheltered behind her canvas until the last possible moment before she had to begin. *He's a jerk. He's a jerk. You don't even like him. In fact, you despise him.* Then her eyes found him. His tall, hard body was chiseled into a perfect male specimen, complete with deliciously golden skin. *Goddamnit!* The sight of him made her stir with hot need. Now she was turned on and overwhelmingly angry at herself. *Why am I such a sucker for punishment when it comes to Ashton King?* She was truly a pathetic disaster and cursed herself for letting him have that power over her.

Consciously making an effort to slow her breathing and her racing heart, she angled her body to more effectively view the models. Sophie refused to let her eyes travel close to Ashton's face. The two of them were posed in a passionate embrace to portray love. Sophie focused her efforts on the girl's form, trying to do justice to her curves. Denying even the slightest glance toward Ashton, she knew his face was angled toward her so she dared not look at him. *I am strong. I am not the same pathetic girl I was in high school. I can do this.*

When the end of class approached, Sophie hastily began packing up her supplies before anyone else. She wanted to make a quick getaway to avoid any interactions with Ashton. She wondered if Ashton and Lucinda kept in touch. He would probably call her up and tell her how laughable Sophie still was three years after high school. Sophie cringed at the thought of the two of them having another thrill at her expense. Physically, Ashton was the most attractive guy she had ever seen. He was tall with a robust athletic build, beautiful bone structure in his face, and a strong defined jawline. His eyes were stormy blue and he had full lips that were made for kissing. He looked like how she always pictured Prince Charming in all the fairytales from her childhood, but he was actually the villain in every other sense.

The sound of his voice as he spoke to someone in the room gave fire to her steps and she gathered her belongings and quickly headed toward the door. She let out a breath of relief as she made her way down the hallway.

"Hey, Sophie." Sophie ignored him, continuing down the hall. "Wait up." Ashton rounded on her. He had his robe thrown on, exposing his tanned, carved chest.

"What?" Sophie surprised herself by her abruptness.

"I noticed that you didn't paint me in your picture. You can't have a picture of love without two people." He raised his eyebrows at her.

"I don't believe in love. I figured I would make a statement." She tried to push past him but he didn't let her pass.

"I know you liked what you saw." He gave her a

boastful smile. *God, those stupid dimples!*

"Always the modest one. Actually, I was shocked that you would actually show yourself in public. I gasped because I thought I was going to throw up." Sophie narrowed her eyes. He was taller than she remembered; he now towered over her. "Why are you even here? Don't you have some stuffy college to attend before you settle into your privileged lifestyle?"

"Ouch." His hand went up to his bare chest and her eyes followed. *Shoot!* Heat immediately filled her cheeks when lust-filled thoughts entered her mind. "That would hurt if I didn't know you were lying."

"I'm not," she said stubbornly, looking past him at her escape route.

"I know you're lying, you always bite your lip after you tell a lie." His eyes lingered on her lips. Sophie brought her hand up to cover her mouth.

"You don't know anything about me." She could feel her emotions swell inside her, choking her.

"If I didn't know any better I would say it was the first time you saw a guy naked. Your cheeks couldn't have turned any redder." He chuckled.

"I have seen plenty of naked men, in fact more than I can count, not that it's any of your concern," Sophie spat out angrily.

Ashton smiled and pointed to her lips. Sophie covered her deceiving mouth again and pushed past him, ignoring the electrical current that seemed to pulse through her with the contact. A tingling sensation lingered where her shoulder had touched him.

"See you never!" she called out behind her, using the words he had always said to her when they were in school.

"Actually, you will see me again. You have to finish that painting, after all," he called down the hall to her retreating form. She would not let him get to her.

Chapter Two

Sophie tried to get the key out of her pocket as she balanced her art supplies. She could hear her phone ringing inside her purse as she stood before her apartment door. Fumbling her things, she managed to kick the door open as everything scattered across the wooden floor. *Goddamnit!* "Hello?" she sighed into her phone. "Mom?"

"Sophie, are you okay?" Sophie could picture her mother's worried expression, the way her brow always furrowed when she thought something was wrong.

"Yes, I'm fine. Just came in the door." Sophie looked down at all her things strewn over the floor. Sophie had always been close to her mother. For most of her life it had been just the two of them. Sophie's mother was only sixteen when she became pregnant. Sophie had never known her father or any other relative.

When Sophie's mother told her family of her pregnancy, she was told to pack her bag and never look back. She was always astounded by her mother's strength. No matter what obstacle was thrown in their path, her mother always found a way, although it was never easy for either of them. It was always a struggle to pay the bills or buy necessities, but no matter how dark things got they always managed to get through.

Sophie remembered when she was five years old and her mother had lost her job. She had been looking for weeks and was unable to find any work. As young as Sophie was at the time, she knew how hard her mother was struggling to keep them afloat. She remembered hearing her mother cry in the middle of the night when she thought Sophie was sleeping.

Sophie remembered walking up and down the streets in front of their apartment looking for coins people dropped. She was so excited with her findings. She surprised her mother by putting it under her pillow so she wouldn't cry anymore. Although it was not much, her mother insisted they buy a treat with it. They went down to the coffee shop and bought a cupcake to share. Sophie loved the smile on her mother's face. It had seemed like it had been such a long time since Sophie had seen her mother happy. The coffee shop owner had put a **'Help Wanted'** sign in the window while they were enjoying their treat. Sophie's mother gave her a big hug. "You are my lucky charm, baby girl." She smiled before she grabbed the sign out of the window and followed the owner.

Even in the hardest of times Sophie's mother always managed to put food on the table for her, even if it was only enough for Sophie. She could remember many times that her mother would slide a plate of food in front of her in their sparse, dimly lit apartment and sit on the other side with nothing to eat herself. Her mother refused to let Sophie share, saying that it was important that she grow up healthy and strong. She had always told Sophie that she would always make sure she would never be hungry no matter what happened. It was a promise she always kept. Sophie remembered pretending she was full so her mother would be able to eat. She never ate until she knew that Sophie had enough. Sophie always treasured her mother's love and strength.

"Okay…well, I was just calling to check on you *and*…to tell you that I mailed the invitations today!" Her mother's excitement brought a smile to her face.

"That's great, Mom! I'm fine. It's just been a long day." Her mother had met her fiancé, Peter, almost two years ago now. Sophie had gotten used to seeing him on her weekend trips home to visit her mom after she moved away to attend school. Peter was a police officer that had pulled her mother over for a broken taillight. They said that it only took that brief moment for them to realize there was something between them. Peter had been in her mother's life ever since. Her mother had dedicated her life to raising Sophie and working as much as she could to pay the bills. Sophie liked knowing that she was finally living for herself. Peter was the first and only man she introduced to Sophie. She had known her mother had dated over the years, but she kept that part of her life separate. Sophie only ever saw the fallout of those relationships.

Sophie was reluctant at first when she met Peter, but he had proven himself over that last few years and over that time Sophie began to accept him. Her reservations fell away and she could see the man that had swept her mother off her feet. She was grateful for Peter's timing in coming into her mother's life—it gave Sophie peace of mind that her mother wasn't alone. Peter gave a new brightness to her mother's eyes that Sophie had never seen before, and that was priceless.

"Don't work too hard, honey."

"Is there any other way?" Sophie responded with sarcastic humor. Since Sophie was able to help her mother with the bills, she did whatever she could. She worked as many hours as possible without letting her schoolwork suffer. She also saved for university from the first paycheck. Sophie insisted on her independence as soon as she was capable, especially now that her mother was finally creating a foundation for her new life, planning her wedding and buying a home with Peter.

"Love you, honey. Call me if you need anything."

"I will. Love you too, Mom." Sophie hung up the phone and reached for her things that still lay haphazardly in her entranceway. When she grabbed her purse from the floor, she shrieked as a furry creature ran between her legs.

***

Sophie banged on her landlord's door without

mercy. She knew he was home; she could hear his television. "Mr. Cleary!" Sophie called through the door. There were only three apartments in the townhouse, which was converted into rentals, and her landlord resided in the lower unit. Mr. Cleary was the perfect embodiment of the worst landlord on the face of the Earth as far as Sophie was concerned. Unfortunately the lack of apartments that she could afford in the downtown area meant that she was stuck with him for now.

"Mr. Cleary, I know you're in there. I need to speak with you." She leaned against the wall in frustration.

"Last week I had to camp out there when my showerhead broke and I am still waiting for the plumber to show up that he promised me. Luckily my boy toy likes the fact that I go over there to shower." Mel winked as she stomped down the stairs in her black lace-up boots that tied all the way up to mid-thigh. Mel lived in the upper floor apartment. Sophie had met her the first day she had moved into the building. Sophie's mother had helped her move and was helping her unpack when Mel walked in to introduce herself. Mel had worn the same boots as she did now, with a tight black leather mini skirt and see-through shirt. Her makeup had been applied so heavily that Sophie could not even picture what she really looked like beneath the layers. Her shoulder length hair was backcombed and sprayed heavily with sparkles. It was during this first encounter that Mel had informed them that she was a stripper and had just come from work. The look of panic on her mother's face was priceless. Sophie had learned quickly that Mel loved making people unsettled.

Two years had passed and Sophie had grown fond of her neighbor and appreciated her straightforwardness. There was no fluff with Mel, and Sophie could always count on her for the raw truth. It had taken many hours of convincing her mother to let her stay, though, especially after they had the luxury of meeting Mr. Cleary.

"Hey, Mel." Sophie sighed half-heartedly. "My furry friends are back."

"Yeah, those furry little shits have been leaving their mark in my apartment too. Let me know if you have any luck with the fat piece of fuck." Mel inclined her head toward Mr. Cleary's door. "Off to shake my money maker." Mel swayed her hips exaggeratedly. "By the way, a little concealer would do those dark circles some good," she said as she continued down the stairs, leaving a trail of overpowering perfume.

"Love you too," Sophie called after her sarcastically.

Sophie jumped as Mr. Cleary's door swung open. "What?" he barked, raking his gaze up and down Sophie's entire body. Sophie stepped back. Mr. Cleary wore a white sleeveless shirt with stains down the front of his round stomach, gray torn jogging pants, and bare feet. What remained of his hair was unkempt and in need of a good washing. He rubbed his unshaven face and looked at Sophie from his dark beady eyes.

"The mice are back. You have to do something about them." Sophie crossed her arms over her chest. She learned long ago that pleasantries did nothing for Mr. Cleary. He took advantage of any niceties to buy himself time.

"I haven't noticed any mice. You sure it wasn't your imagination?" He breathed heavily as he leaned against the door frame. A permanent sheen of perspiration always beaded upon his forehead.

"Oh I'm positive." Sophie narrowed her eyes and tapped her foot.

"I'll check it out," he grunted. If Sophie wasn't already late she would have stayed and made sure he followed through, but she had to leave for work. She knew that nothing would come of their conversation because "I'll check it out" was Mr. Cleary's usual response, which translated to "I'll do nothing." Sophie rolled her eyes as Mr. Cleary disappeared back into his apartment, slamming the door.

***

"I'm here!" Sophie called into the back room as she grabbed her apron from the wall hook.

"Your perfect record is broken, Sophie." Sam shook his head in playful disappointment. He was tall, with a kind smile and attractive charm. Sam wore his dark hair short with a heavy five o'clock shadow covering his cheeks. He was a runner and the effects showed in his slim, toned physique. Sophie had always liked Sam's company. He was always warm and friendly to her.

The other waitresses had always teased her about Sam's infatuation with her; until recently she'd brushed the comments aside, thinking they were being ridiculous. Last week, however, their comments seemed less outlandish. Sophie had walked into the kitchen carrying a tray of plates and accidently walked into Sam. She luckily caught the tray before it slipped from her grasp. His hands found their way on her, helping her find her footing, but they lingered way too long for a helpful hand. The way he looked into her eyes made her breath catch in her throat. Now she wasn't sure what to think. When it came to men, Sophie was completely unsure of herself. Since she'd been old enough to work she'd thrown herself into it. Her mission was to make enough money to pay for school so her mother didn't have to take on a third job. She never allowed time for dating.

Sophie was never good at reading people and tended to avoid any attention that brought the possibility of something more. She didn't have time for dating because she was focused on keeping her head out of the water. Now, when she found herself in Sam's company she feared their relationship had changed. She no longer felt at ease in his company. She preferred keeping her head down and getting from point A to point B without any distractions. There was also the huge fact that he was her manager. Fear of the potential fallout and what that meant for her employment far outweighed anything good that could come of an intimate relationship.

Especially when she listened to the other girls speak of their numerous failed attempts at finding love. Sophie didn't believe that two people could fall in lasting love like in all the fairytales from childhood. The only love she believed in was between a mother and child. She wished she could go back to before she knew of his attraction. It was so much simpler then. Feelings always complicated matters. She didn't like complicated. *Ugh!*

"Anything wrong?" he asked with concern.

"No…I was trying to get my landlord to deal with the mice running rampant in my apartment. I'm really sorry. I lost track of time." She gave him a tight smile, nothing too inviting.

Sam leaned in and placed his hand on her shoulder. She watched his eyes follow the touch of his hand and slowly move back to meet her gaze. "I was…"

"Oh good, Sophie, you're here! I need a break." Megan stomped into the kitchen, hanging her apron on the hook.

Sophie let out a relieved breath, thankful for the interruption. Sam pulled his hand away quickly. Megan raised her eyebrow toward Sophie when Sam turned to leave. Sophie only shrugged in response. She had no idea what to think of it. Sam was attractive, anyone who looked at him knew that, but Sophie couldn't help the uneasy feeling that bloomed within her at the thought of something more between them.

"Don't forget you promised to come out with us tonight," Megan called as she skipped off toward the washrooms.

"Yeah, yeah." Sophie took a deep breath and pushed through the doors out into the dining room. She forced a smile on her face and immersed herself in her job.

The restaurant was one of the busiest in town, which meant Sophie never stopped her entire shift, especially when she worked the evening rush. She liked the fast pace—time slipped away—and before long her shift would be over. The other waiters and waitresses were good company and they had all became close over the two years that she'd worked there. Many of them would get together after work, but Sophie usually passed because she was eager to get home and paint. Painting consumed much of her free time as well as her passion for reading and sewing, all of which were not conducive to a very exciting social life.

"Hottie alert." Lori brushed past Sophie as she nodded toward one of Sophie's tables that the hostess had seated. Sophie approached the table.

"What would you like this evening?" She smiled despite her exhaustion. Her new heels were wreaking havoc on her feet and her skirt suddenly seemed too short as one of the guys skimmed her legs with his eyes before looking up at her.

"That depends on what you are offering." Sophie's smile fell away when she noticed who had spoken to her.

"Seriously!" Sophie narrowed her eyes at Ashton. It irritated her how attractive he was. She tried to suppress the urge to slap his face. *How can you completely adore and despise dimples at the same time?* Nothing like the seduction of evil, it would be safer to throw herself off a bridge than to even admit that he affected her.

"Must be fate." He raised his brows suggestively.

"I don't believe in fate. What do you want to drink this evening?" She turned her attention to Ashton's company, trying to ignore the beacon of awareness that pulled her to him like a moth to a flame.

"You don't believe in fate and you don't believe in love. Tell me what you do believe in, then?"

"I see you've already met my brother." Sophie jumped at Megan's unexpected arrival.

"Your brother?" Sophie tried to recover gracefully, placing a hand upon her chest to calm her beating heart.

Megan introduced the dark haired gentleman sitting beside Ashton. "Sophie, this is Jack, my older brother." Jack winked at Sophie and his smile lit up his features as he reached across the table to shake Sophie's hand.

"It is a pleasure, Sophie." His gave her hand a gentle squeeze. His polite behavior was like a refreshing drink compared to the unrelenting heat that Ashton's presence brought.

"He's coming out with us tonight, along with the rest of these losers." Megan teased the guys at the table. Sophie immediately saw the similarities between Megan and Jack once Megan had introduced him. They both had the same dark hair and similar eyes.

"You're all coming out tonight?" Sophie tried to make her voice sound casual. Her gaze settled on Ashton, who was looking back at her with arrogance. "*All* of you?" she repeated, waiting for specific confirmation from Ashton.

"We can catch up on old times." Ashton leaned

back and looked up at her through his illegally long dark lashes. *He's a jerk. He's a jerk. Don't look at those eyes!*

"You two know each other?" Megan raised her eyebrows, waiting for an explanation. For a moment Sophie thought she saw disappointment flash on Megan's face.

"Yeah, we go way back." Ashton waved his hand to dramatize his point.

"Yeah, way back to *hating* each other," Sophie offered stiffly.

"Hate is such a strong word." Ashton placed his hand on his chest in mock hurt. "I'm sure we can be civil for one night. Can't we, Sophie?"

Sophie watched Megan's smile turn genuine once again. Megan seemed relieved to find out they were enemies. She could see the obvious attraction Megan had for Ashton. The way her eyes lingered on him and the way her voice was slightly off when she spoke to him gave it away.

"You promised, Sophie." Megan nudged her.

Sophie closed her eyes for a moment and took a deep breath. "Of course." She forced enthusiasm for Megan's sake. She had promised Megan that she would go out with the girls for the night. She was starting to feel like this was a ploy to try to hook her up with Jack. Megan had made a few comments about how she thought Sophie would be a good match for her brother. Megan's intentions were starting to unfold, and Sophie was starting to dread the evening to come. She would know better next time not to promise Megan something without getting all the details first.

"So were you two a couple or something?" Megan asked, looking between Ashton and Sophie.

"No, definitely not," Sophie answered quickly, breaking into an awkward laugh. "God, no." She quickly composed herself when she realized how rude she was beginning to sound. Clearing her throat, she tried to redeem herself. "It was never anything like that."

Jack nudged Ashton's arm. "I never thought I would see the day that a girl didn't like Ashton. Well, at least not before he—"

"Hey now." Ashton cut Jack off before he could finish his sentence.

"I can appreciate a woman who can see past Ashton's pretty face." The guy sitting on the other side of Jack smiled at Sophie. "I like you already." It was the first time their friend had spoken up. He was pleasant to look at with an innocent boy next door look. He had neatly trimmed brown hair and friendly eyes.

"Tonight is going to be so much fun." Megan smiled. "I need to get moving before I get in trouble." Megan gave a small wave as she left their table.

Sophie wished she could be as optimistic about tonight as Megan, but when she looked up and caught the wicked glint in Ashton's eyes, she knew she was doomed.

Chapter Three

Sophie didn't have time to make or even shop for an appropriate outfit for the evening, not to mention the lack of funds she currently had. After raiding her closet and coming up short with inspiration the day before, she had asked Mel if she could borrow something.

What was I thinking? Sophie stared at her reflection in the bathroom mirror of the restaurant, annoyed that she hadn't bothered to try on the options Mel gave her before now. They both looked fine on the hanger, but now that she tried them on she realized she should have known better than to assume they would work.

Out of the two dresses, only one covered enough skin to make it appropriate for a public appearance and it was still pushing it. It hugged her every curve in a form-fitting style and was a little too revealing along the neckline for her ample chest. A knot formed in the pit of her stomach with the anticipation of the night to come.

Sophie ran her fingers through her hair,

untangling her loose waves. She always had her hair up for work and class, and she couldn't remember the last time she had worn it down. She hadn't really paid attention to how long it was getting until now as it cascaded down her back in a dark curtain.

"Are you ready?" Megan walked in the bathroom. "Holy shit, Sophie!"

"I know. I borrowed it without trying it on first. Maybe I should just go home." Sophie's voice sounded deflated.

"What's up?" Lori was on Megan's heels. "Wow, Sophie. You look so *hot*."

"I think my brother is going to die when he sees what you were hiding under your uniform," Megan gushed.

"I wish you would have told me that was your plan. I don't like being set up." Sophie tried to keep her mood calm but the uneasy feeling was setting her on edge.

"But you would have said no," Megan complained guiltily.

"Exactly." Sophie glared at her.

"Just tonight. Please…I promise I won't do it again." Megan bit her lip innocently and batted her eyes. "Besides, he's expecting you. You don't want to crush his dreams, do you?"

Sophie rolled her eyes. "Fine." She sighed. "But you owe me."

"Yay! So what's with you and Ashton, anyway? Did something happen between you two?" Megan asked nervously. Sophie knew the question was on Megan's tongue since she had discovered they had history. She was surprised she waited this long to ask.

"No, nothing like that. It was more of a story of hate at first sight. His evil girlfriend made my life hell in school. My high school years pretty much consisted of hiding from the wrath of the great Ashton and Lucinda. It's never a wise thing to make enemies with the most popular kids on the first day at a new school. It means certain doom for your social life."

"Well, I can't see him hating you tonight unless he's gay." Lori turned her lips down.

"Let's go." Megan pulled the door open, leading the way. "You made a great impression on Jack." Megan said. "He thinks you're lovely!"

The girls walked to the club only a few blocks away from their restaurant. The guys had already left. Sophie followed Megan and Lori past the long line that stretched down the street. Apparently they were regulars because the bouncer waved them through without a second thought.

The bar had an alluring interior with a modern, warm feel and a well-planned lighting scheme that gave the perfect atmosphere. The music throbbed, making excitement pulse through the bodies of all the partygoers reveling in the appeal of the moment. It was the perfect backdrop for people to forget what was happening beyond these walls.

"We have to take you out more often. You are a hot guy magnet!" Lori yelled, leaning into Sophie. Her voice barely registered over the music. Sophie only responded with a tense smile. It wasn't long before they found the guys leaning against the bar ordering drinks.

"Hey, big brother!" Megan elbowed Jack and snatched his drink off the counter.

"Hey," he complained, but a smile quickly followed. "Can I get you a drink, Sophie?"

"Um…yeah, sure." Sophie tried to relax. She looked over at Ashton and immediately regretted it. His hot stare was zeroed in on her. She couldn't stop the traitorous thought when it entered her mind of how gorgeous he looked leaning on the bar. He was tall and his shoulders filled his shirt beautifully. The thoughts caused anger to heat her face. She looked away quickly, hoping that ignoring him would be the best solution. *I hate you. I hate you.*

"What would you like?" Jack asked.

"Oh…" She didn't really drink so she wasn't even sure what her options were.

"Nothing hard. She looks like she's a bit of a lightweight." Ashton's gaze wandered to her exposed chest. "Or maybe not." Sophie had to stop the urge to cover her chest with her hands.

"I can hold my liquor just fine, thank you very much," Sophie proclaimed and turned to Jack. "I'll have what he's having." She pointed toward Ashton without looking at him. Her practical side, which she prided herself on, diminished in Ashton's presence. Her turmoil of emotions seemed to cloud over common sense.

"Whiskey on the rocks?" Jack asked skeptically. "You sure you don't want something more…"

"Girly, like a Long Island iced tea?" Lori suggested, holding hers up for Sophie to see.

"No, whiskey sounds good," she insisted. Truth was that she had never tasted whiskey before and she hoped that she would be able to stomach it. She had tasted beer before and a few wines but she didn't really have a taste for either of them so she usually opted out of drinking. The knot in her stomach twisted in warning that she was about to get in over her head, but seeing Ashton standing there with his judging eyes, she couldn't stop her downward spiral.

When Jack placed the drink in her hand, she smiled thankfully and brought it to her lips. The smell of it made her stomach groan in protest but she was determined to drink it out of spite. She took a sip and looked up to see everyone waiting for her reaction. It took everything she had not to make a sour face from the disgusting taste that lingered in her mouth. "It's great." She forced a smile despite the burning sensation in her throat that made her eyes water.

Megan encouraged conversation between Sophie and Jack, playing the obvious matchmaker. Sophie actually didn't mind—in fact she was surprised to discover how much she enjoyed Jack's company. He had a good sense of humor and an easy personality, but as much as she found Jack attractive and appreciated his company, the similarities between him and his sister made it hard to think of him outside the "friend zone."

Sophie made every attempt to ignore Ashton's presence, but as she continued to consume alcohol it was becoming increasingly difficult. Ashton disrupted her concentration and affected her on many levels. All of the deep regressed feelings seemed to surface around him. Even now at the bar with her back turned toward Ashton, she was aware of him.

"Sophie?" Jack brought her back from her thoughts.

"What?" Sophie focused on Jack standing in front of her.

"I must be boring you," he stated lightly with a chuckle.

"No, no, of course not," Sophie said reassuringly. "The whiskey is just getting to me."

"I asked if you wanted to dance."

"Sure, I would love to." Sophie noticed Megan stumble and practically fall into Ashton. He had an amused look on his face as he righted her. Sophie grabbed her drink off the bar and downed the rest of the liquid in the glass and tried to ignore the fire that erupted in her as it flowed down her throat. She found her eyes following Ashton's hands as he placed them on Megan's waist. A twinge of jealousy twisted in her, and she almost gasped in disbelief at her double-crossing emotions. She quickly replaced the feeling with anger, setting her jaw. Anger was safe when it came to Ashton. *Safe and justified*, she reminded herself.

"I think Megan is having a good time." She tried to keep her words light.

"Too good. At this rate I'll be carrying her home. Unfortunately, it won't be the first time," he said with a disappointed tone. "Let's go. I think my time is limited." Jack pushed off the bar and went to whisper something in his sister's ear before turning back toward Sophie. Whatever he said didn't sit well with Megan, who stuck her tongue out and ordered another drink from the bartender.

Sophie followed Jack out onto the dance floor. "Are you sure Megan is safe to leave with *Ashton*? In her condition, I mean?"

"It's not Ashton I'm worried about." Jack led them through the many dancing bodies. Sophie turned back in Megan and Ashton's direction, but she couldn't see them through the sea of people.

Jack knew how to move his body; she found herself giving in to the music quickly and a smile took over her face. She couldn't remember the last time she really let go and enjoyed the moment. The effects of the alcohol were giving her body a newfound confidence.

A new song took over the energy in the room. The beat was slower and more sensual in nature and Sophie found her body pressed against Jack's as more people crowded the dance floor. She felt his hand slide around her waist and pull her closer. *Do I want this?* Jack leaned in to whisper in her ear, but the unceremonious arrival of Megan startled them both. Megan was closely followed by Ashton, who suddenly became a beacon, drawing her complete attention. Megan stumbled on her heels, practically taking out a few bystanders, but Ashton caught her and pulled her close. Megan immediately began to run her hands over Ashton's body seductively, reaching up under his shirt. Sophie could see Jack's body tense because of his sister's display.

"Sorry, Sophie. I had a great time but I have to take my sister home. Do you need a drive?" Jack's concern toward his sister was apparent in his whole demeanor, but he still had a gentle touch as he placed his hand upon her back.

"No, I'm good. Take care of Megan. I had a great time too." She smiled at him when he pulled away to look into her eyes.

Jack's gaze lingered as he looked down at her. He seemed as if he had more to say, but instead he just nodded and turned his attention toward his sister. She watched as Megan and Jack began to argue. He took her arm and led her off the dance floor. Megan was obviously not being compliant with her brother, but at least she had enough sense not to make too much of a scene. Sophie was left staring up at Ashton's imposing form. He raised a brow at her but she didn't wait for his obnoxious remark. Instead, she turned toward the bar where Lori and Matthew had returned to order drinks.

"Hey guys. Megan and Jack just left," Sophie informed them as she took the empty stool next to Lori.

"Yeah, we saw." Matthew shook his head slightly. "Hard to miss."

"It's not an unusual occurrence. Megan doesn't know her limit." Lori dismissed it, though Sophie could tell it was a sore spot. "How's your night going?"

"Good. I'm having fun." Sophie smiled. She turned when another glass of whiskey was slid in front of her. It made her nauseous just looking at the amber liquid.

"What's the matter? I thought you liked it. In fact, your exact words were 'It's great,'" Ashton mocked. She could feel his heat upon her side from his close proximity.

"It is. In fact it's probably the best thing I've ever tasted," she said stubbornly. She sipped the foul liquid and made an exaggerated moan of pleasure.

"I wouldn't do that or you might regret it," Ashton said into his glass as he took a drink.

"What's that supposed to mean?" She turned her body toward him, squaring her shoulders.

"Do you remember the last time you made something look that appealing?" He smirked. Heat flamed through her at the memory. She knew immediately what he was referring to, but tried to force herself to remain unaffected.

It had been four painful months since she started her new school. Lucinda was showing no signs of getting bored with making Sophie the front page gossip. It was after school. Sophie had lingered in the library, waiting for the hallway to clear out. She was heading toward her locker when she stopped at the bake sale table as they were packing up for the day. She recognized the seniors from around the school. They had been raising money for their prom for weeks.

"Can I buy that blueberry turnover?" Sophie asked, eyeing the pastry.

Ashton rounded the corner with his bag slung over his shoulder. The hallway was basically clear now with everyone gone for the day, so the sound of his footsteps echoed as he approached.

"Hey ladies," Ashton charmed. The girls were two years his senior, but they still swooned when he spoke to them. Sophie just kept to herself. She didn't

acknowledge him as she passed over the money.

"Those turnovers look good. Have any more?" Ashton asked the girls.

"No, sorry. That was the last one," the girl apologized.

Sophie turned around and looked back at Ashton.

"Too bad." She called back to him shamelessly. "They are really delicious." She didn't know what got into her. Sophie took a bite of the pastry, doing her best to accentuate how good it tasted. "I think this is actually the best thing I have ever tasted." Sophie turned the corner and continued down the hall. She dropped her books and leaned against her locker. "Mmmm..." The pastry was sinfully good. She took the last bite and licked the icing from her fingers before spinning her lock and opening her locker.

Sophie gasped in shock when Ashton suddenly leaned in next to her. "What are you doing?" She looked up and down the hallway and was horrified to realize they were alone. Her heart beat so loudly she was terrified Ashton would be able to hear it.

"That was mean." He leaned in toward her.

"You would know," Sophie said quickly. She opened her mouth to speak but he cut off her words when he brought his lips against hers. His hands reached up and cupped her cheeks, pulling her into his kiss. She was shocked and overcome with the pleasure of how he felt against her. His tongue caressed the inside of her mouth and she found herself melting against him. She was horrified when a moan of pleasure escaped, bringing her back to

reality. She couldn't believe she had given him the satisfaction. Ashton abruptly pulled back with a smug look on his face and Sophie wanted to scream.

"You're right, it was as good as it looked," he said, licking his lips. "Blueberry is my favorite." She stood in front of him, dazed. She was floored with how desperately she wanted to kiss him again.

"I always knew you secretly wanted me," he boasted.

"I do not!" Sophie gasped. "You just took me by surprise." Her face flamed with embarrassment. She never wanted to disappear so much in her life.

He chuckled at her pathetic display. "See you never." He called out as he walked away from her.

Sophie remembered watching him turn the corner before she let her tears fall. Nothing that Lucinda had ever done to her had left her so devastated. She was crushed.

Chapter Four

Sophie wanted to slap the satisfied look off Ashton's face. "I tried every mouthwash I could get my hands on trying to get the taste of your foul mouth from mine." Sophie narrowed her eyes accusingly.

"If I remember correctly you quite enjoyed it," he argued arrogantly.

"Well, you remember wrong. Next time you try to do something like that you'll regret it. You just caught me off guard."

"Next time? Trust me, I regretted it the first time."

Sophie already knew the truth, but it didn't make it any less painful as he waved it in front of her.

Sophie turned and caught Lori and Matthew watching them. Lori seemed desperate for insight on what was unfolding between the two of them. Sophie tried to seem casual but she wasn't selling it to either of them.

Sophie brought her attention to the drink in her hand. The heat of her anger burned at her skin. "I hate you." Her eyes flicked toward Ashton before she downed her entire glass. Her senses were now numb to the horrible taste and burn of the whiskey. There was only a slight warming in her stomach. Sophie stood up on her unsteady feet and stormed off to the dance floor. The rush of the new liquor fueled her body as she moved. She suddenly realized that she may have overdone her consumption. Her body felt lighter, the room swayed, the music called to her on a primal level, and she no longer felt the uncomfortable press of bodies as she moved to the music.

Strong hands wrapped around her waist, pulling her back against a hard warm body. Her numb state of mind was driven purely by physical response and was no longer processing on a logical level. She knew it was Ashton. Excitement rushed through her at the sight of his hands on her body. She didn't question it. She was fueled by the lust that the music pumped through her. She leaned into him, letting her soft curves press against him. He felt too good to be true, the way his hands moved over her. In her foggy state of mind she couldn't think about anything other than wanting this.

Ashton leaned down against her neck, his breath hot against her skin. It caused an explosion of desire to blossom deep within her, and she reached up to pull him down to her. "Admit how much you want me," he said close to her ear, causing her eyes to snap open. She spun around to face him. Her breath was still heavy with the need. She clamped her eyes shut, overcome with dizziness. She couldn't believe she didn't see this coming. She had actually encouraged him to touch her. Her illusion came crashing down. *Why do I always fall into his stupid trap?*

She ran off the dance floor and headed straight for the exit. She needed to get away from Ashton. He had a power over her that scared her. The cool night air offered little relief as she continued up the street without stopping.

"Sophie!" She heard her name being called. She didn't turn around—she knew who it was. Ashton was probably trying to gloat about the fact that she practically had given herself to him on the dance floor. Embarrassment consumed her and burned away at the effects of the liquor.

She ignored him as long as she could but he remained insistently on her heels. "Why are you following me? If you haven't figured it out, I'm trying to get away from *you*."

"Your friends would kill me if they knew I let you walk home alone." He justified his pursuit. "I know Jack well enough to know he would have my throat. He's a stickler for chivalry."

"Chivalry isn't really your style, is it? Well, don't worry your pretty little panties. I can take care of myself. I always have," Sophie fumed as she heard his chuckle. She didn't want to amuse him. She wanted to cause him great physical harm.

After another block, she swung around to face him. "What do you not understand about leave…me…alone? You're the last person on this entire planet that I want following me home."

"I hardly believe I am the last person, especially after that display on the dance floor," he said in his irritatingly confident tone.

"Grrr…" She picked up her pace, hoping he would back off.

"Did you just growl at me?"

"I hate you!" She looked back and loathed the fact that he had long legs and seemed to be keeping up with her pace easily. *I hate you so much!*

"So you keep saying." She hated that he was so unaffected by her, and she could barely think straight in his company. "*Funny*, I don't believe you."

When Sophie reached her apartment, she grabbed her keys from her purse. "Well, believe it!" Sophie yelled back.

"I'll walk you to your door, that way I know you won't trip and fall on your face between here and there." His tone took on a more serious tone, making her nervous.

Sophie stomped up the flight of stairs to her door. "If you have some big plan to humiliate me even more, then I hate to disappoint you, but there is no audience here. I am at my door. Go away now." When she turned around, Ashton was closer than she expected. He leaned in and muffled her gasp with his demanding lips. The kiss was so unexpected, but she responded greedily before she could register what she was doing. She pulled him closer, lost in a moment of pure physical weakness as she devoured his lips. She reveled in the way he knew how to kiss. In that moment she wanted him with more passion than she thought physically possible until a small breach of clarity shone through her fog of lust. Sophie bit down on his lip until she threatened to draw blood. Ashton pulled back abruptly with a curse.

"I told you you'd regret it." She was determined to gain the upper hand in the situation. She hated the fact that she was breathless and could feel the heat in her face.

A sly smile spread across his face. Sophie noticed his lip already looked swollen from her bite. "Admit how much you want me." He reached out for her, and Sophie slapped his hand away.

"I don't want you." Sophie tried to keep her voice calm but he rattled her.

"You're biting your lip, Sophie. We know what that means."

"I am completely unaffected by you, Ashton King, and I have hated you from the moment I saw you," Sophie stated angrily. "Don't ever kiss me again!" *Why the hell did he just kiss me?* "I hate you!"

His eyes dropped to her lips with a smile. It was an unconscious habit she cursed. Her feelings for him had always frightened her. What did it mean about her character to be attracted to someone who chose to make her life miserable? *I am a mess.*

"I hate you too." He spoke with a tender softness that confused her. Then he turned on his heel and left. *What the hell was that?* Sophie stood in her hallway, completely confounded. She wasn't sure what to make of the confusion that toyed with her thoughts, and the influence of the alcohol did not help the situation.

***

The next morning Sophie woke with a headache. It felt like someone was carving out her skull. She moaned as she crawled out of bed, heading straight to her medicine cabinet for something to dull the pain. Scrubbing her hands over her face, she reached in her shower to turn on the water. She screamed and stumbled backward when she noticed movement in her tub. Two mice were scurrying around, trying to find an escape. "Come on!" she complained as she went to her closet to find a bucket. "Of all days!" *I hate my life!*

Pulling back the curtain, she slipped on her cleaning gloves and tried to grab the furry little creatures. "You little *buggers*!" They evaded her grasp, darting around the slippery surface of the tub. Sophie screamed out in triumph when she clamped down on one of them. When she had them both contained, she set the bucket outside of her apartment door until she could deal with it. Although the bucket was deep, she didn't want to risk them escaping inside while she got ready.

The hot water soothed her tired body, giving her renewed energy. The pain medication was starting to take effect—the prospect of getting through the day seemed more bearable. When she stepped out of the shower and looked at her reflection, memories of the night before came flooding back to her. The thought of Ashton against her lips caused her to cringe. She was disappointed that she had let things get out of hand. The fact that the memory brought heat to her face made it even worse. Her only hope was that she would never see him again. "I am so pathetic," she moaned at her reflection.

Once Sophie was dressed and ready, she collected the bucket from outside. Surprisingly, Mr. Cleary opened after only a few knocks.

"Here, I brought you a present. I'm gonna need the bucket back, by the way." She smirked as she thrust it into his hands. The shocked look on his face as he looked inside was priceless but Sophie didn't stick around, even when he called after her.

The fresh morning air was revitalizing and just what she needed. Her mouth practically watered as she approached her favorite tea shop. Grabbing a tea and bagel, she sat down next to the window to feel the warm sun. Just the smell of the tea soothed her. She searched employment listings on her phone, scanning through the potential opportunities. She would be graduating soon and would have extra time she could apply to another job until she found something more permanent. The restaurant provided a good paycheck, not to mention the tips, but she was tired of living month to month and wanted to put some savings away. She didn't want to be in the position where she would have to ask her mother for help. So far she had been lucky, but a safety net wouldn't hurt.

A text message notification popped up on her phone.

Unknown: Did you have fun last night?

Sophie was confused by the message until she figured Megan probably gave Jack her number. She assumed it must be him, but she wanted to make sure.

Sophie: Jack?

Within a few minutes she had a response.

Jack: Yeah. Anything exciting happen after I left?

Sophie: No. Didn't stay very long after that. How is Megan?

Jack: Hungover but she'll survive. You got home safe I take it?

Sophie: Yep. I survived.

Jack: Did Ashton take you home?

Sophie's cheeks immediately heated at the mention of Ashton.

Sophie: Yes.

Jack: Hopefully he behaved himself.

She wondered if Ashton mentioned anything to Jack about what had happened between them. Her fingers nervously hovered over her phone; she was at a loss as to how to respond. She realized that she had to be straightforward with Jack. She wasn't looking for a relationship and she needed to let him know.

Sophie: I had a wonderful time last night. I

think you are great but I am not looking to get involved with anyone right now. I just wanted to let you know.

A few minutes went by and no response. Sophie nervously sipped her tea. She knew it was the right thing to do because she didn't want to lead him on. Then her phone beeped, drawing her attention.

Jack: I have a confession. My family doesn't know this but I actually play for the other team. I thought we hit it off last night and I think we could be great friends. Is that okay? PS: please don't tell Megan. I obviously haven't enlightened her yet.

Sophie was surprised with his confession and relieved at the same time. The thought did not even cross her mind last night he was gay. His demeanor and the times she caught him looking at her chest did not support his claim, though she was far from an expert on reading people.

Sophie: I think we can be great friends. PS: my lips are sealed.

Jack: Good. BTW Ashton is hot! I know you noticed.

Sophie: Yeah but EVIL!

Jack: He can't be that bad.

Sophie: Sure is. I have lots of stories that will let you know just how much. But right now I am scanning the employment ads to add job #2 to my schedule.

Jack: Looking forward to it. If you need a job I know of an assistant job that just came available. It's not too far from your restaurant. Flexible hours. Great pay.

Sophie: I'm intrigued!

Jack: Let me get back to you with the details.

Sophie: Thank you!

Sophie had enjoyed Jack's company and thought a friendship between them would be a good thing. She didn't really have anyone to chat with on a regular basis. Mel was her closest friend and her schedule was all over the place, with her disappearing for days at a time.

About twenty minutes later, when Sophie was finishing up, her phone beeped with a message from Jack. It had the contact information and a few more details in regards to the job. Sophie decided to go for it. She dialed the number immediately.

"Hello?" a woman's voice answered after a few rings.

"Hello, my name is Sophie Rogers. I am calling for Mrs. Darcy in regards to an employment opportunity."

"Yes, wonderful, this is she. You have such a

lovely voice, dear. We should set up a meeting to discuss the position. When are you available?"

"I'm available today until 3:00, or tomorrow evening," Sophie suggested.

"How about 11:00 this morning?"

Sophie looked at the time; it was 9:25. "Sure, I can make that work. Should I come to you?"

"Yes, dear. That would be lovely. The address is 43 Simons Street."

"I know the street. Thank you, Mrs. Darcy." Sophie ended the call feeling excited about the new employment opportunity. She needed to head home for a quick change before she caught the bus to her interview.

When she approached her apartment door she noticed her bucket sitting against it. She looked in and was relieved to see that the mice were gone. She grabbed the bucket and headed straight for her closet. After a quick assessment of her wardrobe, she selected a black and white floral print skirt with a simple blouse in a muted pastel green. She completed the look with modest black heels. Looking in the mirror, she decided to leave her hair down so she didn't look too formal. She added some blush to her cheeks and a clear gloss to her lips before heading out the door.

Sophie grabbed her phone and dialed her mother's number. When the answer machine picked up, she left her a quick message. Before she tucked her phone in her bag she sent a text to Jack.

Sophie: Heading off to a job interview with Mrs. Darcy. Wish me luck.

Jack: Wow…you don`t mess around. Good luck.

She'd lost touch with the few friends she had in high school after they graduated. Mel was the only person she considered close. Sophie had gotten used to keeping to herself and never really reached out to anyone. Mel was always losing her phone, but she usually just showed up when she wanted to chat, or Sophie would go upstairs if she knew she was home. They had an unusual friendship but it worked for them.

The thought of having someone to chat with regularly had its appeal. She liked the idea of sending Jack a message whenever she wanted to share. This new relationship had its benefits and it felt safe. He only wanted friendship and that's exactly what it was.

Chapter Five

Sophie walked up to the grand house on Simons Street where Mrs. Darcy lived. It was in an older part of the city that had aged gracefully. Large maple trees lined the street, big enough to form an archway down the entire length. In front of Mrs. Darcy's house, stone statues flanked the end of the short driveway supporting a black iron gate. The house was almost as large as the lot on which it sat. Sophie looked up at its stone exterior and couldn't help but be impressed. It was beautiful with so much rich character. The exterior of the house as well as the garden were well cared for. It was absolutely breathtaking.

Sophie walked up to the large wooden door and knocked. A few moments later the door opened, revealing a well-postured older woman, dressed in a beautiful blue dress. Her gray hair was swept up in a perfect chignon with warm, inviting features.

"Hello, dear, aren't you a beautiful sight. I knew you would be lovely from the sound of your voice. Come in." Mrs. Darcy's voice had a buttery quality that made it warm and comforting. She held out her hand and formally introduced herself.

"Thank you." Sophie followed her into a formal living room. The furniture was crisp and fresh but looked as if it could have been original to the house.

Mrs. Darcy poured tea as they discussed the position. She was looking for someone to start immediately to assist in her daily activities, drive her to appointments, and help her organize her social functions. The duties fluctuated based on Mrs. Darcy's daily needs. The hours were very flexible and the pay was more than she had hoped, making it even more appealing.

"I have a feeling this will be a wonderful fit." Mrs. Darcy smiled as she led Sophie on a tour around her house. "You have a good energy about you, Sophie."

"Thank you, Mrs. Darcy. Your home is very lovely. " Sophie looked around at all the beautiful art that was displayed in the home. Mr. Darcy was definitely wealthy. Every detail of the house looked expensive.

"Please call me Margaret." She reached for Sophie's hand, taking it in both of hers. "I am a big believer in fate, Sophie. I learned a long time ago to trust my feelings. We are going to be great friends. I can feel it." Her blue gray eyes sparkled.

"I think so too." Sophie smiled. There was something about Margaret that made Sophie trust her; she seemed so pure of heart. "I should inform you that I don't have a vehicle, will that be a problem?"

"No, definitely not. I have several. When can

you start, dear?" Margaret questioned hopefully.

"Immediately…well, sort of. I currently have another job at a restaurant not far from here, but I can work my schedule around yours. Though, I do have a few more weeks before I graduate art school. I can bring you a copy of my schedule. Once school is out I'll be a lot more flexible."

"That would be lovely. Why don't you come by tomorrow afternoon?" Margaret didn't seem at all worried about a conflicting schedule.

"Thank you, Margaret, it was very nice to meet you." Sophie left with a good feeling about the position.

She pulled out her phone and sent Jack a message.

Sophie: Got the job!

Jack: Congrats.

Sophie: Thanks. I owe you big!

Jack: I will hold you to it ;)

Sophie: Gotta run to catch my bus. Talk soon.

Jack: I hope so.

Mel was shuffling around in Sophie's apartment when she arrived home. "Hey girl!" She hollered from Sophie's small kitchen. She had learned long ago not to be startled by Mel's unexpected presence.

"Do locks ever keep you out?" Sophie complained with a chuckle.

"Nope. How was last night? Did you love the dresses?" Mel came around the corner with a cereal box in her hand. "What one did you wear?"

"Um…I wore the dark red one and it certainly drew attention."

"I know, right? Your boobs must have been busting right out." She laughed. "I was trying to get you laid. I have known you two years and not once have you dated anyone, let alone got any."

"Mission failed." Sophie rolled her eyes. "Besides, you get enough for both of us."

"True." She smiled deviously. "You coming to see my show? You always say you will but you never do." Mel pouted.

"I have never been to a strip club. It's intimidating. Besides, I see enough of you already." Sophie indicated toward her tube top and short skirt.

"We're having a big promo night coming up and I am supposed to recruit some hot friends to make the audience more appealing to the male guests." Mel looked at her sheepishly.

"No way," Sophie barked.

"Oh come on. You don't have to do anything but hang around and look hot. You will get *paid*." Mel knew how desperate Sophie was for cash at the moment.

"Paid?" Sophie looked at Mel skeptically.

"Yes. You'll just be eye candy and I promise you won't have to take anything off." Mel smiled.

"Good, 'cause that wouldn't happen."

"Say yes. You're like the hottest person I know

and you'll make the boys want to empty their wallets and…" Mel buttered Sophie.

"Don't." Sophie stopped the rant of comments she knew was coming. "I'll think about it. When is it?"

"Next Friday night." Mel jumped up and down, wrapping her arms around Sophie. "You're the best."

"I didn't say yes," Sophie reminded her.

"I know but you didn't say no either. Gotta run. You're out of milk, by the way." She said as she slipped out the door.

Sophie sighed and shook her head. Mel always talked her into crazy things. Mel was a wild card that Sophie was drawn to. Her whole life Sophie had felt the weight of responsibility. She never learned to let go and enjoy life. Mel was refreshing and made Sophie realize there was more to life than the struggle to get ahead. It was usual to find Mel in her kitchen in the middle of the night raiding her cupboards, looking for someone to talk to. It was her favorite time with Mel.

Sophie dressed for work in her typical short black skirt and black button-up blouse. Looking in the mirror, Sophie applied gloss to her lips. The memory of Ashton's mouth against hers was a guilty pleasure. She would never admit how much she craved him, but she had a hard time convincing herself it was purely hate that fueled her feelings toward him. Her body wanted to indulge in every pleasure he could offer. She decided there was no harm in letting her imagination run wild.

Sophie grabbed her phone as she headed out the

door. There was a message waiting for her.

Jack: I'm curious about the history between you and Ashton. Tell me why you hate each other.

Sophie: Ugh…where do I start? Actually I should ask before I say anything. How do you and Ashton know each other?

Jack: We met through a mutual friend. Don't worry, we aren't close. My lips are sealed as far as you're concerned. Was it that bad between you?

Sophie: I'm trusting you! It was worse than bad. Ashton and his girlfriend hated me from the moment I arrived at that school. First week they filled my locker with condoms and started the "Sophie the slut, don't get too close or you will catch something" rumor. A direct quote from queen evil herself BTW. Not a good way to be introduced to a new school.

Jack: Horrible.

Sophie: I regret not being able to dish it back better. Instead my main plan of action was to ignore it but I must say it was never very effective.

Jack: I bet you took it gracefully. Not letting it get to you.

Sophie: I wish. Gotta run to work. Can't be late.

When Sophie arrived at the restaurant, she welcomed the rush of customers. The restaurant had always been a popular place, and Sunday nights were no exception.

"Hey, Lori. How's Megan? I didn't see her when I came in," Sophie asked in passing.

"Still nursing her hangover. She didn't come in today. *That* girl does not know her limit, especially when there's a cute boy she's trying to sink her teeth into." Lori rolled her eyes. "I had fun though. How about you? I saw you dirty dancing with the unbelievably hot Ashton." Lori smiled wickedly.

"Oh." Sophie's eyes widened guiltily. She hadn't realized anyone noticed. "I didn't even realize it was him. I was just kind of…"

"Sophie." Lori placed her hands on Sophie's shoulders and looked into her eyes. "As much as Megan is my friend, she is a complete mess. I won't breathe a word of it to her. Megan and Ashton are never going to happen. She's been crushing on him for years now. He barely looks at her but you…holy god, I wish some mega hot guy looked at me like that."

"What are you talking about? We're enemies."

"Whatever." Lori dismissed. "I wish I had an enemy like *that*. Megan is already ridiculously jealous of you and I think finding out that the guy she's obsessed with wants to get in *your* pants will not go over well. You may want to keep it on the down low."

"Why would she be jealous of me? And she's the one who insisted that I go out last night." Sophie was confused about the whole situation.

"Just remember that Megan can get very dramatic." Lori sighed with an apologetic smile before she disappeared through the doors of the kitchen.

Sophie ran the conversation through her mind. She didn't want Megan to feel threatened by her, and she definitely was not going to pursue Ashton.

Sophie was relieved to find out that Sam was not working tonight either. She wasn't sure how she should act around him now that she knew what his intentions were. He seemed to be making his feelings more obvious, or at least they seemed so now that she knew the truth.

The rest of the evening passed quickly and before long they were closing up. Sophie was thrilled with her tips. She had a couple of generous spenders, improving her mood. It was nights like these that made up for the more frugal customers that didn't understand that waiters survived on tips.

On her walk home, she pulled out her phone to see she had a missed call from her mother and a text from Jack. Sophie called her mother to let her know about her new job. Her mother congratulated her and then insisted on getting all the details on Margaret because she wanted Peter to do a background check. Sophie relinquished the information because she knew her persistent mother would attain it one way or another.

Jack: Was that unfortunate condom incident

the worst of it?

Sophie: Hardly. The first of many. I got locked in the girls' bathroom until a janitor found me. Had my clothes stolen from me while I was in the shower. NIGHTMARE. I still have bad dreams about that one. Got my homework stolen many times, had food dumped on me...all the rumors they spread around about me made everyone always stare.

Jack: Are you sure people didn't stare at you because you are beautiful?

Sophie: Haha. No definitely not.

Jack: What did you do when they did all that stuff?

Sophie: Tried to talk to Lucinda many times. That got me nowhere. I tried the whole revenge is sweet path for a while. Not really my thing 'cause I felt too bad about it. Then after that I just hoped they would eventually get bored. Never happened. Didn't even get to my prom.

Jack: Did you want to go to prom?

Sophie: What girl doesn't? I was actually excited about going because someone had asked me, but when he picked me up he tried to take me "parking" instead. I ended up walking home when he kicked me out of the car. Took me 2 hours. Never told my mom I never made it. You are actually the first person I told that pathetic info to. Don't tell anyone!

Jack: Who asked you?

Sophie: One of Ashton's friends. Don't even ask me why I didn't see it coming. He had been nice to me for a couple weeks before. He made me feel special and I fell for it. It turned out to be their best prank of all.

Jack: I might know him. Who was it?

Sophie: You wouldn't know him, but his name was Collin. I was so grateful when I graduated and could move on!

Jack: Yes, I can see why. It seemed like Ashton was a complete jerk. Though, it doesn't seem like the Ashton he is now. Maybe he has changed. Maybe you should give him a second chance.

Sophie: Never! Let's not talk about Ashton anymore. He is your friend and I don't want to come between you.

Jack: I told you we aren't that close. Besides, I like you more. I'm curious about your history.

Sophie: Okay but only because you shared your secret with me. Ashton was the first boy that I had feelings for. I thought he was the most beautiful boy in the world and he hated me from the first moment he saw me. I was pathetic!

Jack: No you weren't.

Sophie: That was the only time that I will ever admit I have feelings for Ashton BTW.

Jack: Have? Is Sophie in love with Ashton?

Sophie: HAD! I HAD feelings for Ashton on some tiny miniscule level when I initially met him and it lasted like 5 seconds. I found a quote one time that sums up my personal take on love: "Love is only a dirty trick played on us to achieve continuation of the species."

Jack: Sounds like the words of a scorned lover.

Sophie: Love is just not for me. It's a fairytale. I am crawling into bed now. Tired from work. Next time we talk about you.

Jack: But I like talking about you more. You are far more interesting.

Sophie: Trust me I'm not and I don't like talking about me. You're lucky you got this much.

Jack: I like talking about you and I appreciate

you opening up.

Sophie: Did Ashton tell you he is a nude model for my art class?

Jack: No. How does he look naked?

Sophie: No comment.

Jack: No comment? How disappointing.

Sophie: Fine…he is not disappointing. Happy?

Jack: Not disappointing…you can do better than that. Give me something else.

Sophie: No and no more talking about Ashton. Goodnight.

Jack: Night. xox

Sophie: xox

Chapter Six

Sophie woke with a start the next morning. She had slept in and was going to be late. "Oh no," she whimpered as she scrambled out of bed and stumbled to the washroom. She couldn't afford to be late for her art sitting this morning. It was the last session, and the painting was worth a substantial portion of her final mark. She flew through her morning routine and settled for running a brush through her hair before twisting it up in a messy bun. She pulled on her favorite oversized T-shirt and jeans before grabbing her supplies and running for the door. She had only a few minutes to make it to the bus stop.

As she rounded the corner, she saw the bus pull away. She cursed the punctual driver and herself for staying up late. She'd given up on the prospect of sleep and did some late night painting of a particular image she could not erase from her mind—Ashton.

Sophie turned when she heard her name called down the street. Mel was leaning out of the upper window of her apartment with a cigarette in one hand and the other waving at Sophie frantically. Sophie sighed as she made her way back toward their apartment.

"I have my boyfriend's car. I'll drive you!" Mel hollered down. "Just give me a sec." She took a long pull on her cigarette before she snuffed it out and disappeared back into her apartment.

Mel shuffled out the front door a few minutes later with oversized sunglasses and an ensemble that was unusually modest for her.

"You're up early," Sophie commented as she watched Mel descend the stairs. Sophie could tell that Mel was tired by the way she carried herself. "Did you even go to sleep?"

"No, I'm too angry to sleep." She huffed. Sophie followed Mel down to where an old black sedan was parked at an odd angle against the curb.

Sophie opened the passenger door and slid into the front seat. The smell of cigarettes assaulted her senses as she sat down in the disturbingly messy interior of the car. Mel reached over and grabbed some garbage by Sophie's feet and threw it into the backseat. "He's a fucking slob, if you haven't already come to that conclusion," Mel complained. Sophie noticed a dark shadow on her cheek.

"What happened to your face, Mel?" Sophie asked with concern.

Mel leaned back in the chair and took a deep breath. She reached up and pulled off her glasses, revealing a dark bruise that darkened the skin beneath her eye. "Corbin," she confirmed.

"Don't do this again, Mel." Sophie's tone was

more demanding than she intended, but she couldn't help her own anger at the sight of Mel's injury.

"Why do they always turn into shitheads after a few months? It's like they use up all their ability to be nice and all that's left is the ability to use their fists to communicate," Mel uttered in frustration. No matter how upset Mel got she never cried. Sophie took Mel's hand in hers and squeezed affectionately. Mel was never one for displays of affection but Sophie knew the odd time when Mel needed it. Mel squeezed back tightly.

"You have to break up with him. You know what's going to happen. You've been here before…you'll see him again and he'll tell you how sorry he is and want to kiss and make up but then it will happen again, and it will be more than just your eye next time." Sophie laid it out for her. She didn't dance around the subject. She had tried that the first time Mel was going through a bad relationship. It was shortly after they had met. Mel ended up in the hospital with broken ribs.

"I know, but—" Mel began but Sophie cut her off.

"What would you do if Mr. Cleary took a swing at you?" Sophie cut in.

"What?" Mel looked confused as she looked back at Sophie.

"What would you do?"

"I would kick him in the fucking balls before beating the living shit out of him." Mel's mouth turned up into a satisfied grin.

"Exactly. You are the toughest girl I know. You don't let anyone else push you around, so don't let the men you date do it. You deserve better than what Corbin can offer you." Sophie smoothed Mel's hair back to get a better look at her eye.

"I'm a fucking stripper, Sophie. What if this is all that I'm ever gonna have?" Mel said sadly.

"You are not *just a stripper*, Mel. You are a strong woman, a daughter, a sister, and my best friend. You deserve as much love as anyone else in this whole entire world. If you don't want to be a stripper, don't. If you do, then don't let it define you. Just do me a favor and don't date customers anymore. Find someone that doesn't see you naked on the first encounter and stay away from the ones that seem to have an addiction problem. Someone good is going to fall in love with you, treat you right, and sweep you off your feet. You just have to stop putting obstacles in your way. Corbin, Billy, and what's his name are no good for you. Start listening to that tiny voice in your head, Mel." Sophie smiled with a warm heart. "I know that warning bells go off when one of those idiots walks up to you."

"You don't sound like someone who doesn't believe in love, Sophie." Mel's small smile brought Sophie relief.

"I don't believe in the whole fall in love and live happily after ever for *me*…but you believe in it and I want you to be happy."

"What is wrong with us? I can't find a man with any good qualities, a drawback to my line of work, and *you*…when are you going to tell me why you are so against believing in happily ever after?" Mel looked up at her with the question in her eyes.

Sophie shrugged. "I have never witnessed happily ever after. My father left my mother before I was born. We struggled through life, trying to survive. I have seen lots of heartache and had my share. I just don't want to risk the pain. It's more trouble than it's worth."

"Wow…we are pathetic and damaged, Sophie."

"True that, Mel." Sophie laughed.

"Tell me though, 'cause I'm curious why don't you take advantage of the fact that you look like a freaking supermodel and hook up with some hotties?" Mel asked in disbelief. "Seriously, the walls in our building are thin and I would have known if you brought someone home with you. I know it's not for lack of intent on the male side, either. They practically drool when you walk by."

"What? No way!"

"*You* are so naïve, Sophie." Mel rolled her eyes as they pulled up in front of Sophie's school.

"I'm not naïve and I really have to go, I'm late. Thanks for the ride, we're going to talk about this Corbin situation later and *stop* smoking, already." Sophie ran up to the front door of the building.

When Sophie walked into the classroom she intentionally kept her eyes from traveling toward the center of the room where Ashton and the other model were posed. "Sorry, sir," Sophie called to her professor, Mr. Walters, as she took her seat.

"You don't need to apologize to me. You are only cheating yourself of time spent on your painting," he responded as he watched her settle in her seat.

"Yes, sir," Sophie replied politely as she readied

her supplies to begin. She gave herself a moment to greedily take in Ashton's gorgeous hard body that looked as if he was carved of stone. Every part of his body looked powerful and delicious. *What am I thinking?* Sophie squeezed her eyes shut and tried to focus on her painting.

A strange heat settled in her core, making her mouth water and her attention waver to sensual thoughts. The canvas in front of her blurred as her mind was solely fixated on Ashton's body. She remembered how his hands felt upon her when they were on the dance floor. The heat of him pressed against her.

Sophie raked her hands over her face. She needed to pull herself together—she was losing her self-control. Sophie forced her attention to the painting in front of her, reminding herself how important this was for her final mark. Taking a deep breath, she began working with the paint until she finished the girl's likeness to her satisfaction. Instead of painting Ashton, she decided to make a bold move. The painting became an image of the woman embracing an identical image of herself. One of the reasons she loved art was the creativity to step outside of rules and structure. She was pleased with the final product and could only hope that Mr. Walters would appreciate the angle she chose.

"I hope that everyone has had enough time to view the models. They will not be joining us again, but should you need more time, next class is open to finish the paintings," Mr. Walters announced at the end of the sitting. Sophie hadn't realized how much time had passed. She was startled when Ashton leaned around her canvas to view her painting.

"I'm disappointed…you stared at me long enough and you didn't even paint me. Though, I must say I do like where your mind is." He smiled wickedly at her.

"Actually I had to improvise because every time I tried to paint you I would feel nauseous," Sophie replied, dismissing him by busying herself with packing up her supplies.

"You're meaner than I remember," he stated with a humorous tone.

"Well, you are *just as mean* as I remember," Sophie spat out.

"And you still want me so bad you can taste it," Ashton declared arrogantly with a raised eyebrow.

"Don't fool yourself. Not every girl that sees you wants you, Ashton." Sophie couldn't hide the color in her face.

He shrugged his shoulders in the same careless way she had seen him do so many times before. "But you do."

Sophie huffed. "Why are you even doing this?" She waved to her painting. "Don't you have something better to be doing with your time?

"And miss this wonderful exchange between us?"

"Was it the model girl?" Sophie's question was met with a bored look. "It was, wasn't it? You were trying to get laid." Sophie rolled her eyes when he didn't try to deny it. "Well, the rest of us live in a world where we have to work toward our future, not waste it away doing pointless things for a thrill.

Please don't let me get in the way of your fabulous time you have planned between the two of you." Sophie waved him away toward the other model, who was still lingering around the room.

"Are you jealous?" The humor in his voice was too much.

"Bite me," Sophie snapped.

Ashton raised his eyebrow. "I can do that." His words pulled at an invisible cord that tied to her inner heat. The way his lip curved up made her want to taste them. "It explains the kiss the other night."

Heat raked across her face. "In your dreams, Ashton." Sophie grabbed her things and headed out of the classroom, not looking back. *I am a confident, grounded woman and I will not let that pompous ass get to me!*

As soon as she was a safe distance away, she found a place to sit and pull herself together before heading to her next class. Pulling out her phone, she sent a message to Jack. It was the first time in her life she'd opened up to a guy and right now she needed him.

Sophie: Ashton is such an ass.

Sophie smiled when he responded almost immediately.

Jack: What happened?

Sophie: Just because he's hot, he thinks that every girl wants to do him, and he is a big fat

jerk.

Jack: Do you want him?

Sophie: Not the point. The point is that he is an arrogant jerk ball.

Jack: Point taken but…

Sophie: But nothing…so when are we going to hang out or are we just going to have a textual relationship?

Jack: Haha. I like that. I'm away on business. This is all you have for now, but I do miss your beautiful face.

Sophie: Okay fine. Strictly textual for now.

Jack: Let's devise a plan to get back at him for being a jerk ball, as you call it.

Sophie: Where have you been all my life? I think I just fell in love with you.

Jack: Gross…girl cooties.

Sophie: Best kind. Any ideas for revenge?

Jack: Sleep with him.

Sophie: Remember that comment I made about falling in love with you? I take it back! That is the most ridiculous plan ever.

Jack: Let him think you are into him. Sleep with him and then give him the cold shoulder. It will drive him crazy.

Sophie: Don't like that plan. Something else.

Jack: Let me think…

Sophie: You do that. Gotta go to class. Talk later.

Chapter Seven

Sophie made her way through the rest of the day. Without Ashton's disruptive presence she was able to regain her focus and turn her day around. The bus pulled up to her stop and she hopped off just as her phone began to ring.

"Hey Hon, I'm glad I caught you. Are you all done your classes for the day?"

"Yep, heading home to change before I head to my new job."

"Peter already knew who Margaret Darcy was. She is a very reputable woman in the community and apparently very well-to-do," her mother said dreamily on the phone. "She comes from old money and was quite the socialite in her day."

"Yeah, I didn't really get the axe-murderer vibe from her." Sophie rolled her eyes.

"Better safe than sorry. I'll let you go so you won't be late," her mother said excitedly. "But first, what do you think of a black and white wedding with touches of red? I was thinking your dress could be red and the rest of the bridesmaids could be black. How do you feel about that?"

"I think that sounds classy and elegant. It will be beautiful, Mom."

"Good. Talk to you later. I love you."

"Love you too, Mom. I'll come out this weekend to help with some decisions."

"Sounds wonderful!"

When Sophie's mother had asked her to be her maid of honor, she was more than happy to accept the role. She wanted to be there for her mother on her special day.

Sophie noticed papers taped to her apartment door when she approached. The first was a notice from her landlord stating that he had hired an exterminator that found multiple infestations needing to be resolved immediately. The building would have to be evacuated for three days while the process was being conducted. The tenants were responsible for finding temporary living arrangements while the problem was being handled. Although she was happy the infestation would finally be dealt with, she was left with the dilemma of finding a place to stay temporarily that wouldn't cost her more than she was willing to pay.

"Three days?" Sophie huffed. She couldn't travel from her mother's house to class for the rest of the week. The distance was too far for a daily commute, especially with the bus system. The next note she pulled off the door was from Mel, her messy handwriting stating that she was staying with her boyfriend for the next few days and not to hate her for not breaking up with him. She also mentioned that Sophie could stay with them if she needed a place. It was an offer Sophie was not going to accept. She did not want to show any support for Mel's decision to forgive her loser boyfriend. "Aw, Mel. What am I going to do with you?" Sophie sighed.

Sophie immediately went to her landlord's door and knocked as loud as she could. After a few minutes of incessant knocking, Mr. Cleary opened the door in his usual rough and unshaven appearance. "What now? I'm getting rid of the pests for you."

"Yes, thank you for that, but I have nowhere to go. I can't exactly afford to go to a hotel for three days. I don't think you can legally just cast us out without any compensation for three days."

Mr. Cleary closed the door in Sophie's face. Sophie resumed banging on the door only to have him return shortly after thrusting a crumpled piece of paper in her face.

"What's this?" Sophie asked, trying to smooth out the paper so it was legible.

"It's a voucher for a motel. I know the guy who owns it. Problem solved," he grumbled before turning back into his apartment and slamming the door behind him.

Sophie sighed, tucking the paper into her purse before returning to her apartment. She had never heard of Econo Rooms Motel before and hoped it wasn't a bad sign. Sophie quickly made herself look as professional as she could with her limited wardrobe. She realized that she would have to make a point of making some clothes that would be appropriate for her new job.

***

When Margaret opened the door, Sophie was immediately reminded why she felt so good about working for her. Margaret's warm energy surrounded her. "Come in, Sophie." She smiled brightly, making her face crinkle with perfectly placed lines that complemented her still beautiful features.

"Hello, Margaret." Sophie entered the grand foyer of Margaret's home.

"My event planner, Karen White, is here to go over the final plans for a fundraiser I am hosting. I would love to get your input." Margaret led her into a formal sitting room. A woman in her mid to late thirties stood before a large display of fabrics and pictures of table settings and floral arrangements.

Sophie helped Margaret confirm all the last minute particulars for the fundraiser that was taking place in a couple of weeks. Everything was planned out to the smallest detail once the meeting commenced. Sophie was surprised how much thought and planning went into one of these events. The menu sounded fabulous and well-known bands were booked for entertainment. The grandness of the event seemed surreal.

"Sophie dear, could you please get us some tea?" Margaret requested once the event planner left. Margaret sat down on the sofa to rest. She looked tired from their long meeting.

"Of course."

Sophie was still reeling through the decisions they had made for the event. The details came together beautifully in her mind. Margaret had told her it was an annual event she held to raise money for heart and stroke research since her husband died of a heart attack three years ago. Sophie gathered from Margaret's kind and loving words that Mr. Darcy had been an exceptional man and loved by many.

When Sophie rounded the corner into the grand kitchen she couldn't stop the yelp of surprise that erupted from her. Her hand immediately went up to silence herself. She hoped Margaret was far enough away to not have heard.

"What are you doing here?" Sophie gasped at the sight of Ashton casually leaning against the counter. A glass of water was raised to his lips and his skin glistened with sweat. *Dear lord!* He had taken off his shirt and thrown it over his shoulder, leaving him dressed only in low riding jogging pants that hugged his narrow hips. She couldn't help her gaze from taking in his tall form. His hard flesh was carved in all the right places, exactly how he had stayed in her thoughts. His perfection would not fade from her mind.

"I should ask you the same thing." If he was surprised by her presence he didn't show any sign of it. Only the hint of his amused smirk graced his features. "But if you must know, Margaret is my grandmother."

"Oh my god! But?"

"My mother's side," he clarified.

She could not believe that the sweet woman she had recently come to know was related to the arrogant, self-serving Ashton King. Now that she knew, it made perfect sense. Ashton was from a very well-to-do family, even referred to by some as local royalty with family ties in politics and involvement in the community. His family owned multiple companies that provided a foundation for the district. It would only make sense that his grandmother would be the graceful, well-known Margaret Darcy.

"This is great…" Sophie mumbled. "I'm just getting tea for Margaret because I'm her new assistant." Sophie forced a smile that she knew did not come across as sincere. Sophie began shuffling through the kitchen looking for the tea cups and tea. The kitchen was huge, and she was making little progress, moving from one cupboard to the next. She glanced occasionally at Ashton, who was watching her with an amused expression. She envisioned punching him in his arrogant face, but her thoughts quickly jumped into running her hands down his lean stomach. *This is insane!*

"You wouldn't happen to know where the tea and cups are, would you?" Sophie tried to force sweetness in her voice.

Ashton straightened up and slid himself further down the counter, revealing the neatly placed tea cups and tea set out on a tray, concealed behind him.

She narrowed her eyes. "How long were you going to make me search before you told me?"

Ashton shrugged his shoulders before turning to place his glass in the sink. "You didn't ask, so I didn't tell."

"Lovely." Sophie rolled her eyes. Grabbing the

kettle, she walked toward the sink to fill it up. Ashton refused to move when she glared at him, forcing her to lean in around him. "You really should go shower. You stink," Sophie lied. He didn't smell terrible at all. His musky masculine scent filled her senses, enticing her.

"Tea actually sounds good. Make me a cup too." Ashton leaned down close, making her splash water on the counter.

"Ashton!" Sophie grabbed a dish towel and wiped up the water. "Did you ever hear of personal space?"

"Yeah, and I've noticed that you like to get in mine." His beautiful, wicked smile spread across his lips. Sophie wondered if it was his dimples that made his mouth so entrancing.

"Don't humor yourself; you're just getting in my way and you can make your own tea..." Sophie trailed off as she heard footsteps approaching the kitchen. She backed away from Ashton.

"I see you found my grandson." Margaret smiled as she entered the kitchen. Her bright eyes came to settle on Ashton with much pride.

"Yes, I have," Sophie affirmed, hoping Margaret didn't catch the conversation between Ashton and herself before she had walked in.

"Isn't she wonderful?" Margaret beamed.

"She is quite something," Ashton agreed. The words rolled off his tongue casually.

"I was just making sure you weren't having any trouble finding your way around. I'll go back and rest these old bones." Margaret turned her warm gaze on Ashton. "Go wash up, dear. I will send for dinner soon and you can join Sophie and me."

Ashton leaned down and kissed Margaret on the forehead lovingly. It was a gesture that surprised her. "As you wish." He smiled before turning to leave the kitchen. "I'll take that tea in my room," he called behind him.

"Yes, of course," Sophie answered politely for Margaret's benefit.

Sophie prepared the teapot and delivered the tray to the living room where Margaret was shuffling through papers. "Here you are." Sophie set the tray of tea down on the table and served Margaret. "Where would I find Ashton's room?" Sophie asked, holding his tea in her hands after stirring a copious amount of sugar into it.

"Second room on the left at the top of the stairs." Margaret had watched Sophie add the sugar to Ashton's tea with a curious expression but did not comment on it.

"I'll be right back." Sophie climbed the grand staircase leading to a wide hallway. Oversized wooden trim bordered the doorways and walls. Many pictures covered the walls that showed Margaret with a man of similar age. Sophie knew it was her late husband. One picture in particular caught her attention. It was not a staged photo like most of the others. It was a candid moment between them. The result was breathtaking and told of their love. It was beautiful.

Sophie continued toward Ashton's room. She knocked on his door that was left slightly ajar, allowing her to peek inside. She did not see Ashton, so she decided it would be appropriate to leave his tea on his desk. The space was very masculine, with dark colors and wood accents. It was also considerably neat with only a few articles of clothing thrown over the furniture. After setting his tea down, Sophie picked up a framed picture of Ashton on his desk. He was probably close to the age when she had first met him, when the emotional roller coaster began.

She heard a sound in an adjoining room, realizing it was an attached bathroom. She quickly tried to replace the frame so it looked undisturbed. In her panic she knocked over a small box that was sitting on his desk. Papers fell out, scattering on the floor. Sophie gathered them and placed them back in the box.

Turning quickly to retreat, she bumped into Ashton, who was standing directly behind her. A gasp escaped her as she made contact with Ashton's damp, impossibly hard flesh. "Find anything of interest?" Ashton asked with cool humor.

Sophie hoped that Ashton didn't notice how her hands lingered on his tantalizing skin. She had to force herself to step back. He smelled of body wash mixed with his own alluring scent; it was intoxicating.

"I...I brought your tea." Sophie forced her voice to sound casual.

Ashton picked up the tea and brought it to his lips. Sophie tried not to smile when he sipped it. A look of disgust crossed his beautiful features when the amount of sugar registered. He looked up at Sophie with his icy blue eyes. Sophie wasn't sure how he was going to react. He set the tea on his desk before leaning in close to her ear. It took all of her conscious effort not to lean into him.

"I will definitely play this game." She could feel his breath against her neck.

"Bring it on. This time you don't have your evil girlfriend to hide behind."

Her body was oversensitized from being so close to him. A swirl of emotions assaulted her and she tried to push them away.

"Oh…there will be no hiding, *Smelly*," Ashton taunted.

Sophie's eyes immediately narrowed when Ashton called her by the nickname that Lucinda so graciously bestowed upon her. Sophie clenched her jaw and tightened her fists to control the anger that surfaced with the unpleasant rumors.

"Yeah…I don't go by that name anymore," Sophie said with heavy sarcasm. "I had a few names that I used to refer to you back then as well, but I fear it would not be appropriate for me to speak those words in your grandmother's home. See you never." Sophie turned quickly on her heel and left the room so she could catch her breath.

The memory of when she became known as "Smelly" for the remainder of her high school years unfortunately remained clear in her mind. It was one of the rare moments that she had been alone with Ashton. He had pulled up a chair and sat down at the table across from Sophie in the back of the library. Hidden away in the corner where people seldom ventured, it was her usual spot, a place that gave her comfort in solitude. Other times she hid out in the art room when her teacher would allow her to use the supplies and she would pass the time painting. Those days were her favorite, when all she had to think about was what color to dip her brush in to create the pictures in her mind.

Sophie looked up at Ashton. "Are you lost? This is called the library. These things are called books." She held up the book in her hand as she whispered sarcastically. Sophie stared back at him with narrowed eyes. He was quiet. Suddenly nervous as to his intentions, she looked around to confirm they were alone. Lucinda rarely let Ashton out of her sight.

"It's just me. I wanted to…" Ashton said quietly.

"There you are!" Lucinda's shrill voice made Sophie jump in her seat. Lucinda's eyes quickly found Sophie and narrowed in contempt. "I knew I smelled something foul," she seethed.

"Always a pleasure, Lucinda," Sophie responded flatly.

"What are you doing back here with Smelly? We were looking for you." She trailed her fingers sensually down his arm.

Sophie wanted nothing more than to return to the pages of her book, but it was impossible with her current company. Normally she knew exactly what to expect from Ashton, but for a reason unbeknownst to her she had seen softness in his eyes before Lucinda arrived. Sophie found herself wondering what would have happened had they not been interrupted. A couple of Ashton's friends rounded the corner to see what was happening. I will not cry! I am strong! They are just words…

He stood up and kicked his chair back into the table with more force than necessary. "Let's go get some air." Ashton turned on his heel and walked away. "See ya never," he called out.

Sophie looked up at Lucinda, who was glaring at her with narrowed eyes suspiciously. "Bye, Smelly." Her laughter lingered behind her as she left the library. It wasn't long after that that her new name circled the school. Who was she kidding—words hurt!

Chapter Eight

Sophie sat at the enormous rectangular table in Margaret's dining room. The table seated twelve easily with the large wooden ornate chairs neatly arranged around the table. It was the most beautiful dining room Sophie had ever been in, with its hand-painted ceiling and lavish woodwork on the walls.

Margaret had ordered food to be delivered to the house, insisting Sophie join her and Ashton for supper. As much as she wanted to go home and gain some much needed distance between Ashton and herself, she did not want to offend Margaret.

"How do you find dinner, Sophie?" Margaret asked as she elegantly reached for her glass of wine with her well-manicured hands.

"It's delicious. Thank you." Sophie smiled. Sophie did not remember tasting food so excellently prepared. Every morsel of food upon her plate was seasoned and cooked to perfection. Sophie glanced over at Ashton, who stared back at her shamelessly. Sophie tried not to squirm under his gaze, but his presence was so potent and his confidence so intimidating. "Could you please pass the salt?" Sophie asked, hoping to ease the awkward moment.

"Sure." Ashton picked up the shaker and then slid it across the table slowly, a smile pulling the edges of his perfect lips.

"Thank you." Sophie studied him suspiciously as she sprinkled the salt over her plate. A loud clanking sound startled her as the top of the shaker fell onto her plate, dumping the contents of the shaker on her remaining food.

"That's not good," Ashton commented with a mischievous expression upon his face. Sophie shot him an accusing look.

"We'll get you some more dinner, dear," Margaret assured her.

"That won't be necessary. I'm already full. I just didn't want to waste anything." As much as Sophie enjoyed her dinner, she didn't think she could eat another bite.

"Mrs. Margaret, there is a phone call for you in the parlour," Charlotte politely informed Margaret. Charlotte was a short round woman with graying hair. Her white apron was crisp and clean, despite the constant work she seemed to undertake. Although Sophie had only known her very briefly, she knew Charlotte never stopped shuffling around the house, making sure things were in order. Her familiarity with the house told of her many years working here.

"Thank you, Charlotte." Margaret excused herself from the table.

As soon as Margaret left the room, Sophie turned toward Ashton. "You think you're really funny, don't you?" Sophie asked, throwing a cold glare toward him.

"I know I am." He leaned back in his chair with a satisfied grin on his face.

Sophie tried to reach under the table to kick him, but the massive table was too big. A chuckle erupted from Ashton when he realized her intent. *Evil can be so seductive. Don't let him get to you!* Sophie leaned back to stretch her leg further, but he still evaded her determined assault. She sat up and stared at him across the table.

"Must suck to be short," Ashton teased, pushing out her chair easily with his foot.

"That's it!" Sophie threw her napkin down on the table before climbing under the table.

"Now this is more like it," Ashton said with enthusiasm.

Ashton moved quickly for his size, dropping down under the table to meet her. They came face to face underneath. Sophie raised her hand with the intention of slapping his face. He grabbed her wrist before she could follow through. He intercepted her other hand as well. Holding both her wrists hostage, he pulled her closer.

"What are you going to do now?" he asked in a breathy voice. His laughter died away and his mood turned serious. The question lingered in the air. Sophie found herself mesmerized by his entrancing eyes and her gaze lingered on his lips. She couldn't think of anything she wanted more than to feel his lips on hers again, teasing her flesh. Her anger was forgotten. She moistened her lips with her tongue as she leaned closer. She looked up into his seemingly hungry eyes. If she didn't know better she would have thought that he wanted to kiss her as well.

"Ashton? Sophie?" Margaret called out. Sophie was so wrapped up in the moment she hadn't heard Margaret return. Sophie jumped in alarm, bumping her head under the table.

"Ouch…I dropped something under the table." Sophie retreated quickly. Sophie could not understand why her body continuously betrayed her in Ashton's presence. All her hard work to keep a level head escaped her when he looked at her with those bottomless blue eyes.

Sophie climbed out from under the table, straightening her clothes. She could feel the blush heavy in her cheeks. "I dropped my…my…"

"Bracelet," Ashton finished for her, tossing her small silver bracelet on the table. She hadn't even realized that it had come off.

"Yes…my bracelet." She retrieved it off the table.

"If you will excuse me, Grandmother." Ashton nodded affectionately toward her before he left the room. He didn't even acknowledge Sophie as he left, leaving Sophie to cringe at her ridiculous behavior. She was making the situation worse by not being able to control her emotions.

Sophie quickly changed the subject to ease her guilty conscience. "I should mention that my apartment building is being resolved of its current…rodent problem." Sophie admitted, embarrassed. "I will be staying at a motel for a few days. I am hoping that it doesn't affect my schedule but I have to figure out the bus route from where

I'm staying. I am hoping to sort it out this evening."

"Why don't you stay here, dear? We have more than enough room in this big house." Margaret beamed.

"I appreciate the offer but I couldn't possibly impose," Sophie demurred. "You have already been too good to me. Dinner was wonderful. I feel confident that I will sort things out. I can be here first thing tomorrow morning. I just wanted to let you know just in case an unforeseen problem does arise."

"Well, the offer remains open, should you change your mind." Margaret smiled and patted Sophie affectionately on the shoulder. "We would love to have you stay with us. Ashton is gracing me with his company for the time being, keeping an old woman company." Ashton was fortunate to have such a wonderful grandmother. She wondered what her life would have been like if she had extended family that consisted of more than just her mother and her. She immediately thought of Mrs. Martin and how much she loved the short amount of time they had together. Sophie returned her smile with genuine feeling.

"Thank you again for the lovely meal, Margaret."

Charlotte shuffled in the room and began clearing the dinner plates.

"Hold on, dear." Margaret placed her hand on Sophie's arm and turned toward Charlotte.

"Could you collect Ashton for me, Charlotte, please?"

"Of course." Charlotte left the room with a nod

and tender smile, her soft humming lingering behind her.

"Ashton will drive you where you need to go tonight. That way you don't have to catch a bus at this hour," Margaret informed Sophie.

"That's not really necessary. Besides, I'm used to taking the bus at all hours. It comes with the territory of not having a vehicle."

"Nonsense. He will meet you out front." Margaret waved away Sophie's excuse. "It's not safe for a girl like you to be out unescorted so late."

Sophie decided not to argue the point with her. "Thank you. I'll see you tomorrow."

"Good night, Sophie."

Sophie stepped out onto the front step and breathed in the cool night air. She pulled her phone from her pocket and realized it was later than she had realized. The afternoon had flown by. A smile graced her lips as she noticed a recent message from Jack.

Jack: I can't think of another option. I am sticking with my original idea of sleeping with him.

Sophie: Argh...remind me never to get you to help me devise any evil schemes. You are a typical man that thinks that all problems can be solved with sex.

Jack: You mean they can't?

Sophie: Funny...BTW Ashton is the grandson

of the woman that I am working for! He is staying with her. Did you know that?

Jack: Actually yes. Sorry about that. I didn't think it would involve Ashton. I knew you would have probably not taken it had you known. I didn't want you to miss the opportunity. Sorry I didn't warn you ahead of time.

Sophie: I guess I will forgive you but you are on probation. Ashton is going to drive me home now. Hopefully he won't drop me off in the middle of nowhere.

Jack: He would never do such a thing.

Sophie: Don't be so sure. I practically threw myself at him a few moments ago. He is probably laughing his head off right now. What is wrong with me? I should hate him. Scratch that. I do hate him.

Jack: You're right, you should hate him…but it sounds like you might not be so against my plan after all.

Sophie: Not going with your plan. Tonight was just a lapse in judgment. Talk to you soon. He is waiting.

Sophie opened the door and climbed stiffly into Ashton's car. She knew the drive would be painfully awkward after she practically begged him to kiss her under his grandmother's table. *So embarrassing.* The realization of her actions were settling heavily and she was dreading being alone with him.

"Just so you know, I only agreed to you driving me because of your grandmother's insistence."

"I know."

The interior of the car smelled so intimately of Ashton, it was as if she were leaning in and smelling his alluring scent against his skin.

Sophie didn't speak a word to Ashton, turning her gaze toward the night sky. Her stomach was twisted with uneasy emotions. Luckily he did not feel the need to make the unnecessary exchange of words either and she was grateful. When he pulled up in front of Sophie's building, Sophie finally spoke.

"Thank you for the drive. Your grandmother is an amazing person and I'm looking forward to working for her. I'm sorry for my actions earlier, it won't happen again. I promise to stay out of your way. In fact it's probably best to ignore each other for the rest of eternity. Thank you and goodnight," Sophie rambled off as fast as she could. She made a quick exit and practically ran to the front door of her apartment.

When Sophie reached the door, she rummaged through her seemingly endless purse trying to find her keys. When her fingers finally brushed the cool metal, she let out a sigh of relief. Sophie startled when someone unexpectedly leaned over her shoulder. "Rodent problem, huh?"

Sophie stumbled backwards. "Holy hell! Are you trying to give me a heart attack?"

Ashton leaned against the frame of her door, crossing his arms with a bored expression. Sophie, on the other hand, struggled to calm her racing heart.

"*What* are you doing here?" Sophie scowled heavily.

"You spoke so fast I didn't understand a word you said...*except* I did catch the part about you wanting to kiss me earlier and how you wished my grandmother didn't interrupt us because you wanted to have mad-hot-crazy sex with me." Ashton tilted his head as a smile played on his lips. Reaching up, he grabbed the top of her door frame. The hem of his shirt pulled up, revealing his hard, chiseled stomach. *This is ridiculous! His stupid stomach is ridiculous. No one is actually built like that! Why does the universe hate me?*

Sophie closed her eyes with a sigh. "Noooo..." she drew out slowly, trying to lid her anger. "I said I would never try to kiss you and I wanted to make sure you knew that. If you thought otherwise, you were mistaken. Have you forgotten that I hate you? People don't try to kiss people they hate." Sophie pushed Ashton's body out of the way and opened her door. When she tried to close it, Ashton pushed his way in.

"I wouldn't rule it out," Ashton said, following her inside.

"How surprising...and *oh my god*! You're coming into my apartment now?" Sophie said in disbelief as she watched him stroll into her small place. "Do you want me to pay you for the ride or something?"

"That depends on what you have in mind for payment." He raised his eyebrow suggestively. It was strange seeing Ashton in her space. It made her apartment seem so much smaller with his imposing form. He seemed genuinely curious about her things as he took everything in.

"Don't touch that!" Sophie grabbed a small sculpture out of his hand he had picked up off the shelf.

"Did you make that?" he asked curiously.

"Yes. And it is very breakable," Sophie scolded.

Ashton walked over to a stack of canvases that lined the wall, flipping through them. "These are actually good." He ran his fingers over the texture of the paint.

"Geez…don't sound so surprised." Sophie rolled her eyes.

"And what is this?" Ashton announced with a satisfied tone.

"What? *Oh my god*!" Sophie rushed over to the painting that sat on her easel, grabbing a large rag she'd thrown over the painting to hide the image. "Could this night get any worse?" Sophie gasped to herself in disbelief. To her horror, Ashton saw the painting she had done of him—*naked*.

"Now why would you paint a picture of someone you hate?" he stated condescendingly.

"It's not you," Sophie blurted out. "It's just this guy that I have a thing for." The words continued to stumble out of her mouth.

"Me," he confirmed matter-of-factly.

"No, not you…why would I have a thing for you? Never, nope. His name is Sam…Sam from my restaurant." Sophie could not believe what was coming out of her mouth. She wanted to scream.

"And this *Sam* looks just like me? With the same tattoo?" Ashton lifted up his shirt to expose the tattoo of the words **'Life is what you make it'** stretched around the left side of his chest toward his back.

"Ah…yep. Quite the coincidence. Why are you here, anyway?" Sophie tried to take the attention away from the painting in question.

"On orders of my grandmother I am to take you to where you will be staying temporarily while they deal with your rodent problem."

"Not necessary," Sophie cut in. "You can leave now."

"If I go home and leave you without making sure you are where you need to be, my grandmother will not be happy with me."

"How is that my problem?"

"It is if I tell her you propositioned me in her very sacred dining room that has entertained many precious family memories over the years."

"You wouldn't!" Sophie gasped in horror.

"I would."

"*Fine*. You are such a jerk. I have to pack. *So*…you have to wait and don't touch my stuff." She was grateful she wouldn't have to take the bus with all her stuff she needed for the next few days, even if it meant spending more time with Ashton. The war of emotions battled on within her as she tried not to pay attention to Ashton lounging on her sofa.

"What? Why are you looking at me like that?" Sophie complained.

"I knew you always had a fucking thing for me…painting pictures, so you could fantasize about me and shit," he said smugly as he stretched his long legs out. "Since I'm here do you want me to pose for another?"

"No! I don't fantasize about you! It's more like the 'and sh—' part."

Ashton sat up with widened eyes. "What did you say? And sh—?" He laughed a deep throaty sound. "Say shit," he coaxed.

"What? I can say it. I just choose not to right now. In fact, I swear all the time, especially when I see you," she proclaimed. Ashton pushed himself off the sofa and stalked toward her. He closed the distance quickly with his long legs. He stopped so close that he stole the breath from her. Reaching out, he touched her bottom lip.

"You lie…especially when you say you don't want me." His breath warmed her skin as he leaned in close.

"You don't affect me and how many times do I have to tell you—I. Don't. Want. You." Sophie stepped back from him so she could remember to breathe. "And for your information, I choose not use certain words. It's a personal choice. I'm ready to go."

***

"Where to?" he asked as he rubbed his hand over

the steering wheel.

Sophie pulled the crumpled piece of paper out of her purse. "Econo Rooms Motel," she read, and then followed with the address printed at the bottom of the coupon. She looked up at him and noticed he was watching her with raised eyebrows. "What are you waiting for? Let's go." Sophie watched Ashton shake his head in disbelief before he pulled away from the curb.

The longer they drove, the more nervous she got about how far away this place was. She wanted to seem completely confident despite her inner turmoil.

When they pulled up to an old dilapidated motel, Sophie held the coupon up to the light. The picture must have been taken years ago. The building now looked in dire need of repairs.

"Stellar place." Ashton's words dripped with sarcasm.

Sophie didn't respond. She pushed open the door and walked toward the main office. A bell chimed overhead when the door opened. A man sitting behind the desk slid his feet off the counter, sending papers fluttering to the floor. His unwashed hair was brushed back off his face in a tangle of waves that met his shoulders. A mustache sat heavily upon his lip and a dark shadow covered the rest of his chin. He wiped crumbs from his shirt, watching Sophie approach the desk.

"Need a room, beautiful?" His words seemed innocent enough, but he gave off a creepy vibe that made her insides twist with anxiety.

"Yes, please," Sophie responded with a small

voice. She glimpsed the small television he had been captivated with when she walked in. She couldn't believe her eyes when she saw a porn playing. *What the hell!*

Ashton pushed through the door behind her, causing the bell to sound again. The man behind the counter eyed Ashton before he addressed Sophie.

"Just you? Or both?"

"Just me." A slow unsettling smile spread across his face. "I have a coupon for my stay." Sophie handed it over to the man. When he took it from her, she pulled her hand away quickly to avoid the unnecessary contact.

"Sorry, sweetheart. This coupon expired ages ago," he informed her before slapping it down on the counter.

"Mr. Cleary, my landlord, gave it to me. He said he knew the owner." Sophie shuffled her feet uncomfortably. She hated the fact that Ashton was standing behind her. She wanted to run screaming from this place.

"My old man died five years ago," he said casually.

"Okay. Your standard room, please," Sophie said quickly. She just wanted the exchange to be over. She would deal with Mr. Cleary later.

She could tell Ashton didn't like this guy either by the way he practically growled under his breath.

"It's one size fits all in these parts, sweetheart." He smiled, dropping a grimy key in her hand.

"Thank you." Sophie quickly left the office with Ashton close on her heels.

"You are seriously going to stay in this shit

hole?" Ashton asked as if questioning her sanity. She ignored him as she walked up to his trunk, waiting to retrieve her things.

"Yes. It's not so bad. It has charm." She tried to defend her decision but her defense was pitiful. She hated this place so much but refused to waste her money on unnecessary luxury. This creepy, rundown motel fit her budget.

"Charm? Fuck that!"

Chapter Nine

Sophie pushed the door open, revealing the dark room. She flicked on the lights when she found the switch. "Not so bad." She tried to encourage herself by staying positive. Ashton came in behind her and set her things on the bed.

"Yeah, it's kind of nice for a piece of shit." As if on cue, screaming erupted from the next room as a couple engaged in a heated argument. Ashton just raised his eyebrows in an *I told you so* way.

"It's just a couple of days. There's even a bus stop just a block away." Sophie tried to keep her attitude positive.

"The one the guy was spray painting a giant cock on when we drove by?" Ashton asked in disbelief.

"It's called freedom of expression. If he feels the need to celebrate his cock, then who are we to say otherwise." Sophie watched Ashton tilt his head. "Don't say anything," she warned.

"Come on. How can I not say anything after a statement like that?" he complained humorously. "Though it is good to know you have nothing against cocks."

Sophie took a quick look in the bathroom, which made her cringe. "Okay. I'm good. You can leave now," she said, walking out toward Ashton. He was pulling the covers back on her bed. A look of disgust crossed his features as he noticed the stained sheets underneath.

"Oh dear," Sophie gasped before she could stop herself. "The chair suddenly looks appealing."

Ashton looked up at her with disbelief in his eyes. "It's your life." He shrugged his shoulders. He stepped back, looking at Sophie before a devilish smile crept over his face. "How do you feel about spiders?"

"Terrified. Why?" Sophie's eyes widened as she stared back at him.

"Because one just crawled on your shoulder." He chuckled.

"What!" Sophie spun around, wiping her shoulders frantically. She jumped up on the bed, trying not to scream out as she searched for the spider. "Where is it?" she cried.

"I think I saw it fall on the bed." He laughed.

Without thinking she jumped off the bed, grabbing onto Ashton and pulling herself up his tall frame. He stiffened under her unexpected move. She didn't care what he thought at that moment, her flee response was triggered and he seemed like the safest option to escape the spider. Pulling herself against him in her attempt to avoid touching the floor wreaked havoc on her insides. Everywhere her body touched his ignited a passionate fire that made her core clench in response. The only sound in the room was her breathing as time slowed down and seemed to stop altogether.

"Oh god! Sorry." Sophie quickly released her hold on him. The spider was long forgotten. The promise of a broken heart pulled at her consciousness. She needed space to clear her head. *Attraction is only a chemical reaction in the brain. These feelings are not real! Get a grip!*

"I would pay anything to know what is going through your head right now." Ashton's words surprised her. She was speechless staring back at him.

Ashton stepped forward, trailing up her arm with his fingertips. "Tell me what you're thinking, Sophie." Her name on his lips undid her.

A moan escaped her when his hand slipped around her waist and grabbed firmly onto her behind. He pulled her body against his, lifting her from the ground until her legs wrapped around his waist. He pressed her back against the wall. "Tell me." He looked down into her eyes, his darker than she had ever seen them, swirling pools of desire. She was putty in his hands as he molded her body to his, pulling, squeezing, and caressing until she could no longer form a rational thought.

"I want…" He gently bit the tender skin of her neck, causing her to cry out in pleasure. "I want this." He wound his fingers through her hair, angling her lips toward his.

"Good," he whispered before grazing his teeth over her lower lip. His erection throbbed against her. She rocked her body against his to satisfy the growing ache deep between her legs. His lips consumed hers—it was demanding, raw, and desperate. It was beautiful and dangerous and desire claimed her like a powerful drug. Both of his hands found her face, pinning her against the wall with his powerful body.

"Fuck, you taste good," he growled almost angrily against her lips before his tongue continued exploring her.

Ashton pulled back. His hooded lids shadowed his eyes. Sophie ran her fingers across his cheek, feeling his chest rise and fall exaggeratedly against her. She twisted her fingers through his soft hair, an indulgence that she had daydreamed about from the first moment she had seen him.

He pulled out of her hold, letting her slide down the wall until her feet met the floor. She immediately grieved the loss of his touch.

"Grab your things. You are not staying here." His tone was suddenly distant. His rejection cut deep.

"I'm staying. What happened to 'it's your life'?" Sophie threw his words back at him.

"That's when I thought you weren't stupid enough to stay. I'm pretty sure that guy at the front desk has quite the rap sheet. Are you sure you want to stay and find out what he's capable of?" Ashton grabbed her things and swung open the door.

After taking the key back to the front desk and informing Mr. Creepy that she wasn't staying, she slid back into Ashton's car. "Where am I supposed to go?"

Ashton took off without answering her question. He drove with purpose, and Sophie did not question it. She had a feeling she knew what his plan was anyway and it was confirmed when he pulled into his grandmother's driveway. She sighed in defeat, climbing out of his car and following him inside. The interior of the house was dark and quiet. Margaret must have already retired for the evening.

"Margaret doesn't know that I'm here. I feel like I'm intruding," Sophie whispered. He stopped in his tracks and Sophie almost collided with him.

"She told me to convince you to come back here anyway. She didn't feel right having you stay at a motel when there was plenty of room here."

"But she barely knows me. I could be crazy," Sophie babbled.

"That's what I said," Ashton whispered back as he led her up the stairs. "This is your room." He placed Sophie's things on the floor and reached to turn on the lamp, casting a warm glow on their surroundings. She couldn't bring herself to meet his eyes as she thanked him.

"Ashton?" she called after him when he turned to leave. He swung around but made no attempt to come closer. "What was that? Back at the motel?" Sophie swallowed hard against the uneasy feeling that hung heavy in her stomach.

"Good night, Sophie." He left the room without another word. Sophie collapsed on the bed, sinking into the soft covers. She pulled out her phone and noticed a new message.

Jack: Stranded in the middle of nowhere?

Sophie: Yes, but not in the sense that you mean.

But I think the literal would be easier right now.

Jack: What happened?

Sophie: What does it mean when you do something even when you know that it will turn out badly?

Jack: It means you're human.

Sophie: I kissed him.

Jack: Did you like it? He looks like he would be a good kisser.

Sophie: Did you know your sister has a thing for Ashton?

Jack: Who doesn't? Don't worry about that. Never gonna happen. She has to realize that eventually. Did you like it?

Sophie: I shouldn't be doing this. I am at his grandmother's house right now. She insisted I stay here. How can I sleep knowing that Ashton is across the hall? Can you say something to make me feel better so I don't cry my eyes out?

Jack: You are amazingly beautiful. Everything about you is too good for him. Don't cry tears for his worthless ass. He probably is so in love with you it scares the shit out of him and he knows he will never be good enough for you.

Sophie: Is it too early in our textual relationship to tell you that I really do love you, all jokes aside? You seem so much different from when we met. I have to confess that I had you pegged all wrong on our first encounter.

Jack: How did you see me?

Sophie: I don't know but I am so glad that things became textual between us.

Jack: Me too.

Sophie: When do you get back?

Jack: Not sure yet.

Sophie: I think we need to meet for coffee or something. Especially after I confessed my love for you.

Jack: Thought you didn't believe in love?

Sophie: For you I made an exception.

Jack: I'm a lucky guy then.

Sophie: Thank you for making me feel better. Night .

Jack: Goodnight Sophie. xox

Sophie scrolled to her other message on her phone. She didn't recognize the number but she knew who it was as soon as she read it.

Mel: You totally hate me, don't you? I can't live without your sense to my chaos. I miss you. Talk to me!

Sophie: Disappointed is more like it. But I would never hate you. You are like an annoying sister that always gets me into trouble. How could I possibly go on without you? ;)

Sophie turned over and stared up at the ceiling. Her phone lit up, drawing her attention from the swirl of thoughts haunting her.

Mel: Thank god u r still speaking to me!

Sophie: How is everything with Corbin? Are you all right? Whose phone is this?

Mel: It's Lips' phone. Things are good. He has been so sweet. Can I just enjoy now?

Sophie: Lips? Stripper friend? You know that I will always be here if you need me even when I don't agree with your questionable decisions. We are not done talking about the Corbin situation.

Mel: Yes. I know. And you are the best. Gotta be on stage in 5. Are you in for Friday?

Sophie: Argh…fine. I better get paid good. And my clothes stay ON.

Mel: Thanks!

Sophie pulled herself from the bed and grabbed a few things from her bag before opening her door and walking across the hall toward Ashton's room. She knocked quietly; after a moment the door swung open, startling her. He stood in front of her with his jeans riding dangerously low on his hips, his bare chest exposing his male perfection. His eyes were dark and caused a nervous sensation to twist inside her.

"Sorry to bother you but I was just wondering what bathroom I should use to have a shower?" Sophie tried to smile, like the tension between them didn't feel crushing. He stepped back and motioned toward the bathroom leading off his room. "Ah…isn't there another washroom I can use?" Sophie asked nervously. She ran Jack's words through her head. There was no way Ashton King was terrified of her. She was just another plaything for a spoiled rich boy to poke and prod to satisfy his curiosity before he moved on to his next experiment.

"No. Not if you want to shower." Ashton walked back toward his bed, turning on the television and tuning her out.

"Okay. I'll be quick." Sophie locked the bathroom door once inside and turned on the water. She brushed her teeth and waited for the water to start steaming. She was nervous having Ashton so close to her while she stripped down. Even with the locked door between them she still felt edgy. When she stepped into the stream of hot water any reservations she had washed away. The water felt wonderful on her skin, the heat seeped into her tense muscles. Picking up Ashton's shampoo, she could smell the familiar aroma that mingled with his own masculine scent. The smell intensified the memory of their kiss and the feeling of him pressing his body into hers. She squeezed a small amount onto her hand and quickly washed herself.

Turning the water off, she moved to open the glass door but noticed Ashton leaning against the counter brushing his teeth. "What are you doing in here?" Sophie gasped, standing behind the frosted glass door. Thankfully it covered her naked body from his view with the exception of her feet and above her shoulders.

"This is my bathroom."

"Yes, but when you said I could use it and I locked the door I was under the impression that I would be alone," Sophie complained.

"You were wrong." He shrugged his shoulders casually, looking at her through the reflection of the large mirror covering the entire wall above the vanity.

When Sophie realized that he was going to take an exceptionally long time brushing his teeth she became cold and restless. "How long are you going to be?"

"I am a strong believer in maintaining good dental health," he said around his toothbrush.

"Can you at least pass me my towel?" Sophie

grumbled.

"I'm busy," he responded.

After a few more minutes of Ashton's painful display Sophie opened the door. She watched his eyes widen in surprise from her brazen act. She wasn't even sure what had gotten into her—this was far from the person she knew herself to be. The Sophie she had been her entire life was modest, focused, and for the most part, avoided all drama. This was technically the first time that she had ever been naked with a guy, but she refused to stand there until he was done playing his game of torment. It was about time she tipped the scales in her favor. She walked up beside him, grabbing her towel from the counter.

He spit out his toothpaste and spun around, drinking her in without any words. She succeeded in the impossible task of making Ashton King speechless. *Score for me!* Ashton couldn't take his eyes off of her as she wrapped the towel around her wet body. He seemed completely awestruck by her actions. "It's not polite to stare and you have a little something right there." Sophie pointed to his chin. Stepping forward, she wiped it away with her thumb. "Good night, Ashton," she called behind her as she left him frozen in place. She had no idea what he was thinking, but she felt triumphant that she'd caught him off guard. A smile played on her lips as she walked back to her room.

***

Sophie dressed quickly the next morning and

went downstairs to find a washroom to brush her teeth and straighten herself up for the day. There was no way she was going anywhere near Ashton's room again. When she heard someone in the kitchen, she decided to see if Margaret was up. She wanted to thank her for allowing her to stay the night.

When she walked in, Charlotte was pulling freshly made muffins out of the oven. "It smells delicious in here, Charlotte," Sophie praised.

"Good morning, Miss Sophie. Want some tea?" Charlotte's warm smile was contagious.

"Don't trouble yourself. I'll get something on the way to class. I just wanted to say good morning before I left," Sophie declined politely.

"No trouble dear, I already made it. Ashton told me you prefer tea over coffee, so I put a pot on for you." She moved to grab the teapot from the counter.

"Ashton told you that I prefer tea?" Sophie was surprised Ashton even knew that. A strange twinge pulled at her insides. *Did I wake up in* The Twilight Zone?

Charlotte gathered a cup from the cupboard. "Here, Charlotte, let me get that. I feel strange having you wait on me when I can get it myself." Sophie took over the task.

"Do you like blueberry muffins?" Charlotte asked, removing them from the hot pan.

"They look delectable, but I really don't feel right about you feeding me as well. Just the tea is wonderful, thank you." Sophie lifted the warm tea to her lips and sipped the soothing heat.

"I can tell you aren't used to being taking care of." Charlotte looked up at her with a look that only a mother could deliver.

Sophie smiled in response. It was true. She had felt it necessary to be independent at an early age. She didn't like to see her mother struggle. "Do you have children, Charlotte?" Sophie asked, leaning against the counter. She saw Charlotte's shoulders stiffen in response and Sophie immediately regretted asking. "You don't have to answer me. I was out of line. Sorry, Charlotte."

"I had a son and he was the light of my life." A sad smile formed on her thoughtful face. "He was killed many years ago in a car accident." Charlotte pulled a picture from her shirt pocket that was well worn on the edges, showing she had carried it close to her heart for many years. She held it up for Sophie. The young man in the picture looked very much like his mother. Charlotte's sadness pulled at her. Sophie could not fathom the loss of a child and the weight that it would have on one's soul.

"I am so sorry, Charlotte. He was very handsome." Sophie passed the photo back to Charlotte.

"Mrs. Margaret is my family now, she is good to me." Charlotte said, picking up a muffin and passing it to Sophie. "Eat. Taking care of people is what I'm good at. You'll have to get used to it." Charlotte's smile had renewed strength.

"Is she trying to refuse your good food, Charlotte?" Ashton's voice was deeper than usual as he leaned against the ornate door frame leading into the kitchen. His hair was mussed from sleep and he looked adorably beautiful. Thoughts of how it felt to run her fingers through its silky strands assaulted her.

Ashton stalked into the kitchen without a shirt to cover his sinful body. Sophie turned her gaze away from him so he didn't become suspicious of her ogling. Regretfully she was sure that the flush of her cheeks made it obvious.

Sophie gasped when he continued to walk toward her, leaning over her to reach in the upper cabinet behind her. "Hey!" Sophie complained. His scent enveloped her. She was trapped against his body and the counter behind her. He leaned down to look into her eyes. "You have a little something right there." He reached up and brushed her bottom lip with his thumb. Sophie's eyes widened from his intimate touch that was meant to throw last night back in her face. She retreated quickly from Ashton, wiping the back of her hand across her lips to erase the sensation of his touch.

"Thank you, Charlotte, for the tea and muffin. I have to leave for class now." She said to Charlotte before heading out of the kitchen.

"I'll drive you," Ashton called as he followed her out into the hallway.

"Definitely not…it's not necessary," Sophie corrected herself for Charlotte's benefit as she left the kitchen and headed toward the front door.

"Great," she muttered as she realized it was pouring. She pulled up her hood before stepping outside. When she started walking she heard Ashton's car roar to life from the open garage bay. Sophie quickened her pace.

When she heard the car pull out she held her breath, waiting for it to pass by, but Ashton pulled up beside her in his sleek black car. "Come on, get in. You're getting soaked."

"Like you care if I get wet."

"Regardless of what you think, I am a gentleman," Ashton insisted.

"On what planet?" Sophie stopped in her tracks and glared over at him. "I don't need you to drive me around." Sophie fumed. Ashton opened his door and hopped out of the car to pursue her on foot. Sophie tried to run away from him but he was much quicker. His arms closed around her waist and picked her up off her feet, carrying her back to his car despite her protests.

"Why are you doing this?" She complained as he sat her down in the passenger's seat.

"Because my grandmother likes you and she likes to take care of the people that she cares about. I want my grandmother to be happy." Sophie stared at him across the car. "And I figure if I'm nice to you, you might show me your tits again." He raised his eyebrows at Sophie.

"Never!" Sophie gasped. "I can't believe you are related to Margaret. She is such a wonderful person and you are—"

"Sexy?" he offered.

"No! More like…"

"Gorgeous?" He grinned.

"No! More like arrogant and pig-headed," she spat out.

"Funny, that is not what every other girl tells me. They seem to find me irresistible."

"I'm not like every other girl then," Sophie proclaimed, crossing her arms across her chest.

"No, you're not." The humor fell away from Ashton's tone as he kept his eyes forward on the road.

"Can we just not talk? I have a headache." Sophie turned to look out the window as Ashton drove.

"As you wish." Ashton did not speak a word the entire way.

Chapter Ten

Sophie tried to concentrate on her work. She was trying to put the finishing touches on her art history project, but her mind would not focus on the words in front of her. Thoughts of Ashton clouded her mind to the point of suffocation. She didn't understand this undeniable attraction she felt for him, knowing how destructive it was to her well-being.

Sophie's phone started vibrating in her purse.

Jack: Did you sleep with him yet?

Sophie: Is that all you think about? Honestly...The idea might have crossed my mind but that's it. I am such a mess right now. Where has my sanity gone?

Jack: REALLY? So are you going to...?

Sophie: No. I like Margaret too much to fuel the fire of hate between Ashton and me. And we all know what happens when you sleep with the enemy. BTW you owe me more than coffee at this point…maybe a nice dinner after coercing all this info from me. I'm not usually a sharer. I hope you feel special.

Jack: I feel very special to know more about the beautiful Sophie.

Sophie: I may be wrong but when it comes to Ashton the rules of the game seem different now that Lucinda isn't involved.

Jack: How so?

Sophie: For the longest time I was convinced that he hated me but now I'm not so sure that hate is the right word. Everything feels different. Maybe it's me who has changed. Maybe it's wishful thinking. I don't really know but there is this new element of attraction I feel from him that confuses me. Can a guy hate and want a girl at the same time?

Jack: Yes but he doesn't hate you.

Sophie: How do you know?

Jack: Didn't you know that us gays have superpowers?

Sophie: Haha. Gotta go to my next class. Later.

Jack: Later. xox

When Sophie walked into the art studio, Mr. Walters called her over for a word. Sally looked like she was about to burst, her words barely contained behind her lips. Sally had witnessed Sophie getting dropped off this morning by Ashton and apparently had been dying to inquire about it.

"I have noticed your approach you took toward presenting your final project. Am I right to presume that you will enlighten me as to why you decided to step so far away from the specifications in your written report?" Mr. Walters paused for her nod of confirmation. "I'm looking forward to your explanation. I must say it was a bold move when it was specifically outlined to include both."

"I know but you always say that art cannot be confined within rules." Sophie smiled innocently.

"Very well, I will await your report before we discuss this further."

Sophie sat down in front of her nearly complete painting. She was pleased with how she had captured the girl's features. Her depiction of the woman embracing the love of herself came across exactly how she intended. Now she needed to come up with a convincing excuse why she didn't include the male model, other than the fact that she didn't want Ashton to have the satisfaction. It was not an option to fail. *I am such an idiot!*

"So?" Sally pulled Sophie's attention from her painting.

"It's not what it looked like. I work for his grandmother and he just gave me a lift this morning," Sophie explained.

"I don't believe it was nothing. He watched you walk all the way into the building with longing in his eyes. That boy has it bad and he is so gorgeous." Sally beamed. "You are so lucky."

"He was probably plotting my demise." Sophie waved away Sally's comment. Watching and hoping she would trip and fall so he could make fun of her was more like it. "We're practically enemies." Sophie ignored Sally's snort of disbelief and began working the paint on her canvas. *Were they still enemies? Do people make out with their enemies? I'm so confused!*

Mr. Walters left the studio open after class for anyone who wanted to stay to finish their work. Sophie took advantage of the opportunity, completing her work to her satisfaction. She slid her finished painting into the rack to dry, taking in the other paintings. Ashton's beautiful body was portrayed in everyone's except hers. Every artist had had their own signature technique used to create his image, but he was well embodied in all of them. He was beautiful and it caused an ache in her. A maddening need for him continued to haunt her. She wanted to run her fingers over every curve depicted in the paintings. His full lips did wonders to hers. They had stirred a desperate heat in her that she could not extinguish. *What is a girl to do?*

***

Sophie sat on the bus, leaning against the window, wondering why Ashton had to come back into her life. Everything had been on course, predictable, and safe before he showed up. The only time she ever took any risk was with her art, or trying to work with a new fabric or design when sewing. Now, she didn't know which way was up. She was drawn to Ashton like a magnet, fearing what would happen should she get too close. He was a walking predicament that terrified and excited her. Every logical part of her wanted to get as far away from him as possible but she feared not seeing him again most of all.

Sophie shook her head in disbelief as her iPod started playing "I Knew You Were Trouble" by Taylor Swift. Ashton was trouble and she knew it. The song was her new theme song for this chapter of her life.

When Sophie arrived at Margaret's, Charlotte informed her that Margaret was resting.

"Is she not feeling well?" Sophie inquired.

"Just tired," Charlotte reassured her before she hurried off to finish up her work. Sophie decided to take the time and familiarize herself with Margaret's schedule. Sophie shuffled through Margaret's contacts—hundreds of names were listed. Margaret had connections to many influential people. It made the handful of names on Sophie's contacts pathetic in comparison. Scrolling through Margaret's schedule, she noticed all the typical appointments to her favorite spa, luncheons, and community events, but there seemed to be numerous doctors' appointments listed. She wondered why Margaret, who seemed so lively, would need to visit the doctor so frequently. She filed away the thought, not wanting to worry about something that may very well be nothing.

Sophie jumped when Ashton walked into the room. His eyes seemed dark and distracted when they settled on her curled up on the sofa. Sophie stood up quickly, straightening her clothes. "Margaret is resting," she informed him quickly. She didn't know why she was acting like she got caught doing something she shouldn't have.

Ashton was dressed in a suit. It was the first time she had seen him in formal attire, and she couldn't help but be impressed by his exquisiteness. He was temptation, strength, and power, and it made her knees feel weak as she looked at him.

"Are you finally trying to grow up and get a real job?" Sophie nodded toward his suit.

"Why would I go and do something like that?" He smiled wickedly.

"You're right. It must be nice to carelessly go about your life chasing girls and squandering your parents' money. What happened to you, anyway?" Sophie regretted asking as soon as she said it. It felt as if she had crossed a line onto new territory.

He moved closer, causing Sophie to hold her breath. "Why do you care?" He raised his eyebrow, looking down at her with his beautiful blue eyes.

"I don't. Just curious what you're doing with your life and why you're here? Did you spend your trust fund and now living off your grandmother?"

"Always so quick to think the worst of me, Sophie." He shook his head.

"You have showed me no other side, so how could I possibly think anything else?"

"Fair enough." He smiled before backing out of the room, leaving her alone again. Sophie collapsed on the sofa, releasing her breath. She was in so much trouble. She couldn't understand why of all the guys in the world she had to have this attraction to Ashton. She had been destined for failure when it came to love, which was why she had avoided relationships thus far. Sophie ran their conversation through her head. *When did I become the mean one? Was it possible that they were so far down the path of cruelty toward each other that neither one of them knew how to find their way back?*

Margaret joined Sophie a short while later. She wore her bright smile despite the dark circles under her eyes. "Ashton told me you like to paint, so I think you might enjoy what I have in store for tomorrow evening, if you're up to joining me."

"If it has something to do with art, I am always interested," Sophie said excitedly.

"Good, it's an art gallery opening. Do you have something formal to wear?" Margaret asked. Sophie looked down at her casual clothes that she had worn to class this morning.

"How formal?" Sophie smiled sheepishly. There was nothing formal in the wardrobe options she had packed before leaving her apartment. Shopping would definitely be in order. A twinge of excitement fluttered through her with anticipation of going to an art show, and one requiring formal wear seemed like it would be very exclusive.

"I'm sure we can figure something out." Margaret smiled warmly. "For the rest of the today we'll take it easy, catch up on a few phone calls.

Tomorrow will be a very full day."

***

Sophie had driven the most luxurious car she had ever been in as she and Margaret made various stops. The responsibly of driving Margaret around in her beautiful car was a little unnerving at first. Sophie took notes and recorded names to ensure she would remember the people she met throughout the morning. Margaret was still very involved in the community for her age.

One of their stops was an elementary school that was planting a garden for the children to learn how to grow their own food. Margaret had been on the committee that had pushed for the project. Sophie smiled when a little girl no older than six years old took her hand and asked if she wanted to play in the dirt.

Before long someone passed Sophie a pair of gloves and she found herself in the mess of it all, digging holes for the children to place their plants. It was an experience that she was thankful for. The children were so excited. The process of growing food seemed magical to their young minds and Sophie realized why Margaret felt so strongly about making a difference in her community.

After Sophie cleaned herself up, she and Margaret headed to a dress boutique. When they walked through the door, Margaret was immediately welcomed warmly by the staff. The interior looked like a glorified lounge. The mostly white décor was immaculate and looked as if it was staged for a magazine shoot with beautiful fresh flowers set out on the tables. Sophie looked around, surprised to see only a few dresses were showcased on mannequins strategically placed to complement the flow of the room. It did not look like any boutique she had shopped in before. Sophie was used to endless racks of clothes to shuffle through.

Sophie sat next to Margaret on one of the pristine sofas, and they were promptly served herbal tea.

"The dress turned out lovely, Margaret. What do you think?" One of the women displayed a dress for Margaret. The royal blue material of the shirted bottom looked as if it would feel like liquid as it spilled over the woman's hands. The bodice was fitted with a high neckline and lace sleeves. It looked beautiful and Sophie couldn't resist touching the soft fabric. She had never felt material that felt so fluid against her skin.

"It is the most wonderful dress I have ever seen. Are you going to try it on?" Sophie asked Margaret.

"I never pass up the opportunity to play dress up." Margaret said before setting her tea down and walking into a dressing room. A few moments later she came out looking amazing in the dress that was obviously made to fit her flawlessly. Sophie couldn't imagine a more perfect dress to display the graceful woman that she was. Her figure still possessed her feminine curves, refusing to fade with age.

"It's beautiful, Margaret." Sophie raved.

"Yes, I think it will do quite nicely. Now for you." Margaret smiled at Sophie like she had a trick up her sleeve. It was the first time that she noticed any similarities between Margaret and Ashton and it made her smile. Margaret nodded toward one of the women before turning back toward the changing room.

"What are you up to, Margaret?" Sophie asked, confused. The same woman came back with a few dresses in hand, presenting them to Sophie.

"Do you have a color preference?" the brunette asked.

"Oh…no, thank you. I am only here to accompany Margaret." Sophie passed on the beautiful dresses displayed for her. The woman furrowed her brow. Her hair was upswept into a sleek style. She wore a pants suit that was very complementary to her figure.

"Bring out a selection please, Donna." Margaret requested, stepping out of the changing room in her original clothes. "It is a formal event tonight so we must dress to impress."

"I would love to try on beautiful dresses, but if they knew what my bank account looked like they wouldn't let me in this store, let alone try anything on." Sophie said nervously.

"Don't worry, dear. I don't expect you to pay for the dress. It is a work function, after all." Margaret insisted.

"Margaret, I appreciate it but I couldn't possibly accept something so extravagant." Sophie lowered her voice.

"This would look darling on you." Margaret held up a red dress, the perfect shade of red that spoke of romance and endless nights. It was beautiful.

Sophie ran her hand over the fabric longingly.

"It should be your size. As well as these." The woman hung up the dresses in the changing room for Sophie to try on.

Margaret had to practically push her into the room because Sophie couldn't get her feet to move. "Try them all on, Sophie. I want to see them."

Sophie closed the curtain and looked at the four dresses. Slipping off her clothes, she first tried on the red dress that slid against her skin with no more than a whisper. She pulled up the zipper that was hidden so intricately on the side. The smallest of straps delicately sat on her shoulders, meeting a fitted bodice that wrapped around her form. The long skirt lay gracefully against her skin, sweeping to the floor.

Sophie pulled the curtain aside and stepped out to the audience that awaited her. "Sophie, you look so beautiful in that dress," Margaret gasped.

"You don't think it's too…?" She indicated toward her cleavage that was displayed. It was nowhere near as revealing as Mel's dress, but she did not feel very professional having her skin exposed.

"No, not at all. You look perfect." Margaret beamed. She turned toward the woman at her side. "We'll need some shoes and a necklace as well."

***

Sophie stood in front of the mirror in her room at Margaret's house wearing the new red dress. Margaret had insisted on buying it, along with the three other dresses, shoes, accessories, and a few pieces of jewelry. She claimed that Sophie would need them for future functions. Margaret wouldn't even entertain the idea of taking it out of her paycheck. She refused to tell Sophie how much they cost. In fact, no prices were discussed or disclosed by anyone while they were there, leaving Sophie to only wonder how much the dresses were.

Sophie sat down on the bed and slipped on her new nude heels before twirling around in the mirror. She felt like a princess and any moment she would wake up and realize that this had been a crazy dream. She had curled her hair loosely and swept it up in a loose low twist with hair cascading from the clip. The jeweled necklace sat on the swell of her breasts and a dainty coordinating bracelet graced her wrist.

Sophie smiled at her reflection after applying the finishing touch of lipstick. She took time to apply her makeup to complement the quality of the dress she wore. She dropped her lipstick into her clutch and grabbed her phone.

Sophie: You should see me tonight. Margaret insisted on getting me a beautiful dress to go to an art show tonight. This does not feel like a job at all. More like a dream. She is way too nice to me.

Jack: I'm sure you are a sight to behold.

Sophie: How is your trip going? Do you know when you will be back, mysterious guy?

Jack: I should know soon.

Sophie: Wish me luck that I don't fall in my heels.

Jack: I wish you all the luck in the world. Have fun tonight. xox

Sophie quickly called her mother and told her about the beautiful dresses and the art show this evening. Her mother's excitement helped quiet the guilt that she was feeling on having Margaret spoil her.

Margaret was speaking to Ashton in the foyer when she made her way downstairs. He was dressed in a tailored suit that was made for his body alone. It was different from the suit he donned earlier. This one was sexier and more appropriate for evening entertaining. His hair was styled perfectly and screamed to have fingers run through it, his presence so demanding that it was hard to pull her eyes from him.

When Sophie looked at Margaret, she smiled back at her like she knew Sophie's secret. Heat flushed her face with her embarrassment. *Note to self...be more discreet!* She didn't want to be seen as silly girl with a crush. Pushing any thoughts of Ashton aside, she tried to focus on the evening ahead. *Please let Ashton be dressed for something else. Please be going anywhere else but with us!*

"Ashton will be joining us this evening," Margaret informed her with a delighted smile.

Damn it! "Wonderful." Sophie said politely; she

was nervous about being around him all night dressed like a god in a suit that made her mouth water and her heart race.

"The car is waiting. Are you ready, Sophie?" Margaret asked.

"Yes," Sophie replied, trying to keep her voice steady.

***

The art gallery opening was an incredible experience. Art was displayed on strategically placed wall panels throughout the large gallery. The building itself was sleek and modern, a blank canvas for the art that was displayed. A full crowd mingled around the paintings and sculptures. Sophie listened to the pieces of conversations that she picked up as she wandered around the room. She loved hearing everyone's personal take on the paintings and sculptures. Margaret had introduced her to many of the guests. They all welcomed Sophie warmly and she enjoyed discussing the art with fellow admirers.

When Margaret grew tired, she rested in a seating area. After Margaret's insistence she was fine and wanted to catch up with some old friends, Sophie continued to explore the art. Sophie sampled the wine, taking in every piece. She only had a few glimpses of Ashton since they arrived; he was keeping his distance. Sophie was grateful considering their surroundings. It was never a good idea to put too livewires together in peaceful surroundings—they were sure to cause a scene.

Every once in a while Sophie would catch sight of him among female admirers. She was disappointed in herself for actively seeking him out when he seemed to be finally giving her the space that she had been convincing herself she wanted all along. There was also the annoying fact that she found herself irritatingly jealous of the women he seemed so captivated with. His laughter would carry to her occasionally, and she found herself moving further and further away so she could ignore him more effectively. *No luck! What did those women have to say that was so god damn funny?*

This is what she wanted all along, for him to ignore her. *This is what I want.* She didn't want to be falling all over him like those other women. She wanted to walk away from him and never think about him again. *Then why do I feel so…upset?*

"Beautiful." A male voice pulled Sophie from her consuming thoughts. She turned around to see a man behind her. Even though his face still held youth, gray was making an appearance in his thick black hair. He was a handsome man and his smile was infectious.

"It is. I think it is one of my favorites," Sophie agreed.

"I was talking about you," he said in a friendly tone that drew her in.

"Oh…thank you." Sophie blushed. "I'm Sophie Rogers." She extended her hand toward him.

"Richard Bently." He folded his fingers around hers. "You look like you enjoy the arts. I have never seen someone look at my paintings with such wonder."

"These are yours?" Sophie gasped. "I love art. I paint as well. I'm just a student but someday I hope to be here." She looked around her. "Or at least somewhere like here." She trailed off with a blush flaming in her cheeks.

"Maybe I could help that dream come true." He reached into his pocket and pulled out his card. "Give me a call sometime and we can meet up and discuss it. I would love to get a look at your work."

"I bet you would." Ashton was suddenly beside them. "She's not interested," Ashton said, pulling the card from Sophie's grasp.

"Yes, I am!" Sophie blurted before turning toward Ashton and glaring death at him. "Sorry, Richard, for my friend's rude behavior."

"Yes, well, I will wait to hear from you."

Richard was already retreating because of Ashton's rude dismissal. "I can't believe you did that," she gasped

Ashton tucked the card in his suit jacket. "You don't want his help. Margaret is ready to go," he said tightly as he turned to leave. Sophie let out an angry breath as she followed him toward Margaret.

Chapter Eleven

When they walked outside to their awaiting car, Margaret had run into an old friend who insisted on taking her home after they shared a quick drink. Margaret brightened greatly with the invitation. After a quick goodbye to Margaret, Sophie climbed into the waiting car. A nervous excitement swelled within her when Ashton climbed in the back with her.

"You looked like you were having a good time tonight." Sophie tried to fill the silence.

"I noticed you staring at me," Ashton responded with a satisfied tone.

"I wasn't staring at you. I was paying attention to where you were so I could avoid you and your groupies," she shot back. "I want that card, by the way."

"No," he answered flatly, turning to look out the window as they drove. He pushed a button on his door, and the privacy screen separated them and the driver.

Sophie unbuckled her seatbelt and slid closer to

Ashton. He looked at her through narrowed eyes. She slipped her hand in his jacket pocket. "I want that card." She searched. He didn't move, instead just watched her with an intrigued expression on his face. The card wasn't where he initially placed it, so she began searching his other pockets. There was nothing in his jacket. She pulled his jacket open. "Where is it?" She was enjoying the search too much, and with the haze of wine in her system she was very brave.

Ashton shrugged his shoulders. He smelled heavenly. Everything about him attracted her like a starving animal to a feast. She couldn't stop herself. The thin fabric did nothing to conceal how tantalizing his hard, hot flesh was underneath his shirt. She listened to his breathing become heavy. He still didn't move to encourage or deny what she was doing as she continued to indulge herself. She was already in over her head, the card temporarily forgotten.

Sophie pulled her dress up and straddled him. His body stiffened under her weight, every muscle tensed with her contact. The feel of him was intoxicating, as if an electrical current surged through her, stirring a desperate heat. Sophie reached up and undid his tie, and then proceeded to undo the top button of his shirt and pulled it open to reveal the warm skin upon his neck. She leaned in and ran her tongue up the length of his neck until she grabbed his ear with her teeth.

"Fuck, Sophie!" Ashton gasped breathlessly. His hands grabbed her behind and pulled her in tighter against him. She could feel his erection throb through the material of his pants.

"I want that card," she whispered against his lips.

"No, you don't," he breathed against her mouth.

Sophie leaned back. "Why?"

"Because of what he expects in return for his help." Ashton released a deep breath, loosening his grip on her.

"What?" Sophie asked, confused.

"He wants this." Ashton ran his finger over the curve of her breasts.

"Why do you think that?" Sophie said in a dispirited tone.

"I know of him and the way he works."

She pulled herself from Ashton's lap reluctantly and returned to her seat as they pulled up to Margaret's house. Ashton kept his eyes on her until the car came to a full stop. He stepped out, holding the door open for her. Sophie climbed out and continued toward the house without looking back. Neither of them spoke.

Margaret was not long returning after them. Sophie greeted her at the door, saying goodnight before Margaret ascended the stairs to retire for the night.

Sophie poured herself a glass of water and sat down at the large island that ran the length of the enormous kitchen. She knew she wouldn't be able to sleep after what happened in the car with Ashton. She looked at her phone and noticed a message from Jack.

Jack: How was your evening?

Sophie: It was wonderful except for the part where now I cannot be around Ashton without losing my head and wanting to get in his pants.

Jack: So nothing has changed?

Sophie: Guess not...it was a really nice art gallery. It was nice to dream that one day it would be my stuff up on those walls.

Jack: It will be.

Sophie: Hope so.

Sophie turned on her tablet and opened up Margaret's schedule to address some changes that Margaret had mentioned before she went to bed. Sophie's shoulders tensed as she heard footsteps coming toward the kitchen. Ashton sauntered in, making his jogging pants and T-shirt look ridiculously sexy. He walked toward the cabinet, retrieving two glasses and a bottle of whiskey. He filled the glasses with ice before pulling out the stool next to Sophie. She glanced up at him questioningly, unsure what his mood would be. He filled both glasses before sliding one in front of her. "Your favorite," he teased. She watched his hands and noticed that even they were sensual and perfect. She couldn't stop thoughts of how they would feel running over her naked body.

"How sweet, you remembered." She said sarcastically.

He laughed then, a deep beautiful sound that

showed a side of him that had always seemed so out of reach. His genuine smile was stunning and perfect upon his strong masculine face. He sipped the amber fluid from his glass like it was water. He didn't mind the burning sensation and strong flavor that made her feel like she was swallowing household cleaner, without the refreshing lemon scent to accompany it.

"Let me see this." Ashton picked up her tablet and angled it away from her.

"What are you doing?" She grabbed at it but Ashton pulled it out of her reach. "You're making me nervous," Sophie complained.

"Don't I always?" He said before setting it back down in front of her. A truth or dare game was displayed on the screen. "Truth or dare?" he asked playfully.

"Oh god…really?" Sophie asked in disbelief.

"Are you chicken?" Ashton baited her.

"Fine…truth," Sophie caved. Ashton picked up the tablet and selected truth.

He leaned in close to her ear. "What were you thinking when you were staring at me tonight?" Ashton asked mischievously, his gaze unwavering.

"That's not what it says. You're cheating." Sophie tried to take the tablet from his hands but he refused to let her take it.

"You said you would play." He raised his eyebrow.

"Argh…" Sophie picked up the glass of whiskey and took a generous sip, causing her to cough through the burning sensation. "I thought you looked nice."

"Nice? Come on. I saw the way you were looking at me." He pushed.

"I thought you looked incredibly hot. *Okay?* Are you happy now?" Sophie said impudently. Heat flooded her cheeks at her confession. "It's not like you didn't already know that."

"I didn't know that you thought that." Ashton's expression softened a bit.

"Like it matters," she added as she rolled her eyes.

"It does." He looked deep into her eyes like he was searching for something. Sophie broke the connection as the heat became too intense.

"Your turn. Truth or dare?" She held up the tablet.

"Truth," he answered without hesitation.

"Do you want to kiss me?" The words were out of her mouth before she realized it. She wanted to take them back immediately but they were already out there, hanging between them.

"Yes," he answered truthfully. "Truth or dare?"

"Dare." Sophie didn't want to make any more confessions that she would regret later. *Was this thing between them still a game?*

A slow smile curled the edges of his full lips. "Take off your shirt."

Sophie took another drink before she stood up. Standing close enough to touch, she brushed against his leg as she slowly pulled her shirt up to reveal her flat stomach. She continued to lift it unhurriedly over the swell of her breasts, revealing her black lacy bra before she pulled it over her head. His eyes turned a dark stormy blue, his expression serious as he drank in her exposed body. He clenched his jaw and she had the urge to lean in and kiss him. To inhale his alluring scent that called to her like a drug. She threw her shirt at him and a playful smile broke across his face. *What is this? How did we even get here? I don't want it to stop!*

Sophie sat back on her stool and grabbed the tablet from his hand. "Truth or dare?" She said devilishly.

"Dare." His voice was raspy and thick. She reveled in the fact that in this moment he wanted her. She could see it in the way his gaze reflected his desire.

"Take off your shirt," she said without even pretending to read the tablet.

Ashton reached over his shoulder and grabbed the material of his shirt, pulling it over his head in one sure motion, discarding it on the floor. A sound of appreciation slipped from the back of her throat, her insides erupting in a fire of desire as she took in all of his etched lines. His body looked as if it was carved from flawless marble.

Ashton sat back down and took the tablet. "Take off your pants."

Sophie slid off her stool, running her fingers sensually down her stomach before her fingers slid under the waistband of her lounge pants. She shimmed them down her legs before kicking them off with a flick of her foot. Ashton's eyes followed the length of her legs.

"Your pants," Sophie breathed quickly. Her own desire made her words heavy in her mouth.

Ashton stood up and disposed of his pants. His

hardness strained against his boxers, struggling to free itself from confinement.

Ashton leaned back on his stool and reached down with a powerful arm and pulled her stool as close as it would move against his. Sophie reached out and touched his chest—the bare flesh felt unreal under her fingers as she traced his lines. He was the embodiment of all of her desires.

Ashton's heavy lidded gaze watched her. He looked as if he was drunk on the lust that flowed all around them and through them. She couldn't imagine anything she wanted more than having him against her. Ashton tucked a lock of hair behind her ear, running his fingers down her neck. It caused a rush of goosebumps to cover her skin. His finger continued slowly down her chest and over the swell of her breasts before he hooked his finger under her bra, pulling her toward his lips. He lifted her onto his lap, molding her soft curves to his hard body. Her flesh was overly sensitized and everywhere she touched him felt incredible. It was mind blowing and completely new territory for her. Her hips moved of their own accord, driven by her primal need.

Sophie moaned against his lips. "I want you," she said into her kiss. He groaned in response as if he took pleasure in her words.

Sophie pulled back from the kiss. "What are we doing?" Sophie whispered, looking into his eyes.

"What feels right," he whispered back.

"Does it? Feel right to you, I mean?" she asked with searching eyes. His hand cupped her cheek, holding her close.

Footsteps down the hallway startled them. Sophie slid off Ashton's lap and she grabbed her clothes off the floor before she darted toward the pantry door, shuffling inside before she swung the door closed. She tried to even her breath and slow her wild heart. *I can't believe I was making out with Ashton in Margaret's kitchen! Holy hell! What am I doing?*

Sophie peered through the narrow opening that still allowed her to spy into the kitchen. Ashton stood, shrugging on his pants before sitting back down on the chair. He acted like he couldn't care less if he was caught making out in his grandmother's kitchen. *Was this normal behavior for him?*

"Charlotte? You're up late." Ashton turned to acknowledge her entrance.

"Just getting a glass of water, dear. How are you?" She tilted her head in concern as she noticed Ashton's flushed appearance. Ashton shrugged his shoulders and glanced toward the pantry door. Sophie stepped back from the opening. "Do you want to talk about it?" Charlotte asked as she patted his shoulder.

"No, not right now." Ashton smiled at her.

"Later then," She said before walking toward the hall. Once her footsteps faded, Sophie stepped out of the pantry.

Ashton ran his fingers through his hair and downed the rest of his glass. They both just stared at each other. *Did he regret what just happened? What the hell just happened? I am terrified!*

"I guess we owe Charlotte for saving us from

doing something we would have regretted." Sophie sighed. She wasn't expecting the sharp look he threw her way, like she had wounded him with her words.

"Yeah," Ashton responded coldly, "but it never hurts to put another notch on my belt." He tilted his head with his familiar steely, cold gaze. The old Ashton was standing in front of her. Now looking into his eyes, all she could see was the person that only felt passionate about hurting her.

Sophie narrowed her eyes angrily. "You won't be adding my name to your list of conquests, Ashton King. Whatever this is between us was just a momentary lapse in judgement."

"We'll see. You *did* just admit that you wanted me, after all." He leaned against the counter smugly.

Sophie stormed out of the kitchen, leaving him to gloat in his annoying victory. He finally got her to admit that she wanted him. She wanted to crawl under a rock. How could she not see what he was doing? Her chest ached as she was suddenly racked with sorrow. When she got to her room she crawled on the bed, pulling the covers up over her head and cried until she had nothing left. Her phone vibrated; reaching for it, she noticed Jack had sent her a message.

Jack: Are you asleep?

Sophie: No. You're up late. Work stuff or late night partying?

Jack: Couldn't sleep. I wanted to talk to you.

Sophie: I'm glad you want to 'cause I need you right now.

Jack: Rough night?

Sophie: You could say that. I wish you were here. I really need a friend to tell me that everything is going to be okay.

Jack: If I was there with you I would wrap my arms around you and not let go until I saw a smile on your beautiful face. Even if it took hours, days even...

Sophie: What about months?

Jack: Um...months? Joking. As long as it takes.

Sophie: Do you know why I don't believe in love?

Jack: Why?

Sophie: Because it doesn't believe in me. What is wrong with me? There is too much bad history between me and Ashton. I would be a fool to think it would turn out as anything other than a complete disaster. I just don't know how to stop wanting him and I don't think he knows how to stop hating me. I am so confused!

Jack: He doesn't hate you. You will probably find out that he has been secretly in love with you from the first moment he saw you.

Sophie: Ha! If only you knew, you wouldn't say that.

Jack: You'd be surprised.

Sophie: Have you ever been in love?

Jack: Yes.

Sophie: And? What happened?

Jack: I will get back to you on that.

Sophie: That's all. At least tell me what it feels like. So I know…please.

Sophie waited for a response but as the minutes passed, her eyes grew heavy. She laid the phone against her chest and let her eyes close. The vibration of the phone startled her away from her drowsy state. She held up the phone.

Jack: It's like…hearing the most amazing song you have ever heard and no matter how much time passes or how many other songs you hear it's the only one you want to listen to, sing to, dance to. No other song makes you feel the same. It is the rhythm of your heart from the moment you hear it.

Sophie: *I think that is the most beautiful thing I have ever heard. And you have found your song?*

Jack: *Yes.*

Sophie: *That makes me happy.*

Jack: *Me too.*

Chapter Twelve

The next morning Sophie noticed a note from Charlotte saying she'd left to pick up groceries and run some errands. Sophie made some tea and settled in to read the newspaper. She got nervous as the morning proceeded with no sign of Margaret. She had morning appointments booked in her schedule. When Sophie could wait no longer, she walked up to Margaret's door and knocked. She was only met with silence. She didn't feel it appropriate to enter Margaret's room without permission.

Sophie decided to wake Ashton. She stood outside his door for a moment, wondering if she should disturb him. She ran her fingers over the groove on his door and remembered what happened between them last night.

Sophie remembered Jack's words from last night when he described what love felt like. The feelings that Ashton stirred in her were raw and powerful. She found herself wanting to play his song over and over until she knew every word so she could sing it always. She didn't believe in love but Jack's words seemed so fitting for how she felt about Ashton. It seemed so unfair to have no control over your own emotions and how these feelings were leading her mercilessly down a destructive path.

When she knocked on Ashton's door, she heard a moan of protest. She waited to hear movement but she was only met with silence. She turned the handle and pushed it open cautiously. The light from the hallway spilled into his room, illuminating his still form upon the bed.

"Ashton?" Sophie walked quietly over toward his bed. "Ash?" she whispered again.

She touched the warm smooth skin of his bare shoulder. "Ashton?"

"What?" He groaned. "Come to finish what we started?" he said, pulling the covers back to expose his gorgeous body. Sophie's eyes hungrily took him in.

"You wish." She pulled herself back to reality. "Margaret isn't up yet for the day and she has appointments this morning. I knocked but she didn't answer. I didn't want to go in. I'm worried. What should I do?"

Ashton kicked his blankets off and climbed out of bed. He wore only his boxers—she was washed with memories of last night and how close she came to giving herself to him. He was too sexy to pull her gaze away as he pulled on his pants. She was mad at herself for telling him that she wanted him last night, but it was the truth. Every part of her wanted him in so many ways. She wanted to know every part of his body. She wanted to know the Ashton that Margaret knew and loved. She wanted to hear him laugh, to be the one to make him laugh, tell her about his day and his life, and most of all she wanted him not to hate her. She watched him disappear through his door to check on Margaret.

Sophie sat on the edge of Ashton's bed, unable to bring herself to leave. The room smelled of him and it soothed her. The sheets were warm from his body and she had to stop herself from curling up in his bed to see what it would feel like to be wrapped up in him. Sophie stood up quickly when he leaned into his room. "Cancel her morning appointments and make an appointment with Dr. Reynolds. He should be in her contacts." He continued down the hall.

"Ashton?" she called, following. "Is she okay?"

"She'll be fine." Ashton stopped walking suddenly. Sophie couldn't react fast enough, colliding with him.

"Sorry," she muttered as she tried to right herself. Seeing him standing in the hall, his bare chest bathed in the light, his hair in sexy disarray from sleep, was breathtaking. To her horror she was literally falling all over him. She stared up into his eyes. "And I should apologize for last night."

"What about last night?" His voice gruff.

"For saying that I would have regretted it. Even knowing what it would have meant to you, I wouldn't have regretted it." She whispered her secret. She felt like she needed to say it and so she let the words fall from her lips as she looked into his deep blue eyes.

"What would it have meant to me?" He clenched his jaw. There was a hint of challenge in his low voice.

"Nothing." Sophie shrugged casually. She turned on her heel to walk away.

"Sophie?"

"Don't, please. I don't want you to say anything. I just needed to tell you. I have to go and make some phone calls."

Dr. Reynolds agreed to meet Margaret at 1:00 p.m. that afternoon. Margaret slept for most of the morning before she came down in time to leave for the appointment. Sophie only managed to get her to eat a plain piece of toast and a small cup of tea before they left. Despite her tired eyes, Margaret looked every bit of the well-groomed woman she always was. She wore a dark blue pants suit with a white blouse.

"Are you trying to impress the doctor?" Sophie teased as they pulled up to the doctor's office.

"Well, he is a very handsome man, but no. When you're my age you always have to look your best because anything else can be scary." She chuckled lightly.

"I can't imagine you looking anything but beautiful, Margaret," Sophie assured her.

"Too kind, dear." She took Sophie's hand and gave it a loving pat before she opened her door to leave.

"Are you sure you don't want me to come in with you?" Sophie's worry was obvious in her tone.

"I will be fine. I'll call you when I'm done," Margaret insisted.

Sophie waited for Margaret to disappear inside the building before she left. She took the opportunity to finish her final report that correlated with her painting. She drove to her favorite tea café not far from where she dropped off Margaret. Once inside, she found her usual place in the corner. Sitting in the oversized armchair, she wrapped her hands around her large tea, warming her from the inside as she sipped. Sophie pulled up her file titled, *Love, the Greatest Fable of All Time*. She'd started her report only days ago, but the words flowed like a steady stream, pouring her thoughts upon the pages. To her, the idea of romantic love was unrealistic. To believe in something that was determined by unpredictable feelings that were as fluid as the ever flowing ocean would be unwise. It made no sense to her that people would put so much faith in the idea of love when there was no guarantee. History was full of art created under the belief that romantic love existed for them, but just as many that proved it did not. You have to love yourself because you are the only one who truly can; everything else is only a temporary illusion. Once she finished her report, she found the nearest printing location to ready it for submission. Sophie was already finished when Margaret called her phone.

Sophie was pleased to see that Margaret already looked better when she picked her up. Her color had returned and her smile was more genuine. "How are you feeling now?" Sophie asked as Margaret slid into the front seat.

"Like myself…just tired from this annoying bug I have. What's this?" Margaret asked, pointing to the cup of coffee sitting in the cup holder.

"I got it just in case you needed it." Sophie shrugged.

"Oh I do. You are an angel," Margaret raved.

Margaret decided to retire to her room for the afternoon when they arrived home. Sophie left to run a few errands and drop off her report. She was officially done with all of her classes, and it felt great to turn in her last piece of work. When she returned to Margaret's, she curled up with a book, staying close should Margaret need her. Sophie's phone rang, pulling her from her pages.

"Hey, Mel," Sophie answered.

"Don't say I told you so," Mel whispered in a hurried tone.

"Mel? You're scaring me." Sophie stomach dropped.

"Last night he drank way too much. *Surprise,*" she ended with angry sarcasm. "It's like he doesn't stop."

"Where are you? Did he hurt you?" Sophie's words were rushed as panic tightened her throat.

"That ass keeps marking me up. How am I supposed to make any money covered in bruises?" Mel fumed but kept her voice low.

"Where is he?" Sophie questioned.

"He's here. He's all right now, begged my forgiveness and all that shit I'm tired of hearing. He thinks I forgave him. I want to leave but I'm scared that he'll go berserk if he sees me trying to get my suitcases out the door. He won't let me out of his sight even to go to the washroom. I think he has a feeling I might take off."

"What do you want me to do? Can you leave

your stuff?" Sophie asked hopefully.

"No, I need my things, and if I leave it he'll probably burn it or something," Mel protested.

"I'm gonna come and get you. Where is his place?" Sophie was determined to get Mel out of that situation.

"It's that old shit hole on Merrill's street. Thanks, Sophie, you are the one person I can always count on."

"Always, be there soon."

Sophie hung up her phone, knowing she needed to get to Mel as soon as possible. She walked across the hall to Ashton's room and knocked on the door. She'd heard him come back earlier from his run. "Come in," he called distractedly.

When Sophie opened his door he was on his computer. Whatever he was doing was demanding of his attention; he didn't look up as she walked in. "I have to call you back, Gabe," he said before ending his call.

"What would I have to do to let me borrow your car?" she blurted.

He looked up at her with a surprised scowl. "A lot...and don't tell me you want to borrow my car to run off to a booty call with that Sam guy."

"What?" Sophie was confused by his comment until she remembered telling him she had a thing for Sam from work. "No...I should have known better than to ask you." Sophie sighed as she turned to head downstairs. She knew the bus came every twenty minutes.

"Sophie...wait!" Ashton called from the top of the stairs. He was pulling a sweater on over his head, his hair still damp from his shower.

"I don't have time, Ashton, I gotta catch the bus."

"Stop running away from me, please…why do you need my car?" His voice was pleading. "I can tell you're upset about something. I wouldn't have given you a hard time if I knew it was important."

Sophie took a deep breath and stared back at him, unsure of her next move.

"I'll drive," he said before walking past her and heading for the garage. Sophie followed him quietly. She didn't explain until she slid into the passenger's seat. "My friend Mel is in trouble with an abusive boyfriend. I have to get to her." Sophie felt a tear slip down her cheek. She was terrified for Mel.

"Where?"

***

Sophie knocked on Corbin's apartment door. She felt better knowing that Ashton was with her. He looked intimidating standing beside her with his tall, solid build. A stern scowl weighed upon his features, making him look fierce. Ashton was a strong contrast to her own small, non-threatening presence. He made her feel braver walking into the situation.

No one came to the door but Sophie could make out muffled voices from within. Mel hadn't answered her phone when Sophie tried calling back. She was getting worried the situation might have took a turn for the worse.

"Who did you call, *bitch*?" Sophie stilled when she heard the angry male voice break the silence.

"No one." Mel's voice sounded small. "I didn't call anyone." Her words were followed by a scream that caused Sophie to panic. She banged on the door frantically, screaming for Mel to open it. Ashton threw the weight of his body into the door. His shoulder met it with a resounding crack, giving way to the force of the blow. Sophie's eyes immediately found Mel, her hand against her reddened cheek. Tears washed down Sophie's face without restraint. She wanted to run to Mel, but Corbin stood between them. The shock of their intrusion melted from his face to show rage rolling off him in crashing waves. He threw his beer bottle against the wall, glass showering down to the floor.

"Who the *fuck* are you?" Corbin hollered with a raw voice. He looked bleary-eyed and his appearance was scruffy. He was no longer the well-groomed charming guy that had swept Mel off her feet. His true colors were shining through and they were far from beautiful. Sophie felt guilty for letting her friend fall so deep into this horrible situation.

"Get Mel and get out of here," Ashton ordered Sophie, keeping his eyes on Corbin.

"She ain't going nowhere with you. She's *mine*," Corbin sneered.

Ashton was a good half foot taller than him, but Corbin was too drunk to notice he was at a serious disadvantage. His unfocused gaze didn't register the danger Ashton presented. The scale was tipped in Ashton's favor, but Corbin was unpredictable—his fuse was obviously short and he had no sense of mind in his intoxicated state.

"Let's get your stuff." Sophie reached out for her. Mel shot a nervous glance toward Corbin before slowly moving toward Sophie. Corbin growled before taking an exaggerated swing at Ashton. He stumbled clumsily in his drunken state, allowing Ashton an easy opening. His fist met Corbin's face, knocking him back onto the floor amongst the broken glass. Blood exploded from Corbin's nose, running down his face and staining his white shirt.

Sophie hurried Mel down the hall to gather her things. The sounds of the struggle between Ashton and Corbin carried down the hall, fueling their steps. Mel threw all her things in her bag, zipping it quickly before running to the bathroom. Corbin's bedroom was in the same cluttered, untidy state as his car. Clothes covered the floor and spilled from his closet. Mel slid all her things off the bathroom counter, dropping them into another bag.

Sophie took it from Mel's shaking hands. "Is this everything you need?" Mel merely nodded. Sophie took her hand in hers and led her back down the hall.

Corbin's unconscious body was sprawled out on the floor. The girls looked up at Ashton, who was shaking out the pain in his hand. "He wouldn't stop coming at me. I had to put him out."

Mel walked up to Corbin, giving him a kick in his side. "Goodbye, fucker. Hope you have a shit life." Mel turned around and looked at both Sophie and Ashton. "Let's get the hell out of here."

Sophie crawled in the back seat of Ashton's car,

wrapping her arms around Mel's shoulders. Mel was no longer shaking; relief allowed both of them to relax slightly. Sophie soothed her friend and waited for her to break the silence.

"From the look of you, you must be the guy that has been making Sophie act all weird lately." Mel was the first to break the heavy silence.

"*Mel.*" Sophie's eyes widened in disbelief. "She obviously doesn't have a filter." Sophie sighed, her eyes meeting Ashton's in the rearview mirror.

"Are you going to tell me who the hot guy is?" Mel insisted.

Sophie could tell Ashton was enjoying this.

"I just started working for his grandmother. He offered to drive me," Sophie explained, hoping Mel would not dig any further. "Enough about me. Are you okay?" Sophie could see fresh bruises forming on Mel's arms and her lip was swollen.

"I'll be fine. Just need to sleep." Mel let her shoulders collapse into Sophie. "A motel would be heaven right now." She sighed. "Thank you for coming to my rescue, Sophie and knight in shining armor guy."

"Anytime, Mel." Sophie smiled. "I'm just glad it's over. No more Corbin, right?"

"Right," Mel confirmed whole-heartedly.

Ashton pulled up in front of the motel Mel requested. Sophie was relieved to see it didn't look like the place Mr. Cleary had recommended. Ashton parked the car and told the girls to wait while he checked on availability. He came back a few minutes later with a room key in his hand.

Sophie flicked on the lights, flooding the room

with a warm, low light. It smelled freshly cleaned, with inviting décor and crisp looking linens on the bed. Ashton set her bags on the bed before he excused himself to make a phone call.

Mel was in the shower when Ashton returned with a couple bottles of water and food from the vending machine. "These were the healthiest options," he said, placing them on the table. "I didn't know if she would be hungry." Sophie folded the last of Mel's clothes that had been thrown in her bag and placed them neatly on top of the dresser.

"Margaret called and asked if everything was all right. Charlotte must have mentioned that we both took off in a hurry."

"What did you tell her?" Sophie asked curiously.

"I told her we were on a date." Ashton looked at her as if he was curious what her reaction would be.

"What? Why?"

He shrugged. "Seemed better than the truth."

"Was she mad?" Sophie asked nervously.

"She actually told me not to mess it up. Apparently she has little confidence in my moves." Ashton shook his head in disbelief.

"Actually I was going to mention something about that," Sophie teased. "I mean truth or dare...come on."

"As I recall, you enjoyed yourself." Their light conversation suddenly turned intense. His penetrating blue eyes looked as if they were undressing her, causing Sophie to practically melt to the floor. Mel opened the bathroom door and the moment dissipated. She narrowed her eyes suspiciously at Sophie and Ashton. She was wearing pajama pants and an oversized sweatshirt that floated on her small frame, making her seem so much younger. "I thought you two would be making out or something. Your sexual tension is suffocating."

Sophie left the comment alone. "How are you feeling?"

Mel crawled into the bed. "I feel like I could sleep for days."

"Ashton got you some food in case you're hungry." Sophie offered a bottle of water and a granola bar from the table.

"Thanks, I can't remember the last time I ate." Mel pulled back the wrapper and devoured the bar.

Sophie climbed onto the bed and snuggled in next to Mel.

"Thank you." Mel smiled sadly, tears clouding her eyes.

Sophie wrapped her arms around Mel and leaned back against the headboard of the bed and let Mel shed all of her tears while rubbing her back. Mel eventually drifted to sleep, completely exhausted.

Ashton sat quietly in the armchair. He was quiet as time passed into the late hours. "Are you thinking this is the worst date you've ever been on?" she whispered.

"No." His voice was sleepy, his features relaxed and handsome. He had run his hands through his hair a few times, making it messy and irresistible at the same time. "You can go home. I'm going to stay in case she needs me," Sophie offered.

"This chair is actually very comfortable." He smiled lazily back at her.

Sophie wasn't sure when she had fallen asleep, but when she woke up the lights were off and Ashton was asleep in the chair. Mel was still curled up against Sophie's side, her breathing deep and even. Sophie slowly slipped out from under Mel, pulling the covers up over her shoulders.

She quietly opened the closet, removing an extra blanket that was neatly folded on the shelf. She quietly walked over to Ashton, unfolded it, and laid it over his long legs that were stretched out in front of him. He looked so peaceful in sleep. The streetlights cast a soft glow into the room, highlighting his relaxed features. He was breathtaking. She couldn't think of a face more flawless than his. The memory of his kiss caused her mouth to tingle with recollection. His full lips knew how to dance with hers expertly, like they knew all her secrets. He really was a knight in shining armor tonight, saving both of them from the horrible situation that Sophie would have walked blindly into.

Sophie looked up, noticing his eyes were now open. She froze, wondering how long he had been watching her gazing at him. He lifted his hand and gently touched her fingertips with his. It was the lightest contact but the effect was immobilizing. He intertwined his fingers with hers, pulling her down against him. Sophie didn't resist, climbing onto his lap and laying her head against his chest. He smelled of everything wonderful as she melted against him. "Thank you for tonight," she whispered. He didn't say anything, only pulled the blanket up over them, wrapping her in his warmth.

She fell asleep to the rhythm of his heartbeat.

Chapter Thirteen

Sophie woke when she felt a gentle touch brushing her hair from her face. She slowly opened her eyes, remembering where she was. Her body was curled around Ashton's in the chair. "Sorry…I didn't mean to fall asleep." Her voice barely cooperated in her drowsy state.

"Don't apologize," Ashton whispered.

"What time is it?" Sophie pulled herself up.

"Still early, but we should get going."

Sophie wasn't certain what to think of her night curled up in Ashton's lap. She didn't question why he pulled her close. She took comfort wrapped in his arms and fell into a deep, satisfying sleep. She wondered what he thought having her curled around him the entire night. She was in unknown territory with Ashton. Ever since he came back into her life she had been trying to figure out the new set of rules when it came to him and her.

Sophie woke Mel to tell her that she had to leave, promising to call later to check on her. She slipped out of the room and followed Ashton to his car. The sun was relentlessly bright and intense for the early morning, promising a clear and beautiful day.

"Mel is a colorful character," Ashton said when Sophie hopped in the car.

"That's a good way to describe her." Sophie tilted her head thoughtfully. "Most people say she's brash, crazy, and even scary." Sophie chuckled.

"That description works as well." He nodded thoughtfully. "How did you guys become friends?"

"She lives in my apartment building, which is why she's also temporarily homeless. I think we should be able to move back home tomorrow. Then you will be rid of me, at least during the evenings." Sophie hated how nervous she sounded. It was one thing to be a mess on the inside but she didn't want Ashton to know.

Ashton grew quiet for a moment before he spoke again. "You wouldn't have just been another notch on my belt."

Sophie wished she had her sunglasses to hide behind. She was terrified her emotions were written all over her face. She was surprised there was no more humor in his eyes. "Why? Is there no more room left?"

He tilted his head and bit his lip in a very sexy expression. "Do you think me some kind of man whore?"

"Does it matter what I think?"

"Yes."

Sophie didn't know how to respond to his words. She found herself freefalling without any way to save herself from the inevitable impact.

"I think…that I don't know what I would have done without you last night. Thank you." She smiled at him. Suddenly too shy to hold his gaze, she turned away and watched the landscape change as they drove.

"I'm glad I could help."

Sophie was relieved when they got back and Margaret was still asleep. She didn't want her thinking they were out all night, especially if Ashton actually did tell her they were on a date. Sophie showered and dressed quickly with the hopes that she would be able to speak to Margaret before she left for the day.

Margaret came down into the kitchen as Sophie was helping Charlotte clean up some dishes from breakfast. Margaret shook her head with a laugh.

"She's a stubborn girl, Miss Margaret—always insisting on doing my job." Charlotte chuckled.

"I'm just doing my part," Sophie defended herself. "I'm glad I caught you before I left for class. Your schedule is all cleared for this morning. Karen sent you an email with some questions about the fundraiser. We can get back to her by the end of the day, and Mr. Graves wanted to reschedule your meeting from yesterday to this afternoon. He says he has some things he wants to run by you and doesn't want to wait."

"Very well, dear." Margaret smiled appreciatively. "What would I do without you ladies in my life taking care of me?"

"Relax this morning, Margaret, have a bath or something. We can save the world after lunch," Sophie teased.

"A bath does sound nice," Margaret said wistfully.

Sophie flew through her morning of classes. Most of the professors had lost interest in trying to push their lectures until the very end. Everyone's mind was occupied by the summer ahead, planning their adventures. Everyone except for Sophie, who planned to work every opportunity she had to make her savings account slightly less pathetic.

She called Mel the first opportunity she had, hoping she was already up.

Mel answered the phone after the first ring. "Tell me you slept with that man god you brought last night," she said.

"Glad to see you're back to your old self." Sophie rolled her eyes.

"I know you're rolling your eyes at me, Sophie, but seriously, does he have a brother, or cousin, anything?" Mel rambled.

"No, only child, and I don't know of any extended family. Sorry, but if you want a shot at Ashton, go for it." Sophie didn't have any claim on him but a small part of her hated the idea of Ashton being with someone else.

"Yeah, right. I saw the way he looked at you. He looks at you like you're the only girl in the world. I mean, did you see my tits in that shirt last night? Not one look."

Sophie laughed. "You're wrong. I don't know what we have but it's far from ever being *anything*."

"Riiiggghhhttt. You know I love you, right?"

"Yep."

"Good. Stop being stupid!" Mel barked into the

phone.

Sophie sighed. "I gotta go."

"Dream boat paid for me to stay tonight too. I'll be here till tomorrow when I have to face the world again and go to work."

"Are you sure you're up for work after what happened?" Sophie questioned. Mel's relationship with Corbin had taken its toll on her. It was the first time Sophie had seen Mel so vulnerable.

"I'm fine. I'm not letting that asshole have the satisfaction of interfering with my life anymore. You're still coming, right?"

"Ugh…yes." Sophie sighed in defeat. Any hope she had that Mel would forget died away.

"Good. Give hottie a big thank you kiss for me right on the…"

Sophie cut her off. "Gotta go! Bye."

Before she tucked her phone away she sent a message to Jack.

Sophie: Home yet?

Jack: No, no yet.

Sophie: Are you really away or are you avoiding me?

Jack: Never. I'd rather spend time with you than be here.

Sophie: I spent the night with Ashton. Not what you think. We just slept…at least I did. He helped me with a friend. I saw another side of him.

Jack: And?

Sophie: I don't know. I just know when I was sleeping against him I felt like I was home. Is that weird?

Jack: No.

Sophie: Anyway do you want to hear something crazy? I agreed to work at a strip joint tomorrow night for my friend Mel. Not taking clothes off but it will be my first time there. Getting nervous now that it's getting close.

Jack: What! Why would you do that?

Sophie: She asked. Maybe it's time to do something a little crazy. I always play it safe and besides it's hard to say no to Mel. She makes everything sound like the greatest idea ever. They just want extra girls mingling for the event. It seems simple enough.

Jack: Probably not a good idea. Being around a bunch of rammed up guys. NOT good.

Sophie: Are you worried about me? Sweet but I am a big girl. I will be fine. I already agreed anyway.

Jack: Cancel.

Sophie: Nope.

Jack: What place?

Sophie: Be happy that I am gonna shake things up a bit and stop being boring.

Jack: What place? Safe is good. Safe is very very good and you are far from boring.

Jack: Don't do it.

Jack: Seriously don't do it.

Jack: Sophie?

Sophie didn't bother answering his text. Jack seemed so adamant about her not going through with it. She wasn't going to change her mind. She'd already told Mel she would. Sophie tucked her phone in her purse and headed toward the bus stop. She had a lot of things to do this afternoon with Margaret before her shift at the restaurant.

When Sophie walked into the restaurant that evening it was busy as usual. She grabbed her apron and set to work. She tried to pretend she didn't notice Sam's subtle looks. When she caught him watching her she gave him an innocent, friendly wave. The evening passed quickly with the rush of customers.

Megan flagged her down when she walked into the kitchen. "Hey, Sophie, Jack is at the bar asking for you."

"I didn't know he was back. Thank you." Sophie beamed, heading in his direction.

Jack looked up and noticed her approach. An adorable smile brightened his entire face.

"Sophie. How have you been?"

"Great! Why didn't you tell me you were back?" Sophie questioned excitedly.

A baffled expression crossed his features. "I just got in this afternoon. I came here tonight hoping you would give me a second chance after running out on you last time."

Sophie bumped her shoulder into his arm. "Of course. How do you want to make it up to me?" Sophie teased playfully.

"Any way you want." He suddenly seemed nervous.

"Ooh, how about that expensive dinner you promised me?" Sophie wiggled her eyebrows. Jack's confusion wiped away his smile. "Have you forgotten already that you owe me for telling you all my secrets?" Sophie searched for recognition in his expression, anything that indicated he knew what she was talking about. "Do you have any idea what I'm talking about? Our texts?"

"Texts?" His expression confirmed that he had no knowledge of the conversations. *Oh god.*

Sophie's stomach twisted with the realization that Jack was not the person she had been texting. She suddenly felt sick to her stomach. "Excuse me, Jack. I suddenly don't feel well." She could feel all the color drain from her face as she flew toward the bathroom.

"Sophie?" Jack called after her.

Pushing the door open to the washroom, Sophie locked herself in a stall. She tried to take deep, calming breaths but panic had a tight hold on her.

The bathroom door opened. "Sophie?" Lori called hesitantly as she walked in.

"Yeah?" Sophie's voice sounded brittle.

"Sam said you didn't look well. I wanted to check on you." Lori's feet stopped in front of the stall door. "I saw you talking to Jack. Is everything okay?"

"Yeah…I just need a minute. Something came over me all of a sudden." Sophie leaned against the wall. Someone was playing a sick joke on her and she was devastated. She pulled her phone from her pocket, skimming through the conversations she had when she thought it was Jack. She knew without a doubt who was capable of this deception. She cringed at the thought she actually believed Ashton had actual real feelings for her. She was such an idiot. She knew he was trouble but she invited him in anyway.

"I'll get you a glass of water," Lori offered.

A few minutes later Lori returned, passing the glass under the door. "Thanks," Sophie managed. She tried to sip the cold liquid but it wouldn't pass the lump in her throat.

"Sam said he would drive you home. It's pretty much the end of the night anyway. I can handle your stragglers and I won't even steal your tips." Lori attempted to make her laugh with her teasing tone.

"I think I'll have to take the offer." Sophie squeezed her eyes tight. "But keep the tips." In the two years since she had started working there she had never missed time or left early. She took pride in the fact that she was dependable, but in this moment she had to admit defeat. She'd had the rug pulled from beneath her. She couldn't bring herself to face the customers and pretend that she wasn't completely devastated.

"I'll let Sam know. He'll probably jump with joy at the chance to spend time with you. I hope you feel better soon," Lori added before she left. "And I'll let Jack know you're leaving. He's been lingering around waiting for you."

When Sophie came out of the washroom Lori was handing Sam her purse and sweater. "Thanks, Lori," Sophie managed. She felt like she was going to cry any moment. "And thank you for taking me home, Sam."

"Anytime." Sam smiled warmly as he led her out toward his car.

"I'm really sorry to abandon ship and make you leave to drive me home as well. I feel really bad about it." Sophie looked over at Sam. She could only see his darkened features until a car passed by, lighting up his face.

"It's really no problem. I'm glad I could help. Considering this is the first time in two years that you have had to leave early, I-I mean. I think you're a-a great employee. Don't worry about anything. Just feel better," he stammered through his words. He reached over and patted her on the leg, letting his hand linger. His touch didn't cause heat to rush through her body. It didn't make her breathless and desperate like Ashton's did, but it felt nice.

Sophie could see longing in Sam's gaze. He was no longer trying to be discreet, his eyes searching hers for some sign of approval.

Sophie wondered if it would be possible to feel even a fraction of the passion for Sam she felt for Ashton. She thought about taking his hand and going down a path with him that would lead her far away from Ashton. She tried to focus on Sam but all she saw was red in her haze of anger and complete shock that were both warring for center stage.

She placed her hand on top of Sam's, tentatively testing the waters. "I really appreciate you taking me home." She smiled. The feel of his skin was warm under hers. She could see him visibly relax with her gesture. When she touched Ashton, all sense dissipated and she was left with instinct that was driven with need. When she touched Sam, her conscience would not quiet, whispering words of uncertainty. Maybe if things were different she could have found happiness with Sam, but Ashton had stolen that from her. Her body mourned the heat, desire, and intensity that was missing with Sam. It wouldn't be fair to him; he deserved better.

"Nice house," he said, looking up in admiration.

"It's actually my boss's house. Well, my other boss. I'm staying here while my apartment is being rid of its rodent problem." Sophie made a disgusted face.

Sam laughed. "I'll get your door." He walked around and opened it for her, offering his hand to help her out. The air felt thick between them, making her uncomfortable. He stepped closer, looking into her eyes. Sophie was suddenly nervous he would kiss her. "I hope you feel better soon." Sam tucked her hair behind her ear.

"Sam…I…" Sophie began tensely.

"Don't say anything right now. Just know that I want to get to know you, spend time with you. I'm a very patient man, Sophie." Sam leaned in and kissed her forehead.

Sophie relaxed and let a smile fade her nervous disposition. "Thank you, Sam."

"Good night, Sophie."

Sam didn't drive away until Ashton swung the front door open. "I thought you were gonna call me when you were done working so I could pick you up." He glared at the taillights of Sam's car as he drove down the road.

"Sam offered." Sophie shrugged her shoulders. He was upset and raked his hands through his hair, making him look irresistible. The thought tried to dissipate her anger, but she held on tightly.

A scowl formed on his face as he studied her. "Sophie—" Ashton began. Sophie cut him off. She was tired of his lies.

"Goodnight, Ashton." She turned and headed toward her room without another word. She did not want to start a fight in Margaret's home, and the emotions swirling inside her threatened to burst though the seams. She didn't know if she would be able to control herself if she let them slip. She adored Margaret too much and she didn't want to cause any disrespect.

Inside her room she threw herself on the bed and pulled her phone from her pocket as it vibrated against her hip.

Jack: Sophie?

She stared at the screen, blatantly aware that it was no longer Jack on the other side of their conversations. Her heart beat so loudly that she could feel it in her throat. She was angry. She wanted to show him that she was not going to be toyed with.

Sophie: I'm here. What are you up to?

Jack: Nothing. You?

Sophie: Actually I'm glad I have you to talk to. I don't think I can resist my attraction to Ashton anymore. All I think about is having him in my bed and running my tongue over his entire body. I get wet just thinking about his naked body.

Sophie hit send and felt the evil grin play on her lips, but the realization that there were no lies in her words made her breathing deep and her fingers tremble. Ashton didn't respond for a moment and she thought she would lose her nerve.

Sophie: Seriously, if he were to come to my door right now I would not be able to control myself. I long for him to please my body in every imaginable way.

She had power over him in one sense, anyway. She knew that he responded to her sexually before and she was going to see how far she could push him. She wanted to turn the tables. After a few long moments of silence she heard a gentle knock on her door. A victorious smile sprang to life upon her lips. She climbed off her bed, flipped her hair around, and pinched her cheeks before she walked toward the door. She looked down and decided to unbutton her work shirt, exposing her slinky camisole underneath. It plunged dangerously low, exposing the deep valley between her breasts.

She opened the door slowly to Ashton's tall frame filling the door. She tried to be as seductive as she could. "Yes?" she whispered. "Do you need something?" She had no idea where she was pulling this from. It was a part of her that she had never indulged before. She trailed her fingers along the soft flesh of her exposed cleavage.

Ashton's breathing was deep and his eyes dark as he watched her. "Do you want to come in?" She bit her lip playfully as she kept her gaze intently on him. He hesitated for a moment before he brushed past her, walking into her room.

"Have a seat." Sophie motioned toward her bed. "I am just getting changed, if you don't mind?"

"No." His voice broke. "No, go ahead." He sat down on the edge of her bed, his eyes following her with desperate need. She almost lost her nerve looking into his beautiful face. She wanted him with a fierceness that scared her, but she would never have him like she wanted. It was time she toyed with him to even the scales.

Sophie unbuttoned her pants, turning around and letting them slide down the length of her legs, bending over seductively to discard them. A sharp intake of breath from Ashton reminded her that she was in charge of this situation, and having power over this sexy, powerful man thrilled her. When she stood up she could feel his body behind her. His hands slipped around her waist, greedily taking in her body with his keen hands.

"What are you doing to me?" he whispered against her neck. The heat of his breath caused fervor to charge her body. *Him? The question is what does he think he's doing to me?* She thought angrily. She knew she had to remain focused. She refused to fall under his spell again.

She spun around, pushing him back toward the bed. He relinquished to her demand until he collapsed onto her bed onto his elbows. Sophie straddled his waist, pressing her body against his. Her hands explored him as she rocked her hips against his groin. He could not hide his excitement. Ashton's breathing quickened as he let her have his way with him. She skimmed her lips along his jawline, gently nipping at his chin.

"Say that you want me," she whispered against his lips. His eyes were enchanting as they drank her in. He growled as she sucked his bottom lip in her mouth. She lost herself for a moment as their lips caressed in a beautiful dance of pleasure. Sophie pulled back for a breath, pushing him down until his back was pressed firm against the bed.

Sophie lifted her camisole over her head. Her fingers lingered on the clasp of her bra. "Say that you want me," she demanded in a heady whisper.

"I want you…I want you." He pulled her down against him. "I fucking want you," he whispered against her skin. Reaching around, he flipped her over so her back was on the bed. He kissed the sensitive skin of her neck, slowly traveling down toward her chest.

"What name do you want me to scream out when you take me?" Sophie asked soberly.

He stilled, looking at her in confusion, his lips swollen from their kiss.

"Ashton or…*Jack*?" She couldn't help the pain that seeped into her words.

Sophie watched Ashton's face fall. "*Fuck*." He pushed himself off the bed. She instantly missed his heat, the feel of him against her. She didn't feel the satisfaction that she hoped she would. Instead she felt only pain. She was heartbroken.

"I ran into Jack tonight at the restaurant. By the way his eyes were roaming my body, looked like he forgot he was gay," Sophie bit off.

"Sophie. I'm sorry. I didn't mean for it to go that far. I was…" He seemed lost for words.

"Sorry for *what*, Ashton? I don't want to hear it. You have always tried to make me miserable from the moment we met. Well, congratulations, you succeeded once again."

"Sophie." Ashton stepped closer.

"Don't." Hot tears streamed down her face. "I hate you, *Ashton!*"

"I never hated you…I don't think it would even be possible," he whispered quietly. Sophie stared at him through a veil of anger. There was nothing he could say in this moment to lessen the hurt and pain that was suffocating her.

"You need to leave now!"

"Sophie, please let me…" Ashton pleaded, reaching for her. "I can't think clearly around you. I made a mistake. I just wanted…"

Sophie cringed away from him when he reached for her. "There is nothing you can say to me right now," she snapped. "I have been on this stupid roller coaster for far too long. I want to get off. Leave."

Ashton turned on his heel and walked from the room. She locked her door. Sliding down to the floor, she let her tears fall. Why did she feel like it was the end of the world? Why did it feel like she would never catch her breath and that she was surrounded in darkness when the lights were still on?

Chapter Fourteen

Sophie got up early the next morning and packed her things, regretfully leaving the new dresses hanging in the closet. Margaret had bought them for her, but she didn't feel right taking them with her. When or if she would need them again she knew where to find them. She slipped down the hallway as quietly as she could.

She stopped at a small table where Margaret displayed many framed pictures. There was one in particular she was looking for. She picked up the smooth black frame with the picture of Margaret and her late husband that displayed the intensity of their love by only the look in their eyes. The picture captured every year, every laugh, everything they built together in their marriage. This was her proof that love really did exist for some people. She could see it as plain as the people in the picture. It made her want to believe one day she could be so lucky.

Leaving a note on the kitchen counter, she let Margaret know she had left to move her things back to her apartment and she would be back later in the day to take her to her doctor's appointment. She didn't think she could handle running into Ashton anytime soon. The pain was too raw and she needed to distance herself to begin the healing process. Mel had called last night, telling Sophie that they could move back in whenever they wanted because their apartments were officially vermin free. The timing couldn't have been more perfect.

Sophie barely managed to carry all her things to the bus stop. Luckily the bus driver was polite enough to help her lift them onto the bus. When she finally made it up to her apartment she collapsed from the weight of her things, exhausted. Her apartment was a welcome sight after days of being away. It was nowhere near the same level of finery as Margaret's exquisite home, but it was all hers and she loved it. The comforting smell of her paints filled her senses. She took a deep breath—she was home. Her paintings covered her walls, surrounding her with bright, beautiful colors. Sophie collapsed on her bed, watching the intricate paper mobile she created that was suspended from the ceiling over her bed. It had taken her weeks to complete every paper bird that was wired to look like a flock of birds spiraling into the sky.

She looked at the painting of Ashton, still half covered by the cloth she had thrown over it. She slipped off her bed and walked over, removing the cloth to reveal the painting in its entirety. A pain twisted in her chest looking at his handsome face. She remembered what it felt like to have her lips against his. To feel his rough unshaven face against her soft skin, his hands playing her like a beautiful song, making her want to scream out and sing along at the same time. *Never again.*

Sophie's phone rang, jolting her from her thoughts. She went to retrieve it from her purse, knocking over a bolt of red fabric. "Hello?" Sophie didn't recognize the number.

"Hello, Sophie…it's Sam. I know it's early but I just wanted to check to see if you're feeling better. I noticed on your schedule you're not in till Monday night, so I just wanted to call since I won't see you till after the weekend." Sam's voice seemed nervous on the other line.

"Yes, actually I am doing much better. I'm going to my mother's this weekend to help her with wedding plans."

The conversation flowed easily with Sam once he warmed up. Sophie thanked him for calling, trying to keep the direction of their exchange as innocent as possible until she figured out if she could actually give Sam a fair chance. Could she date someone she worked for? It was probably against the rules, despite the fact that no one else seemed to abide by them with all the hook ups that happened at the restaurant. Sophie wondered if she actually cared for Sam enough to enter into a relationship with him. She had avoided relationships her whole life, should she give one a chance? She knew that deep down her main reason would be to distract her from Ashton. *Ugh. Why does my IQ plummet when it comes to the male species?*

Hanging up her phone, she unconsciously began playing with the red fabric that she had bought weeks ago. A smile spread across her lips. She had no idea what she was going to do with Sam, and absolutely no idea how to forget about Ashton, who haunted her every waking thought, but at least she could always figure out what to do when it came to fabrics and paints. It was a language she knew how to speak fluently—she needed to create. She needed to purge the energy that had been building within her.

Pulling the fabric from the bolt, she grabbed her scissors and set to work. She was inspired by the new intense emotions that she had discovered—she had met desire on an entirely new level and she wanted to give it form. Sophie worked away the rest of the morning.

It was nearly noon when Mel came bursting into her apartment. "It's so good to be home!" she bellowed. Sophie was in her kitchen eating a bowl of cereal, wearing dress pants and a sleeveless blouse with a very delicate pattern only appreciated on close inspection.

"Where are you off to, hot stuff? Going to entice a well-to-do business man into leaving his family to run off with you?" Mel asked, wiggling her eyebrows. She grabbed a bowl and joined Sophie.

"Close. I'm going to work and make my own fortune." Sophie smiled.

"Not as exciting and definitely not as fun," Mel replied with an evil smirk.

"Yeah, the funny thing is I have this thing called a conscience. It makes me do things that are morally right," Sophie said with light sarcasm.

"*Conscience,*" Mel drew out slowly, rolling the

word around in her mouth. "Never heard of it. Anyway, if Joe talks to you tonight, make sure you say no to whatever he asks you."

"Who is Joe?" Sophie asked tentatively.

"My boss. Just saying if he approaches you with anything, just say no. Like asking you to entertain certain guests, or I don't know…get up on stage, join the payroll. Just make sure you say no," Mel ordered.

"Don't worry. The only thing I plan on saying tonight is no," Sophie assured her.

"Good. I'll keep an eye on you, but if at any point you want to leave, go ahead. I'll make sure you still get paid." Mel patted her arm. "Thanks for coming tonight."

"Sure. Did Corbin try to contact you?"

"I learned from my last relationship to avoid telling them where I live." Mel's shoulders dropped.

"Good. Hopefully that was the last of him."

"We both know that would be way too easy." Mel looked up at Sophie. There was fear in her eyes, a fear that Sophie felt as well. "Let's just hope that he won't be sober enough any time soon to try and find me."

"What if he comes to your work?" Sophie asked nervously.

"They're used to dealing with crazy there. That's where I'm probably the safest."

"What about the police? Can they do anything…?" Sophie let her words trail away with the glare that Mel gave her. "Nevermind."

Mel had told her before that she would never go to the police for help. When she was younger, she'd tried to file a complaint against someone at the police station. When she divulged the fact that she was a stripper, the officer made it seem like she deserved the trouble. She'd walked out and never looked back.

Sophie took Margaret to the doctor again that afternoon. When Sophie asked about her appointment, Margaret dismissed any reason for concern, saying it was just for routine test results, putting Sophie's mind at ease. Luckily she didn't run into Ashton while she was at the house. The longer she went without seeing him the better, allowing the memory of him on her skin to fade. She needed time.

Standing in front of her mirror in her apartment that evening, Sophie pulled the red fabric over her head and slipped the dress that she made down over her curves. The material had just enough stretch to hug her body, stopping just above the knee. Her hair was curled in long, loose flowing waves, cascading over her shoulders. Her makeup darkened her eyes, making them smoky and sexy. Grabbing her red lipstick, she drew it over her lips, finishing the look. She felt devious, like she was breaking all the rules. She was unleashing the part of herself that came alive with Ashton's touch. She wanted to be daring, strong, and take back her confidence.

Picking up her phone, she erased all the messages from Ashton telling her not to go tonight. Her fingers lingered over the buttons before she decided to send him a message.

Sophie: F**K OFF!

Ashton: You can't even swear in writing?

Sophie: Go to hell.

Ashton: I'm already there.

Sophie: Good. Stay there.

Ashton: Don't go tonight.

Anger fueled Sophie's steps, throwing her phone into her clutch she shoved her feet into her heels before walking out her door. Mel was on her way down the stairs from her apartment when she met her.

"Definitely say no to everything anyone says to you tonight," Mel said with wide eyes. "Where has this girl been hiding? I like her."

"Too much?" Sophie questioned, suddenly unsure if she should have glammed herself up so much.

"Hell no! I like this side of you, but I won't be making any tips tonight because all eyes will be on you." Mel beamed. "Let's go."

When their cab pulled up in front of their destination, Sophie's heart fluttered madly in her chest. The exterior was sleek, black, and discreet, other than the silhouettes of females in the windows. A large bouncer dressed in black with a fierce expression on his face stood at the door eyeing everyone that approached. Mel jumped out of the car and skipped toward the front door. The bouncer's scowl melted into a smile as he watched

Mel approach.

"Hey, beautiful." He laughed, velvety and deep, from his large chest.

"Hey, Dustin." Mel stretched up on her toes to kiss his beautiful dark skin. "This is my favorite girl in the whole world." Mel motioned toward Sophie as she introduced her to the bouncer. "Sophie, this is Dustin."

"I can see why she's your favorite girl." He said genuinely. His manners were refreshing as he shook Sophie's hand. "Nice to meet you, Sophie."

"You too, Dustin." Sophie offered politely.

"This must be your first time. You seem really nervous." Dustin chuckled. Sophie didn't even notice she was shaking until she looked down at her hands.

"She's gonna be one of the crowd minglers tonight." Mel threaded her arm through Sophie's.

"Don't worry, Sophie. We'll keep an eye on you," he said reassuringly.

The music pulsed through the interior of the club. It was dark with low seductive lighting. Small platforms with lights running along the edges were sporadically placed throughout the bar, each displaying a girl twisting her naked body around the dance poles. Only thongs stood in the way of displaying all their secrets to the thin crowd that was dispersed through the establishment. "It will be packed later. It's still early," Mel yelled beside her over the raging music. The bartenders were stacking up endless rows of glasses behind the bar, readying for the evening guests. "Come with me. I want you to meet Kate. She's going to be on the floor with you. You guys can hang out." Mel's words were music to her ears. Having someone to talk to would be wonderful, a distraction from focusing on where she was. The girls on stage greeted Mel as she passed, each of them seemingly as comfortable naked as someone who was completely clothed.

"Mel!" a stout man shouted as he walked toward them. His hair was wiry with unkempt curls. His large dark eyes were the only good feature upon his face. "Hello, who's this?" He held his hand out toward Sophie.

"Joe, this is my friend Sophie. She's helping us out tonight." Mel introduced Sophie to her boss.

"Very nice to meet you, Sophie." He smiled widely, showing his crooked teeth.

"You too." Sophie shook his hand as he looked her over like an object.

Mel gave her an apologetic look. "You were looking for me?" She pulled Joe's attention away from Sophie.

"Yeah, Cindy didn't show up again. Can you cover her?"

"Yeah sure. I have to show Sophie around. I'll come see you in a bit." Mel grabbed Sophie's arm and pulled her along.

Mel gave Sophie a brief tour, showing her the main stage where Mel would be performing later, and the area that Sophie was supposed to mingle around. The décor was just as eye catching as the entertainment; everything was sparkles and lights.

Mel introduced Sophie to Kate, another girl that would be working around the crowd, enticing the customers to open their wallets. Kate was short with voluptuous curves. She loved when men looked at her. Her hair was curled into tight bouncy ringlets and her lipstick was a bright pink like the dress that squeezed her to the point it looked likely it would pop off. Sophie couldn't help but smile at Kate's enthusiastic mood. She was ready to take on any man brave enough to approach her big personality.

It didn't take long for customers to start filling the bar. Sophie sipped the sweet drink that the bartender had poured for them. Kate had greedily sipped through four glasses in the past hour as they chatted. Sophie was too wary of what was happening around her to let go and enjoy herself. She hadn't seen Mel since she left to go backstage to get ready. The acts had begun on the main stage, and Sophie was amazed with how the girls danced so confidently with so many male eyes greedily watching their every move. The room filled to capacity as people poured in from the streets. Sophie soon found it hard to move around without pushing through the bodies.

Kate flirted with countless men, chatting easily like it was the most natural thing in the world to be surrounded by horny men. Sophie was grateful that Kate took the attention from her nervous disposition.

"Excuse me?" Sophie turned around and looked into the deep brown eyes of a tall, well-dressed man not that much older than herself. "It looks like you're not enjoying that drink. Can I offer you something else?" He was handsome in an unconventional way. His features were sharp but worked together to create a memorable face.

"Um…sure. Thank you," Sophie accepted gratefully.

"What would you like?" He smiled to reveal straight white teeth.

"Not sure, but something less sweet would be great."

"Sure thing." He leaned against the bar and ordered Sophie and himself a drink. He was tall and his athletic narrow form indicated that he knew how to move his body. With two drinks in his hand, he turned around and held hers out for her.

"Thank you."

"I hope you don't think that I'm being to forward, but I think you are the most beautiful girl I have ever seen." He seemed so much more confident now. "Are you a model or something?"

"Me? No, definitely not. How many drinks have you had?" Sophie laughed off his comment. She never really knew how to respond when people gave her a compliment. Her cheeks heated with embarrassment.

"Just starting." He held up his drink and took a generous sip.

"This is so much better," Sophie said appreciatively after trying her drink. It didn't take her breath away like the last one that tasted more like a dessert.

"Do you come here often?" he asked cautiously.

"No. It's actually my first time. I'm here with my friend." Sophie turned around to see Kate doing shots at the bar with a couple of rowdy men. They began chanting her name as she plowed through the row lined up on the bar for her.

"She seems to be having a good time. I'm Cale, by the way." He held out his hand.

"Sophie." Sophie slipped her small hand in his and he brought it to his lips.

"Excuse me, miss?" Sophie turned to see one of the waitresses standing beside her. "The guy at the end of the bar told me to give you this."

Sophie looked over in the direction the waitress indicated and noticed Ashton. He was leaning casually against the bar. He stared back at her as he sipped his drink.

"It's water." The waitress shrugged with an awkward look upon her face.

"No, thank you," Sophie declined. She turned her attention back toward Cale, who was looking back and forth between Sophie and Ashton.

"Please don't tell me he's your boyfriend," Cale asked with a tilt of his head toward Ashton.

"No, he's not." She pulled the straw out of her glass and discarded it on the bar before she tipped her drink up to her lips and drained the entire glass. "This is really good."

A smile curled the edges of Cale's lips. "Let me get you another."

"Sure. I feel like having fun tonight." Sophie refused to look at Ashton at the bar, but every once and a while she would find herself subject to his dangerous, dark glare from the other side. He was impossibly attractive, like the devil promoting how pleasurable sin could be. *Why the hell can't you leave me alone?*

After a few drinks Sophie's guardedness slipped away and she let herself enjoy the evening, no thought to the future or what lay outside of here and now. The waitress made a few more attempts at offering her water from Ashton but she declined every time. "Suit yourself. He keeps paying me a shit load of money to keep offering it." The waitress strutted away to serve other customers. She shot Ashton an evil glare as she downed her drink and then turned back to Cale. He was now flanked by a couple of his friends. She didn't even know their names, nor did she care to ask. She was past the point of caring about formalities. A new drink would always appear in her hand after she finished one. She lost track of who was giving them to her.

When Mel finally came out on stage, Sophie screamed her name. Mel winked back at Sophie. Mel was as comfortable as the other girls upon the stage, moving her body in the language of sex. It was really quite beautiful if it wasn't cheapened by the men hollering and whistling to her.

"A friend of yours?" one of the guys asked. Sophie couldn't even keep track of who was speaking anymore. Her senses had suddenly become clouded together.

Sophie found herself at the edge of the stage. Mel crawled over to her seductively before leaning in to speak to her. "You are going to get yourself in trouble, girl in the red dress." She leaned back and continued her dance.

"I'm having fun." Sophie washed away Mel's concern. Their exchange scemed to get the crowd worked up, the commotion grew louder.

"It was a bad idea bringing your naïve butt in here," Mel said, artfully dipping down to speak before standing back up to continue her dance. Sophie watched Mel signal someone across the room. Sophie turned away from the stage to see who it was, but dizziness was pulling at her, causing her to stumble.

"Here." Cale wrapped his arm around her waist and pulled her against his body. His need for her pressed against her side, causing her to suddenly realize she may be in over her head. He grabbed her breast, fondling her. "Why don't we go somewhere more private?" he whispered in her ear.

Sophie put her hand against his chest and tried to push him away but he was too strong. "No," she slurred. He reached with his other hand and cupped her behind. "Hey!" Sophie objected.

Ashton was suddenly there in a blur, his hand on the collar of Cale's shirt. "Don't *fucking* touch her," Ashton demanded. She had never seen him so enraged.

"Who the fuck are you?" Cale tried to remove Ashton's grip on his shirt. He immediately stopped his resistance when two bouncers approached the scene. Sophie felt relief as she watched Cale and his friends retreat.

The guy from the door leaned in to talk to Sophie. "This guy says he knows you. Said he's taking you home. Is that true?" Sophie looked up at the bouncer, trying to remember his name.

"Dustin?" she asked for confirmation.

"Yeah. Should I get Mel? Or is this guy okay?" Concern lined his face as he pointed behind him.

She looked over his shoulder. Ashton stood there with a scowl on his face, looking back at her.

Sophie took in his large, seething form. He personified everything appealing in the male body, powerful, handsome, strong, and incredibly sexy. Unfortunately he was a huge jerk. *Oh my god I drank way too much. This is becoming a bad habit.*

"No…don't get Mel…I know him," Sophie managed, surprised she managed to get her heavy tongue to cooperate.

Sophie walked toward him, swaying her hips exaggeratedly. She smiled when his eyes slid down the length of her dress. When she was close enough she grabbed his shirt, pulling him closer. He smelled delicious. "*You* said you wanted *me.*" She looked directly into his eyes. "I won this sick little game."

"Yes," he admitted as his eyes dropped to her lips. "You did."

Chapter Fifteen

Sophie tried to resist the rousing of her body. She was tired and the morning light was too bright as it pulled her from sleep. She brushed her hair from her face before stretching. Her hand ran up a warm hard body, it felt marvelous under her fingers. A delighted moan escaped her lips before reality cleared her mind. Sophie sat up abruptly, looking down at Ashton sprawled out asleep in her bed. She untangled her legs from his, trying to retreat from her bed as quickly as possible. She couldn't even appreciate how perfect he looked in only his underwear laying on her colorful, girly sheets. He looked too large for her double bed with his feet hanging off the end.

Ashton began to stir when she bolted ungracefully from bed. He lifted his head and raked his hands down over his face. "What's wrong?" His voice was deep from sleep.

Sophie looked down and noticed she didn't have any clothes on. "I'm naked," Sophie gasped.

"I know. It's fucking awesome." He smiled

lazily. Sophie grabbed a blanket off her bed and tried to cover herself. "Don't get shy now." He groaned when his eyes could not ravage her bare flesh.

"Did we…?" Sophie motioned between them. "Did we have sex?"

"You don't remember?" He leaned up on his elbows.

"Oh my god." Sophie began to panic. She grabbed her duffle bag and started throwing clothes in from her closet and dresser. "Oh my god," she repeated as if a broken record, each one building in her panic.

"What are you doing?" Ashton sat up and watched her dart around the room.

"I have to go to my mother's. I told her I was going to stay with her this weekend…I gotta go. Oh my god." Sophie rushed into the bathroom, locking the door behind her and leaning against the counter, taking a deep breath. She couldn't remember how she got home last night or anything else that apparently happened once they got there. She was so confused she didn't know how she should feel—disappointment, fear, anger? They all swirled in her stomach, causing her to feel uneasy. *This is a nightmare!* She closed her eyes and took deep calming breaths. A knock on her door caused her to yelp in surprise. "Sophie? Are you okay?" Ashton's voice was hesitant. She could feel him standing close on the other side of the door.

"Yeah. Be out in a minute." Her voice sounded pathetically small and terrified. Gathering all her courage, she opened the bathroom door.

Ashton was pulling his shirt down over his sculpted torso when Sophie stepped out of the washroom. Suddenly more than anything she wanted to remember what it was like when they were together. She spent so many hours fantasizing about being with him and when she finally did she didn't even remember it. He looked back at her with an unreadable expression. She didn't know what she was supposed to say in this situation. She didn't know what she said to him last night and the thought terrified her.

"It's probably best for you to go," Sophie confessed. The look in his eyes immediately made her regret it, but the truth was she needed time to think. She felt like she was losing control, struggling to stay above water.

He clenched his jaw, staring back at her with his dark eyes. "You asked me to stay last night." He let his anger slip into his voice. The pain in his expression chipped away at her anger. He got what he wanted, he should have been relieved to have an excuse to leave, but instead Sophie was left feeling like the bad guy. She held onto the tears that threatened to fall.

Ashton turned on his heel and walked out of her apartment without even glancing back at her. He took all the air from the room when he left. She wrapped he arms around herself and released the tears that were waiting to fall. It was the perfect ending to her tragic obsession with a boy that was destined to break her. She couldn't have written a better ending if she tried. Never knowing what it was like to have him take her in the most intimate way possible, she would always be left wondering.

***

Her mother's face was a welcome sight after surviving the bus ride torturing herself with thoughts of Ashton. Her head felt heavy from the night before. She had checked her phone constantly the entire drive with the ridiculous hope that he would send her a message, anything just to know that he thought of her for even just a moment since he left her apartment.

"Sophie, love. Come in." Her mother wrapped her arms around her tight, forcing the tears to resurface. "I'll make us some tea and we can talk about it." Her mother wiped a tear away from Sophie's cheek. She could see her own eyes in her mother's, the same light green, though her mother's always seemed more soulful and welcoming. Even lined with years of laughter, worry, and days lying in the sun, they were always so captivatingly beautiful.

Sophie sat at her mother's small round kitchen table covered with wedding brochures and magazines. It looked like everything had been attacked by sticky notes. Her mother sat a large steaming mug in front of her before grabbing a tub of ice cream out of the freezer, pulling the cover off, and sticking two spoons in.

"You are the best mom ever."

"It's because I splurge for the good stuff." She smiled brightly, scooping a big spoonful of the rich, flavorful ice cream. "Tell me why you're upset."

Sophie grabbed the other spoon and scraped the ice cream along the surface, making it curl in on the spoon. She let it melt on her tongue. "Yummy. It seems like forever ago we had ice cream like this. I applaud your choice in flavor, by the way." Cookies and cream was always their favorite.

"I picked it up when you said you were coming home this weekend. I didn't realize then how much we would actually need it." She smiled her concerned mom smile Sophie had seen so many times growing up. It was familiar and comforting, a reminder that her mother was always there for her. "I'm gonna guess that it's a boy causing these tears."

"Yes…A very frustrating, irritating…"Sophie trailed off.

Her mom reached over and squeezed her hand. "Well, this conversation sounds familiar. I think you used those same words before. Don't tell me we're discussing Ashton King again?"

Sophie sighed. "The one and only. He's up to his old tricks again. He's Margaret Darcy's grandson. I unknowingly walked right into having him in my life again. I can't escape him."

"I don't know your history other than the few things that I have weaseled out of you over the years, but a boy who invests that much time in anything is interested, trust me. One day you'll find out what is truly in his heart."

"I don't know what scares me more, finding out you're right or finding out you aren't." Sophie collapsed on the table. "I know it's not good to want to be with him, but I do anyway. One moment he's the same mean guy he was in high school, the next…I want to be with him so much it hurts sometimes. I don't know which way is up anymore."

"Is my baby girl in love?" Her mother raised her eyebrow suspiciously.

"*No*," Sophie growled her denial. "He just makes me feel lost. I just need him out of my life so I can think straight."

"I know that I tainted your view of love, it breaks my heart knowing what I put you through, but even after all those years of failed, horrible relationships I finally found love, making all that pain worth it. Do you think that all of this would start making sense if you just opened up your heart and see where it takes you?"

"I'm scared."

"Aren't we all? Just promise me that you won't miss out on one of the greatest parts of life because you're scared of getting hurt."

"Mom…he hates me," Sophie said discouragingly.

"I sincerely doubt that. Do you want me to beat some sense into him?" her mother teased. "I could get Peter to arrest him under some bogus charge."

"Don't offer that because I might take you up on it," Sophie said thoughtfully, licking her spoon. "He has so much power over me. I have never actually given him my heart and yet he finds a way to break it time after time. What happens if I actually do give it to him? These feeling are too deep, too wide, too everything. Can I survive it?"

"It certainly sounds like love." Her mother

placed her hand on her shoulder. "I would do anything for you, you know that, right?"

"I know…let's focus on planning your wedding. That's what I want to do right now." Sophie sat up straighter in her chair. She was amazed how much better she felt being with her mom. "Thinking about Ashton just makes me feel angry right now."

"Okay, but this conversation is not over." Her mother leaned in to give her a hug.

A couple hours later Sophie and her mother were buried in all the magazines her mother had spread out. They were going over every detail of the plans while the music selection for the reception played in the background. Her mother had downloaded popular wedding tunes and the list included music from every genre. They laughed and sang along to "Sex Bomb," turning it up and dancing around the kitchen.

"Seriously, Mom, you have to at least play some music from this decade," Sophie said, falling into her chair.

"I know but that one is definitely in." She laughed.

"I'm a lucky guy to come home to two of the most beautiful women in the whole world." Peter walked in the kitchen dressed in his police uniform. He had salt and pepper short cropped hair, deep brown eyes, and a square jaw. Sophie watched her mother's face light up when he walked into the room, like he was the most handsome man she had ever seen.

"Hey Peter." Sophie stood up to give him a hug.

"Hey Sophie, you have no idea how happy I am

to see you. Your mother is driving me crazy talking about every little detail of the wedding." He patted her on the head like she was a little girl after he hugged her tightly.

"Hey there, Peter, watch it. You don't want me turning into bridezilla," she warned.

"Not even possible, Rachael." He wrapped his arms around her mother and kissed her on the head before looking over at Sophie. He mouthed to Sophie so her mother couldn't hear that she was already a bridezilla. Her mother caught on when Sophie laughed and elbowed him jokingly in the stomach.

"Hey now, you might break your elbow on my abs of steel." He laughed.

Sophie couldn't wipe the smile from her face as her mother and Peter danced around the kitchen floor. He spun her around, dipping her so low her mother squealed with delight before he kissed her silent. It was beautiful to see her mother so happy. Peter showed her how much he cared for her in every touch, every smile, and every look.

Peter grilled his famous hamburgers for supper, and they spent the evening sitting under the stars, enjoying each other's company. It was the first time that she really spent an extended period of time around Peter and her mother together. They both asked endless questions about classes finishing up, her new job, and about her painting.

Her mother teased her about it being the first time she had seen her in a long time without paint staining her hands or smudged through her hair. Peter fit so perfectly, like they were always waiting for him to come along to complete their little puzzle. She was so glad her mother found someone she wanted to spend the rest of her life with. They moved like magnets, an invisible force always drawing them closer.

Peter excitedly spoke of his tales fighting crime. He loved doing his part to keep people safe; she knew that look in his eye when he spoke about his job. It was the same look she donned when she held a paintbrush in her hand. It was the feeling that warmed you from the inside out when you realized that you had found your purpose in life, knowing without a doubt that you are doing what you were created for.

When the night eventually won the battle and they could not resist the temptation of sleep anymore, Sophie retreated to the spare room in her mother's small two-bedroom rental house. The room had only been Sophie's for a short time before she moved into her own place to attend school. When she crawled into bed she checked her phone for any messages before she went to bed. There was a frantic message from Mel, actually multiple messages. Sophie called her back and let her know that she was fine and staying with her mom this weekend. After a couple of choice words from Mel, who ranted on about leaving her hanging all day, Sophie said she would see her on Monday.

There was another message that made Sophie's stomach drop when she noticed it was from Ashton. It was a voice message, and when she listened to the sound of his voice it made her insides ache. "Hi Sophie…I don't really know what I should say, but from the look on your face this morning, sorry is probably where to start. I apologize for last night. I don't even know what to say to make this better. Have a good time with your mother and I guess I'll talk to you later."

Sophie dialed his number with shaking fingers. His beautiful deep voice answered after the first ring. She liked the thought that he was waiting for her call.

"Hey Sophie." He spoke cautiously like he didn't know what direction this conversation would take."

"Why did you lead me to believe you were Jack? Did you think that I wouldn't find out? Was it your intention to make me feel like a complete idiot?"

There was a moment of silence before Ashton spoke. "When you thought I was Jack…I just went for it. I thought I might be able to figure out how to get close to you. I don't know what I was thinking, Sophie, but I fucking loved that you started opening up to me."

There was a stretch of silence that lingered between them until Sophie spoke. "I was thinking about last night and there is a favor that I would like to ask." Sophie tried to sound confident.

"Sure." His tone eased slightly.

"When I get home tomorrow night, will you come over to my place?" Sophie tried to keep her words smooth but they felt like they wavered as they flowed from her lips.

"Are you planning to beat me up?" His tone turned lighter. Sophie let out a breath of relief and they both stared to relax.

"No, actually, I was hoping you could give me a

play by play of what happened last night because I don't remember…I wanted to know what it was like…being with you." Sophie's words dropped off like the ground fell out beneath them. She quieted, waiting for him to respond.

"*Okay*." He drew out the word in confusion. "Let me get this straight. You are asking me to come over to your house tomorrow night to sleep with you?"

"Ah…yes? I won't be home till around ten, though. I'm not sure if that's too late." Sophie's words trailed off.

"I'll be there."

Sophie went to bed with a smile on her face. It was not possible to find a happy ending with their history, but at least she would know what it was like to have him physically. Maybe it would finally ease her desire for him. Maybe being with him was what she needed to get over him. Nothing else seemed to work so far. Excitement and anxiety of what was to come made it hard for her to fall asleep.

***

The next day Sophie and her mother browsed the local dress shops. Her mother was still unsure in regards to her dress. With her wedding less than two months away she was getting nervous.

"What do you think?" Her mother stepped up onto the platform in front of a large mirror. It was the eighth dress she had tried and none of them brought out the reaction Sophie was waiting for.

"You aren't smiling," Sophie commented as her

mother twirled around to show off all the details of the dress.

"It's just…I have a certain style in mind and I can't seem to find it in my budget." She scrunched up her face in the mirror, making Sophie laugh.

"If you let me know what you want I could try and make it for you," Sophie offered.

Sophie watched her mother's face light up. "Really? Are you sure you have time for that?"

"Of course. We can go look at fabrics if you want."

"Yay! You make the most beautiful things." Her mother hopped off the platform and disappeared into the changing room. "Before we leave I want you to try on the dress I picked out for you," she said from behind the curtain.

Sophie and her mother both agreed on the dress she had selected for her. It was a strapless red dress, similar to the dresses she'd already selected for her bridesmaids, only they were in black, although hers was more elaborate than the simple design of the others, having lace detail around the bodice. The bottom flowed gracefully around her thighs.

The fabric store brought back so many memories as she walked through the familiar aisles. She hadn't been to this store since she had moved. She and her mother shuffled through all of the material that was suitable for a wedding dress. She gravitated toward the off-white material, trying to create more of a vintage design. Sophie lifted up a soft material that caught her eye.

"Perfect!" her mother agreed. Before they left the store they had also found some elegant lace that paired with the fabric beautifully. Her mother couldn't have been more excited.

Sitting in the cake shop, her mother sketched out the basic idea she had, giving Sophie the direction she needed to create the dress. She had never fashioned a wedding dress before but the idea of it was not new to her. She had created many dresses and she was confident that it would turn out. They were served tea by the woman who had brought out samples of the different flavors of wedding cakes available.

"Peter likes everything, so I knew he would be useless helping me make this decision." Her mother chuckled. "He even says he loves my burnt pancakes."

For as long as Sophie could remember, her mother had always burned the pancakes she made—she was easily distracted and had a habit of putting the burner on high. "You guys are perfect for each other."

"I know. I am so happy, Sophie." Her mother grabbed her hand. "Sometimes I think it's too good to be true and that I'm going to wake up and this is all a dream."

"I love you, Mom."

"I love you too, baby girl." Her mother smiled warmly. "I have a surprise for us to do when we leave here. We're going to get our nails done. I booked an appointment for us. It's the place that's doing our hair and makeup for the wedding."

"Sounds good to me. So does this French vanilla cake." Sophie savored the taste. "With the strawberry layers."

"Yeah…it's my favorite too."

Chapter Sixteen

Sophie looked down at the pale pink color being applied to her nails while she listened to the endless one-sided conversation from the girl painting them. When Sophie sat down she recognized the girl from somewhere but she couldn't place her. She didn't have to wait long to make the connection. As it turned out, Marsha had gone to high school with Sophie.

Marsha felt it necessary to fill Sophie in on all the latest gossip she had recently heard from their graduating class. Her face was fuller than it had been in high school but other than being slightly heavier, she looked the same as Sophie remembered her. Marsha used to follow wherever the excitement led, changing friends like someone changes clothes. Her natural red hair was untamed and pulled back into a frizzy mess on the top of her head and her makeup looked like she couldn't decide on a certain idea, so she blended different techniques together to create an awkward look that did nothing to enhance her features.

The names Marsha mentioned washed over Sophie. She barely recognized most of them. She nodded politely as Marsha paraded on endlessly. It was only when Ashton's name came into the conversation that Sophie perked up.

"Apparently he just came into town and beat the…" Marsha looked around to see who was watching her before she continued. "…shit out of Collin. Collin looked horrible with two black eyes and a busted lip, but if you ask me that creep deserved it, always treating girls like they were objects."

"Does anyone know why Ashton beat up Collin?" Sophie asked curiously. In the back of her mind she wondered if it had anything to do with her confession of what Collin had done to her on prom night. It was nice to think that Ashton would defend her honor, but she didn't read too much into it. It could have been anything. For all she knew Ashton and Collin were still friends and could have had an argument about anything.

"No…who knows? I hadn't seen Ashton in a while. He left right after high school, traveling and working for his father and all that. You know, off being the gorgeous golden boy that he was."

Sophie shook her head like she had no idea what Ashton was up to. "Yeah, well. You can probably recall we weren't on great terms." Sophie shrugged.

"Yeah, *whatever*." Marsha rolled her eyes. "Everyone knew that Ashton had a thing for you. What boy didn't?"

"What are you talking about?" Sophie was completely confused by her statement.

"Every guy in our entire school was enamored by you but no one would dare even approach you because they were scared of Ashton, who had threatened them all to back off." Marsha widened her eyes as she purged her gossip.

"Ashton hated me," Sophie objected.

"No one knows why you guys had this weird hate thing going on when it was clearly not the case. The only thing I could figure is that he was trying to keep Lucinda off your case. That girl would have torn you apart if you had stolen her man. As bad as she was to you, it could have been much worse."

"I highly doubt that. That girl loathed me and made me miserable."

"Because her boyfriend only had eyes for you," Marsha explained. "How did you not know all this? Did you seriously think he hated you?"

"Yes, of course I did. I know he did. He and Lucinda always found ways to make sure I knew it," Sophie defended herself.

"Think whatever you want, I guess. You probably just have to point at a guy to have him come with his tail wagging." Marsha's tone was almost bitter as she released Sophie's hands. "I, on the other hand, have to practically pay a man to even look in my direction."

"Thank you, Marsha." Sophie smiled politely, taking the opportunity to leave. Marsha was becoming a little overwhelming and she was anxious to leave.

***

Sophie enjoyed a meal with her mother at their favorite restaurant before she left that evening. Her mother and Peter both insisted on driving her home. Anticipation twisted her stomach in knots on the ride home. She texted to see if Ashton was still coming over to her place, he responded with a quick yes. A nervous excitement made her unable to sit still. The ride home seemed to last forever before Peter pulled to a stop in front of her apartment. After saying goodbye to her mother and Peter, she headed inside. She had told Ashton to come at ten, leaving her enough time to shower and get ready before he arrived.

Once in her apartment she quickly unpacked her things, straightened up her place, and then jumped in the shower. Trying to calm her nerves was not an easy task. She felt as if her skin could not contain her, so much untamed energy rattled through her. She took care in selecting her underwear and slipped on a night dress that made her feel sexy. The thin material clung to her body and the narrow line of lace that lay over the top of her breasts was very complementary. Once she had dried her hair she checked the time and realized she had only minutes until Ashton would arrive.

When his knock sounded through the room she was too nervous to walk toward the door. After his second knock she took a deep breath and forced her legs to move. Turning the door knob, she pulled it open to reveal Ashton. His tall powerful frame filled her line of vision and she found it hard to remember to breathe. He looked like he belonged to a fairytale as the impossibly handsome prince that sweeps the girl off her feet. She felt more than swept in that moment, blown away was a better description. She realized she wanted more than anything for Marsha to be right.

"I was beginning to think you weren't home." He smiled.

"I'm home," Sophie confirmed nervously.

He tilted his head with a crooked smile. "I see that." He stepped into the room and closed the door behind him. Sophie tried to stop her legs from shaking. "So, I'm not exactly sure what you want of me," he stated, standing before her with a curious expression.

"First, I want to apologize for how I acted yesterday morning. It was overwhelming waking up with no memory of what happened the night before and I panicked."

"Understandable," he responded as he leaned against the door frame.

"And…I want you to show me what happened…step by step, if possible," she said as heat pulled at her cheeks, making them feel heavy when she spoke. "I know this may seem ridiculous to you but I can't stand not knowing how it went down between us." Sophie waved her hand between them nervously.

"Went down?" He chuckled. Sophie could feel his power as it radiated off him, calling to every part of her. He reached down and took her tentative hands, placing them around his neck. Leaning down, he grabbed hold of her bottom and pulled her body up into his arms. "This is what happened first." He breathed hotly against her ear.

"Are you sure we didn't talk first?" Sophie said breathlessly. She tried to keep her body from shaking but to no avail. He smiled at her nervousness.

"You might have said something like the fact that you think I am ridiculously handsome and you want me to take your clothes off." Ashton's tone was dangerously playful. He was enjoying himself. She could see it in his eyes.

Sophie's eyes widened. "I said that?" She gasped.

"Yes." He leaned in and grazed his lips across her cheek.

"What did you say?" Sophie's heartbeat was wild in her chest.

"I said…okay." She could feel his smile against her neck.

"You just said *okay*? That's it?" Sophie narrowed her eyes and pulled back to see his face.

He shrugged innocently. "Then I said…*goodbye dress,* as I did this." Ashton let her slip out of his grasp without realizing he still had hold of her night dress, pulling it up over her head.

"*Ashton*?" Sophie inhaled sharply, covering her body the best she could with only her arms. Her lacy bra and panties left little to the imagination.

"You said you wanted a play by play." He tossed her dress to the side when she tried to grab for it.

"I do," Sophie relented. "Is this really what happened?"

"Yes," he said, looking down at her shamelessly, his eyes taking in her every curve. She let her arms fall to her sides, liking the way his eyes took her in.

"Are you going to tell me that I confessed all my feelings for you and threw myself at you?" Sophie narrowed her eyes at him, searching his expression for the truth she was looking for.

"Yes, exactly. I thought you said you didn't remember." Ashton tilted her chin up toward him, leaning in close. "This is the part where you kissed me."

Sophie took a deep breath and raised herself up on her toes, her fingers grabbing hold of the material of his shirt and pulling him down as her intended kiss ripened her lips.

"Oh…before you kissed me you said you wanted me. You should probably say that now if you want this to be a true representation." His lips curled up deviously.

"This isn't exactly what I had in mind. I thought it wouldn't be so…me being so…" Sophie tried to pull away but Ashton grabbed her by the arms, pulling her in closer.

"Ask me what I said then."

"What?"

"Ask me what I said after you said that you wanted me so bad you can't stand it?" he said, this time his eyes were serious as he looked into hers.

"I really said that?" Ashton only nodded. The intensity in his eyes was making her insides tighten. "What did you say then?" she whispered, not breaking their eye contact.

"I said…I wanted you more." Sophie gasped at his confession. It was unexpected and she hadn't realized how much she wanted to hear those words until he said them. He closed his lips around hers, impatiently exploring her mouth. Sophie melted into him, pulling herself up to deepen their kiss. He pulled her up like she weighed nothing at all, pressing her body against his. Sophie wanted to memorize everything about him. How his hair felt as she ran her fingers through it, how his strong shoulders tensed with her touch. How it felt like she was the only girl in the world when he kissed her.

Sophie hadn't even realized that Ashton had moved them to the bed, she was so lost in the way his lips pleased hers. He sat down on the bed with her straddling his lap. A giggle erupted from Sophie as they tried to situate themselves.

"I like that sound," Ashton confessed as he grabbed her hand and kissed each knuckle. "You put a song on when we got to the bed." He nodded toward her iPod sitting on her nightstand.

Sophie felt a scowl form upon her brow. "What did I put on?"

"I'll show you." Ashton reached over and grabbed the iPod. Turning it on, he scrolled through the playlist.

A smile spread across her face as she noticed his lips moving as he shuffled through the music.

"What?" He looked up at her. He was handsome with his entrancing blue eyes and hair that was all disheveled from Sophie running her fingers through it. He looked so sexy that she leaned in and kissed his lips gently, slowly. "Mmm…you taste so good," He confessed. Her insides tightened in response to his words.

"This is it." He pushed play and "Don't Cha" by the Pussycat Dolls began playing.

"*This* is what I put on?" Sophie raised her eyebrow in disbelief.

"Yep." He grinned.

"What did I do then?"

"You danced." He leaned back on his elbows and nodded toward the floor behind her.

"What? I danced?" she asked with serious doubt.

"Yes, I'm serious. You danced your sexy little heart out."

Sophie took a deep breath and stood up. She shook her head for a moment. "Fine…don't laugh at me." She narrowed her eyes accusingly.

"I wouldn't dare." He raised his hands slightly off the bed.

Sophie moved slowly at first, trying to get past her nerves. She closed her eyes and felt the music call to her body. She smiled to herself as she fell into a groove. "Like this?" she asked, opening her eyes.

He stared back at her with dark eyes, nodding to her question. Her confidence found her as she got into the music. Turning around, she moved her hips to the music. "What did I do next?" she asked as she danced along sensually.

"You took off your bra." His breathing was deep as he continued to watch her with utter amazement.

Sophie reached up and watched his eyes follow her hands to unclasp her bra. "Like this?" she asked, slipping the straps off her shoulders.

"Yeah." His voice cracked sexily.

She turned around and let the material slide down her stomach before she threw it at Ashton playfully. A smile broke his serious expression, sitting up like he was being pulled toward her.

"Now what?"

He nodded toward her panties. His eyes thirstily drank in her flesh like it was intoxicating.

She slid her hands over her breasts and continued down her stomach before sliding her fingers under the lacy fabric, pulling them down her legs. He leaned toward her as he lost the battle to keep his distance. She turned around and shook her behind playfully in front of him.

"Did I do this?" she asked with a sly smile upon her lips.

"Fuck," Ashton growled, standing up.

"Hold on." Sophie backed up. "So I was completely naked and you had all your clothes on?"

He looked down at himself and then reached up to pull his shirt over his head. "No..." Sophie stopped him. "Let me." He relaxed his shoulders and let his hands fall to his sides.

Sophie stepped forward and grabbed the hem of his shirt and slowly pulled it up to expose his hard stomach. "I want to touch you, Sophie." He breathed roughly, like he was in pain. His hands clenched in tight fists at his sides.

"Be patient." She pulled his shirt up and kissed a trail of soft, delicate kisses along his chest. He leaned down so she could reach as she pulled the fabric up over his arms. He was so much taller than her. She bit her lip as she studied him.

"I don't think I can wait anymore...I've been waiting for a long time." His voice was so deep it pulled at her; she recognized the need in his voice, matching the intensity of her own.

"One night is not a long time," she teased.

Ashton watched as Sophie undid his belt. He took over the task, sliding his pants down, then kicked them off. Sophie needed to see all of him, the last piece of the puzzle that created his perfection. She pulled his boxers down to meet the same fate as his pants, freeing him of the restraint. He was magnificent, the perfect representation of a male body. Her need made her insides turn liquid. He pulled her body against him, kissing her feverishly, like a man that had been denied too long and was now driven by pure wild need.

Lying her down on the bed, he leaned over her, kissing her cheek and continuing down her neck. Nerves suddenly uncoiled through her, making her stiffen under him. "What's wrong?" He looked up at her through heavy lids as his body pressed her legs apart.

Sophie placed her hand on his shoulder. He didn't take his eyes off hers, searching for an answer to her question. "Did it hurt?" she asked in a small voice.

"What?" Confusion clouded over his expression. "What do you mean? Holy shit, Sophie." He retracted quickly and sat on the bed beside her. He looked over at her with desperate eyes. "Are you a virgin?"

"Ummm…yes. I mean I was until last night…so technically not anymore." Sophie tried to smile but it felt too awkward on her face. "I was upset that I didn't remember my first time…that's why I wanted to do this."

"How are you still a fucking virgin?" Ashton

squeezed his eyes tight.

"There was never anyone I wanted to be with until now…and I'm not a virgin anymore, remember?" Sophie leaned up, running her hand over his shoulders.

He pulled away from her touch. Standing up, he grabbed his underwear and pulled them on.

"I don't understand," Sophie asked with confusion.

"I can't take that from you, I didn't know. *Shit.* Sophie…I wouldn't have done this shit if I knew. We didn't have sex last night. You asked me to come in…we kissed, but you were too drunk so we didn't do anything. You asked me to stay, so I did. You took off your clothes and I fucking didn't complain. I just wanted to be with you." He grabbed his pants off the floor and pulled them back on. "I keep pulling this same fucking shit because I don't know how to stop. I can't think straight when it comes to you."

Sophie was too stunned to say anything. She grabbed the blanket from her bed and covered herself. After Ashton pulled his shirt down over his head he looked at her, waiting for her to say something but words failed her.

"I'm sorry. Don't you have anything to say at all? Yell at me at least." He stood there silently waiting for her to say something but she couldn't. She had no words. *"Fuck!"* he cursed angrily before storming out of her apartment.

Sophie fell back on her bed. She felt like everything had been taken away, but at the same time she had received a wonderful gift. Torn in two different directions, she didn't know how to react. She was relieved to find out she didn't have sex for the first time and not remember it, the devastation of what she thought she'd lost didn't really hit her until she realized how overwhelmed with relief she was to find out it wasn't true. She also realized as she lay on her bed watching the birds flutter overhead, when Ashton had walked out the door he took her happiness with him.

Sophie slowly crawled off her bed and pulled on her robe before she retrieved the picture she had taken from Margaret's house. Walking over to her easel, she set the picture down and grabbed a canvas from the stack on the floor. Painting always cleared her head and right now she could barely think. She focused on capturing what the picture so beautifully displayed. She wanted to capture their song.

Chapter Seventeen

Sophie awoke the next day plagued with exhaustion from her sleepless night. She spent most of the night hours sitting in front of her painting, watching her brush slowly creating the exact likeness. She was terrified to close her eyes and dream of Ashton. She was fragile and couldn't risk letting herself fall to pieces. She stayed in the shower until the water wrinkled her fingers, completely saturating her with hot water, but still it wouldn't wash away the ache.

She couldn't decide if she was mad at his deception when all she could think about was finishing what they started. The only thing she could figure was that she needed time. She needed space. She needed to think, and when she was with him it was impossible. She was driven by instinct when she was close to Ashton. Everything about him drew her in, his smell, his body, and the way his perfect lips called to her. Why did things that were bad for her have to be so tempting? It was like she was set up for failure.

Sophie's hands shook when she knocked on Margaret's door that morning. She was relieved when Margaret answered the door because she wasn't prepared to see Ashton. "Good morning. I can tell you're feeling better." Sophie smiled, relieved when her tension fell away.

"I am actually feeling very well this morning. Let's get some tea, shall we? I am in need of some caffeine." Margaret said brightly.

Sophie followed Margaret into the living room where Charlotte was placing a tray of tea on the coffee table. "Good morning, Sophie," Charlotte welcomed brightly. "How are your mother's wedding plans going?"

"Very well. We finalized the cake choice. All the bridesmaid dresses are ready and my dress fit perfectly, no adjustments needed. I'm actually making my mother's dress. I need to get started on that and I have to plan my mother's bachelorette tea."

"I didn't know you could make a dress." Margaret eyes lit up.

Sophie shrugged her shoulders. "I made what I am wearing. I've made lots of dresses but this will be the first time I make one that elaborate."

"Amazing. A girl of endless talents," Margaret raved.

"I wouldn't go that far." Sophie shook her head.

"Tell me about this bachelorette tea for your mother." Margaret sat down on the sofa and motioned for Sophie to get comfortable.

Margaret was always so interested in what Sophie had to say that it made her comfortable opening up. Sophie wondered if this was what it would have been like growing up with a grandmother. Being with Margaret reminded her of the time she spent with Mrs. Martin. She had made such a big impact on Sophie's life and would always have a place in her heart. Sophie felt lucky to have known two strong, loving grandmotherly figures since her actual grandmother turned her mother and her away long ago. She didn't understand how someone who was supposed to love you could send you away in your time of need. Looking at the kind-hearted woman sitting across from her she couldn't imagine Margaret turning away her own child. Her love seemed unconditional and true, the way love is supposed to be for your children.

Sophie found herself talking about her mother having her at a young age and not knowing her own grandmother or any of her family members. Margaret never judged or let the smile fall from her face. Sophie loved how gracious and understanding she was. In turn, Margaret shared with her.

"When I was little I used to imagine having a grandmother just like you," Sophie confessed.

"I'm glad you came into our lives, Sophie. I'm grateful that I got to meet such a beautiful soul. Your mother must be so proud."

"She always made sure I was well taken care of, even when we had no money. I always felt like I was her favorite thing in the whole world." Sophie said thoughtfully. "She's a wonderful mother."

"I think we need to work together to make your mother the most wonderful bachelorette ever."

Margaret said warmly.

"I can't ask you to do that, Margaret. I appreciate it, but…"

"I insist. I love parties and I have just the location in mind," Margaret said enthusiastically.

"But—" Sophie tried to argue.

Margaret cut her off again. "Please humor an old woman. I want to do this."

"Thank you, Margaret." Sophie smiled. "Can I ask you something?"

"Of course, dear."

"What is Ashton like? I know this seems silly but I think we may have gotten off on the wrong foot and sometimes I wonder if I really even know him."

"Ahhh…" She said knowingly. "My Ashton has always been special and close to my heart. He is very strong minded." Margaret chuckled. "Very intelligent. When there was something he wanted he went after it. He is strong and beautiful with a very hard shell but inside…" Margaret reached over and placed her hand on Sophie's knee. "Inside he has a lover's heart just like his grandfather. That man loved with a fierceness that scared me, but it was magical, so very wonderful. I see my husband's heart in that boy. He is the light in this old woman's life." Margaret sat back in her chair, reliving memories that surfaced.

"He sounds like he was a wonderful man, your husband." Her heart was swelling with sadness for Margaret's loss of such a great love.

"He was," Margaret said thoughtfully. "It was the greatest gift, being loved by him."

"It sounds beautiful." Sophie could only imagine the kind of love that still had such a strong hold long after the person was gone.

"If you will excuse me for a moment." Margaret moved to stand up but stumbled, grabbing for the arm of the sofa.

"Margaret?" Sophie helped Margaret regain her footing. "Are you feeling all right?"

"Yes, dear…just a little dizzy. I will be fine." She patted Sophie's arm. "I'm just going to go and rest these old bones. Could you cancel my lunch with Mrs. Lockhart?"

"Sure. Do you need me to get anything for you?" Sophie was concerned. Suddenly all of the times she questioned Margaret's health all piled on top of her and she couldn't help but worry that there was more to it than what Margaret was telling her.

"No, thank you." Margaret assured before she left the room.

Sophie walked into the kitchen and made herself a cup of tea. Out of curiosity, she looked up the contact information for Margaret's doctor. She wanted to pacify her uneasiness about Margaret's health. Sophie searched through webpages looking for information on Dr. Reynolds—what she found caused her stomach to twist in dread. Dr. Reynolds was a renowned oncologist. Sophie stared at the screen, trying to find fault in her findings. Everything she uncovered only justified her fears. The doctor's current office location was the address Sophie had dropped Margaret off to the other day for her appointment. Her fingers shook as she quickly closed her computer when she heard footsteps coming down toward the kitchen.

Charlotte rounded the corner. "I just checked on Margaret and she said you could leave for the rest of the day…work on your mother's dress, maybe," Charlotte suggested. "She's just going to rest."

"Maybe I should stick around in case she needs anything." Sophie tried to make her voice casual, not wanting to let her discovery be suspected. She didn't know what Charlotte knew but Sophie suspected that she might be the only one in the house that was kept in the dark.

"I promise I will call. I can handle things as they are now."

***

Sophie was so preoccupied with thoughts of Margaret she was caught off guard by Mel standing in her apartment. "Mel! You scared me." Sophie dropped her bag and placed her hand on her chest.

"Why are you so jumpy today?" Mel asked, standing in front of the painting of Ashton, lain against the wall. Sophie was unsure what to do with it.

"Nothing…I'm just distracted." Sophie waved her hand dismissively.

"Thinking about that?" Mel raised her eyebrows as she pointed at Ashton's likeness. "Did you sleep with him yet?"

"No, I didn't sleep with him." Sophie sighed, falling back into her sofa.

"Why on earth not?" Mel sunk down beside her.

"Didn't you work last night?" Sophie furrowed

her brow.

"Yes."

"Why are you awake right now?"

Mel moaned and leaned back against the sofa, throwing her arm over her face. "Corbin came into the club last night. The guys stopped him, nothing happened, other than him getting thrown out, but I'm still nervous. Dustin drove me home last night and searched my place for me before he left, but still I can't feel comfortable knowing that he's out to get me. I tried to sleep but I wake up with every little noise. I'm just so nervous he's gonna find out where I live."

"Stay here," Sophie offered. "Lie down and get some sleep. You look exhausted. I'm just going to be working on my mother's dress."

"Thanks, Sophie. You're the greatest." Mel slapped Sophie on the leg before jumping up. "Oh look!" Mel grabbed her purse off the sofa and rummaged through it before she pulled out a small white envelope that Sophie recognized immediately. "Your mother loves me after all." Mel had a ridiculous smile on her face.

Her mother didn't mention that she was inviting Mel to her wedding, but Sophie was thrilled that she did. Mel was her closest friend and even though Mel always made her mother nervous, her mother knew how important Mel was to her.

"What's not to love?" Sophie made a note to call her mother later to thank her.

The hours flew by as Sophie worked with her mother's material. She constantly checked her phone to make sure that Margaret wasn't trying to get a hold of her. When she had the general shape of the dress constructed, she fixed it on the mannequin to make some adjustments.

"Wow…looking good." Mel yawned as she climbed out of bed to see Sophie's progress.

"It's taking shape at least." Sophie nodded. "I ordered us a pizza. It should be here any minute."

"Yum. I'm *totally* in love with you."

"I know." Sophie laughed. "I'm awesome."

Sophie and Mel ate until they were stuffed and talked until it grew dark outside. When Mel left for work Sophie organized her things for class the next day and realized she must have left her report at Margaret's house. Grabbing her purse, she decided to head over. It gave her a reason to check on Margaret, anyway. Luckily the bus was still running at its regular intervals before the schedule changed to evening hours. She didn't have to wait too long before the bus pulled up. Once the late evening hours arrived the bus goers tended to change from the working class to a more rowdy group who weren't always good company.

When she arrived at Margaret's, Ashton answered the door. She hadn't prepared herself to see him; her thoughts were occupied with concern for Margaret. It was like being hit in the chest when she looked into his eyes. "Margaret isn't here."

"Is she okay?" Sophie's eyes widened nervously. "She didn't feel like herself this afternoon."

"She's fine." There was no playful humor in his eyes. He was quick to the point and Sophie wasn't sure how to act with him.

"I think I left something here…" Sophie started.

Ashton stepped back before she could finish, opening the door for her to come in. He turned and strode toward the kitchen. Sophie walked in and closed the door behind her and followed after him. The last place she remembered seeing it was in the kitchen when she took her computer out. "Looking for this?" He closed the folder and slid it down the counter toward her.

"Did you read it?" Sophie asked in a small voice, looking at her report sitting in front of her.

Ashton shrugged his shoulders as he filled a glass of water, drinking the entire glass before he turned around. "Didn't care for it much."

"It's my opinion." Sophie grabbed the report and tucked it in her bag, taking out the tablet. She selected the truth or dare app that Ashton had installed and slid it toward him. He looked up at her with his sexy, curious stare. He was dressed in well-fitted jeans and a thin gray shirt that made him look irresistible as usual. Sophie was pretty sure that he could make anything look amazing. "Truth or dare?" Sophie asked, staring back into his eyes.

"Truth." He looked at her challengingly.

"Are you staying with your grandmother because she's sick?" Sophie's words tumbled out in a rush.

He looked taken back. "Yes," he finally answered.

"Why didn't she tell me?" Sophie continued. "Why didn't *you* tell me?"

"You already asked your question. My turn. Truth or dare?" he asked as his intense eyes were on her.

"Truth."

"Do you really believe that *shit*?" He pointed to her report tucked away in her bag. "About romantic love being a myth?"

"Yes," she answered, breaking eye contact. "Who else knows she's sick?"

"My parents, Charlotte, me, and now you." He stepped closer to her, leaning against the counter. "Were you relieved when you found out you didn't sleep with me?" Sophie felt her heart quicken in her chest. She had no idea how to attempt answering that question; her own thoughts had refused to settle since last night, leaving her conflicted. "Yes or no?"

"Yes," she whispered. He didn't respond, only nodded slightly.

"How sick is she?"

Ashton pushed himself off the counter. "She'll tell you when she's ready," Ashton said as he walked away from her.

"Ashton? I'm not finished playing," Sophie called after him.

"I am," he called back, not even turning to look at her.

Sophie followed him toward the staircase. "Ashton? Wait, please." Ashton grabbed the railing and stopped, as if contemplating his next move. "I don't know what to say but I don't want to leave things like this," Sophie beseeched. There were so many things that she wanted to say to him but she couldn't put it in words. She didn't think she could survive the explosive emotions that he inflicted in her. "I'm so confused. I don't understand what this is between us." She looked up at him with pleading eyes. She wanted him to shed some light on what was happening.

"There is no us," he said coolly before heading up the stairs.

"Thanks for clarifying," she called after him angrily. Sophie couldn't contain her anger as she stomped out of the house and closed the door with more force than necessary.

The next few days leading up to Margaret's fundraiser, Ashton avoided her in every way possible. Sophie never saw him in the house during the day and she didn't stick around in the evening to find out how angry he was with her. The thought of a confrontation made her nervous. Ashton made it very clear he didn't want anything to do with her. Although she missed him desperately, she figured it was for the best to let things lie. Sophie found herself hovering over Margaret, trying to make her comfortable. She didn't know if she was being too obvious but she was worried.

Mel had stayed at her place every day since the incident. Sophie was grateful for the company because it distracted her from wallowing in her thoughts. She wished she could dismiss Ashton from her thoughts as easily as he did her. Sometimes it felt like it hurt too much to breathe. She knew this was coming. It's why she'd avoided getting involved with anyone for so long. This pain was the result of her own stupidity and she could blame no one but herself.

She finished the last of her classes for the term. When Sophie passed in her report to Mr. Walters he skimmed the title and raised his eyebrow.

"A strong opinion for someone so young," he

commented, skimming through the pages. "Should be an interesting read. Maybe someday you'll be able to prove yourself wrong."

"Maybe." She smiled sadly. Sophie walked out of her classroom knowing that she was finished with school. The last three years were over and now she had to look ahead to establishing her life.

When Sophie arrived home from the restaurant to get ready for Margaret's annual fundraiser that evening, she noticed a delivery man standing on the door step.

"Miss Rogers?" he asked when she approached.

"Yes?" Sophie answered curiously.

"This is for you." The young man in a gray uniform held up a garment bag and a couple of boxes were tucked under his arm. "They are from a Mrs. Darcy. She said that I needed to stay here until I delivered them directly to you because you would need them for this evening." He seemed nervous as he waited to follow her into the building.

"Thank you. Come on in." Sophie opened the door and he walked in behind her. "Were you waiting long?"

"Naw. I'm getting paid so it doesn't matter. Where should I put these?" His voice cracked when he spoke and his neck became red and splotchy.

"Oh, honey, you're home." Mel walked over in only a tank top and tiny boy shorts. She wrapped her arms around Sophie. She knew what Mel was up to immediately. Mel always liked to get a rise out of people, especially those who were easy targets. She tried to keep the smile off her face as Mel ran her tongue up Sophie's cheek seductively.

"Hurry up and get naked. I've been waiting for you all day," Mel said enticingly as she ran her hand down Sophie's body before she turned toward the delivery boy. His eyes were wide with delicious wonder. "I'll take that." She held out her hand to him.

His hands shook as he reached out to pass the garment bag to Mel and then placed the boxes on the counter. He kept his eyes on the girls as he walked toward the door. Giving a nod, he fumbled for the doorknob and slowly slid out of the doorway.

"Mel, you are evil. That poor guy." Sophie laughed.

"I think he jizzed in his pants." She wiggled her eyebrows deviously before breaking into laughter. "It will give him something to tell his friends. What is all this, anyway?" Mel waved at the packages.

"Dresses that Margaret bought me for functions like tonight's fundraiser." Sophie unzipped one of the garment bags.

"Wow, she likes you," Mel commented excitedly, running her fingers over the smooth fabric. "What one are you wearing tonight?"

"The black one, I think," Sophie said, pulling it out of the bag and holding it up in front of her. "What do you think?" Sophie asked. The dress was floor length with a slit up one side to expose her leg to mid-thigh. The top was a halter style with a tasteful open back.

"Hell yeah. Love it."

Sophie showered and primped herself. Instead of her usual moisturizer she smoothed on scented lotion with a shimmer, giving her skin a nice glow. Sophie styled her hair in loose waves, pulling half of it up in a twist while leaving her hair long down her back. She layered her eyes heavy with a smoky shadow and added color to her lips before sliding the dress over her head for the finished look.

"You look like a goddess, Sophie. Here put these on." Mel handed her a pair of silver earrings.

"Thanks."

"What happened to that stack of paintings you had in the corner, the bright colorful ones with the flowers?" Mel pointed to the corner that had been her storage area in her small apartment.

"Oh. I forgot to tell you. I offered them to Margaret to auction off for the charity event. I thought I would put them to good use."

"You're crazy. You could have sold those pictures. People pay lots of money for paintings like those. You probably just gave away enough money to buy a car."

"I can always paint more." Sophie shrugged. "It just felt like the right thing to do. Besides I have so many more that I can sell."

Chapter Eighteen

When the limo pulled to a stop, Sophie looked through the window at the most expensive looking hotel she had ever seen. The exterior looked like a modern take on a stone castle, dropped in the middle of the city, surrounded by sleek looking buildings with exteriors consisting of mostly glass. A long row of cars lined the street, awaiting their turn to pull up to the front of the hotel. *Wow.* A gentleman in a suit held the door open as Sophie followed Margaret out of the car. Flashes surrounded them as photographers captured the guests exiting the vehicles. Sophie nervously trailed Margaret as they walked along the carpeted path leading up to the grand entrance.

The event planner, Susan, closed in on them as soon as they entered the building. The poor woman looked frazzled and close to breaking down in tears. Sophie tried to pay attention to Margaret and Karen's hushed conversation, discussing the minor problems that arose in case she could be of assistance, but she was too distracted by the grandness of the hotel. Exquisite flowers covered every surface, filling the space with pleasing aromas. It was as if they were walking through a garden. Everything was immaculate and considered to the smallest detail.

All of the guests were led into a large room through grand double doors. Wine and appetizers were being served to the awaiting guests before the main dinner and auction to follow in the dining room. Women of all shapes and sizes were draped with stunning fabrics, anchored in the room by the staple black suits of their dates standing by their sides. A pianist played a soothing rhythm that flowed over the constant hum of the voices lingering in the air. A large chandelier hung overhead and beautiful swags softened the walls.

"This is such a beautiful hotel," Sophie finally said when she found her words. A few guests who knew Margaret had joined their small group. Sophie found herself wandering when Margaret became preoccupied with old friends. She exchanged pleasantries with other guests that acknowledged her as she passed. She took in all the details of the room. The fabrics paired with the walls had an embossed pattern that could only be truly appreciated up close. She couldn't help but run her fingers over it, memorizing the beautiful design. The paintings were heavily textured and all of the objects in the landscaped views flowed into the next, blurring all of the edges to a dreamy finish.

Sophie could feel the energy change in the room even before she noticed who walked in. She turned to see Ashton. A blonde girl in a very short dress hung off his arm and laughed shrilly at something he whispered in her ear. Her dress was covered in sparkles and reflected the light at every angle. She looked like a glittery disco ball. Sophie tried to ignore the jealousy that stirred within her. She met eyes with Ashton briefly before turning away. Sophie turned back to examining the freshly cut flowers lining the tables of the room.

"I would love to see the world through your eyes." Sophie couldn't stop her eyes from widening at the gentleman who came to stand beside her. Sophie looked up into the darkest eyes she had ever seen. His rich brown hair was styled in a sleek manner that complemented the expensive looking suit he wore. He was striking and Sophie couldn't help but appreciate his allure. He was not as breathtaking as Ashton but he was quite impressive in his own right.

"I was just trying to guess what flowers they were." Sophie smiled with reddened cheeks.

"I must admit that I couldn't take my eyes off you since you walked in the room. I have been to many of these events and yet this is the first time that I have seen you. It's nice to see a new face, especially one so lovely." He was confident and smooth. It was hard not to be drawn in by his charm.

"Thank you. I am here with Margaret Darcy. I started working for her recently." His compliment made her turn a deep shade of red. "My name is Sophie Rogers." Sophie offered her hand.

The dashing stranger was quick to take it in his own, lifting her hand up to his mouth. He kissed her softly and looked up at her with his captivating eyes, making Sophie even more nervous. "Xavier Peirce," he offered.

"*Peirce.*" Ashton was suddenly standing beside them. His bottle blonde with telling roots stared around the room in a daze—her gaze slid over everyone around her. Nothing seemed to hold her attention for more than a few seconds.

"*King,*" Xavier replied with equal malice. "I heard you were back in town. Got tired of working for Daddy?"

"At least *I* work." Ashton's smile dripped with ill intent. There was obvious dark history between the two, and Sophie didn't want to stick around to find out how far things would go. Sophie noticed Ashton's blonde was staring at her, and all Sophie wanted to do was withdraw from the suddenly very uncomfortable encounter.

"It was nice to meet you, Xavier. I should go find Margaret. If you will excuse me." Sophie couldn't breathe the air—it had become as thick as mud with the tension.

"Let me walk with you," Xavier offered. Sophie's eyes unconsciously found Ashton's, that were narrowed and directed at Xavier.

"That would be lovely," Sophie replied, turning away so she didn't have to see Ashton and his date all over each other. She took Xavier's arm when he offered. She didn't know what got into her but it made Xavier more appealing knowing that Ashton didn't like him.

"How do you and Ashton know each other?" Sophie asked Xavier as they made their way through the crowd. Xavier glanced back toward Ashton.

"Our families know each other, and we surf at the same beach." Xavier shrugged his shoulders. "And he used to date my cousin. So naturally I hated him." Xavier smiled.

"Don't tell me that your cousin was Lucinda?" Sophie bit her lip nervously as she looked up at his face.

"You know Lucinda?" Xavier tilted his head as he studied her.

"No. Forget I asked. I need to get a drink." Sophie's eyes sought out a server pouring glasses of wine. "Excuse me." She headed straight toward it.

"Sophie, wait." Xavier was close on her heels. "Let me guess…you were a victim of my Luce's wrath?"

"Something like that." Sophie pointed toward the white wine the server set down on the table. "Please," she added.

The server poured the clear sweet liquid into the glass. Looking up and noticing Sophie's encouragement, he continued pouring until the glass was completely full.

Xavier chuckled. "Oh yeah. She hated you, didn't she? My cousin was never good when she felt threatened. I love her, but she is a shallow bitch." He shook his head. "What did she do to you?"

"Let's just say it was enough." Sophie sighed. She didn't want old memories to ruin the mood of the evening.

Sophie was relieved when someone started

directing everyone into the dining room. She told Xavier that she would see him later and left quickly to find Margaret. Ashton and Blondie were in Margaret's company. "There you are, dear." Margaret waved.

Sophie tried to smile back but it wasn't as sincere as she would have liked. Blondie was rubbing Ashton's arm and she couldn't help the irritated feeling that grated on her. "You did a fabulous job, Margaret, this is amazing," Sophie praised as she took in the dining room and the decorations.

"You helped too," Margaret offered.

"Don't give me any credit for this." Sophie shook her head. "This amazing night was well planned out before I came into the picture."

When they sat down at their table she noticed regrettably that Ashton sat directly next to her. "I should switch to the other side of the table so you can sit next to Ashton," Sophie offered Margaret. Her heart beat too fast at the idea of sitting next to him and watching him flirt with his date.

"Don't be silly, dear. Have a seat," Margaret dismissed lightly with a graceful wave of her hand. Ashton pulled out Margaret's chair for her to sit. Sophie went to pull out her own chair when Ashton reached over and placed his hand over hers. She looked up at him, a sinking feeling settling in her stomach when their eyes met. Sophie averted her eyes, sliding her hand out from under his touch. Sophie nodded politely before sitting.

When they were all settled at the table, Sophie felt a gentle touch on her exposed back. She knew it was Ashton toying with her. Old habits die hard, apparently. Her heart beat loud enough to drown out her surroundings.

Sophie tried to keep her attention focused on Margaret and her friend, Mrs. Lockhart, sitting on Margaret's other side. Sophie came to find out the two had been friends for thirty years. Their past was apparent in the way they spoke to each other. They had long developed a strong foundation for their friendship. Sophie wondered how Mrs. Lockhart would take the news when Margaret finally told her that she was sick. It was apparent from their conversation that Mrs. Lockhart was unaware of any health issues Margaret was suffering. That feeling in the pit of Sophie's stomach returned. Sophie had no idea how sick Margaret was and the thought worried her. Ashton was resistant to give up the information and Margaret did not seem ready to share, leaving her in the dark. Sooner or later she knew she would not be able to hold her tongue and she would start asking questions.

Ashton moved his leg so it was touching Sophie's. She didn't want to pull away at first. She was reluctant to break the connection that caused a sensual heat to warm her. Sophie looked over at Ashton's date. Sophie watched her for a moment, observing the pair. Her favorite answer to most of what he said was "That's cool," and soon it began scraping on Sophie's nerves. She was like a broken record. Ashton didn't show any indication that he minded Blondie's annoying presence at all. Sophie figured he was probably thinking about what he was going to do with her later and the thought made an angry twist of jealousy run through her. *Why am I tormenting myself?*

As soon as everyone was seated, salad was served. It looked like art upon the plate. The sweet dressing was drizzled over the perfectly ripe fruit and Sophie enjoyed how all the flavors came together beautifully in her mouth. A gasp escaped Sophie's lips as Ashton's hand daringly grazed her leg, along the open slit. His fingers left a trail of fire over her skin.

"Are you okay, dear?" Margaret looked at her with a puzzled expression.

"Yes. Sorry." Sophie tried to smile innocently. She reached under the table and removed Ashton's hand from her leg discreetly. Ashton continued to persist with his exploring fingers throughout the meal. Sophie's attempts to keep his hands to himself without drawing attention proved useless and eventually she let his fingers do their bidding. They drew heat from her center that flowed through her entire body, making her skin flush.

A soft moan escaped her lips to her own horror as Ashton's touch became more explorative. *Don't play his game! You are such a stupid girl falling for this again!* She looked over to see a satisfied grin turn the edges of Ashton's lips. Blondie was obliviously eating her dinner. Margaret, on the other hand, was looking at her when she turned in her direction.

"You're all flushed, dear. Are you feeling all right?" Margaret asked deep with concern.

"Yes…I…I just have a bit of a headache. I might be coming down with something." As Sophie said the words, Ashton's hand slipped under the fabric of her skirt and dipped dangerously between her legs, caressing her sensitive skin. "Ah…If you will excuse me." Sophie stood abruptly. She headed toward the washroom quickly. She passed the main washroom and continued toward another that she saw further away from the dining room. She needed to catch her breath and needed to be alone. *I need rehab for my sick addiction to the man that will be my downfall.*

Sophie pushed open the door and walked into the washroom, quickly looking under the stalls to see if she was alone. When she saw no one else she leaned against the counter, releasing the breath that she was holding. She could still feel Ashton's touch on her leg and between her thighs; it made need pulse through her. The bathroom door swung open and Sophie pushed off the counter quickly when she saw Ashton stalk inside. His eyes were dark with purpose.

"Ashton? You can't come in here." He moved dangerously close, cupping her cheeks and angling her face toward his. "Don't," Sophie whispered. "You can't just kiss me whenever you feel like it and then walk away. I can't keep doing this."

"Then get out of my *fucking head,*" he pleaded. He stepped back, searching her eyes.

"Your date is out there waiting for you," she said. "You should go."

"Do you want me to go?" Ashton asked, tilting his head.

"Yes," she answered quickly.

"I would believe you if you weren't biting your

lip." Ashton let a cool smirk form on his lips. "But have it your way. I'm sure Marilyn will be more willing anyway." His tone turned wicked.

Sophie couldn't help but be hurt by his words. "Yeah, I'm sure she'll think it's *really cool*," Sophie spat at him. Ashton started laughing and they both lost the edge of their anger. His smile was beautiful.

"What the fuck is this?" Ashton whispered. Sophie was surprised to see her turmoil reflected in his eyes. *What the hell? Is he struggling with this as well?*

"I don't know how to answer that. Everything I feel is so closely tied with anger. I'm still so angry, Ashton. I wish I could get past it, but I don't know how. I don't know how to let my guard down when it comes to you. I don't know if I can or if I want to."

Ashton nodded tightly. He swung the door open and left. Sophie wasn't even sure what to think. Her mind was left hazy like she had too much to drink but she was completely sober.

When she composed herself she made her way back to the dining room. Ashton was turned toward Marilyn, engrossed in conversation, and she was grateful.

"How are you feeling?" Margaret asked as Sophie sat down.

"I'm okay now, just needed to get some air." Sophie said reassuringly, which seemed to appease Margaret. Dessert was served moments after she sat down. Blueberry turnovers were beautifully plated to look like exotic desserts.

"They're Ashton's favorite." Margaret looked at

her grandson adoringly. "He eats them like they're going out of style."

Ashton was looking at Sophie when she glanced at him. "Funny, huh?" He raised his eyebrow. Picking up his turnover he took a bite. "Mmmm…so delicious."

Sophie's face erupted in red with the memory of the first time he kissed her.

When he finished his, he pointed toward Sophie's untouched plate. "Are you gonna eat that?" Sophie only shook her head. "Too bad. These are really good." There was no denying that Ashton was using her words from that day. "I think this is actually the best thing I have ever tasted." His gaze was piercing as he stared at her. She was relieved when someone stood up to the podium and called everyone's attention.

Sophie found it hard to focus on the auction; sitting so close to Ashton she found it hard to relax. She didn't want to feel something as terrifying as the emotions that Ashton produced in her. There were so many beautiful items presented to the crowd and the amount of money being offered surprised her. People laid down thousands of dollars like it was change for coffee. There was sculptures, paintings, vacation packages, designer purses, jewelry. The list of items went on and each one of them were purchased at a steep price. When Sophie's paintings came up, she nervously sat up straighter, leaning forward in her chair.

Margaret reached over and patted Sophie's hand, which was gripping the edge of the table so hard that her knuckles were white. "So exciting." Sophie was too nervous to respond.

The set of paintings were a colorful collage of abstract flowers flowing over the three separate canvases in a rendition of an endless field of summer. The sunlight flowed down like liquid, spilling around the blooms like a river washing the color throughout its entirety.

The auctioneer set the starting price at five thousand dollars and Sophie's hand went up to her mouth to stifle the sound of shock that escaped her lips. Sophie jumped when Ashton lifted his hand and made his bid. "What are you doing?"

"Bidding," he said flatly.

"Don't," she argued.

"Try and stop me." He raised his hand again and the bidding continued to rise. Sophie watched in a daze as the bidding flowed through the room. When the price was up to twelve thousand, Ashton went to raise his hand again. Sophie reached over and took his hand in hers.

"You are not allowed to buy it. I don't want you to have it." When he moved to raise the other, she grabbed it too before anyone could notice. Leaning in toward his ear, she went to whisper for him to stop being ridiculous. Her hands held his in his lap and he responded to her touch. His erection was obvious as it strained against his pants. She inhaled deeply against his neck, inhaling his masculine scent. *"Oh god,"* Sophie moaned in appreciation. *Why did I just say that? He smells so good!* She swept her lips over the soft skin of his neck before she could process what she was doing. He leaned in toward her, but she retreated quickly, pulling her hands away from his. Sophie immediately chastised herself for how that would have looked to everyone at the table. Marilyn had a confused look on her face. Luckily, Margaret seemed unaware of their exchange.

Sophie forced a smile when Margaret turned to acknowledge her, placing her hand gently upon Sophie's shoulder. "Your painting was a big hit. You have a bright future ahead of you." Sophie didn't know who had made the final bid because she had been fantasizing about running her tongue along Ashton's remarkable skin. She had completely blocked out the happenings around her. She could feel Ashton's eyes on her but she refused to look at him for the remainder of the auction.

When the bidding was done, Margaret was swept into endless conversations from those who sought her. Some faces Sophie recognized from mingling earlier and others were new. She exchanged pleasantries and joined in the conversation occasionally but she was feeling too drained to enjoy herself.

"Goodness me, I forgot that you weren't feeling well." Sophie was unusually quiet but not because she felt ill. It was because she practically crawled into Ashton's lap when only a short time before told him she couldn't do this. *Great, now it's me that's sending the mixed signals.*

"I'll be fine, don't worry about me." Sophie tried to dismiss Margaret's concern. "It will pass."

"Ashton, can you take Sophie home?" Margaret turned to Ashton when they approached. Marilyn was still hanging off his arm like she was scared to let him go.

"I'm fine, Margaret," Sophie interrupted. "Really, I am. I would much rather stay and see you home."

"You need to take care of yourself or you are no good to me." Margaret smiled teasingly.

"We're leaving now anyway," Ashton offered.

"What if you need me for something?" Sophie asked Margaret. If she was being honest with herself, leaving with Ashton terrified her.

"Nonsense. I'm just going to gossip for a while. I'll get a ride home with Betty." Margaret wrapped her arms around Sophie in a warm embrace. "You should know the gentleman who bought your painting is well-known in the art industry." Margaret winked.

"Really?" Sophie's eyes widened.

"Now go." Margaret chuckled. "Let us old people talk."

Sophie held onto the excitement that surfaced with Margaret's news. It was much better than trying to shuffle through the chaos that plagued her when it came to her current thoughts of Ashton. Sophie left the dining hall and quickly exited the building. She was trying to avoid any more awkwardness with Ashton.

"Have a good evening." The doorman opened the door for her as she approached. When the night air hit her it was very refreshing. She took a few deep calming breaths to settle her nerves. Sophie could feel her shoulders tense when Ashton and Marilyn's voices neared. She turned and offered a tentative wave. "I'm just going to grab a cab. Good night, Marilyn, it was nice meeting you. Have a good evening." Spinning, she headed toward the line of cabs waiting on the side of the street.

"Sophie," Ashton called after her. Turning, Sophie noticed his approach.

"I need to just go home and clear my head. It's not good for me to be with you right now. Go with your date. She's waiting for you." Sophie opened the door and climbed into the car before he had the chance to respond. She looked back up at him through the door window. His expression was wounded, making her insides twist uncomfortably. *Remember, distance equals safety.*

On the ride home Sophie couldn't help but scroll through all the texts from Ashton when he was posing as Jack. She wondered if his words held any truth among the lies.

Chapter Nineteen

When Sophie arrived home, her mind was too restless to consider sleep, despite the late hour. Instead, she spent her hours on her mother's dress, sewing all the intricate handwork. She worked until her fingers were sore and her eyes were heavy. Concentrating on her needlework kept her mind busy. She didn't want to think about how Ashton tasted when his lips were on hers, how his body responded to her, or her own undeniable attraction to him. She was managing just fine until "Don't Cha" by the Pussycat Dolls came on. She jumped from her seat and turned off the music. She was too tired to relive that moment.

When the first rays of morning light started filtering into her apartment, Mel came barrelling in covered in sparkles. "Good night…or technically good morning," she called to Dustin, who remained on the threshold of Sophie's apartment.

"Hey Dustin!" Sophie called to him.

"Morning, Sophie!" He waved politely. "Lock this door behind me," he insisted before closing the door.

"Yes, sir." Mel chuckled before flipping the lock. He was becoming a regular occurrence in Mel's life and Sophie was happy she was finally interested in a well-rounded guy.

"You look like hell," Mel said as she turned on Sophie. "Did you sleep at all?" Mel hung up her purse on the hook by the door. Most of Mel's daily things were now in Sophie's apartment. She had been staying with Sophie since the night Corbin came to the club. She alternated between sleeping on Sophie's sofa to making Sophie share her bed. "*Hello,* Sophie?" Mel tilted her head. "Earth to Sophie."

"I didn't sleep…but I think I am now. I just haven't realized it yet. I was working on Mom's dress all night."

"Wow! Did you ever. Looking at that dress makes me want to get married." Mel looked closely at the lacework.

"Bed now?" Sophie asked.

"Yes. I'm tired from shaking my awesome booty." Mel laughed.

As soon as Sophie placed her head on the pillow she felt herself drifting.

"Sophie?" Mel whispered. "I put my notice in tonight." Sophie opened her eyes and smiled. "I want to do better for myself."

"I'm proud of you. What are you going to do?"

"Get a job where I get to keep my clothes on." Mel giggled.

"Good start." Sophie smiled and closed her eyes.

"Thank you for making me want to do better for

myself."

"You deserve the best."

***

When Sophie arrived at the restaurant later that afternoon she readied herself for the supper rush that would soon fill the restaurant. She had slept the entire morning with Mel curled up beside her. When they both woke up they ate leftover pizza while Mel scanned the "Help Wanted" ads in the paper. She had found a couple she was interested in and was eager to start the process. Sophie wondered if Dustin had anything to do with her new outlook. Their phone calls had become a regular thing and Mel seemed quite taken with him. Mel excitedly told Sophie that Dustin had been accepted into the police force and he was starting his training next month. Her eyes always lit up when she spoke of him. Sophie hoped with all her heart that this new road would lead to Mel's happiness. At least her outlook on police officers was bound to change if she was dating one.

Sophie's customers covered everything from families with small children to groups of rowdy men, drinking their fill of beer and watching the game on the televisions that were suspended from the ceiling. The restaurant was large and consisted of a bar section and a dining room where the families normally gravitated. Though, on busy nights people took seats wherever they could get them and the bar crowd normally spilled over into the dining section. Sophie was normally in the bar area; she had her regular customers that usually requested her and Friday nights brought many familiar faces.

Sophie took the order from a group of regulars. All four of them were married but that didn't stop them from their playful flirting. Sophie smiled and played along. They came almost every Friday night and Sophie knew all of them by name. When she turned from their table to enter their order, Sophie caught sight of Ashton leaning against the bar. She stopped in her tracks at the unexpected sight of him staring shamelessly at her.

Megan leaned over the bar, drawing Ashton's attention. Sophie was grateful for his distraction and headed back toward the kitchen. She had an awkward conversation with Megan earlier in regards to not wanting to date her brother, Jack. She found herself dancing around the truth when Megan insisted on digging into the matter. Somehow the conversation always steered toward Ashton and she couldn't help the guilt that swirled within her. She could tell Megan had her suspicions but how could Sophie possibly go about explaining the chaos between Ashton and her? She felt it better just to pretend there was nothing to talk about.

Sophie tried to busy herself and ignore Ashton but she kept meeting his gaze across the crowded restaurant. He stood out in the sea of people with his height and piercing beauty. His intense blue eyes could literally make anyone swoon. When things died down and he wasn't showing any signs of leaving any time soon, Sophie decided to confront him.

"Why are you here?" Sophie leaned over his shoulder. She couldn't help but appreciate how his T-shirt hung over his muscled back. She watched the other women around the bar discreetly steal glances at him, their eyes hungry for what a man like him could do to them.

"I needed a drink," he stated simply. He leaned his body back into her. She didn't know if it was intentional or not but she didn't move away.

"No Marilyn tonight?" Sophie teased.

"No, she got a little upset when I called her by someone else's name last night while things were heating up," he said. How easily it seemed he could shrug off women. *Reality check!*

"Too many to keep track of, huh? I feel so bad for you," Sophie said.

"No, just hung up on one in particular. Unfinished business, you know."

"Hey, Sam." Sophie cut off Ashton's words as Sam approached them from the inside of the bar. Sophie greeted him warmly. Sam had been true to his word and hadn't pressured her into giving him an answer to his request to spend time together. She had told him she needed time and he was being very giving. Sophie couldn't help but notice that Sam's smile fell from his lips when he surveyed what was happening between Sophie and Ashton.

"This is Margaret's grandson, Ashton," Sophie introduced. "Ashton, this is Sam, he's the manager here."

"Ah…Sam. I have heard so much about you. In fact, Sophie tells me she has quite the crush on you. Did you know that she painted a picture of you?"

Ashton spoke with evil intent.

"Ashton!" Sophie cried out, horrified. "Sam...I didn't paint a picture of you. He's joking. That would be creepy." Her face burned with embarrassment.

"She did, I saw it. Sophie has been dying to ask you out but she's just too nervous. We should all go out after her shift. What do you think, Sam? It would be a good way to break the ice."

Sam looked completely lost for words but a smile pulled at his lips with the offer.

"It can be a double date. You and Sophie and me and..." Ashton looked around the bar. When he noticed Megan approach, he reached over and grabbed her. "Megan."

The biggest smile Sophie had ever seen exploded across Megan's face. "What's going on?" She tried to talk through her smile and the words sounded awkward.

"The four of us are going out on a double date after work." Ashton declared. Sophie could see Megan melt into his hold.

"I don't think this is a good idea." Sophie shuffled her feet nervously. "You probably have plans." She offered Sam an out.

"No, I think it would be nice," Sam encouraged.

"Great." Sophie tried to seem happy for his sake. She was angry, embarrassed, and a number of other things.

"It's so adorable how nervous you are," Ashton pressed. She felt anger heat her skin.

"I have to get back to work," Sophie excused herself, biting her lip so hard she tasted blood. For the rest of the shift Sam kept watching her and it made her uncomfortable. Ducking into the kitchen, she pulled her phone out of her purse.

Sophie: I can't believe you did that! So mad right now.

Ashton: Just helping out...I know you have a crush on him. You can thank me later. I have something in mind.

Sophie: Never. And I don't have a crush on him.

Ashton: Stop denying your feelings...oh right...you don't have any.

Sophie: Haha so funny. You're the heartless one. Fine. I will go on this stupid date. But I'm not talking to you.

Ashton: I will be too busy with my date to notice you anyway.

Sophie shoved her phone back in her purse and finished her shift. The rest of the evening flew by, the dread of their double date growing. She watched time slip away until her last customer thanked her as they walked out of the restaurant. Ashton stayed at the bar, chatting with the employees as she worked. He didn't acknowledge her for the rest of the shift and that was fine by her because she was fuming.

The four of them decided on a place not far from the restaurant. Sophie had never been there before but it was well-known, especially for late night crowds. It was a tavern-style bar, with a rustic wooden interior and lots of tables scattered throughout the interior. Groups of people sat and enjoyed the music and each other's company. Sam and Megan mentioned that the nachos were amazing and recommended they order some for their table.

After Sophie's shift had ended, she freshened up in the bathroom. She hadn't brought a change of clothes but luckily she had worn a black dress that was appropriate for their destination. It was a fitted, cap sleeved design that was very simple except for three buttons that ran down from her neckline. She ran her fingers through her hair and applied some gloss to her lips. When she looked at her reflection she opted to undo the top two buttons, allowing the swell of her breasts to be exposed. Ashton said that he was going to ignore her but she wanted to make it hard for him.

Sitting in the tavern now, she was glad she did. She found Ashton's eyes noticing her reveal. Megan was so enamored with Ashton she practically drooled on him, leaning as close as she could get without crawling into his lap. Sam sat nervously beside Sophie and slowly warmed up after a few drinks. Ashton pulled out his phone and a moment later hers buzzed in her purse. Sophie pulled it out and read what Ashton had sent.

Ashton: *Do up your buttons before Sam gets*

the wrong idea.

Sophie: It was your idea for this date and maybe that's what I'm going for. I want to find out what I have been missing.

Sophie was trying to be discreet as she typed her answer, continuing to chat with Sam after saying it was a message from her mother. When she hit send she saw Ashton glare over at her. He seemed angry, he didn't even try to engage with Megan, who looked over at Sophie, trying to figure out what was behind the tension that was building between Sophie and Ashton. Ashton insisted on glaring daggers and Sophie ignored him, refusing to let her eyes settle on him.

Sophie focused all her attention on Sam, leaning in and touching his arm. When she moved to shift closer, she realized Ashton had put his foot up on the bench between her and Sam. Sophie tried to push it away but he was unmoving. He didn't flinch as Sophie reached up his pants and pinched his leg. When Sam leaned in and told her he was having a wonderful time, the guilt surfaced. She was leading him on and it was completely unfair. She smiled and then excused herself to go to the washroom.

Sophie stood in the bathroom for a few minutes to clear her head before she opened the door to return to the table. She was surprised to come face to face with Ashton in the hall, leaning against the wall. It was just the two of them standing in the dark narrow hallway. He pushed himself off the wall.

"What?" she asked angrily. "Bored with your date already?"

"Don't sleep with him," Ashton ordered.

"It's none of your business who I sleep with," Sophie bit back. "Go back to your date. It was your idea to play matchmaker, after all."

"I told her I didn't want to be with her and she stormed out." Ashton shrugged his shoulders. "Tell Sam to go home, you don't want to be with that stiff."

"You have no right to tell me what I should do." She stepped forward and stabbed her finger against his solid chest. "If I want to bring him back to my apartment and show him what a good *'dancer'* I am, that's *my* business."

"Fuck no." Ashton grabbed her finger. "He can't have you because *I* want you." He stepped forward, pinning her against the wall. Looking down at her, he slipped his arm around her waist. Sophie didn't resist. *I want you too!*

"Ashton!" She pressed against his chest with her hands, trying to force space between them. He refused as he steeled himself against her attempt to escape. He brought his lips down toward hers, only a breath away. "Tell me you want me to kiss you," he whispered against her lips. Everywhere his body touched hers, a tingling heat spread through her. Her body acted of its own accord, arching toward him. Ashton's hands ran up the length of her body before cupping her face. "Tell me to kiss you...please. I need this," Ashton pleaded against her lips. The scent of him was intoxicating, causing her instincts to take over, clouding her mind. *How can I say no when every cell in my body is screaming yes?*

Her hands reached up and grabbed the hem of his shirt, her fingers gliding over the rippled flesh of his stomach, and he took a deep ragged breath in response. "Kiss me," she whispered. The words were barely past her lips when he claimed her mouth, pressing his body into hers. His tongue explored her mouth like she was the most delicious thing he had tasted and she lost herself in the passion, returning the fervor.

"Wait..." Sophie pulled back, breathless. "Sam...I need to talk to Sam."

"No need." Sam's voice was angry. He was standing at the entrance of the hall, staring at them with a mixture of anger and disappointment. Sophie had never seen him look so devastated.

"Sam!" Sophie pushed away from Ashton. "I'm sorry, Sam...I—"

"Don't bother. I think we can call it a night." Sam turned on his heel and stalked away.

"Sam!" Sophie started after him but Ashton grabbed her arm.

"Let him go."

"But I hurt him." Sophie let her shoulders drop.

"He's a big boy, he'll get over it. Besides, he's not your type anyway."

"And *you* know what my type is?" Sophie raised her brow at him.

"Yes...me." Ashton reached up and tucked her hair behind her ear.

"You're impossible." Sophie shook her head and took off after Sam. She felt horrible for what she had done to him. She couldn't leave things like they were. She walked quickly toward the exit and out onto the sidewalk. She saw him walking down the street and she ran after him. When she neared him she called out his name. "Sam! Please, let me talk to you."

He kept walking and said nothing, only glancing back at her. Sophie could see the pain in his eyes. "I never meant to hurt you. I don't know what's going on between Ashton and me. I've known him for years and he'd always hated me…he caught me off guard."

"He doesn't hate you now," Sam said in a clipped tone but his pace slowed and it gave Sophie some relief knowing he was willing to hear her out.

"That's just it. He's just playing with me and I'm stupid enough to fall into his trap…I just need you to know that I care for you, Sam, but I can't give you what you need from me. I should never have agreed to come out tonight. I can't leave things like this between us. I value our friendship."

Sam stopped and turned toward her. "I need to know if we could ever be more than friends." Sam looked at her, his eyes full of emotion.

"Sam." Sophie took a deep breath before she continued. "I have thought about what it would be like to be with you. You're a wonderful man, with so many good qualities. You deserve to be loved and you need to know that I could never give you that. It would be selfish for me to enter a relationship with you knowing that there's nothing for me to give. I gave my heart to someone a long time ago and it was broken beyond repair. I learned the hard way that love isn't for me. Please understand." Sophie couldn't believe the confession she made to Sam. It came directly from her heart and it was a truth she had buried deep.

"I appreciate you telling me this. You will always have my friendship, Sophie, but I just need to clear my head. I have always hoped we could be more. I just need some time, okay?" His shoulders were drooped and he looked defeated, but the force of his anger had passed.

"Okay." Sophie said softly. Sophie watched Sam continue walking down the street. She jumped when Ashton moved into view beside her.

"*Oh my god.*" Sophie put her hand against her chest. "You scared me."

"Who was he?" Ashton asked, standing beside her.

"What are you talking about?" Sophie asked thoughtfully as she watched Sam turn the corner and leave her line of view.

"Who did you give your heart to?"

"*You heard that*? Do me a favor and forget it." Sophie sighed and headed down the street. She wanted to be home.

Ashton easily kept up beside her. "Come on. I want to know."

"You weren't supposed to hear that and I don't want to talk about it. In fact, I want to walk home and not talk at all."

"Fine. We don't have to talk."

After Sophie realized he was going to keep walking with her she glowered at him. "Are you planning on following me all the way home?"

"I'm not following you. I just happen to be going in the same direction." He smirked.

When Sophie turned onto her street she looked over at Ashton, who had an amused expression upon his face.

"You didn't have to walk me home."

"I figured I might as well since I'm going to the same place." His deep blue eyes looked at her and she had to stop herself from being drawn closer to him, still her feet from wanting to move toward him. She had no control when it came to him. *Why am I drawn to such an arrogant jerk who always takes whatever he wants with no consideration for the destruction he causes?*

"You're not coming to my place."

"Yes, I am. We need to talk."

"I don't really feel like talking right now." Sophie pushed open the front door and continued to her apartment.

"I know something else we can do then," Ashton said suggestively as he followed her in spite of her protest. He pulled out his phone and pushed some buttons before holding it up to show the truth or dare screen. "Truth or dare?"

"Dare," Sophie responded, turning around to stand in front of her door, her arms crossed.

"Let me in your apartment." His lazy crooked smile was adorable and sexy and she knew there was no way that she was having a quiet night to herself.

Sophie unlocked her door and swung it open wide behind her as she walked in. Ashton followed and closed the door behind him. *This won't end well.*

Chapter Twenty

"Truth or dare?" Sophie spun around to face Ashton. He was leaning against the door watching her under his dark lashes that the dim light caused to shadow across his cheeks.

"Truth," he answered confidently.

Sophie let her purse slide off her arm and land on the floor. She let out a breath before she spoke. "Why did you hate me so much?" It was the question she'd wanted to know from their first encounter when he had pulled her hair and left her heartbroken. She had fallen into his beautiful blue eyes when she first saw them looking at her and placed his mark on her heart.

"I never hated you."

Sophie choked off her breath in disbelief. "Do you seriously expect me to believe that? After all that you did to me."

Ashton pushed off from the wall. "Do you want to know what I *fucking hate?* I hate the fact that when I first met you I fucking panicked because I had everything figured out. I had everything where I fucking wanted it. I had more girls than I could have possibly wanted begging me to pay attention to them. Then you walk into the class with your pretty dress and worn out red shoes. You were the most beautiful girl I had ever seen. I couldn't fucking breathe sitting behind you, wanting desperately for you to turn around so I could see your eyes because they were amazing. I had never wanted anything so bad in my whole entire life and I wasn't ready for it."

Ashton closed his eyes tightly and took a deep calming breath. "It wasn't me who pulled your hair, it was shithead Collin, but I couldn't say anything. It was the first time in my life I didn't know what to say. I knew I was in fucking trouble when I looked up and saw Lucinda watching me when I was practically crawling over my seat to get closer to you. I knew she was going to rip you apart. I could see her evil intentions brewing so I did the only thing I thought would make her back off. I let her think I hated you…I let you think I hated you too because I knew I couldn't have you and it pissed me off." Ashton ran the back of his fingers tenderly along Sophie's cheek.

"You were the only one that believed it. Soon I welcomed your hatred because it's all I deserved from you. It became our only interaction, my only way of getting close to you. I tried to keep Lucinda off your case but it would only make it worse on you. You seemed so content with hating me and it was all I could do not to kiss you every time you were close. You were all I could think about. You were all I wanted and I couldn't have you." Ashton stopped talking and looked at her. He seemed vulnerable standing before her with his words in the air. It was the first time she had seen his cockiness stripped away and he let her see what was inside of him. He ran his hand though his wavy blonde hair. He was too beautiful to be real as he poured out his feelings. The shock of his words stilled her body. She didn't know how to process what he was saying.

"Do you how many blueberry turnovers I've eaten since I kissed you that day?" His words were soft and raw. "I just don't know how to stop this cycle."

"Me either. I don't know how to let my guard down around you. I'm scared of getting hurt." Sophie shook her head slowly, and a tear fell down her cheek. Ashton brushed it away. He looked at her with his endless blue eyes, so much feeling stirred within them. "Truth or dare?" he whispered.

"Truth," she said softly. The word felt strange in her mouth as she tried to sort through the storm of emotions that raged through her.

"Who did you give your heart to?" There was fear in his eyes as he looked at her. She realized that he was just as afraid of getting hurt as her and still he opened up, making himself susceptible to the pain.

"You," she whispered. "I have only ever wanted you."

Sophie ran her fingers down his chest, making sure he was really standing here in front of her. He wrapped his arms around her and pulled her close. She slid her arms around his neck as he lifted her off the ground, her legs wrapping around his narrow waist. He held her like she was weightless and she loved the fit of their bodies. She loved how he felt against her, all of her soft flesh molded against his hard body, and it made her yearn for more of him. Desire flourished within her and she wanted to taste him.

Sophie sucked on his full bottom lip and his reaction was primal and urgent, demanding more. She pulled away and looked up at his expression that now reflected his lust and desire.

"This thing that we're doing, whatever it is…maybe we should stop. I work for your grandmother. What if it ends badly?" she whispered against his ear.

"Can we stop?" he said breathlessly, his voice heavy with longing.

"Yes. No. Maybe. I don't know."

"What if I told you that I don't want to stop…that I can't stop?" He kissed along the sensitized skin of her neck.

"I'm scared," she admitted, looking back at him with the same intensity.

"I am too, but I can't stay away from you, I can't stop thinking about you. Just the thought of never touching you again…I need you…I want you…I—"

Sophie broke off his words as she kissed his lips. He growled into her mouth. Holding onto her he moved them into her apartment.

Sophie felt the softness of her bed against her back as he laid her down. Leaning over her he trailed kisses down her neck and chest to the reveal of cleavage she had teased him with. His hand skimmed up her thigh and under the fabric of her dress, squeezing her flesh.

"Wait." Sophie pushed him up so she could look at his face. His hair looked tousled from her fingers and his incredible lips were swollen from their kiss.

"You owe me a strip dance." Sophie's playful smile pulled her lips. Ashton's grin made his eyes light up as he pushed off the bed. "I get to pick the song," Sophie declared as she grabbed for her iPod. She scrolled through her list and laughed as she selected "Sexy and I Know It" by LMFAO.

Ashton arched his brow as he recognized the song that started playing. As Sophie watched him start to move to the beat of the music she wondered if there was anything Ashton could not do well. He was so in control of his body, moved so confidently. Sophie laughed as he carried on with her. He was familiar with the song and knew exactly how to utilize it. He pulled his shirt off over his head and Sophie took in his strong, gorgeous body. When he flexed his muscles, Sophie's mouth watered. Ashton pulled his belt from his pants and kicked them off.

A gasp escaped her as Ashton jumped on the bed. "You stopped laughing." He nipped her ear as he leaned in over her. "I love the sound of your laugh."

"I don't feel like laughing anymore." She was surprised how serious her tone sounded.

"What do you feel like then?" He looked down at her hungrily.

"I feel like…" Sophie reached down and grabbed the hem of her dress and wiggled it up her body, pulling it over her head.

"I don't feel like laughing either." He took in her body beneath him, raking her with his gaze. "I feel like kissing you."

"Then kiss me."

Ashton pressed his lips against hers. "I also feel like taking off this." Ashton slipped his finger under the strap of Sophie's bra.

"Then take it off."

Ashton unclasped her bra and threw it off the bed. "You are so beautiful," he whispered between his kisses. His hands explored her body, raining kisses over her skin and leaving a trail of burning need. "And I want to take these off." He ran his fingers down the curve of her hip and cupped his hand over her bottom as he grabbed the fabric of her underwear.

"Then take them off." Her voice was now harsh with desire as her hands memorized the lines of his shoulders and the solid curve of his back. The feel of his powerful body over her made her feel a pleasure like no other. The feel of his naked flesh upon hers made the whole world fade away and left her intoxicated with pure bliss.

The realization that there was nothing between their bodies, skin on skin, made Sophie's head reel with longing. Ashton's desire pressed against her soft flesh and she arched her body off the bed to meet his. Her body hummed with pleasure but her mind was clear. She wanted and needed this with a fierceness she couldn't even begin to understand.

"I want you more than I ever wanted anything," Ashton said against her lips.

"I want you too, I want this...I want you inside

me," Sophie panted in response.

Ashton tensed over her, his muscles hardened under her touch and his mouth claimed hers with a new vigor. "Are you sure?" He pulled away and looked into her eyes. Sophie looked at his handsome features, his strong jawline, full lips, perfectly straight nose, and endless blue eyes and she realized he was the only one she ever wanted to be with. His were the only lips she wanted to kiss. She reached up and ran her fingers along his cheek and traced his bottom lip.

"I have never been more sure of anything," she whispered before she pulled him against her to kiss him, to taste him. To breathe in his scent and feel everything that is him upon her. His song was the most beautiful thing she had ever heard and she wanted to play it forever, to live in this moment always.

Ashton took care with her body as he slowly built her pleasure, his lips grazing her flesh, his tongue pulling warmth from her core as she reacted to his touch. He explored her like he was discovering her secrets. Sophie soon writhed for release from the frenzy of desire that took over her. Sounds of her bliss slipped freely from her lips, in turn causing Ashton's own excitement to build. When Ashton pressed against Sophie's slick heat as he entered her, Sophie gasped from the sensation of feeling too full as she stretched around him.

"Are you all right?" He stilled, noticing her discomfort as he pushed slowly into her core. The heat of his breath tickled the sensitized skin of her neck.

"Yes…don't stop…" she panted.

Ashton leaned down and took Sophie's nipple in his mouth. The sensation made her melt around him, allowing his presence inside her to turn into another sensation. Pleasure erupted inside her as if the discomfort was pulled away, exposing the building of pure bliss. A primal need took over as she thrust her hips against his. His growls of pleasure encouraged her as they both brought each other toward release.

Ashton opened her eyes to sensations that left her soaring, a feeling that lingered as she leaned against his chest. Her fingers lazily traced the deep grooves of his stomach. He had been so gentle with her. The moment couldn't have been more perfect and she would never forget giving herself to Ashton. "Wow…if I had known what I was missing…" Sophie smiled against his chest, surrounded by his scent and his heat as he held her close.

Ashton chuckled. "Yeah, me too." Sophie raised her head from his chest and looked up at his face. "It's different with you," he explained.

"Good different?" Sophie asked, biting her lip nervously.

"Yes, good different." He kissed the top of her head. "Very good different…incredible."

"When did you get this?" Sophie read the words of his tattoo: **'Life is what you make it'**, as she traced the letters wrapping around the side of his chest.

"When my grandfather died." Ashton's voice was low when he spoke.

"Margaret told me about him. He sounds like he was such a wonderful man." Sophie smiled thoughtfully.

"He was. He used to say it a lot. It reminds me of him."

Sophie sat up and slid her leg over his waist, straddling him. His smile was beautiful and his eyes were shining with emotion. She wanted to paint him like this, capture this moment on a canvas for her to always be able to gaze upon. Ashton ran his hands over her breasts and down her stomach. "You're perfect." He whispered.

Sophie's eyes widened when she felt him harden beneath her. The sound of the door opening caused them both to still.

"Mel." Sophie breathed against his neck. Ashton wrapped his arms around her and pulled the blanket over their heads.

"Hey, Ashton," Mel called.

"Hey, Mel," Ashton returned with a chuckle.

"I'm glad you guys finally did it. The sexual tension between you two was unreal."

"Mel!" Sophie gasped from under the blanket.

"*What?* It's true and you know it."

Ashton's laughter ruptured from his chest and Sophie loved the sound and feel of it as he lay under her. Her whole life Sophie tried to believe that she didn't need love but Ashton had always made her doubt it from the first moment she met him. She could no longer deny that it had any hold on her. She had been swept up in the frenzy of emotions Ashton caused in her. She was in love with him. She wanted to listen to his song forever, remember all the words, and set her life to the beat.

***

When Sophie opened her eyes the next morning she found herself alone in her bed. She sat up holding the sheets over her chest, Ashton was gone. She slid out of bed, retrieved a night shirt, and pulled it over her head. She walked into the living room separated only by a partial wall, allowing a couple of minimal archways to separate the apartment into designated rooms. Mel was still asleep on the sofa. She looked so innocent, not at all like the firecracker she was when she was awake. Sophie couldn't help the ache that twisted her insides. Ashton had left her without saying goodbye. She picked up her phone, hoping he left a message explaining his departure. There was nothing.

Last night she shared something with Ashton that she thought was truly the most beautiful thing she had ever experienced. She wondered if Ashton had meant the words he'd said to her last night. She wanted it to be real, wanted to believe every word that he said.

Thoughts of Margaret began to trouble her. Fear that something happened made her fingers dial her number in a hurry. It rang twice before Charlotte answered. "Miss Sophie. How are you?"

Sophie was washed with relief at Charlotte's pleasant tone. "Hello, Charlotte, just making sure that Margaret doesn't need me today."

"Her daughter, Bridgette, Ashton's mother, is in

town visiting her. She and Marcus are taking her out to lunch today," Charlotte informed her.

"Wonderful. Tell her to call me if she needs me." Sophie was relieved that Margaret was well but it didn't ease the sadness. She had always tried to convince herself that her attraction to Ashton was only physical but she knew she had been wrong. Last night only revealed how deep her affections for him ran. *What if Ashton realized it was just sexual attraction for him? What if that's all he wanted?*

Sophie turned her music on and tucked the iPod into her panties. She slipped onto her stool in front of her easel and set to work finishing her painting for Margaret. Painting always cleared her head and she needed it now more than ever. Before long the world faded and she was completely focused on her painting.

Sophie startled when someone slid their hands around her waist. She relaxed when Ashton's delectable scent suddenly enveloped her. She leaned back into him as his lips skimmed her neck. His hand reached down into her panties where her iPod was. *Thank god!* After taking his time retrieving it he pulled it out and turned it off. "You look so hot right now," he whispered in her ear.

"Where were you?" Sophie relaxed.

"Getting breakfast." He smiled against her neck. "What's this?" he asked when he noticed what she was painting.

"Oh…" Sophie suddenly felt guilty for having stolen Margaret's photo. "I was going to surprise Margaret. To say thank you for letting me stay and for giving me a job…" Sophie trailed off.

"It's incredible." Ashton looked at the painting. "I was there that day when this picture was taken. My grandmother arranged us all to get together to have a family portrait done. The photographer took this picture when they were wrapping up. I guess she saw something…"

"Beautiful," Sophie finished.

"Yeah. She'll love the painting, Sophie." Ashton kissed her on the cheek. A sad smile graced his lips and she wondered if it was painful looking at the picture of his grandfather. It was obvious they had been close before he passed.

"Something smells delicious," Mel moaned from the sofa. Ashton and Sophie smiled at each other. Mel tumbled off the sofa and dragged her feet to the kitchen.

"I went to the bakery around the corner. I didn't know what you ladies would want so I got some of everything." Ashton said, rubbing the back of his neck.

Mel opened up one of the bags sitting on the counter. "Holy fucking shit, that smells like heaven." Mel reached in the bag and pulled out a croissant. "Still warm," she squeaked. Taking a big bite, she looked in the other bag. "Oh Sophie, there are blueberry turnovers. Your favorite," Mel said with her mouth full. She grabbed one out of the bag and passed it to Sophie.

Sophie and Ashton both looked at each other before they laughed. "I had one a few years back that was the best thing I had ever tasted and since then I can't get enough."

A crooked smile pulled at Ashton's lips before

he leaned in and kissed her softly on the lips, pulling gently on her bottom lip. "I know what you mean."

When all three of them had their fill and were sipping on their tea, Mel announced anxiously that she had some news. "I just want to say that last night was my last night as a stripper and today is my first day—well, technically unemployed, because I haven't actually gotten a new job yet—but it's a start, right?"

Sophie smiled. "Cheers." They all toasted Mel's announcement with their tea. "We should celebrate."

"Let's go to the beach!" Mel suggested excitedly.

Sophie looked at Ashton. "Do you want to go to the beach with us today?"

"I can't think of a better way to spend the day." Ashton said, putting his arm around Sophie's shoulder. A smile spread across her face that she couldn't undo. She was ridiculously happy and Ashton was the cause of it.

Chapter Twenty-One

The sun was gloriously hot as its rays spilled heat down upon them. Not a cloud was brave enough to occupy the same sky on the bright beautiful day. The beach was full of bodies soaking up the heat and cooling themselves off in the waves that splashed upon the shoreline. The beach was massive and stretched as far as Sophie could see. She couldn't remember the last time she had enjoyed the ocean and the beautiful sand of its shores.

Ashton stuck his surfboard into the sand near the water before pulling his shirt off over his head. Sophie couldn't help but stare at his sinful body. She noticed she wasn't the only one enjoying the view. Mel gave her a nudge. *"Good god."*

"Yeah, I know." Sophie said.

Dustin joined them for their adventure to the beach. He dropped Mel's bag on the sand. He noticed the girls watching Ashton and decided to pull off his own shirt. Mel and Sophie smiled at each other. "Dustin, you are definitely the hottest guy on this beach." Mel patted him on his muscled arm. Dustin was fit and obviously no stranger to the gym.

It was the first time Sophie had actually seen Mel and Dustin together for any amount of time. She could see the romantic relationship developing between them despite the fact that Mel claimed them still to be only friends. They had known each other for a long time and it showed in the way they trusted each other. He grabbed Mel into a hug, picking her off the ground. "I love this girl." He squeezed her playfully. Mel screamed in delight before settling in a fit of giggles.

Ashton looked over at Sophie from under his blonde waves of hair and dark lashes. He looked mischievous and sexy when a smile formed on his lips. "Come here." Sophie pulled off her sun dress and laid it on her bag, revealing her mismatched bikini. The top was a pink and white floral halter style and the bottoms were pink with mint green stripes. It was her favorite bathing suit and she hoped Ashton would like it. It wasn't as sexy as Mel's deep red barely there bikini, but she loved the way it played her curves. He stared at her as she approached, making her feel a little self-conscious. His eyes followed her every move.

"You look delicious." Ashton said when she stopped in front of him. He reached down and scooped Sophie up in his arms before she could respond, heading for the water. She screamed as he splashed through the waves. Sophie clung to

Ashton's neck as he walked in deeper.

"You wouldn't throw me in," she said with wide eyes. The waves splashed, sending water to spray over them.

"Wouldn't I?" Ashton laughed.

Sophie tightened her grip around his neck, holding herself tight to his body as they playfully struggled. "That's it." Ashton dropped down in the water, submersing them both completely into its cool embrace. They both came up laughing. Sophie brushed her hair out of her face as Ashton held her close. He looked down at her with eyes the same color as the water that surrounded them. His tanned skin begged for her touch as she ran her fingers over his chest. "Can I do that to you?" He smiled. Sophie giggled before Ashton leaned down and kissed her slowly at first, testing her reaction of the display of affection in public. He deepened the kiss when she responded to him. He tasted of salt and his own enchanting flavor.

Their moment of sweet indulgence was broken when they both turned toward the shore where Dustin was chasing Mel into the water. They both crashed into the waves and went under the water only to resurface, splashing water on each other.

All of them enjoyed the water until the girls decided to lie in the sun for a while. Dustin asked Ashton to show him how to surf and the girls were entertained watching Dustin struggling to stand on the board. Ashton's movements were so controlled on the board. Sophie found herself mesmerized by him. Since she had met him she wanted to know what it would be like to be his object of affection and now, since last night when they finally told each other how they felt, he looked at her like she was the most beautiful girl in the world. Every time their eyes met he grinned like an excited kid and it made exhilaration course through her, making her feel weightless, like she could float away in the slightest breeze.

"You got it *bad*," Mel said as she sat up to flip over.

"Look who's talking. I see you flirting with Dustin every chance you get." Sophie sipped her water bottle while watching Ashton.

"I flirt with everyone, *remember*? But with you…you look at him like he's everything you have ever wanted wrapped up into a very attractive package," Mel said dreamily. "It's magical."

Sophie turned around to see Mel's face. Her large sunglasses covered most of her face. "Magical? Okay where did my Mel go?"

"Come on. You fell in love with the guy when you first met him without even knowing it and then you find out that he felt the same way all this time. What's more magical than someone who was supposed to be the enemy to be the one to prove love exists for the girl who never believed?"

"*Quiet*, and he didn't say he loved me, by the way. He just told me he didn't hate me." Sophie gave her a warning look.

Mel rolled her eyes. "Oh Ashton, you have shown me the light," Mel said in mock dramatization, her hand against her heart. "I love you soooooo much."

"Stop before he hears you." Sophie tackled Mel

to try and silence her. Sophie tried to cover Mel's mouth but she was too evasive. They both ended up in a fit of giggles, tangled on the towels.

"As much as I hate to break up this incredibly hot display, your ice creams are melting," Ashton said from the edge of the towel. "And I think you're drawing a crowd."

"Yum!" Mel lit up as Dustin passed her a cone and sat down next to her.

"Thank you," Sophie said, taking the cone.

"So I saw you watching us out there, do you want me to give you a lesson?" Ashton sat down beside Sophie and leaned back on his elbows. He looked sexy with his large muscular form stretched out beside her. It made her picture him back in her bed and the wonderful evening they had shared together. Sophie looked over when Mel screamed because Dustin had made her smear her ice cream on her face.

"I think I'm better on the beach. It looks like it could be potentially dangerous for me." Sophie laughed.

"I wouldn't let anything happen to you." Ashton nudged her with his shoulder.

"Oh yeah? Well, I have a confession to make. There is a reason that I practice the arts and not physically demanding activities. I'm not the most coordinated person," Sophie admitted. "It looks like it takes more skill than I am capable of."

"I have a confession to make as well." He moved closer to her so their shoulders touched and it sent a tingling heat through her. "I am jealous of your ice cream."

"Why would you possibly be jealous of my ice cream?" she asked in mock innocence as she seductively licked it and moaned in enjoyment.

"You're gonna get it now," Ashton teased.

"What are you gonna do, because you already threw me in the water." Sophie raised her brows.

"This." He leaned over and bit Sophie's bottom lip. The pull caused heat to rupture within her. She reached up to stop him from pulling away and kissed him deeply.

"Get a room!" Mel yelled.

***

The intense heat shone down upon them as Sophie lounged on her towel. Ashton had lain down next to her and his breathing had slowed to a deep, even pace. She watched his peaceful physique, the perfect lines of his muscles and how they moulded his skin in the most enticing ways. *Will I ever tire of looking at him? I can't imagine.*

"Who's that walking this way?" Mel asked.

"Xavier." Sophie frowned in surprise. "I met him at the charity auction the other night."

"Wow. Another hot admirer?" Mel whispered with her eyes locked on his approaching form. His skin glistened from the lingering water upon his tanned flesh. His wet dark hair hung around his face. Sophie thought it suited him more than the swept back style he had sported at the charity auction. His features were almost menacing but he was definitely handsome, and his smile softened his features. Sophie heard Mel's hum of approval as he neared their towels.

"Ladies." He welcomed them before turning toward Sophie. "What a pleasure seeing you again, Sophie."

"You too." Sophie offered. "These are my friends Mel and Dustin." Mel flashed one of her brilliant smiles. Dustin, who was lying on his stomach, only lifted his hand in a lazy wave, nowhere near as enthusiastic as Mel's welcome. "And you know Ashton."

"You're blocking our sun with your fat head. Why don't you move to the other end of the beach, or better yet leave?" Ashton said suddenly. He turned over and sat up.

"I came to speak with Sophie. I didn't have a chance for a proper goodbye when we met the other night."

"Goodbye," Ashton bit off coldly, wrapping his arm possessively around Sophie.

Sophie gently hit his arm before turning to address Xavier. "That was my fault. I wasn't feeling well," Sophie said, fully aware of the tension between the two.

"Well, I'm glad to see that you're feeling better now." Xavier smiled sinfully, watching the interaction between Sophie and Ashton.

"Yes, I am, thank you."

"Well, I'm off to take advantage of the waves. If you care to join me…" Xavier's words were cut off by Ashton.

"Not gonna happen." Ashton gave him a cold stare that translated even through his dark sunglasses.

"Another time then, Sophie." Xavier winked at her before turning to leave.

"Fuck off," Ashton added.

"Oh, Ashton, I hear that you and Lucinda have been spending time together recently. Just can't get enough of her, I guess, right?" Xavier grinned slyly. "Well, I'm sure you would be interested to know she just arrived." Xavier nodded toward the parking lot. Everyone turned to see where he indicated. Sure enough Lucinda was heading toward the beach. Sophie hadn't seen her since the day she had graduated high school. After all that time she still got a bad taste in her mouth at the very sight of her. She suddenly felt sick to her stomach. Sophie looked at Ashton, whose eyes were watching Lucinda approach, his expression unreadable as he stood up. Her high that she had been experiencing since last night was suddenly brought to an abrupt end. *What did Xavier mean by spending time with Lucinda?*

Lucinda sauntered up the beach, her figure barely concealed under a very revealing string bikini. "X," she called to her cousin. She dropped her bag and wrapped her arms around Xavier. When she pulled away her eyes fell on Ashton. "Hey, Ashton." She snaked her arms around his waist. Sophie couldn't stop the shocked expression on her face. So many scenarios ran through her mind and the one that stood out above all others is maybe this had all been a sick joke played on her. In her mind it was suddenly high school all over again.

Ashton stayed rigid in Lucinda's hold. "You know Sophie." He waved his hand toward Sophie.

"And these are her friends, Mel and Dustin."

Lucinda turned to observe the three of them. "How cute." She waved dismissively.

"You didn't mention you were coming to the beach." Lucinda ran her hand down his chest, with the sweetest of smiles that Sophie had only ever seen Lucinda direct at Ashton.

"Come on, Luce," Ashton stated irritably, pulling her hand off his stomach.

"Well, I'm suddenly feeling like maybe I got enough sun today." Sophie stood up.

"Sophie, wait," he said, stepping out of Lucinda's embrace.

"Let her go. We have so much to talk about and she was always such a bore, anyway. Don't you remember what you used to call her? What was that again?" Lucinda didn't even turn around to look at Sophie.

"What the fuck are you doing, Luce?" Ashton said impatiently.

"Now that you mention it, Sophie…" Mel grabbed her towel and flung it up into the air, spraying sand over Xavier, Lucinda, and Ashton. "I'm ready to go now." Mel smiled evilly.

Lucinda screamed out, "You bitch!"

"No, actually, I think you have proven to be the *bitch* here." Mel stalked forward. Dustin grabbed her by the waist before she could get too close.

"Time to go," Dustin said quickly. "Come on, little firecracker."

"Let me go." Mel struggled against his hold.

"Sophie, don't go." Ashton tried to wipe the sand out of his eyes.

"The beach is too crowded for me and I really would like to be alone right now." Sophie tried to keep the tears from falling, taking deep breaths. She took off across the beach toward Dustin's car. Luckily the door was open and she slid into the backseat.

She heard Mel's angry bellows float in the air around the car. "I will gouge your eyes out if you come any closer."

"Better listen to her, man. Just give her some time," Dustin offered. His strengths as a bouncer surfaced and he tried to find a peaceful resolution.

"Fuck!" Ashton cursed. "Sophie, just let me talk to you!"

Sophie grabbed the door handle and pulled it open. She stepped out of the car and captured Ashton's frantic gaze. They all stopped talking and watched her.

"That was just Xavier being the ass he is. I didn't know she was gonna be here," Ashton called to her.

"I don't think I can trust you, Ashton. The scars are just too deep." Sophie slid back into the car before her eyes started to water.

Mel slipped in next to Sophie. "Are you okay?"

"Yeah...I just want to go home. I have seen enough Lucinda to last a lifetime." Sophie sighed.

Dustin started the car without a word. "Thank you, Dustin. Sorry about the drama," Sophie spoke quietly.

"I had four sisters. *That* was drama. *This* is just keeping it real." Dustin flashed her an easy smile.

Mel grabbed her hand. "You were too kind when you spoke of Lucinda before. That girl is a supremo bitch."

"What have I gotten myself into? I should had stuck with my original plan and intended on being a spinster for the rest of my life. Stayed far away from Ashton and all the trouble he brought into my life. I knew I was gonna end up being hurt. Seeing them both together again just set me off."

"He was a very enticing package." Mel squeezed Sophie's hand. "I must admit he seemed pretty upset just now."

"Good," Sophie said, deflated, as she watched the scenery pass by her window. The only place she wanted to be was home. "I guess maybe I overreacted but what are the chances that Lucinda would just show up today?" Sophie looked out the window. "Ashton makes me act like a crazy person and that scares the hell out of me."

Sophie floated through work that evening. Things with Sam seemed somewhat normal except for the sad smiles she received on occasion but it didn't feel awkward. She was just grateful he wasn't angry with her. Megan, on the other hand, refused to speak to her. She suspected Sophie and Ashton had become more than the enemies they had claimed to be. Sophie didn't bother trying to engage to deny or confess anything to Megan. She let her think whatever she wanted because Sophie lacked the heart and energy to deal with it. Everyone else was oblivious to the chaos in Sophie's life, making them all the more appealing to deal with. Time flew by and before she knew it she was heading home to her apartment.

Sophie shuffled through her text messages as she

opened the door to her apartment. There was a voicemail from her mother asking her to call and a handful of texts and voicemails from Ashton asking her to call him. She took a deep breath when she walked in her apartment.

"What's that smell? Is it…"

"Cookies!" Mel finished Sophie's sentence. She rounded the corner from the kitchen covered in flour. It was streaked across her cheeks and dusted on her clothes. The display brought a smile to Sophie's face.

"Come try them." Mel skipped back toward the kitchen. "I thought it would be a good idea to have a stock pile of comfort food after today."

"They smell delicious." Sophie praised as she observed the cookies spread out over the counter. "How many did you make?"

"Didn't know what you would feel like so I made lots of options."

"Wow." Sophie took a bite of the cookie Mel waved in front of her. It was a buttery shortbread with an icing glaze that melted in her mouth. "Wow. These are amazing," Sophie gushed.

"I know. Wait till you try the double chocolate." Mel made Sophie try every kind, which she obliged eagerly. They were all delicious and Sophie found it hard to pick a favorite.

"How did I not know that you could bake like this?"

"I am a girl of many talents." Mel winked before her smile fell from her face. "I worked in my parents' bakery for years until my Dad decided to treat himself to one of the girls that worked there.

She was actually younger than me. After that everything went to shit. I haven't spoken to my piece of shit father since and my mom is angry at the world. I can't stand to be near her. My family is all around, upside down, inside out, and all colors of fucked up." Sophie hated seeing the pain in Mel's expression. Mel slowly started opening up to Sophie more and more and Sophie looked forward to the moments when Mel let her close.

"We all have our issues. Sometimes a messy past makes us better equipped to handle the future. When I look at you I see someone who has the strength to take on the world."

"What would I do without you, Sophie?"

"We make a good pair, don't we?" Sophie smiled. "Why don't you sell your cookies? These are so amazing."

"I have always loved to bake. It makes me happy." Mel looked lost in thought for a moment. "You really think I could sell them?"

"Yes. They're delicious."

"You've given me something to think about." Mel twisted her lips. "Mel the baker? Oo la la. I like it, especially if I get to wear a hat. Maybe I should work on my French and try and pull off the whole French pastry chef persona with a cute little outfit."

"Maybe you should start with a business plan first and pick out the outfit later." Sophie laughed.

"You're no fun, but you have to admit I would look cute in a baker's hat."

"Of course. No argument there," Sophie agreed with a smile, taking another bite of cookie.

After Sophie had eaten an obscene amount of

cookies for her supper, she decided she should respond to Ashton's messages that had repeatedly lit up her phone.

Sophie: I just need some time.

Ashton: I promise that I didn't know she was going to be there.

Sophie:...I want to believe you.

Ashton: Don't let it ruin last night. It meant a lot to me. You mean a lot to me.

Sophie: Then give me time.

She just needed to unwind from the events that had taken place in the last twenty-four hours. It was a whirlwind of highs and crashing lows and she needed to sort through the emotions. She told him she needed to finish her mother's dress and that they would sort things out later. He didn't seem very pleased, but finally accepted her request.

Chapter Twenty-Two

The next day Sophie wasn't scheduled to work. She took advantage of the time to finish the intricate details of her mother's dress. The dress was piecing together nicely and she could envision what her mother was going to look like as she walked down the aisle. Sophie's fingers caressed the smooth, lush material and the lacework as she made every stitch. She took her time making sure that the seams were flawless and as perfect as her mother deserved.

Mel woke up earlier than usual. She was slowly adjusting to more regular hours since she was no longer working late nights at the club. She curled up on the sofa with her laptop, keeping Sophie company as they both worked on their projects. Soothing music was playing in the background and they each took turns making tea. It was almost noon when Sophie stepped back and admired her work.

"All finished," she declared.

Mel hopped off the sofa to regard the finished

product. "Holy fucking shit balls. Your mother is going to die when she sees this dress."

"I hope she likes it. I want it to be perfect for her." Sophie fluffed the skirting and ran her fingers over the seams, making sure she didn't miss anything.

"You are fabulous. Everything you do is fabulous…and that's why we should go into business together." Mel's eyes widened with hope. "I've been doing some research. I think we should open a tea and cookie shop. Ever since you mentioned it yesterday it has been running through my brain over and over. It feels right. I think we should go for it."

"Wow. Okay. I need to think about it."

"Yay!" Mel hugged her.

"I said I would think about it."

"I'm just excited you didn't say no. I thought you were gonna laugh in my face," Mel confessed.

"Thought about it." Sophie chuckled. Mel gently slapped her arm. "I was joking. What we have to do is make a plan and see how feasible it is."

Sophie and Mel sat down for the rest of the afternoon trying to put together a business plan. Sophie was surprised how much experience Mel had with how a bakery runs from her family's business. The Internet gave them access to endless information about starting up similar companies and what's involved. After researching costs, the start-up fees added up.

"I think I gave up stripping too soon. I might have to go back to work for a while." Mel sounded a little deflated.

"We'll figure it out, but the thing that's working against us is the fact that that neither one of us is familiar with running a business. Let me talk to Margaret and ask her if she knows a good business consultant we can hire and iron out the details before we try to approach anyone for financing." Sophie added some more notes to their growing list.

"I'm starting to get some savings from the amazing pay from Margaret. She has a lot of contacts and she's been involved in a few local companies. It wouldn't hurt. Until then, you can figure out what we'll be selling. The red velvet cookies and the thumb drops are definitely in, they are highly addictive. I hope you realize this business could be very bad for our waistline." Sophie laughed.

When they finally stopped working, night had already taken over the sky and the stars were struggling to make their appearance through the city lights. After all their research they were both in a good head space for what they had to work toward if they were going to make this a reality.

"Are we really gonna do this?" Mel asked, curled up beside Sophie in their dark apartment.

"Yes. I think we are." Sophie admitted. "Let's go for it. What do we have to lose?"

"All of our money."

"True. I guess if it doesn't work out I'll have to join you on stage for your comeback show." Sophie laughed.

"I highly doubt Mr. Hot Ass will let you back into that place, let alone up on stage after last time."

"I have no idea where that's going. He could be

long gone by that point." Sophie said sadly.

"God-boy looks at you like you're the key to unlocking the mysteries of the universe. I highly doubt he has plans to go anywhere."

"I don't feel like the key to his anything." Sophie laughed Mel's comment off.

"I'm serious."

"I don't want to talk about it."

"Fine. What is your mom gonna say when you tell her that you're going into business with the crazy stripper?"

"I was thinking I might not tell her." Sophie laughed. "Seriously though, I think she's warmed up to you. It has been a couple of years now. I mean, who doesn't eventually fall for your delightful character?"

"True."

***

The next day Sophie arrived at Margaret's early. The morning was unusually warm for the early hour. The night air brought no relief and the day threatened to bring an unruly heat. Sophie was glad she'd decided to wear her pale green sundress. It was lightweight, making it perfect for hot days. She always received compliments whenever she wore it because it matched her eyes. She wanted Ashton to notice her, despite Lucinda's arrival and what it potentially meant. As much as Sophie tried to push him from taking center stage in her mind, she couldn't stop her heart from thumping to the beat of Ashton's song. Sophie ran her fingers through her hair before she knocked on the door.

"Good morning, Miss Sophie," Charlotte said brightly as she swung open the door. "How are you this morning?"

"Great. Yourself?" Sophie asked, stepping into the house and looking around.

Charlotte chuckled. "He's not here, dear. He went back to his place, but I'm sure he'll be back soon. That boy is such a doting grandson to Mrs. Margaret. Never too far away."

"Oh. I wasn't looking for him," Sophie denied.

"Of course." Charlotte smiled, seemingly unconvinced. "Margaret is in the sitting room having her tea."

Margaret was dressed and ready to take on the day when she walked in. "Good morning. How was your weekend?"

"It was great. I didn't know that Ashton had a place around here." She found herself speaking before she could stop herself.

"I'm surprised he didn't tell you. He found a place shortly after he moved back into town and had it renovated. It turned out beautifully."

Sophie decided to change the subject. Margaret was far too perceptive and she didn't want to expose her feelings for Ashton. She didn't know what Margaret would think of her lusting after her grandson. She didn't want to upset her. "I finished my mother's dress yesterday. She's coming up this week to try it on. I'm keeping my fingers crossed. I'm very nervous."

"I'm sure she'll love it, I know what you're capable of and I have no doubt that it's a beautiful dress." Margaret smiled, sipping on her tea. "I have some good news for you," Margaret said mischievously. Sophie couldn't help but smile at Margaret's lively mood. "Sit and pour some tea." Margaret waved her toward the other armchair adjacent to her own. Sophie sat down and let herself sink into the cushions.

"Okay, spill." Sophie encouraged now that she was settled.

"Mr. Heshman, the gentleman who purchased your paintings at the auction, contacted me and requested to meet with you. He's interested in showing some of your work in his gallery."

"Really?" Sophie couldn't help the ridiculous smile that consumed her face. "He wants to show *my* work?"

"Yes, dear." Margaret chuckled with amusement. "I told him you would contact him today and set up the meeting."

"That would be a dream!"

Sophie was barely able to hold the phone as she dialed Mr. Heshman later that morning. She was so nervous that she had to concentrate on keeping her voice steady and professional. He was a perfect gentleman on the other end of the line, going over details of what he had in mind. He was making changes at his gallery for a scheduled reopening. He wanted to present some new, fresh work and thought Sophie's style was the perfect fit for what he was looking for. Mr. Heshman made an appointment with her to view her other work. When Sophie hung up her phone, she was overcome with excitement.

"Yay!" she said to herself in disbelief. It was every artist's dream to be recognized and given the opportunity for exposure.

"Someone just got good news." Ashton's velvety voice startled her. She turned around to see him standing in the kitchen behind her. He wore a dress shirt and fitted blazer that was paired with jeans—a style that looked incredibly hot on him.

"Oh. I didn't know you were here." Sophie's voice was slightly higher than she intended, making her want to cringe.

"What's this?" He picked up a business card that Sophie had sat on top of her things. "Business consultant? Planning on conducting some business?"

Sophie grabbed the card from his hand and tucked it inside her bag. "Maybe. It's someone Margaret suggested. I heard you have a new place nearby." Sophie turned back to meet his gaze, changing the subject.

"Yep."

"You didn't tell me." Sophie suddenly realized how little she knew about his life.

He shrugged his shoulders. "We were busy talking about other things and busy *not* talking." He smiled but the feeling did not translate to his eyes.

"The man who bought my painting at the auction wants to display some of my work at his gallery," Sophie blurted out. The news was too much to keep to herself and she wanted to share it with him.

"That's great news." Sophie watched the curve of his lips and found herself wanting to feel them upon her. Ashton stepped forward as if reading her thoughts.

"Don't." Sophie tried to pull back. He looked down at her with a pained expression, as if her rejection physically hurt him. "Yesterday when I saw you and Lucinda together it scared me and made me question what I'm doing."

"No. Don't question anything. There is nothing between me and Lucinda. I told you that none of that was real." Ashton looked at her pleadingly.

"But it felt real to me," Sophie whispered. Ashton's hand caressed her cheek and his thumb gently traced her bottom lip.

"I'm sorry for any pain that I ever caused you," he whispered.

They both turned abruptly as Charlotte hurried into the kitchen with a panicked expression. "Come quickly. It's your grandmother." Charlotte exchanged a worried look with Ashton before all three of them hurried toward the sitting room.

Margaret was leaning against the arm of the sofa when they walked in the room. Her normally flawless upswept hair was disheveled and she looked pale, accentuating the dark circles that had developed under her tired eyes. "I'll be fine." Margaret looked up at all their stricken faces. "I just slipped." She waved her hand lazily, trying to brush off any concern.

"She collapsed when she tried to stand." Charlotte told on her despite the look Margaret gave her. "I helped her get up."

"Sophie, call her doctor and tell him that we're on the way." Ashton was immediately at Margaret's side.

"Of course." Sophie hesitantly backed away. Fear closed in on her; she was still clueless as to what was ailing Margaret.

"I told you I'm fine. I just need a moment to collect myself," Margaret insisted.

"Stop being so stubborn," Charlotte ordered Margaret. "We aren't going to ignore this, Margaret." It was then that Sophie knew how deep Margaret and Charlotte's relationship ran. Charlotte's concern was for that of a loved one, not just an employer. The years they had spent together formed a bond between the two women.

Dr. Reynolds' receptionist informed Sophie that he would see her upon arrival without consulting the doctor first. Sophie was surprised by how accommodating the doctor was.

After her phone call, Sophie found Ashton helping Margaret in the passenger's side of her car. "Dr. Reynolds will see her when she arrives at his office."

"Good." Ashton closed Margaret's door and moved around to get in the driver's side. His features were set and determined.

"I want to come," Sophie declared. Ashton hesitated for a moment until he opened the rear door. "Thank you." Sophie slipped in the back of the car. "How are you feeling now, Margaret?" Sophie asked, reaching over the seat and placing her hand on Margaret's shoulder.

Margaret reached up and covered Sophie's hand with hers. "I will be fine, dear. Don't worry about this old woman."

"Too late."

***

Sophie sat in the waiting room next to Ashton. Neither one had said a word since they were told to wait while the doctor examined Margaret. Dr. Reynolds' office was sleek and modern with everything in its place. White on white was the color scheme of the waiting room and nothing spoke of comfort. Sophie couldn't help but think of how some colorful paintings upon the walls could change the feel of the room entirely from the cold sterile feel that was exuded now. A row of magazines were fanned out on the table in front of them, with all the latest gossip displayed, but Sophie couldn't bring herself to focus on anything that could distract her from her thoughts. Margaret had been quiet on the ride, which only intensified Sophie's worry.

Sophie watched Ashton's knee bounce nervously beside her. Sophie didn't know what to think; she had no idea how ill Margaret was, and sitting in an oncologist's office waiting for word didn't do anything to ease her concern. She had so many questions that were struggling to reach her lips but Ashton's sombre mood made her refrain.

Sophie reached over and took Ashton's hand in hers, intertwining her fingers in his and giving a comforting squeeze. He looked up at her then, his eyes a deep blue glazed with unshed tears. The worry for his grandmother was written all over his beautiful features. Sophie smiled softly and leaned in against his shoulder. He released her hand and wrapped his arm around her shoulders, pulling her closer. They stayed like that until the doctor came out to speak to Ashton. They both stood quickly as Dr. Reynolds approached.

Dr. Reynolds was a well-kept man with salt and pepper hair and a strong jaw. He wore his success in the way he carried himself. He seemed a gentleman in every sense of the word. Sophie couldn't help but notice how his white medical coat was cut to show that even in his late forties he still maintained his prime physical form. He was a very impressive man and it was easy to fall for his genuine charm.

"I feel it necessary to move up your grandmother's surgery. She has agreed to be admitted immediately."

Ashton nodded in agreement. "Can we speak with her?

"Of course. Follow me." They followed Dr. Reynolds to his examination room.

"I owe you an apology, Sophie, for not telling you of my health dilemma earlier. I wanted to save you any unnecessary worry." Margaret reached out toward Sophie.

"You owe me no such thing," Sophie disagreed. She took Margaret's hand in her own.

"I have been diagnosed with ovarian cancer." Margaret smiled sadly as she squeezed Sophie's hand. "Fortunately it has been discovered early enough. I have no plans to let this beat me. I have every intention of dancing at my grandson's wedding one day." Margaret smiled at Ashton, who was standing quietly by her side. "Now…" Margaret sat up straighter, turning her attention to Dr. Reynolds. "Let's get me better, shall we?"

"Yes, we shall." Dr. Reynolds' smile was authentic and it made all three of them relax under its effect. His belief in Margaret's recovery convinced Sophie to relax and to stop the panic that held her in its grip. They had hope that Margaret would recover well.

Chapter Twenty-Three

Sophie sat in her apartment staring at a painting she had just finished, making sure the colors blended to her satisfaction. She wanted it to be perfect for when Mr. Heshman came to view her work. She had managed to create a stock pile of canvases over the past year and was happy with the selection she could place in his gallery. Even though her skills as an artist had been confirmed many times over by her professors and other people in the industry, self-doubt seemed to pull at her, questioning what Mr. Heshman would think of her pieces. This was the moment she was waiting for, to have herself out there for the world to see. She only wished she felt more confident instead of vulnerable.

When Sophie got home from the restaurant, Mel wasn't home. She had left a note on the counter saying that she wouldn't be back until tomorrow, complete with a winking smiley face at the bottom.

The smiley face confirmed she was with Dustin. Sophie placed the business consultant card on the counter with their business plan and other paperwork they had gathered. A smile lightened her face; she was excited with the possibility of owning a business. She knew it wouldn't be easy but she didn't mind the challenge. Work was something she was always willing to throw herself into.

Sophie called the clinic. She wanted to check up on how Margaret was feeling. Her surgery was scheduled for tomorrow and Sophie was nervous. The nurse informed her that Margaret was sleeping and didn't want to disturb her. Sophie tried to call Ashton as well and was only met with his answering machine. Sophie decided to distract herself with a painting she wanted to finish.

Sophie turned her iPod up as loud as she could stand it and sat in front of her painting. She wanted to drown out the worries that haunted her. Warmth pulled at her skin to the point of discomfort—the day had been relentless. Sophie hopped off her stool and checked the air conditioner. The air that was being pushed into the room was warm. *"Come on!"* Sophie complained as she turned it on full but it only continued to push warm air through its vent. "Great. I guess I have a date with Mr. Cleary tomorrow," Sophie mumbled to herself. Sophie struggled to open the old wooden case window that groaned as she managed to pry it open. "That will have to do." Sophie sighed. Unfortunately there wasn't even the slightest breeze.

Sophie pulled off her shirt and pants. It brought some relief without her clothes. She tucked her iPod in her bra and went back to her stool. Taking down her finished painting, she grabbed a new canvas and set it up. Ideas flashed through her mind. She loved looking at a blank canvas and letting her mind get inspired to transform it. Sophie became lost in her creation. A gentle caress against her shoulder startled her and her paintbrush slipped from her hand, luckily missing the canvas as it dropped to the floor. Sophie pulled out her earphones and turned around.

"Ashton!" Sophie cried out. His arms wrapped around her tight, his lips teasing the sensitive flesh of her neck.

"I am so turned on right now," he whispered against her ear, sending shivers through her.

"How did you get in?" Sophie looked up into his face. His eyes were dark and beautiful. It always amazed her how handsome he was as he looked at her hungrily.

Ashton nodded toward the open window. "You weren't answering your phone and I saw your light was on, so I climbed up."

Sophie's eyes widened. "Guess I better not leave my window open anymore. I don't want strange guys climbing in my window."

"No, you don't." Ashton's smile melted her. "I needed to talk to you. You scared me yesterday." The fear in his words tore at her. Sophie reached up and ran her hands over his hard chest. His hands cupped the sides of her face before he brought his lips down to kiss her forehead and pull her close.

Sophie pulled back and saw the desperation in his eyes. She never expected to have this much of a hold on Ashton. It was a new concept for her and she still expected to wake up from this dream. The elation of this realization made her head swim and her need burn in white hot fury. She pulled herself up and crushed her lips against his. Sophie grabbed handfuls of his shirt, pulling him closer even though there was no space between their bodies. Ashton lifted his shirt over his head and let go of his hold only long enough to discard it before his hands found her again.

Ashton lifted Sophie, pressing her against his hard body, and walked toward her bed, laying her down. "You are so fucking beautiful." He stood up to discard his jeans on the floor. She could feel her skin heat under his gaze. He leaned over her and kissed her lips softly before trailing down her neck. "I'm yours," he whispered against her skin, making a smile blossom on Sophie's swollen lips. *This has to be a dream! Don't wake up. Don't wake up!*

"And I am yours," she whispered in response. Ashton leaned up to see her face.

"That's the best thing I ever heard." His happiness was infectious. Sophie touched his face. "And you are the best thing I have ever seen." Ashton reached behind her to unclasp her bra. "I feel like I'm going to wake up any minute, because this feels too fucking good to be real."

Ashton slid his hand down her body, discarding her underwear on the floor with the rest of his clothes. Sophie was addicted to the feel of his body against hers. She loved the taste of him, his smell, and his touch. Her fingers played every line of his body as she took advantage of the sensuality he embodied. Ashton pressed himself between her legs. "You feel so good." Everything he did brought her intense pleasure, as if he knew the secrets of her body.

"Knowing I was your first makes me very happy." Ashton looked into Sophie's eyes. "The other night was the best night of my life...thank you."

"I know how you feel." Sophie ran her fingers over his hard stomach and let her touch wander further. She was intrigued by how beautiful his manhood was as it pulsed with desire. She leaned down and kissed him there, inviting him into her warm mouth. Sophie began to slowly explore him, memorizing the feel of him as she found pleasure in giving Ashton pleasure.

Ashton growled as she released him and then climbed over his body to straddle him. His hands never left her skin as she eased herself onto his steely length. "Say you're mine," Ashton whispered heatedly.

"I'm yours." Sophie leaned down and whispered against his lips. "Only yours." A moan escaped Ashton's mouth as Sophie began to move against him, his body wound tight underneath her. Sophie responded to the pleasure he gave her, losing herself to the intense feeling that captured her. When Sophie cried out in release, Ashton followed immediately and they both collapsed against the bed.

The feelings she had for Ashton were magical, beautiful, and captivated her beyond anything she ever imagined. She lay beside him and ran his fingers over his tanned, perfect skin.

"I think I am addicted to you." Ashton's voice was raspy from their passionate exchange.

"I can live with that." She moved closer to him and nuzzled his neck. His smell was so enticing, his heat comforting, and everything about him enchanted her. She knew without a doubt that she was addicted to him as well but admitting how deep her feelings ran scared her. A part of her was still scared of getting hurt. "I'm glad you broke into my apartment tonight."

"Me too…let's go get an ice cream." Ashton looked at her playfully. "It's hot as shit in here."

"Now?" Sophie giggled at his sudden playful mood.

"Yes, right now. I want to take you out for ice cream." He stood up and pulled on his pants. Sophie watched the way his muscles rippled. It was sinful how strong and attractive his body was.

"Ice cream does sound good, but so does staying in bed." Sophie smiled wickedly.

"Oh, we'll be going back to bed after, just not this bed. I want you in *my* bed." He grabbed Sophie's hand and helped her stand, pulling her against his chest and kissing her on the top of the head.

"Your place?"

"Yes, my place. I want to see what you look like in my bed."

***

Ashton had taken Sophie to a late night diner

that had a ridiculously large selection of flavors. Sophie stared through the glass, trying to narrow down her choice. "Wow…I think I will go with the…cookies 'n cream…or no, make that mint chocolate chip." Sophie looked up to see Ashton watching her with an amused grin on his face. "What?"

"You look so adorable right now." He winked as he leaned against the counter.

"Adorable? Seriously? That is what you call little kids." Sophie huffed with a furrowed brow.

"You are definitely adorable and sexy as fuck. Come here." Ashton reached for her arm and pulled her against his chest and nipped at her neck.

"Hey!" Sophie giggled. "We have an audience." Sophie widened her eyes and nodded toward the few late night customers that were scattered through the small diner. There was a man dressed in a suit, his tie loosened and hung haphazardly around his neck; he was completely lost in his computer. An older gentleman sat tucked in a booth reading a paper with a half-eaten piece of cherry pie sitting in front of him. There was a middle aged couple sitting together next to the window sharing a late night meal of burgers and fries as they chatted casually. They seemed to be the only ones that even seemed to notice her and Ashton's presence, looking up occasionally with polite smiles.

"What?" Ashton looked around the diner consisting of about fifteen tables and booths lining the back wall. It was small and in need of some updating but it was cozy and welcoming. You could tell that whoever owned it had taken care of it, but it had aged like the owner.

"They look like they could use some entertainment." Ashton's look made her knees weak.

"How did you know about this place and its many flavors of ice cream?" Sophie asked.

"When I was little my grandfather always brought me here. My favorite times were when I slept over. I always had trouble sleeping as a child and he would bring me here in my pajamas no matter how late it was. I naturally thought that was the coolest thing knowing that my mother would have a fit. My grandfather believed ice cream solved every problem." Ashton said thoughtfully.

"Wouldn't that be nice?" Sophie smiled at the thought of a young Ashton sitting with his grandfather eating ice cream in one of the booths.

"Sorry for keeping you waiting. Did you decide yet?" An older woman with vibrant red hair streaked with white shuffled out from the back room carrying supplies. She set them on the counter before turning her full attention toward them. Despite her age a youthful brightness shone in her eyes and lit up her features.

"Yes, we have." Ashton smiled with recognition.

"It's been a long time but don't think I don't know who you are, *Ashton King*. Get your handsome self over here and give this old woman a hug." She came around the counter with her arms spread wide. "It's good to see you, and who have you brought with you?" She smiled at Sophie. "She is absolutely gorgeous. Where did you find such a lovely girl?"

"I know. I can't believe my good fortune." Ashton smiled. "Colleen, this is my girlfriend, Sophie. Sophie, this is Colleen. Colleen has the best selection of ice cream in the whole city."

"I know what's important. The ice cream is what keeps all the best customers coming back." Colleen took Sophie's hand, giving it a gentle shake.

"It's nice to meet you, Colleen." Sophie loved the woman's energy and instantly adored her.

"The pleasure is all mine, sweetheart."

Sitting in a booth, Sophie and Ashton enjoyed their ice creams. Sophie was in a state of bliss. Every time Ashton looked at her she felt like she was the most important girl in the world. His eyes followed her and a sexy smile teased her. She noted their late night ice cream adventure as one of her favorite evenings of all time. The conversation between them flowed effortlessly and the excitement only built with the promise of things to come when Ashton brought her back to his place. She loved how he leaned toward her, or reached for her hand. Every touch made her desire more.

After a farewell to the friendly waitress, Sophie followed Ashton out into the warm night air. Ashton's hand found hers and he brought them up to his lips. When they reached his car he pulled her against his chest. Sophie's fingers stroked the hard ridges of his abs beneath his shirt to indulge in his sensual flesh.

"You're driving me crazy, Sophie," he whispered hotly in her ear, making goosebumps flash across her skin.

"Oh yeah?" Sophie laughed.

"Yes, it's so hard to keep my hands to myself. I can't think straight around you. I just want to touch you…and taste you." Sophie shivered from his words as they caressed her skin.

"I don't remember you being the public display of affection kind of guy. Don't get me wrong, I'm not complaining." Sophie leaned into his embrace.

"I wasn't until you. I can't get enough." Ashton gently bit the skin of her neck, causing a flash of needy heat to overcome her.

"We should probably go to your place now," Sophie said breathlessly.

"After you." Ashton reached around her to open her door.

On the drive to Ashton's place Sophie saw a small storefront building that had a lease sign in the window. The building had character with its brick front and large showcase windows. "Can you pull over?"

"What's wrong?"

"I just want to see something."

When Ashton pulled over on the side of the street, Sophie slipped out of the car and approached the building. The interior was dark and she couldn't see anything inside but she could see potential in the location and the appearance of the storefront.

"It was a pizza shop…why the interest?" Ashton stepped around her to see her face, studying her expression.

"Wouldn't you like to know?" Sophie teased. "Just interested for future possibilities." Sophie pulled out her phone and took a picture of the sign. She looked up at Ashton, who was waiting for her to explain. "Mel and I have plans…well, we are in the very beginning of the planning stage, but still, this place makes me excited. It would be perfect."

"You and Mel are making plans? Should I even ask?"

"We're opening our own strip joint. I want to give it a try." Sophie tried to sound serious but Ashton's expression turned almost panicked as he stared at her. "I was joking…are you nervous I would make a fool of myself trying to do my "Don't Cha" routine for the world to see?"

Ashton looked visibly relieved with her confession. "No, I was thinking that I was going to have to buy up every available piece of real estate in the city to prevent your little business endeavor."

Sophie's face fell in shock. "I was that bad? Geez."

"No, just the opposite. That was so fucking sexy. I don't want anyone else to see you take your clothes off except me. I'm a very selfish person, Sophie, and I don't like to share. I don't want to share you with anyone…ever." Ashton stepped closer, leaning down so he was a breath away from her. His smell was heady, causing her whole body to need him with an intensity that ravished her. She was completely lost in him and she knew there would be no going back. "You're like a drug, Sophie." He grazed his lips over her cheek, running his fingers through her hair. His nearness caused her insides to heat, caused her heart to race, and her mind to fog. She was lost in the lust he ignited in her in a white hot fury. A moan escaped her lips as he ran his tongue along her neck. "My. Place.

Now." Sophie practically melted from his arms when he pulled back. It took great effort to keep her legs beneath her. Ashton opened her door and she slid in like she was made of liquid.

The ride was short to his place and Sophie was grateful because his eyes made her skin heat and she couldn't find any words. The sexual energy between them was intoxicating. This passionate lust was a new experience for her. Her body wanted him like he was breath for her lungs. *Is this love? Whatever it is, it feels absolutely amazing!*

Chapter Twenty-Four

Ashton pulled his car up in front of a beautiful sleek building. A doorman approached once they came to a stop. Ashton swung open his door and stepped out. Sophie's door was opened by a man with an inviting demeanor.

"Thank you," Sophie said softly.

"My pleasure. Do you have any bags that you need assistance with, dear?" The man was probably in his forties with graying hair and a perfectly trimmed mustache.

"Got it, Alfred," Ashton answered before Sophie could. He had already retrieved Sophie's small duffle bag from the back of the car. Sophie was surprised to have a doorman assisting them. He seemed to be on familiar terms with Ashton, anticipating that Ashton would toss his keys. He grabbed them easily when they soared through the air in his direction.

"Very well. Have a good evening, miss." The

doorman bowed respectfully.

"You too. It was nice to meet you. I'm Sophie, by the way." Sophie offered her hand. The man seemed amused as he accepted her hand.

"Charles, but you can call me Alfred if you like. Ashton seems to think it more fitting. I won't tell you what I call him. I fear it would not be appropriate for a lovely lady such as you to hear. Though, I will tell you it is definitely not Bruce Wayne." He winked.

"Hey now. Be nice. Don't scare her off." Ashton reached over and grabbed Sophie's hand, pulling her along with him. Another man was holding the main doors open for them as they walked toward the entrance.

"Where are we?" Sophie whispered, walking into the grand building. A beautifully decorated lounge presented before them—it looked professionally decorated with exquisite art covering the walls and a large desk made of marble stretched out to the left with a woman sitting behind it. The building was impressive.

"Good evening, Mr. King." The woman behind the counter practically salivated as they walked past. Sophie watched the woman's eyes linger on Ashton.

"Evening." Ashton nodded as he kept his pace quick. Ashton seemed oblivious to her interest. Sophie decided against acknowledging the woman, whose thoughts were written all over her face.

"This is where I live. Well, on the top floor, actually." He pressed the elevator button impatiently.

When the elevator doors opened, Ashton pulled her inside. Sophie looked around the mirrored interior. She looked up and caught his darkened eyes locked on her in their reflection, his jaw clenching. Her face heated from the intention that was painted on his expression. As soon as the doors closed completely his hands were on her. Her bag dropped to the floor and he lifted her up easily, pinning her between his hard body and the cool mirrored wall. He greedily roamed her body with his hands. His fingers reached under the hem of her shirt and browsed her sensitive flesh teasingly.

"Should we be doing this? There might be cameras in here or something." Sophie panted from the desire that now coursed through her, robbing her of breath.

"There are cameras but I don't fucking care. I can't wait to touch you."

"Ashton!" Sophie gasped, trying to pull her shirt back down and right herself. The elevator beeped and the doors began to open. Ashton reached down for her bag before he turned around and grabbed Sophie, throwing her over his shoulder.

"What are you doing?" Sophie couldn't help the laughter that spilled from her.

"Taking you to my bed," Ashton announced. Sophie looked around at the beautiful foyer that presented before two grand white doors. Ashton pushed a sequence of numbers into a keypad before he opened the door and walked in.

His hand cupped her bottom under her shorts and she squealed out in laughter. "Ashton! Put me down. I want to see your place." From what Sophie could see from her view over Ashton's shoulder the place was wonderful. Full height windows ran along the outside wall, giving an incredible view of the city below.

"Sure. You can see my place but we start with my room," he said playfully. Sophie screamed when he dropped her on the bed.

"Is this how you bring all the girls into your place?" Sophie laughed as she sat up on his bed.

"I have never brought another girl to this place before. You are the only girl I want in my bed." Ashton leaned down to kiss her lips. The city lights shone in the massive window that covered an entire wall in his room, casting a glow over his body. She ran her fingers over the magnificent bone structure of his cheek. She couldn't help but appreciate his perfection.

Sophie pulled away from the kiss. Reaching down, she pulled her shirt up over her head. "I want you," Sophie whispered as she let him take in her flesh. She pulled the straps of her bra down off her shoulders before reaching back and unclasping it.

"I want you more," he whispered, watching her. Sophie was driven by the heat and the desire to be with him that overcame her.

Sophie slipped off his bed and stood in front of the window so she was cast in the lights that shone upon them. She unbuttoned her shorts and slid them down the length of her legs. Her panties followed. She stood in front of him completely naked and heated with the need for his touch. "Don't move," she whispered as she approached him.

Sophie walked toward Ashton, who stood

watching her, unmoving with clenched fists. His gaze followed her like a predator watching his prey. She stepped behind him and reached for his shirt, pulling it up. Ashton reached back over his shoulder, pulled his shirt off over his head, and dropped it on the floor. Sophie's hands skimmed his waist as she ran her hands around to the hard rippled flesh of his stomach. She loved all the grooves that her fingers dipped into. She reached for the button of his pants as she pressed her breasts against his back and his breathing became deep and labored.

Sophie slipped his pants and underwear down, freeing him of any confinements of clothing before she circled him and took in his body. "Have you figured out what this is between us?" Sophie whispered.

"What do you want it to be?" he responded, watching her closely, his hands still by his sides.

"When I walked into that classroom when I saw you the first time, I wondered what it would be like to kiss you…I wanted to. I wanted to be the girl that held your hand and cheered you on from the sidelines as you played. I was jealous of Lucinda for having you."

"You should never have been jealous of Lucinda. Every time I kissed her I imagined it was you. You were out of my reach but it didn't stop me from wanting you. Now that I know what it's like to be with you I don't ever want to be with anyone else." Sophie ran her hands down his lean hard stomach, causing Ashton to take a sharp intake of breath. "Let's forget about the past and concentrate on the future."

"That sounds like a good plan to me." Sophie whispered. "I want you to touch me."

"Good, 'cause I was going out of my fucking mind." Ashton pulled her naked body against his as he lowered her onto the bed. Sophie delighted in the feel of his lips all over her. If this was love then she was now a believer. She wanted him, she needed him, and he had become a part of her heart.

Sophie's head spun as he moved down her body, teasing her with his lips and explorative hands. He continued until he met the over-sensitized skin between her legs. His tongue explored and his hands caressed until Sophie lost touch with reality. She fell deep into a pool of pleasure and came undone.

***

The next morning Sophie woke with a smile on her face. When she opened her eyes she felt Ashton's arm wrapped around her. She could hear his soft even breathing, indicating that he was still asleep. As much as she wanted to remain wrapped in his comfortable embrace, it was getting late and she was scheduled to work at the restaurant. When she moved, Ashton's arm tightened around her. "Are you trying to sneak out on me?" His voice was thick with sleep and he sounded so incredibly sexy.

"As much as I would love to spend the day with you in bed, I have to work." Sophie laughed as he pulled her closer to him.

"Do you still not believe in love?" he whispered

against her neck.

"Are you trying to make a believer out of me?" *Because you already did!* She wasn't ready to make that kind of confession yet. Sophie turned around to see his face. He leaned up on his arm to look down at her. His hair was messy and it made her smile how delectable he looked. His eyes were so bright blue and she wanted to know everything about him, all his secrets.

"Maybe." He leaned down and kissed her arm before looking up at her from under his thick dark lashes. Sophie ran her fingers through his soft hair. "You look so beautiful in my bed," he confessed as Sophie played with his hair.

"I like your bed."

"I also want to know what you look like in my shower," he said with a mischievous tone.

Sophie's eyes widened before he grabbed her by the waist and pulled her off the bed. He carried her out of his room toward the shower. "Ashton! What are you doing?" Sophie laughed as he hugged her against his chest. Sophie wrapped her legs around his waist as he carried her. She couldn't resist taking the opportunity to nibble on his ear as she leaned in close to him. He grabbed his toothbrush off the counter and slathered it with toothpaste before he stuck it in his mouth and went to turn on the shower, all while refusing to let her down. Sophie laughed and squirmed in his hold as he kissed her with his toothpaste covered mouth. She grabbed his toothbrush from his mouth and placed it in her own and proceeded to brush her teeth. "That's so fucking hot. I am never getting a new toothbrush," Ashton commended. Sophie kissed him back, making him laugh deep. It was the perfect sound and it melted her insides. He walked them into the hot water of the large tiled shower. Under the soothing stream of water he kissed her passionately, deeply like he could never get close enough. She knew because she felt the same about him. *This has to be real! I want to stay here forever.*

After the shower that Sophie knew she would not soon forget, Ashton offered to drive her to work. She gladly accepted because it meant she could have that much more time with him.

When they got in the car, Ashton reached over and ran his hand over the bare skin of her leg. She was wearing her black skirt and white button up blouse, which was pretty much a standard for her work attire.

"Don't start something you can't finish, sir." Sophie stopped his hand from reaching under her skirt.

"The backseat is roomier than it looks." Ashton raised his eyebrows suggestively.

"You know you never did tell me how you ended up posing nude for my art class," Sophie said when the question suddenly came to mind.

Ashton smiled. "Truthfully…I found out you were in that class and the opportunity arose. So I decided to go for it."

"You did it to see me?" Sophie was shocked at his confession.

"You sound surprised."

"Well, I am. Were you hoping that I would see your hot body and not be able to resist?"

"Yes. I told you I always had a thing for you," he stated wickedly.

"What about the girl?"

"I was trying to make you jealous. Did it work?"

"That depends on if you slept with her." Sophie raised her eyebrows.

"Naw. Not my type. She practically threw herself at me. I like girls to pretend they hate me." Ashton pulled up to the front of the restaurant. "Do I need to go in and tell Sam that you're off limits?" His mood turned suddenly serious as he looked past her into the restaurant.

"Nope. Not necessary. Things are good between me and Sam now that he knows I don't want anything more than friendship." Sophie leaned over and gave Ashton a kiss before she opened her door.

"Do you want me to pick you up?"

"No. I don't know what time I'm getting off, but I'll call you tomorrow before I go visit Margaret."

"Sounds good."

When Sophie walked into the restaurant she could see the beginning of the lunch rush start to accumulate, filling up the tables. She walked into the back room to put her bag in her locker when she was intercepted by Lori, who seemed slightly anxious.

"You look like you are going to say something I won't like," Sophie stated before Lori had a chance to speak.

"There's something I wanted to tell you before you hear it from someone else." Lori twisted her apron in her hands.

"Okay…" Sophie encouraged hesitantly.

"Well…I know Sam has had this thing for you. Lately he's been sulking around. I'm not sure what exactly happened between you two but last night I asked him out for a drink. I felt bad for the guy…I had a great time and I think he did too. I just want to make sure it's okay with you before I ask him out again. I'm not rushing into anything, especially since I know he's still hung up on you, but I thought maybe I could win his attention if we spend time together…" Lori looked up at Sophie with an awkward smile, unsure of how to continue the conversation without some feedback from her. "I need to know that I'm not competing with you, because if that's the case, I wouldn't have a chance."

"Nothing happened between Sam and I, and nothing will happen. We're friends and that's all it will ever be," Sophie insisted. "I think it's wonderful that this might be the beginning of something between you two. I want you both to be happy."

"I feel so much better. I didn't want you to get mad at me. There's already enough drama with Megan having the hate on for you right now." The relief was evident in Lori's posture. "She's convinced that you stole Ashton King from her, by the way." Lori shook her head. "I have no idea what's going on, but from the way that Ashton looks at you, I wouldn't blame you for falling for him."

"We are actually seeing each other." Sophie looked at Lori guiltily. "How exactly do I break the news to Megan without her trying to kill me?

Lori's mouth hung open. "I knew it was only a matter of time."

"For what it's worth, I had fallen for him a long time ago. I just didn't know what it was then," Sophie confessed.

"Megan has to accept it eventually—we can hope anyway." Lori patted her on the shoulder.

Sophie worked up the courage through the rest of her shift to break the news to Megan. She felt like she owed it to her to let her know even though Sophie was fearful of how Megan would react. When their shift wrapped up, Sophie took the opportunity. Megan did not take the news well and Sophie had to dodge a few glasses before Megan stormed out of the restaurant.

"I don't want to know what that was about," Sam said as he came out of the back room to see what the commotion was about. "Please tell me no one is injured." He looked at the broken glass on the floor.

"No injuries," Sophie assured. "I'll clean up the mess."

"Give her a month or two, she'll move on to her next obsession." Lori tried to cheer Sophie up as she helped with the cleanup.

Sophie sighed dejectedly. "I hope so but until then I think I have to watch my back."

"Megan is mostly bark. I wouldn't worry too much about her bite." Lori shrugged.

"It seemed more than just bark as the glasses were flying at my face. She barely missed me."

***

When Sophie walked in her apartment after work she was met with a beautiful aroma. She let her purse slip from her shoulder and took in the flowers that were displayed throughout the apartment. The drama from work was suddenly forgotten.

"Do you have a magic vagina or something? Seriously, this guy is in love with you." Mel came skipping over toward her. "Here." Mel passed her a card.

Sophie,
A reason to believe in love.
Ashton

Sophie couldn't help the excitement that coursed through her. It was a beautiful gesture. Sophie pulled out her phone.

Sophie: My apartment smells beautiful…thank you. A bit much but very much appreciated.

Ashton: You're welcome. I am trying to make you a believer and nothing is too much when it comes to you.

Sophie: It might be working.

Ashton: Good. I wanted to make those beautiful lips smile.

Sophie: Mission accomplished.

Ashton: I wish I was there to kiss them.

Sophie: Me too…tomorrow.

Ashton: Definitely.

Sophie was inspired to paint looking at all the flowers displayed around her apartment. She sat in front of her easel, deliriously happy. The memory of his touch still energized her, lingering upon her skin. She wanted to transfer her feelings on the blank canvas in front of her to represent how she felt.

Chapter Twenty-Five

Sophie and Mel had arranged to meet the business consultant that Margaret had recommended early the next morning. The meeting went well. John Marshall, the consultant, seemed to be optimistic about their endeavor, especially knowing Mel had actual experience working in a bakery. He reviewed their business plan, making only minor adjustments. John even indicated he might have potential investors. Sophie and Mel took it as a sign that they were on the right path.

***

"It's perfect!" Mel spun around in the building Sophie had found.

"There is a definite advantage to having a building that's already set up with some of the necessary equipment. This will substantially help with the start-up costs, not to mention making the process that much easier." Both Sophie and Mel fell in love with the place. It offered the perfect character and location they were looking for.

"A fresh coat of paint and some minor tweaking and this place will be ready to go," Mel squeaked out in excitement.

The landlord agreed to their terms, allowing them to make the necessary renovations that would be required. Mel and Sophie were able to make the first payment with savings and the landlord agreed to give them a month to finalize further financing. John was incredibly helpful in the negotiations, finding terms that worked well for everyone. John was working out the final details with an investor and was confident that everything would firm up. Everything seemed to be falling into place.

When they left the building, Sophie decided she would head to the hospital to visit Margaret before visiting hours were over. Sophie called ahead, letting Margaret know she was heading in. She sounded wonderful on the phone and even proceeded to let Sophie know that she was no longer on a liquid diet. Sophie laughed and took the hint that Margaret was looking for something to eat other than hospital food. Before she left, Sophie sent a quick text to Ashton, letting him know she was heading in to visit his grandmother.

Sophie decided to get off the bus a couple of blocks away from the hospital to pick up Margaret's favorite coffee and pastries. Sophie pulled out her phone again to see if Ashton had responded but was disappointed to discover there was still no response.

Walking into the coffee shop, her senses were

assaulted with the very rich flavor of coffee. The smell reminded her of Margaret. It was always a favorite stop they made in their daily schedule. Sophie got in line behind an older couple who were trying to make a choice in what type of croissant to get with their coffee. Sophie found their playful banter endearing.

She looked around the café as she waited her turn, taking in the people that filled the seats when her eyes fell on Ashton on the other side of the room. He didn't blend into the crowd because of his striking appearance. People's attention was drawn to him, his presence was so magnetic and remarkable. The company he was keeping made her stomach feel like lead. Across from him in the booth was the one and only Lucinda. She couldn't help the ache that made her insides twist. She watched Lucinda flip her hair flirtatiously and reach out toward Ashton's arm. They looked happy in each other's company.

The mocha colored walls felt like they were closing in on her; the painted coffee mugs that ran along the wall seemed to shift around her as if her world was suddenly tilting in the wrong direction. Everything felt wrong—even the smell of the air suddenly made her nauseous. Ashton stood up and Lucinda followed suit, straightening her very short skirt. She smiled before leaning in to kiss Ashton on the lips.

"Miss?" Someone tapped Sophie on the shoulder and she turned to see that it was her turn at the counter. The girl behind the register was staring at her impatiently and Sophie couldn't bring herself to form words. She was trying to hold herself together, she felt so brittle.

"Sorry," Sophie mumbled as she backed out of line. Her eyes found Ashton again but this time he was looking straight at her, a shocked expression on his face. She turned to leave as fast as she could. The air outside offered little relief when she pushed through the doors. She focused on putting one foot in front of the other. Sophie flagged down a cab that was passing.

Sophie didn't turn around when she heard Ashton call her name. She didn't respond when he touched her arm. She couldn't bring herself to look him in the eyes. She could feel herself shatter on the ground beneath her.

"Sophie please…it's not what it looked like."

Sophie reached for the cab door. "That seems to be the going excuse when it comes to you and Lucinda." Ashton reached for her hand and she pulled it away. "Don't touch me!" She climbed into the car and tried to pull the door closed but Ashton held it open.

"Don't leave like this," he pleaded. "Don't keep running away from me."

"It was stupid of me to think that I could just forget the past. I'm done being hurt by you," Sophie spat out angrily. "This thing with you and Lucinda is clearly not over if you keep finding your way back to each other. I feel like a fucking yo-yo with you. I'm up one minute and down the next, but guess what? You pushed me too far this time and I finally snapped.

"Congratulations, Ashton, you finally broke me.

I don't want to be with you. I can't be with someone that secretly meets up with their ex, who hates me. How do you think that looks? Seeing you there together, so friendly with each other, both with stupid smiles on your faces? Then the final straw was that lovely fucking kiss. What the fuck was that? Actually, I don't even want to hear you try and explain yourself out of this. I don't believe any of the shit that comes out of your mouth. Your word means nothing to me because I can't trust you. You're not the person I thought you were." Sophie tried to swing the door shut behind her but Ashton held it open.

"You just swore," Ashton said in disbelief.

"That's what you got from all of that?"

"No, but…"

"Fuck you!" Sophie pulled the door so hard it slammed closed. She pushed the lock down before Ashton pulled on the handle.

She told the driver to take her to the hospital, completely ignoring Ashton.

"Are you okay, miss? That was quite the argument." The driver kept glancing at her through the rearview mirror as they drove the short distance to the hospital. It was barely long enough to justify getting a cab but she had to get distance between her and Ashton as soon as she could.

"Yes. Sorry. Just give me a second to pull myself together." Sophie took a deep breath.

"Take all the time you need." The middle aged man seemed nervous about her emotional state. When she finally got her tears to stop falling she reached for her purse. "It's on me, miss, no need to pay. Just feel better.”

“Thank you.” Sophie’s voice wavered. She knew she should probably just have gone home but she knew she would regret not visiting Margaret, who was expecting her, and she feared that if she went home there might be a chance that she could not bring herself to leave again.

Everything felt wrong, her skin felt too heavy upon her and her head felt too light. The ground beneath her feet was too hard and the air around her too thin.

Sophie stood outside Margaret’s hospital door trying to get control over her emotions, trying to bury the pain that assaulted her. She could feel her phone vibrating in her pocket but she couldn’t bring herself to pull it out. She knew Ashton was trying to call her and she felt too broken to face him now. She was here for Margaret. Taking a deep calming breath, she tried to pull all of her frenzied emotions in tighter against her heart so they wouldn’t show through. Sophie held onto a basket of sweets that she had bought from the gift shop downstairs. Her hands felt numb as she grasped the handle of the basket until it groaned in distress. Finally when she felt as ready as possible, she knocked. When Margaret called for her to enter, she pushed the door open and forced herself to seem unaffected by the storm of emotions brewing inside her.

“Sophie,” Margaret welcomed warmly when she entered. It did offer Sophie some relief knowing that she was doing so well. She was sitting up with a magazine upon her lap. “It’s good to see you, dear.”

"You look beautiful. Are you sure you just had surgery?" Sophie tried to be light but she could hear her words fall heavy to the floor.

"Come sit. I'm a little sore but other than that I'm doing great. The doctor feels good about the surgery and my recovery, so I couldn't ask for more," Margaret assured her.

Sophie placed the basket on the table next to her bed. "In case you need something sweet." Sophie smiled and reached in to wrap her arms around Margaret. "I was worried about you. I'm glad things went so well." When Sophie went to pull away, Margaret held onto her, giving her an extra squeeze.

"Tell me what's wrong?" she whispered, holding onto Sophie. She let her go to look into Sophie's eyes.

"I'm fine." Sophie tried to sound sincere but she felt her lip tremble. "Nothing that needs to be discussed right now. When do you get to leave this place, anyway?" Sophie sat down beside Margaret's bed and took in the white room around her.

"It could be as early as tomorrow but what I would really like to know is why there is so much sadness in your beautiful green eyes."

Sophie shook her head as she avoided Margaret's gaze. "You would think that they would have clued in that a little color on the walls could make this place a little less stark and depressing," Sophie said thoughtfully.

"Sophie? Look at me." Margaret reached for her hand. "I want you to talk to me."

Sophie looked into Margaret's eyes and felt her resolve crumble. "My whole life I told myself not to fall in love because I would only get hurt. I saw my mother hurt so many times. I didn't want to feel that." Sophie reached up and wiped a tear that fell down her cheek. "I thought I could avoid it…I *should* have avoided it." Sophie didn't want to tell Margaret who she was talking about because she didn't know how Margaret would feel about her being with her grandson. "It's my own fault for believing that it could end any other way."

"What happened?" Margaret held onto Sophie's hand.

"I stopped on the way here to get you your favorite coffee and he was there with his ex-girlfriend. And she's not just some girl. She made it her life's mission to make my life miserable in high school. I saw them kiss. I ran out without the goods…sorry." Sophie wiped away the tears that ran freely down her cheeks. "You probably really would have enjoyed a caffeine fix right now." Sophie took a deep calming breath.

"Come here." Margaret offered her arms for an embrace. Sophie leaned over and fell into Margaret's comforting hold. "We can't have the good without the bad, unfortunately. I know that it hurts right now but if there is something that I have learned over my many years it's that the pain is worth it…I never did like that Lucinda girl." Margaret patted her arm.

Sophie pulled away and looked at Margaret with wide eyes. "You know?"

"Yes, dear. I don't know why he was meeting her. That's something only Ashton will be able to tell you. Though, one thing that I do know is when my Ashton came to me years ago and told me about a new girl at his school, I could see it in his eyes that you owned a piece of his heart even then. He told me that you were the most beautiful girl he had ever seen. Since that first day he spoke of you, you have never been far from his mind. I think he reserved his heart for you since that very first day. Maybe things are not as they seem."

Sophie shook her head. She wasn't really sure how to proceed with the information that Margaret had just told her. "I don't understand. Did you know who I was when you hired me?"

"Yes." Margaret sighed. "He didn't want you to know but it was actually Ashton who told me you needed a job. He arranged everything. Though, I am so very grateful you came into my life. I knew instantly why you meant so much to him. You need to keep in mind that fate brought the two of you back together for a reason. When you open yourself up to love it makes you vulnerable to pain."

"I wish you were right, Margaret, but I fear this crazy road that Ashton and I are on has come to an end. I'm not strong enough for this."

"I don't know the history you and Ashton share. I know that it hasn't been easy for either one of you. You are one of the strongest people I know. You just have to decide how hard you're willing to fight."

They both turned toward the door as it swung open and Ashton stood there filling the frame of the door. He was out of breath but looked relieved when his eyes fell on Sophie next to Margaret's bed.

"Let me explain…please." Ashton walked up to her, kneeling in front of her.

"Wait." Sophie placed her hand on his shoulder. She could feel his shoulders tense, unsure of her intentions. "Will you come outside with me?" she asked. He stood and reached for her hand. She let him take it.

"Of course." He pulled her hand up to kiss it. His contact made the tears sting her eyes because this would be the last time she held his hand. Being close to him made it impossible to think clearly, to know what was best.

"Goodbye, Margaret. I'll call you later," Sophie managed. Margaret only offered a gentle nod. Sophie knew it was because Margaret knew where Sophie's thoughts were.

Sophie led him down the hall to a group of chairs that were away from any commotion, giving them privacy. She sat down and waited for him to take the seat beside her. She looked into his beautiful blue eyes that were full of questions. She would have loved the opportunity to stare into them every day for the rest of her life but it was not meant to be. Sophie leaned over and kissed his lips softly. She pulled away when he reached up to pull her close. "This is my goodbye."

Ashton grabbed her hand. "Don't do this." He was desperate and it tore at her already broken heart. "I didn't know she was going to kiss me. It didn't mean anything."

"You have no idea what high school was like for me. From my first day I was basically shunned by everyone. No one would talk to me because of lies that Lucinda and you spread. It doesn't matter why you did it. It hurt, every moment of every day was painful for me because no one would even talk to someone that Lucinda and you hated for fear that they would be turned on as well. I thought I could get past it, and what we shared was wonderful…but seeing you and Lucinda together again, not once but twice, made me realize that it still hurts too much. I can't do this. I don't want to hurt like that again. We shouldn't be together, this was a mistake. How could we ever have expected a happy ever after to come from something that was born of so much hatred?"

"No…don't," Ashton begged.

"It doesn't matter why you were with her, Ashton. It doesn't change the fact that I don't love you." Sophie couldn't bring herself to look at him.

"No. Don't say that," he pleaded.

"Goodbye, Ashton…just forget about me. We will both be better off." Sophie pulled her hand from his and walked away. She wasn't strong enough to stay any longer. She knew the words she spoke were a lie. She now believed in love. Her heart loved him with a desperation that scared her and she needed to break free of the hold before it destroyed her. Walking away from him was the hardest thing she had ever done. She could feel his eyes on her like a weight. She walked past the bus stop and kept going; she didn't want to stop. She walked until her feet hurt and the sun began to set. She avoided all the people that passed her by. She could tell they watched her, could see her pain written all over her. She didn't stop until she saw her apartment building cast in the glow of the streetlight. She entered her apartment. Closing the door, she dropped her purse and shoes and headed toward her bed, where she crawled in without a word.

The tears began anew now that she was in the comfort of her bed. The smell of Ashton lingered on her pillows. She sobbed as the empty ache in her chest tightened its hold. She was too late. She hadn't stopped herself before she hit bottom.

Sophie felt the bed shift as Mel crawled in and wrapped her arm around her. Mel didn't speak a word; Sophie was grateful because there was no way that she would be able to respond. Sophie let herself drift off into a restless sleep because she had come undone.

The next morning the sun was harsh as its light flooded her apartment, taunting her and trying to lure her from sleep. Sophie pulled the pillow over her head and refused to wake to the world. Mel had risen with the beginning of the day and was trying to be quiet as she shuffled around the apartment and left. Sophie got up and closed all the windows, pulling the curtains tight to block out the sunshine before climbing back in bed.

Sophie slipped in and out of sleep as she tossed and turned under her covers, hiding from the world. The idea of getting up and facing the fact she needed to put herself back together was too much. She waited for the pain to fade but it held on so tight it made it hard to breathe.

Sophie wasn't sure what time it was when Mel came back into her apartment. Sophie didn't bother to open her eyes. "Your mom called me. She left a couple of messages this morning and got worried when you didn't return them." Mel's voice was thick with concern.

"Please tell me you didn't say anything." Sophie's voice was dry from thirst.

"I couldn't help it. She has this way of getting information out. She's sneaky, but all I said was that you weren't feeling good. You should call her. She'll drive out here if you don't confirm you're still alive. I think I still freak your mother out a bit." Mel reached up and pulled the blanket down, brushing Sophie's hair from her face. Sophie could see the worry creasing Mel's features. "I'm only giving you this one day to mope. That's all you get but you still have to call your mother and let her know I didn't kill you and cut you up into tiny pieces."

"Okay," Sophie whispered. Mel grabbed her phone and passed it to her before she went to retrieve a glass of water to sit on Sophie's nightstand.

"Drink this," she demanded.

Sophie looked at her phone and noticed her mother's missed calls, not to mention a call from Margaret and many from Ashton. He had left many text messages as well. A message from Ashton used to excite her but now they only made her sad. She was surprised how late the hour was as the day was already fading into night.

Ashton: I'm sorry.

Ashton: I need to talk to you.

Ashton: Call me please.

Ashton: You don't need to love me. I just want to be with you.

Sophie couldn't read anymore. She erased all of the messages from Ashton before she called her mother.

"Mom?"

"Honey, I was worried about you. Mel told me you weren't feeling well."

"I'm okay. Mel is taking care of me. Are you still coming this week to try on your dress?" Sophie didn't want to broach the topic of why she wasn't feeling well because she knew she wouldn't be able to hold herself together.

"I was hoping to come tomorrow. Does that work for you?" Her mother had a cautious tone, like she was trying to read between the lines.

"Perfect." Sophie forced some enthusiasm into her voice. She wasn't sure if her mother believed her or not.

"Okay…how are you feeling now?"

"Better. I should be as good as new tomorrow."

"Good, and I want you to tell me all you have been up to. Do you need anything?"

"No, I'm good."

"Tomorrow then. Love you."

"Love you too, Mom." When Sophie pressed end and let the forced pleasantry for her mother's benefit melt away, she was left with her overwhelming sadness.

Mel was good and let Sophie stay in her bed for the rest of the evening but the morning came entirely too fast and she still did not feel ready.

Chapter Twenty-Six

Mel pulled back the covers. "Noooo," Sophie moaned.

"I told you I would give you yesterday to sulk around and not get out of bed but now it's a new day." Mel walked into the bathroom and turned on the shower before she grabbed Sophie's toothbrush and slathered it in an obscene amount of toothpaste. "Here. Brush your stank teeth and wash your stank body so we can go out and grab some breakfast while I tell you what John said when he called this morning. He had some important information about a certain business that we're trying to start."

"Okay, Mom," Sophie moaned sarcastically before she rolled out of bed.

"Did you just make a joke? Thank the lord she isn't completely lost to me!" Mel cried out dramatically.

The hot water soothed Sophie as it ran over her; it did not wash away her sadness but it gave her enough to conjure the strength to get dressed and start the day. Sophie couldn't help but smile when Mel blasted "Single Ladies" by Beyoncé. It made her want to be happy again but the road seemed so long. Mel hadn't pressed for details but she knew it was only a matter of time. She just hoped she would be ready.

Sophie stared at her reflection in the mirror. The dark circles under her eyes spoke of her inner torment. Her face seemed strange to her, her skin looked pale and her lips were dry. She powdered her face with some color and rubbed some gloss over her lips, hoping it would disguise her emotions that seemed to seep through her skin.

***

Sophie looked at her plate of food. She was hungry but the food didn't taste like it should. It left an aftertaste in her mouth that made it hard to swallow. She realized her broken heart affected every part of her body. She felt like a stranger in her own skin. It was a version of herself that she didn't care for. She fought the urge to call Ashton and beg him to take her back. Though, if it hurt this much only after their short time together, she wondered if she could survive when he would grow tired of their relationship and leave, like so many men had left her mother over the years. Flames eventually burnt out. *I wish I could go back to my safe boring life when Ashton was in the past and I was wonderfully sane. At least I think I do...*

Sophie tried not to think about Ashton and

Lucinda and the way things looked in the coffee shop. *Do I believe Ashton? Should I believe him? Can people die from emotional turmoil?* He made her feel too much and it terrified her. *Am I insane? I feel like it.*

"Do you want me to kick his ass? You know that I can," Mel said bluntly as she reached over and took a hash brown off Sophie's plate and popped it into her mouth.

"No. I just want to move on and learn from my mistake." Sophie sighed. She pushed her plate away and leaned back in her chair.

"Was that Lucinda bitch involved, because I would love to take her down?"

"All I want is for you to tell me what John said when he called." Sophie rested her chin in her hands.

Mel sat up straighter, a brilliant smile on her face. "John said that the investor he has been in contact with is keen on investing in our business. We just have to put a proper business proposal together and then he plans to finance it completely. John wants to meet with us to go over the details but this is perfect for us. We can get started right away. Nothing can stop us now."

"That is amazing." Sophie felt a real smile touch her lips. This was just what she needed to distract her. She would focus everything on establishing their company and eventually she hoped that her heart would heal.

"The more you love them the harder it is to let them go. That's how I know I have never been in love yet because I was always glad to walk out when the time comes."

"What about Dustin?" Sophie furrowed her brow. "I thought you guys were a thing?"

"Maybe…he wants to take it slow and see how things go." Mel let out a long slow breath. "When I'm with him I feel really good but he's too…"

"Safe?" Sophie added with a raised brow.

Mel smiled and shook her head. "Yeah…it's strange for a guy not to want to jump my bones as soon as he can. It makes me question if he's really into me. Does that seem weird?"

"You're used to idiots, so of course it will be strange to be with someone who's looking for more than a free ride, but you have to want to be with him for it to work."

"I really like him and maybe that's what's making me nervous. I keep waiting for him to turn on me or something. He took me out to eat the other night and he didn't expect anything in return. I'm not used to it."

"That's what you need and deserve, Mel. You need to get used to it. No more losers from loser town. That was the old Mel. You are now a businesswoman with standards. No more turning back now."

Mel reached over and grabbed Sophie's hand. "You're the best friend in the whole world."

"I know." Sophie squeezed back tightly.

"We are all colors of messed up, you know. I don't know how to recognize a good man when I see them and you're scared to let yourself fall in love, so you run away from it even when it comes in the hottest package known to man."

"But we're going to make the best business partners," Sophie encouraged.

"Damn fucking right. Let's kick it." Mel jumped to her feet. "We have lots of shit to do before we can start selling our cookies." She winked.

***

Sophie felt drastically better when her mother arrived that afternoon. She knew there was no way she could hide it from her. The truth of her broken heart was written all over her.

"Sophie, darling! This is the most beautiful dress." Her mother's face lit up as she looked down at the dress; the fit was almost perfect as her mother spun around in front of the full height mirror in Sophie's apartment. Her mother ran her fingers over the material and her smile shone brighter than the sun. Sophie placed a couple of pins into the material for some minor adjustments but she was very pleased how well it fit. Tears started to fall from her mother's shining eyes. "I love you so much. This is more than I ever imagined." She gathered Sophie in her arms and squeezed tight. "Are you going to tell me why you're so sad?" her mother whispered in Sophie's ear as she kept her arms secure around her shoulders. She pulled back and looked into Sophie's eyes that were also filled with tears.

"Mom? How do you know that it is different with Peter than with all the others?" Sophie kept her hands busy fussing with her mother's dress. When her question left her lips her mother reached for her hands.

"There are no guarantees in life but I know that my heart wants to be with him even with the risk. He makes me happy and I want to spend whatever time that I can by his side. All I can do is hope that we will have the rest of our lives together."

"Don't you think it would be easier not to risk it? Why would you want to give someone so much power over your life? What if your heart gets broken and you can't put the pieces back together again?"

Her mother tucked Sophie's hair behind her ear before lifting Sophie's chin to look into her eyes. "It doesn't mean that you give someone power over you. It's opening up your heart to someone and finding a connection. To find meaning in our lives that makes us happy and stronger. I like my life with love even if it meant I had to suffer many failed attempts. If you don't take the risk because you're scared of getting hurt, then you could miss out on something beautiful. Our hearts are strong, even if it doesn't always feel like it. Don't cheat yourself because you are afraid."

"What if I can never really forgive Ashton for what he and Lucinda did to me? What if I can't get past it? Seeing him with Lucinda makes me feel like the vulnerable girl I was back in high school. I run as fast as I can in the opposite direction, literally. I'm just waiting for them to reveal this has been a joke the entire time but…when he looks at me I feel loved. He makes me feel alive."

"I wish I had the answer for you. I don't like how he treated you. I hate that he made you suffer but if you love him you have to figure out if it's worth the risk to make it work. Eventually you have to stop running and face it. You are no longer that little girl anymore. You are a strong, independent woman. Take control of your life."

"You're right." Sophie hugged her mother tightly; the comfort of her mother's embrace was exactly what she needed. "I love you, Mom."

"I love you too, baby girl, more than you will ever know." Her mother held her. "You are my favorite person in this whole world and I don't like seeing you sad."

"I'm gonna be okay." Sophie wiped her eyes. "I like this more mature version of you, Mom."

"It was about time, don't you think? I only wish I could have made the debut years ago." Her mother squeezed her hand. "It would have helped my mothering skills."

"I wouldn't change a thing," Sophie insisted. "Mel and I have some good news for you."

"It's about time this sappy love fest was over," Mel piped in. Sophie laughed because she noticed Mel's watery eyes. "And don't worry, she's not gonna tell you that we're lesbian lovers." Mel smiled evilly.

Sophie couldn't help but laugh and her mother followed suit. Laughing felt good, she wanted to find her happiness again.

Her mother listened excitedly as the two of them told her of their business plan and the immediate plans for the cookie café. Sophie's mother's reaction was encouraging as she asked questions. Sophie and Mel planned to spend the rest of the day finishing the business proposal for the investor and organize the renovations that had to take place. Dustin's brother, Christian, was a contractor and agreed to take on the project. The plumbing did not need to be altered and only minor electrical was required to acquire proper outlets for their equipment.

"And your job at the restaurant? And with Mrs. Darcy?" Sophie's mother asked.

"I'll give my notice at the restaurant once our financing is official and my job with Margaret is flexible."

"I am proud of you girls. This is exciting and you seem to have all your bases covered. I hope to be your first customer."

When Sophie's mom left, her spirits were considerably lifted. It was nice to focus on something other than the upheaval within her heart.

Sophie and Mel spent the rest of the afternoon making phone calls to confirm their numbers before sending their final business plan to John. When they were finished, Sophie called Margaret to get an update. Margaret was excited to announce that Ashton was on the way to take her home. Sophie made plans to meet her at her house. She was planning to stay with Margaret for a couple of days until she was healed, taking a couple days off work from the restaurant. Hearing Margaret speak Ashton's name brought an ache to her chest. She hoped that she wouldn't run into him because she knew how difficult it would be. She wasn't ready yet.

When Sophie arrived at Margaret's house, she was surprised to hear so many voices coming from the sitting room. "Hello, Charlotte," Sophie greeted as she set her bags down in the entrance way.

"Ashton's parents are in town visiting Margaret. They're expecting you." Charlotte gave her an encouraging wave toward the voices.

"I don't want to intrude. I'll let them have their family time."

"Nonsense. They have been looking forward to meeting the girl that Margaret and their son are always fussing about."

"What?" Sophie suddenly felt terrified.

"Go on. I'll put your bags in your room," Charlotte insisted.

Sophie forced her legs to walk into the room. She was nervous to meet Ashton's parents. Sophie suddenly wished she had worn something nicer than her favorite jeans and a pale green T-shirt, when her eyes settled on two finely dressed people. Sophie recognized them as Ashton's parents immediately. Ashton had his father's dominating presence with amazing bone structure, with his mother's coloring and bright blue eyes. They turned to study Sophie as she entered. Sophie forced a pleasant smile on her face, ignoring the nerves clawing at her insides.

"Hello, Sophie," Margaret welcomed her. She was sitting on the sofa with a blanket over her legs, resting. Sophie was relieved to see her coloring had improved even more since yesterday. Both Ashton's parents stood up as Sophie approached. Ashton's father extended a hand as she neared. His features reminded her of Ashton.

"Nice to meet you, Sophie. I'm Marcus and this is Bridgette. We have heard so much about you."

"Hopefully only the good things. It's nice to meet you too. I have grown rather fond of Margaret and you have a wonderful son as well," Sophie offered politely. They smiled welcomingly in return.

"So you think I'm wonderful?" Ashton's voice startled her as he approached her from behind.

"Ashton? I didn't know you were here." Ashton's smell enveloped her. He leaned down and kissed his grandmother's cheek before coming to stand next to his parents.

"I can see why Ashton is so captivated by you. You are quite the vision," Bridgette complimented.

"Thank you, Bridgette. You are too kind."

Sophie looked up and caught Ashton's eyes on her. She knew that the truth was he was the one that captivated her. Her resolve was crumbling.

"Sorry to interrupt but I wanted to see if Sophie wanted this with her." Charlotte entered the room carrying the wrapped canvas with her. "Or in her room with her bags?"

"My room is fine. Thank you, Charlotte."

"Is that a painting? I have heard of your wonderful talent," Bridgette asked, eyeing the large package.

Sophie felt her face heat. She hadn't intended to make a big deal about the painting she had made for Margaret. "Yes. It's just something I did for Margaret. I was planning on giving it to her later," Sophie tried to dismiss nonchalantly.

"Did you paint me something?" Margaret beamed, making her appear youthful.

"Yes. I wanted to thank you for all that you have

done for me," Sophie offered nervously.

"You are so sweet." Margaret reached for Sophie's hand, giving her an affectionate squeeze.

"Bring it here, Charlotte," Bridgette requested.

Sophie had to stay her fingers from twisting a hole in her shirt. Ashton looked slightly amused at her anxious behavior. Ashton leaned in next to her. "You look sexy as hell when you're nervous." His breath against her ear made her insides melt. She wanted to taste his lips. She was defenseless against his charms. *I have to be strong! I can't keep falling into this cycle that will have me running scared because I don't know if Lucinda still has a claim on him.* How could she protect her heart when it so willingly wanted to sacrifice itself up for slaughter, even with the memory of him and Lucinda so vivid in her mind from the coffee shop?

"Can I open it?" Margaret asked, looking at the painting excitedly.

"Oh…of course, it's for you. You may open it whenever you like." Sophie noted everyone's eyes on her, especially the hot gaze of Ashton. Sophie held her breath as Margaret untied the sting, pulling back the paper to expose the picture that she created. Margaret's hand immediately went to her mouth to stifle a gasp. For a moment Sophie's heart felt like it stilled in her chest, unsure of what Margaret would say. Sophie watched as tears filled Margaret's eyes.

"It's beautiful." Margaret sobbed gently. "You have captured everything about him that I loved more than life." Margaret ran her fingers over her late husband's features so lovingly it almost pained

Sophie to watch. The look in Margaret's eyes spoke of the love she held for him. Sophie looked up and noticed Bridgette's tears as well.

Marcus gently touched Sophie's shoulder. "Thank you." The appreciation in his eyes was touching. She hadn't realized how much the picture would affect those who knew the man in the painting.

"Yes. Thank you for this. This is the closest I have felt to him since the day he left this world." Margaret smiled through her tears.

"I'm glad you like it." Sophie's heart swelled, these people loved him very much, and it was written on all of their faces.

Ashton ran his fingers gently down the length of her back, giving Sophie shivers. She wasn't sure why Ashton insisted on touching her. She had said her goodbye but she couldn't bring herself to stop him. He stood too close, his addictive smell called to her. His face was so perfect it was impossible not to want to look at him, to want to touch him. If only he would give her some space to clear her head of his spell. Sophie answered Marcus and Bridgette's questions, and let them know her paintings would be displayed in Mr. Heshman's art gallery. "It is so good knowing that Margaret is being well cared for." Bridgette touched Sophie's forearm. "And I have never seen my son so taken with anyone like he is with you. We have been looking forward to meeting you."

Ashton cleared his throat as if warning his mother.

"We will be back tomorrow, Mother." Bridgette

leaned down and kissed Margaret's cheek. "Call if you need anything."

"Of course. Good night, love." Margaret smiled.

After Ashton's parents left, Sophie made tea for Margaret and then helped her upstairs so she could ready herself for bed. Margaret grew tired and wished to retire early. Sophie helped Margaret into bed, giving her the pain medication she needed.

"Ashton will not be able to let go, he's too far gone. I can see it in his eyes when he looks at you." Margaret looked up at Sophie thoughtfully. "My husband used to look at me like that." Sophie wasn't able to respond; she could only smile sadly. "He told me you don't believe in falling in love." Margaret took Sophie's hand. "You should know that it believes in you."

Sophie sighed. "Goodnight, Margaret. I'll keep my phone on all night. Just call me if you need anything." Sophie slid the phone on Margaret's nightstand closer to the bed so it could be reached easier.

"Think about what I said."

"I will."

"Goodnight, Sophie."

Chapter Twenty-Seven

After Sophie got ready for bed she grabbed her robe and quietly left her room to go downstairs to make more tea. The house was quiet. Charlotte had gone to sleep and Ashton had disappeared earlier in the evening, no word to his whereabouts. *I hope Ashton went home.*

When Sophie entered the kitchen she was surprised to see Ashton sitting at the table with a bottle of whiskey in front of him. *Crap!* His hair looked as if he had repeatedly run his fingers through it and his eyes were noticeably bloodshot. He didn't say a word as Sophie walked in, only leaned back in his chair. His blue eyes were dark and were trained on her as she grabbed a tea cup before sitting across from him.

Sophie wrapped her fingers around the whiskey bottle and pulled it toward her. She let the amber liquid fill her cup. The smell made her stomach turn but she wanted to do exactly what Ashton was doing and take the edge off her emotions.

"Ask me truth," Ashton broke the intense silence.

"No. I don't want to play." Sophie tipped her cup up and swallowed the harsh liquid.

"I do. Ask me why I was with Luce." He grabbed the whiskey and filled his own glass.

"I don't want to know." Sophie shook her head. She didn't want to know anything that involved Lucinda.

"Please."

Sophie slipped her robe off her shoulders and laid it over the back of her chair. She walked over to Ashton, who was watching her without a word. She slid her leg over him and straddled him in his chair. Looking into his eyes, she ran her fingers through his hair. He closed his eyes and a single tear slipped down his cheek. Sophie leaned in and kissed it away softly. He stayed still beneath her. Opening his eyes, he studied her through a haze of stormy blue.

"I dare you to kiss me," Sophie whispered. His eyes fell to her lips before he leaned in and took them. Ashton stood up abruptly, taking her with him. Pressing her body into his, he deepened their kiss. He started walking out of the kitchen with Sophie in his arms.

"Where are you taking me?" Sophie whispered.

"To my bed," Ashton said with purpose.

"Why do you always feel the need to carry me?"

"Because I don't want to let you go."

When Ashton laid her upon his bed she was surrounded by his scent like a warm blanket. Ashton slipped her night dress over her head, exposing her. His lips rained her with pleasure as he savored her.

Leaning over her, Ashton looked at her with his mesmerizing blue eyes, searching for answers. Sophie ran her fingers over his cheek and touched his full lips. Her body responded to every touch he gave her. He was a musician and she was his instrument. His expert fingers played into her pleasure like a beautiful song. He took her with sad longing, like he knew that she would still not open her heart to him.

Ashton held her close as he entered her, his usual playful demeanor far from reach. They were both falling apart.

Sophie lay against Ashton's chest, her body satisfied beyond measure but her heart already mourning him. She'd only given in to her desires one last time. Ashton was quiet as he ran his fingers gently along her back. Sophie didn't even realize she was crying until Ashton reached down and wiped the tear from her cheek with his thumb.

"I was offered a job contract overseas for an undetermined amount of time," Ashton said quietly.

"What about your new place?" Sophie turned her body to look up at his face, running her hand along his body, memorizing the feel of him beneath her.

He became quiet for a moment as he trailed his fingers along the curve of her shoulder. "Tell me to stay here with you and not take it." Ashton reached up and ran his fingers through her hair.

"I can't do that," Sophie whispered, another tear escaping her. She sat up and grabbed her night dress and slipped it over her head. Ashton raked his hands over his face and sighed.

"Can't or won't?" He leaned up on his elbows.

"Both."

"Sophie." Ashton grabbed her wrist, stopping her from climbing off the bed. "I'm in love with you."

Sophie leaned in and kissed him, desperately savoring his taste with tears blurring her vision. When a sob escaped her lips, she pulled away and from his bed. "I can't do this if Lucinda is a piece of the puzzle. Can you guarantee me that you will never see Lucinda again and that she doesn't mean anything to you?"

He didn't respond immediately. Torment crossed his features. "Tell me you love me and we can figure everything else out. It's not what you think it is with Lucinda. I just need you to trust me for a little while longer."

"I can't."

"Love me or trust me?"

"Both."

"Then I guess this is it." His eyes dropped to his lap. Sophie needed to leave, the room suddenly felt suffocating. Walking across the hall, she closed and locked her door. She climbed into her bed and checked her phone to make sure Margaret didn't need her before she pulled the covers over her head. She cried until her body gave way to exhaustion and she fell into a sleep consumed with dreams of Ashton.

The next morning Sophie felt like a ghost of herself as she crawled out of bed. She went to check on Margaret, who was still asleep. She pulled the door closed and walked quietly down the stairs and entered the kitchen where Charlotte was baking bread. The smell made her mouth water.

"It smells amazing in here."

"Are you feeling all right, dear? You look pale." Charlotte looked at her with concern. "I will put some tea on for you." Charlotte plugged in the kettle.

"Yes. Just didn't sleep very well." Sophie smiled half-heartedly.

"Seems to be a trend this morning. Ashton left a short while ago. It looked like he hadn't slept at all." Charlotte shook her head.

"He's gone?" Sophie frowned.

"Yeah. He said he had to take care of some things before he caught his flight later. He took a job offer that started immediately. He'll be back for goodbyes later. He didn't want to wake Margaret too early."

Sophie suddenly had no appetite. Ashton mentioned a job overseas but she didn't realize it was so soon. She knew that she should be relieved because this is what she wanted. Ashton admitted that Lucinda still meant something to him but she couldn't help but feel sick to her stomach. The more she was with him the harder it was to let go.

Charlotte understood Sophie didn't want to talk, saying no more about it as she set tea in front of Sophie and went about her business. When Sophie finished she went to wake Margaret to ready herself for the nurse's arrival for a routine checkup.

The day flew by as Sophie's thoughts were consumed with her pain of knowing that Ashton was leaving. It made her question everything she was doing. His confession of love wound so tightly around her heart. She only wished it was enough for him to walk away from Lucinda but apparently it wasn't.

Sophie had a meeting with Mr. Heshman midafternoon to view her artwork. She made sure she was back at her apartment with enough time to lay out all her paintings to view easily.

"These are incredible. I would like to display them all," Mr. Heshman commented as he stood before the work spread out around her apartment. "The colors and the details are amazing. This is exactly what my gallery needs to give it a fresh look." Mr. Heshman was a tall man with a slim build. His facial hair was trimmed in a very unique manner that gave him an artsy look with his thick framed glasses. He was excitable by nature and warm in his approach. Sophie knew immediately that she liked him. He had a very endearing energy about him.

"Sophie, you are such a pleasure. Thank you for this opportunity. I will arrange someone to pick up these paintings over the next few days and then we will be in contact to discuss appropriate pricing for each piece. I assume you are willing to part with everything should the price meet your satisfaction?"

"Of course. Except for one painting. I don't wish to sell this piece." Sophie indicated the painting of Ashton that drew her eye no matter where she was in her apartment.

"Ah…this one holds special meaning," Mr. Heshman acknowledged with understanding. "Well, I would love to display it regardless. If you are willing to part with it temporarily, that is?"

"Yes. That would be fine," Sophie agreed.

"It was a pleasure, Sophie. I would be interested in showing any future pieces that you create. Please be in touch. I think this arrangement will suit us both very well if your work is received as well as I anticipate. I have been in this business long enough to recognize unique and wonderful talent when I see it. I would also like to set up a photo shoot to get your picture taken. People are always interested in discovering the artist behind the canvas and you my dear, are too lovely not to show off."

"Thank you, Mr. Heshman, for this wonderful opportunity." Sophie shook his hand.

"Please call me Falon."

The meeting went better than she expected. She was excited with the possibilities this arrangement could bring for her. Mr. Heshman had very good connections in the art world. Painting was something that she knew she was supposed to be doing. When she sat down in front of her easel she had no doubts, she was made for expression with art. Sophie loved the feel of a brush in her hand and the smooth glide of the paint as it spread across the canvas.

"That went well." Mel walked up beside her and nudged her side.

"It was probably all the cookies you kept feeding him." Sophie laughed. The apartment smelled of vanilla from Mel's creations.

"I needed an unbiased opinion. He certainly liked the oatmeal ones."

"Or maybe the half-dressed girl that kept feeding

them to him." Sophie nudged Mel back.

"What? These shorts make my butt look hot." Mel defended her insanely short shorts with an innocent smile and flutter of her eyelashes.

"That's because you can *see* your butt." Sophie laughed and shook her head. "I'll drop that paperwork off to John on my way back to Margaret's. She loaned me her car."

"Well, aren't you just weaseling your way into that woman's heart," Mel said as she dropped a bunch of cookies in a paper bag. "Here you go. Test some out on your rich friends and see how they like them."

"Thanks," Sophie said, grabbing the bag from Mel and the folder with their finalized business proposal.

"Take care of yourself, Sophie. We got a business to start and the circles under your eyes are scaring me." Mel placed her hands on her hips.

"See you tomorrow."

"Oh…I think I will move back into my place today. I am paying rent after all."

"Are you sure? You know that you are welcome to stay as long as you want."

"As much as I love your sofa," Mel said sarcastically, "I'm ready for the next step. Besides, things between me and Dustin are getting serious and I don't think you want us making sweet love on your sofa."

"Very true. Glad we're on the same page."

Margaret's recovery was going well and Sophie noticed she was getting her energy back. Sophie smiled when she noticed her painting was hung over the fireplace in the main sitting room. "It's like it was always meant to be there." Margaret said. "Marcus hung it up when he was here earlier. They are heading back home and were sorry that they couldn't see you again before they left."

Sophie felt bad that she had intentionally avoided coming over when they were here but she couldn't bring herself to face them. She felt like they were disappointed in her for having walked away from Ashton. He had told them before he had left to take his job that they were no longer together. "I'm sorry that I missed them. They are so lovely."

"I think they're still holding onto the hope that the two of you will get back together," Margaret said with a sad smile.

"Ashton and I not being together is the best for everyone in the long run," Sophie declared.

"I have to disagree and I know that Ashton feels the same way. I'm not sure what happened between the two of you but the look in his eye when he said goodbye to me today was not the look of someone who wanted to leave." Margaret smoothed the blanket over her lap.

"There's too much history and heartache between the two of us," Sophie admitted.

"I think that the only thing that his heart has known is love for you." Margaret said. Sophie sat down on the chair beside Margaret with a sigh. "But unfortunately it is not always enough. I'm sure everything will unfold as it is supposed to in time." Margaret smiled like she was holding a secret.

"I suppose." Sophie frowned. *His heart unfortunately also knows something for Lucinda…*

"The heart is a very complicated thing," Margaret said thoughtfully.

***

Sophie kept herself busy for the weeks leading up to her mother's wedding. Margaret had received positive feedback from her doctor in regards to her recovery and success in removing all cancerous tissue from her body. They were now monitoring her closely and making sure her progress continued. Within a couple of weeks she was back to her usual busy self, booking her schedule with events and meetings to continue her work in the community. Sophie admired her strength. Margaret had even helped Sophie plan her mother's bachelorette tea that came together beautifully. Margaret had arranged for it to be hosted at an elegant country club. The staff served the most delicious sweets and sandwiches to accompany their tea. All of the women in her mother's life came together to celebrate their friendships and wish her mother well in her new life with Peter. Her mother had many friendships that developed over the years that filled the void of family she did not have. Sophie knew most of them. They were all familiar in her childhood memories. Sophie couldn't wish for a better group of people to be in her mother's life.

Falon had arranged for her pieces to be picked up. Her apartment felt bare after all the paintings were packed up and shipped out. The gallery opening date was set and Sophie looked forward to seeing how her work was received. The financing had also been finalized for their Cookie Café and Mel and Sophie were preparing for their grand opening to take place a week after her mother's wedding. The work on the building was close to completion. Their menu was confirmed after consuming an insane amount of cookies and perfecting recipes that kept the girls up late for many nights.

Sophie stood in the small office in the back of the café that smelled of fresh paint. Two small desks were sitting in the room with a couple of filing cabinets. The girls decided on warm, inviting colors for their café and were very pleased now that they were covering the walls.

Sophie held a letter from their investor. They had not dealt with the company personally. All their dealings had gone through John, who operated as the middleman. Sophie was grateful the investors were taking a chance on their new company. Without the financing this would not have been possible. Sophie had written a letter to thank them for the opportunity, making it possible for them to open their new business. She had given it to John to deliver and was surprised she had gotten a response. Sophie sat down in her chair and opened the letter.

Dear Sophie Rogers,

Thank you for your letter. You presented an opportunity I could not refuse. It is an investment that I know is well made.

I look forward to hearing of your success.

Sophie flipped the letter over in her hand. There was no signature or name assigning the letter to a person, only the company logo in the upper right corner. She ran her finger over the crown emblem. It was familiar somehow as she traced the lines. She had seen it somewhere before her dealings with John but she could not place it. Suddenly the realization hit her. She had seen it on some of Ashton's paperwork. It was his family's company. *Holy crap!*

Sophie grabbed her phone. She had to know for sure. The phone rang three times and she almost lost the nerve and hung up but then Ashton's voice rattled her. She missed him so much that the mere sound of his voice pulled tears from deep inside her.

"Sophie?" He spoke her name. It had never sounded so beautiful to her ears. She forgot to answer when she became wrapped up in how much she missed him. "Are you all right?"

"Yes...I just wanted to know if it was you that invested in our company."

She was met with silence on the other line. "It's what I do. I make investments."

"Would you have done it if you didn't know me?" Sophie asked.

She heard him sigh on the other line. "Just let it be, Sophie."

"Why did you do it? There is no guarantee that this company will make any profit."

"I don't fucking care about the money, Sophie. I wanted to help you...just a second." Sophie heard him speak to a woman in muffled voices before coming back on the line. "I have to go, Sophie."

She couldn't help the jealousy that twisted in her stomach even though she had no idea who was with him. She wanted to be there beside him. "I miss you," she whispered.

"Don't say things you don't mean. Goodbye, Sophie." Tears slipped down her cheek as she listened to him hang up. She had no idea where in the world he was right now, she only knew that wherever it was, her heart was with him. She let her phone slip from her fingers and fall into her lap as the tears flowed freely. *Why did I say that? Either get in or get out.*

"Did you see the arms on the guy out there? What's wrong, Sophie?" Mel sat in her chair and wheeled herself closer to Sophie.

"It was Ashton who gave us the money." Sophie wiped her tears from her face.

"Then he's smarter than I gave him credit for." Mel tried to brighten Sophie's mood. "How can he go wrong investing in two hot girls selling their cookies?"

Sophie couldn't help but laugh through her tears.

"I miss him so much, Mel, it hurts." Sophie welcomed Mel's embrace when she offered it. "Why couldn't he love me enough to walk away from her?"

"So much for not falling in love." Mel patted Sophie's shoulder.

Sophie took a deep shaky breath. "Ashton moving away was a sign that this was never going to work anyway. How can he really love me when he admitted to still having feelings for Lucinda?"

Mel looked at her with an unsure expression on

her face. "I have no fucking idea. I don't think things line up the way they are supposed to unless you make them. You think about things way too much—it even makes me confused. I just know that you can't just keep staring at that painting of him hoping that he'll crawl out of it."

"I know," Sophie sighed. "What time is it? I have to head into the restaurant for my last shift." Sophie stood up and took a deep breath and dried her face.

"Okay. We'll talk about this later…you're not gonna do anything stupid like tell him we don't want his money right?" Mel asked nervously.

"It's a little late for that."

"Good," Mel said relieved as she leaned back in her chair. "Though, maybe you should ask him to explain what is going on with Lucinda. It might make this whole situation clearer."

Chapter Twenty-Eight

When Sophie walked into the restaurant for her last shift she felt a mixture of sorrow and anticipation. She had an attachment to this place after spending so much time within these walls. She had gotten the job when she moved here two years ago. Even though people had come and gone, there were still some she worked with who had been constant in her life during that time. Even with the recent drama with Megan, she would miss this place. There was also the excitement to be entering a new chapter in her life. She knew that this job was only supposed to be temporary. It was never a long-term plan and now life was leading her down another path.

Megan had avoided Sophie since her outburst and Sophie was grateful for it. She wanted to get her job done without having to watch her back. Sophie managed her tables and things moved rather uneventfully through the evening until Sophie approached her last table of the night. Lucinda was sitting in a booth by herself, waiting for her.

Sophie felt her stomach drop as she looked at Lucinda staring back at her. Sophie turned on her heel to find one of the other waitresses to serve her, when Lucinda called after her.

"It's not what you think. I just want to talk to you…promise." Lucinda didn't have the usual menacing energy that she usually exuded. She looked smaller than Sophie remembered her with her shoulders rounded and her small frame tucked behind the table. The only thing Sophie could read was the sadness that had settled around her. Her strawberry blonde hair was cut shorter than Sophie remembered, falling just below her shoulders. "I don't want to start anything."

"I hope you realize it's a little hard for me to believe that with our history." Sophie looked around the quieting restaurant. Sighing in defeat, she slid into the booth next to her. "Talk then," Sophie said with reservation.

"Okay, where do I start? This is not easy for me but I owe Ashton." Lucinda fidgeted with her hands like she was nervous. The gesture surprised Sophie. "My whole life I was never really good at anything but I had my looks and that seemed to get me what I wanted. It's all anyone seemed to care about. Everyone looked up to me and I won't lie, I loved the attention. I loved the power that I had over people but it didn't matter how much makeup I wore or what outfit, I always knew Ashton saw through it all. I wasn't a good person but he stayed with me anyway. He always took care of me…especially when my father died. My father was the only person besides Ashton that saw something more in me than what was on the outside. When he died I was devastated."

Sophie stayed silent as Lucinda spoke. She wasn't even sure where this conversation was going but she found this side of Lucinda endearing. It made her seem real. "I had only just started going back to school after his death when you showed up and something changed in Ashton. There was a fire in his eyes when he looked at you I had never seen before, no matter how much I tried to win his affection. You were this perfect person that I worked so hard to convince people I was. I hated you so much…" Lucinda said the words but they lacked true conviction, as if the feeling was lost to them now.

"He always tried to convince me that he didn't have feelings for you but I knew he was trying to protect you. That is what he has always done. He protects those he cares about. I was a horrible person and I wanted to destroy everything about you because you were everything I was not. He fell for you in one instant. I saw it when you walked into the classroom. I knew he wouldn't break up with me because he knew I needed him. I was struggling with my father's death and I took advantage of his loyalty when I should have let him go. It was me who made up all the rumors and then told everyone it came from Ashton. You believed every word and I loved it. The only reason he was mean to you was because it was the only time you ever acknowledged him. You would fire up. Any other time you would keep your head down and ignore him. To be honest, I was scared you would take Ashton from me and he was all I had."

"I didn't mean to make you feel that way, Lucinda. I just wanted to be left alone," Sophie interjected softly.

"I know. I was a bitch. Fuck it, I'm still the biggest bitch ever but I know I needed to do this. Ashton doesn't deserve this and…neither do you." Lucinda looked a little pained at her confession.

"The day you saw me and Ashton together at the coffee house, we had come from the clinic. I recently found out I'm pregnant. The guy I was with took off when he found out. My mother doesn't want anything to do with a daughter who is pregnant out of wedlock because it doesn't fit into her life plan. I am no longer her perfect little girl. I have no one…except Ashton. He said he would help me out. He drove me to the clinic but I couldn't go through with it. He promised to keep my secret until I can wrap my head around what I'm going to do. He doesn't love me, Sophie, he never did. Not in the way I wanted, at least. I have always felt like a little sister to him that he wanted to protect because he saw the sad, damaged girl on the inside. I knew you were in the coffee shop, that's why I kissed him. The part you missed was when he told me that his heart belongs to you." Lucinda took a deep breath. "He's miserable right now because of me."

"Lucinda—"

"Let me finish before I come to my senses and say something about your ridiculous shoes or something," Lucinda cut her off. Taking a deep breath, she continued. "I have always come between him and what he wants and I don't want to be that girl anymore. I know he loves you and that I have once again gotten in his way. Despite what you might think, I do want him to be happy."

"I appreciate you coming here and saying this, Lucinda. I have to admit this seems very strange to have a conversation with you that was not intended in some way to bring me harm, but I definitely could get used to it." Sophie smiled sincerely. She knew how difficult this must be for Lucinda. "I don't know if it is even possible to fix the mess I made between Ashton and me, but I would like to start over between us."

Lucinda looked at Sophie with a confused expression. "Do you really mean that?"

"Yes, of course. We aren't in high school anymore. Let's leave the past in the past."

"I would like that." Lucinda eyes glistened with unshed tears. "You probably think I deserve the mess I have gotten myself into." Sophie was taken aback by Lucinda's confession. There was desperation in her words that scared Sophie. Lucinda felt lost and alone, it was written all over her. "Why are you being nice to me after all I put you through? This is your chance to hit me while I'm down." Lucinda took a shaky breath.

"My mother raised me as a single mother, so I know how hard it can be. No one should be alone." Sophie reached over and put her hand over Lucinda's. "You are strong and you will get through this."

Lucinda stared at Sophie's hand touching hers. "I don't have any friends, you know." A tear fell down her cheek and she quickly wiped it away. "Or family anymore…"

"For what it's worth, you have me," Sophie encouraged.

Lucinda looked at Sophie with a shocked expression, like she couldn't believe what Sophie just said. Lucinda leaned over and hugged Sophie tightly. "That means a lot. Do you think you can ever forgive me?"

"I already have." Sophie was surprised by Lucinda's affection but she could see that she was broken and Sophie wanted nothing other than to help her. She let go of all the pain Lucinda caused her, letting it fall away. She was amazed to see how deep the relief ran as the weight lifted off her shoulders.

"Ashton will wait for you. He has always been waiting for you since he first saw you. I'm sorry for the way I treated you. You're a good person, Sophie."

They were interrupted when Lori approached their table with a cake in hand and a big bright infectious smile. "Sorry for interrupting but we wanted to wish you good luck, Sophie. We're going to miss you here." Behind Lori's beaming face was everyone else from the restaurant standing behind her, surrounding their table. Sophie looked at everyone who was standing before her to wish her well. She was surprised to see Megan in the group since they hadn't spoken since the incident.

"Thank you. This is so nice of you guys." Sophie

laughed as they set the cake down in front of her.

"You're always welcome back, Sophie," Sam offered brightly as he wrapped his arm around Lori's shoulders. Sophie looked at Lori, who winked at her. Things had progressed between Lori and Sam and Sophie could tell from the looks on their faces that they were happy.

"I love you guys, and don't take this personally, but I hope I never have to come back," Sophie teased, causing everyone to break out in laughter.

"We knew you weren't a lifer." Sam patted Sophie on the shoulder. Lori leaned in and hugged Sophie tightly. "I'm gonna miss you. Don't worry about Megan—she already found a new obsession." Lori nodded toward Megan, who stood beside a new server who had started last week. He was handsome with a rugged appeal, reminding Sophie of a good old fashioned farm boy. Megan had her sights set. If only the poor boy knew what he was in for.

Lucinda stayed while everyone shared the cake and had a few drinks. She seemed friendly and made an effort to mingle with Sophie's friends. When the evening wrapped up, Sophie walked Lucinda out to her car. "Thank you for tonight, Sophie."

"You're welcome. You will stay in touch, right?" Sophie asked, still a little unsure about this new development between them.

"Actually, I have an ultrasound tomorrow..." Lucinda trailed off. She suddenly lost her nerve.

"I'll be there. Let me give you my number," Sophie jumped in, hoping it was what Lucinda was fishing for.

A bright smile spread across her face. "Really?"

"Really." Sophie confirmed.

Lucinda wiped tears from her eyes. "Stupid pregnancy has me all emotional." Sophie was surprised when Lucinda suddenly wrapped her arms around her, squeezing her tightly.

"I honestly never thought we would be here," Sophie confessed.

"I know. It's weird but nice." Lucinda pulled away. "Am I still allowed to tell you how horrible your shoes are, because they really are horrid?"

Sophie shook her head and smiled.

***

"Have you totally lost your *fucking mind*? You can't be serious…tell me you're not serious." Wide-eyed disbelief pulled at Mel's features as they stood outside their cookie shop.

"I'm serious. That's why I'm late." Sophie said. She knew that Mel would have a hard time processing the fact that she had a change of heart where Lucinda was concerned.

"Are we talking about the same cold hearted bitch who made your life miserable? *That* Lucinda?" Mel was waving her hands around dramatically. She looked at Sophie like she had just grown another head.

"Yes, the same Lucinda. I want to help her and I really think we can be friends. Just give her a chance," Sophie insisted.

"What? Are you expecting me to go to her next

doctor's appointment with her too and hold her hand? Be all buddy-buddy with her after what she did? I don't think so," Mel fumed. "Now there is no question you lost your mind."

Sophie grabbed her hand. "Mel, you are my best friend. I need you to understand. I forgave her for the past and I told her that I would be her friend. She's pregnant and alone without any family to help her. This feels right and I need to do this. Please be supportive. Everyone deserves to be loved."

"Argh…don't look at me like that…fine. As long as you promise to love me the most and she won't weasel her way between us. 'Cause if she tries to steal you away from me, it doesn't matter if she's pregnant. There are plenty of places to hit a pregnant woman without harming the baby, like that bitchy face of hers." Mel stomped her foot.

"That's all I ask and who could possibly replace you?" Sophie smiled.

"So true." A smile took over her angry composure and melted it away. "It's funny that you think everyone else deserves to be loved except yourself. You deny yourself the one thing that will make you the happiest."

Sophie didn't know how to respond. Mel was right. She was denying herself the love she felt for Ashton for no other reason than for fear of things she could not control. When Sophie sat beside Lucinda in the hospital room, holding Lucinda's hand, watching the new life growing within her, Sophie realized that she had it all wrong. Love was not something to be scared of. Looking at that little baby she knew it deserved to be loved. That strong little heartbeat was ready to take on life. Sophie knew she shouldn't live her life in fear of what she might lose but instead she should live it for what she could gain. That little baby was proof that hearts were strong and should fight for love because it was what gave life.

"Anyway, we have lots of work to do." Mel climbed up the ladder and pulled down the tarp that was covering their sign. "What do you think?" Mel waved toward their café triumphantly.

Sophie looked up at the sign that was on display for the world to see. "Wow. It looks amazing." Bold lowercase letters spelled **'eat my cOOkie!'** It made her smile to see their vision brought to life. The two o's in the word cookie looked like two large chocolate chip cookies.

"We will talk more about the whole Lucinda thing later but we have a store to put together before your Mom's wedding tomorrow. Come on."

Sophie grabbed a sign they had made up with the opening date and set it out on the sidewalk before she walked back inside to tackle the set up now that the renovations and painting were complete. They were ready to put the final pieces together and make it presentable for opening day only a week away.

***

"That's it. I'm buying a car!" Sophie announced when the bottom of the box gave out and all of the contents dropped onto the floor of the bus on their way home.

"For the love of god, yes!" Mel agreed as she

374

began collecting their papers scattered around their feet. Mel and Sophie had worked all day and the store was now ready to open. The shelves were stocked with supplies and everything was lined up and prepared for opening day.

"What a day…so tired," Mel moaned as she sat down and leaned her head on Sophie's shoulder. Sophie looked around the bus and noticed the other people sitting around them. Most kept to themselves, tuned into their phones and computers and oblivious to anyone else around them. She made eye contact with a man sitting on the other side of the bus, whose eyes were already on her when she looked his way. He was dressed in a pair of jeans and a ragged looking T-shirt. Sophie gave him a polite smile but turned her attention away quickly when he in exchange gave her a very suggestive, creepy expression. It was all she needed to put her plan into motion.

When the bus pulled up to the next stop, Sophie stood up. "Come on."

"What are you doing?" Mel gasped in surprise. "This isn't our stop."

"I'm going to buy a car," Sophie said in a determined tone.

"Right now?" Mel questioned in confusion.

"Right now," Sophie confirmed.

"Okay. This is exciting!" Mel said, following Sophie off the bus. "This is so unlike you…but I like it!"

"Yeah." Sophie smiled at Mel. "Someone told me that I need to do what makes me happy. Right now, a car would make me happy." She winked at

Mel.

"Does that mean you're gonna call him?" Mel asked hesitantly, her eyebrows raised in anticipation.

"One step at a time," Sophie said.

"What happened to using Mrs. Money's car?" Mel skipped beside Sophie.

"I feel guilty using Margaret's car when I'm not working. She pays me way too much as it is, I'm not taking her car. Besides, that thing is worth more than I'll make in my entire life. I'm nervous driving it down the street when I have to pick up her dry cleaning."

"What does guilty mean? I don't think it's something I have ever experienced before." Mel smiled her signature mischievous smile.

"I'm going to give Peter a call and see if he has any advice for buying a car. I think the pair of us will be the perfect equation to be deceived by a sleazy car salesman."

"Sophie? Is everything okay?" Peter spoke quickly on the other end of the line. Sophie had never called Peter before, so she understood his initial response to assume something was wrong.

"Yes. Everything is good. Are you busy?" Sophie suddenly felt nervous.

"No, Sophie, what's up?" She heard the relief in his voice.

"I am standing in Dan's Cars lot, trying to buy a car but I realized I don't know what I'm doing. Mom is as clueless as me when it comes to cars…I was hoping…"

"I'm actually not too far from there," Peter broke

in. "Give me twenty minutes."

"Thanks, Peter."

"Sure thing," he said before he hung up.

"Peter said he would stop over in twenty minutes. Well, we might as well go see what Dan has for us today," Sophie said as they walked into a car lot with a banner *'Dan's Cars'* overhead. There were rows and rows of cars in every color and make lining the square of pavement that designated the used car lot. It looked strangely out of place surrounded by tall office buildings.

"Ooh…look at this one." Mel leaned down and ran her hand seductively over the hood of a faded gold colored car. It looked decades old with oversized dice hung from the rearview mirror. "We would look like porn stars driving around in this beast."

"It looks more like a boat than a car." Sophie shook her head. "I'm going for more of a sophisticated look." Sophie laughed as she continued to eye the cars. It wasn't long before a man in a suit sauntered out to ask them if they needed any help. He wasn't that much older than them. His charm was turned on and he was ready to impress.

"Hello, beautiful ladies. How can I help you today?" The man's face was covered with a few days' growth and his thick wavy hair would make any girl jealous. He had a slyness about him that seemed appropriate for the typical car salesman persona she pictured.

"I was hoping you could show me what my options are."

"It would be my pleasure. I'm Dan." He held out his hand and Sophie took it.

"I'm Sophie, this is Mel. Would you be the Dan from the sign?" Sophie pointed behind her.

"*That* Dan is my father. I'm the new and improved version." He winked playfully.

Sophie followed Dan around the lot as he showed her different options. Mel loved Dan's attention and she made sure he noticed her. Sophie tried not to giggle at Mel's attempt to seduce the best deal from him. Sophie didn't know the first thing about cars or whether to trust the smooth talker in front of her. She was grateful when Peter's police car pulled into the lot.

"Hey kiddo." Peter stepped out of his car in full uniform.

"Hey, Peter. Thanks for coming." Sophie smiled.

Peter engaged with Dan and quickly narrowed Sophie's options down based on what she had in mind. Before Sophie knew it Peter had found her a great deal. Peter insisted on having his own mechanic confirm the condition of the vehicle. He was the closest thing she ever had to a father. It was nice having his support.

Once the deal was finalized Sophie opened the door of her new car and slipped in behind the wheel. "It's official. I am a car owner." Sophie beamed.

Peter chuckled. "You look good behind the wheel but *no speeding*," he warned jokingly.

"Yes, Officer," Sophie laughed. "Peter?" Sophie's tone suddenly turned serious. Sophie looked in her rearview mirror to see that Mel had moved on to flirting with Peter's partner. She had to admit Mel had a talent. She turned back to Peter. "I wanted to say thank you for being there for my mom. I know how much she loves you."

Peter reached in through the window and placed his hand on Sophie's shoulder. "I love your mother very much and I will always be there for her as long as she'll have me. That goes for you too, Sophie. I like that you called me today."

"Me too." Sophie squeezed his hand, still on her shoulder.

"I have to get my partner out of here before he gets in trouble," Peter chuckled, nodding toward Mel and him.

"Good idea," Sophie laughed. "Thanks again."

Peter smiled. "You're welcome. I'm glad I was nearby. Be safe and I'll see you tomorrow for the big event."

"Bye Peter!"

Mel jumped into the passenger's seat a moment later. "This is awesome," she squealed.

"I know." Sophie ran her hands over the steering wheel before she turned the key in the ignition. She buckled her seatbelt.

"I forgot how delicious a man was in uniform." Mel looked back at the police car pulling out of the parking lot.

"He's married, with a baby on the way." Sophie raised her eyebrows.

"I know, he told me. Don't worry, I'm not gonna jump his bones. I just appreciate hot men. Besides, I gotta keep my options open in case Dustin and I don't work out." Mel's enthusiasm waned.

"How are things going with you two?" Sophie asked with curiosity. It seemed like it had been awhile since Mel said anything about their relationship.

"We had a fight," Mel blurted.

"And…" Sophie encouraged her to continue.

"I told him to fuck off and I ran out on him. That was a few days ago. I don't even remember how it started. I haven't answered his calls." Mel sulked and collapsed back into her seat.

"Maybe it's time you should," Sophie gasped.

"Yeah, you're right. I miss him like crazy and I want to get laid." Mel sighed. "Drop me off at his place?"

"Definitely." Sophie turned the music up in the car and a big smile spread across Mel's face as well. They sang along with the radio and laughed until they pulled up in front of Dustin's.

"Thanks, Sophie. Do me a favor and call Ashton. It's nice to hear you laugh again but you still look so sad. I feel like you're gonna shatter at any moment."

Sophie only nodded, unable to bring words to the surface with the mention of Ashton's name. She watched Mel disappear into Dustin's apartment but she didn't leave, instead she pulled her phone from her purse. She stared at the screen for what seemed like a long time before she decided to send Ashton a message.

Sophie: Truth or Dare?

The seconds felt like minutes as they slowly

ticked by…

Ashton: Truth.

Sophie: When are you coming back?

Ashton: I don't know.

Sophie: Your turn.

Ashton: I gotta go.

I'm too late!

Sophie: Please ask me! I pick truth…

Ashton: Bye Sophie.

Sophie: You made me a believer.

Ten minutes.
Twenty minutes. *Respond already!*
Thirty minutes…*please say something.*
One hour…

Chapter Twenty-Nine

Sophie looked in the mirror, retouching the gloss over her red stained lips. It was the exact same color as her dress. It was the day of her mother's wedding and they had spent the entire morning at the spa indulging in beauty treatments, styling, and primping. She looked at her hair as it fell in perfect waves around her shoulders with the top swept up into a beautiful clip her mother had bought for her. It was the first time that Sophie had her makeup professionally done and she loved how the colors played around her eyes.

The contrast to her perfectly polished exterior, the chaos it shielded inside couldn't be more opposite. She smiled at herself in the mirror, trying to make it as genuine as she could. Her mother deserved perfection on her wedding day but everything reminded her of Ashton. *I screwed it all up and now it's too late. He didn't even respond.*

Sophie picked up a bottle of perfume from the

counter. The sweet aroma brightened her thoughts. It was a smell that accompanied countless memories of her mother when she was growing up. She always wore the same scent and it gave Sophie an overwhelming sense of comfort. Sophie wanted to make sure this day was perfect for her.

A knock on the door startled her. She opened it, gasping in surprise when Mel burst into the washroom.

"Mel! What are you doing here?" Sophie didn't even try to contain her shock.

"You sounded a little off this morning. I wanted to check on you." Mel was dressed in a beautiful black and white patterned dress. Sophie smiled at the transformation into a sophisticated woman. The fitted dress accentuated her natural beauty without having her body on display. Her hair was in a sleek style and her makeup soft.

"You look gorgeous, Mel," Sophie complimented. She loved the fact that Mel wanted to impress her mother.

Mel looked down at the dress, smoothing it over her hips. "Yeah, I clean up all right." Mel shrugged. "You're not so bad yourself. No one would be able to tell that you have cried yourself to sleep for the last few weeks.

Sophie dropped her eyes to the floor. "I can't call him. I can't not call him. I feel like I'm stuck." Sophie took a deep breath to stay the tears that threatened to fall. *I will not ruin my makeup! I will not ruin my mother's day!*

"Why can't you just call him, Sophie?" Mel looked at her like it was the simplest solution in the world.

"Because…what if he's better off without me? What if he already moved on? What if he doesn't want me anymore? He didn't respond to my text."

"Sophie, you're being ridiculous!" Mel stomped her foot. "I just want to slap you. He. Still. Wants. You."

"How do you know? He could be moving on and dating other people for all I know…wait? How could you possibly know that?" Sophie looked at Mel with an accusing look.

Mel widened her eyes and then tried to casually dismiss Sophie's question by turning her attention to the perfume on the counter. "Ooh…what's this?"

"No way, Mel. You look guilty. What did you do?" Sophie grabbed her arm and turned Mel to look at her.

"Don't get mad, okay?" Mel said sheepishly. The guilt rolled off her and it made Sophie nervous.

"How can you tell me not to get mad if I have no idea what you did?" Sophie leaned on the counter and took a deep calming breath.

"I may have called him." Mel's lips turned up in an awkward smile.

"You called Ashton?" Sophie gasped in shock. "When? How could you do that? What did you say? What did he say?" The questions tumbled out of Sophie's mouth without end.

"Last night. You have been miserable since he left. I didn't know what else to do. Don't be mad, please. I watched you pick up the phone a million times. I know you wanted to call him, so I did it for you."

Sophie squeezed her eyes shut. "I think I am going to cry…slap me." Sophie breathed tightly.

"What?" Mel asked unsurely.

"Do you know how expensive this makeup was? Seriously, slap me so I don't cry." Sophie opened her eyes and looked at Mel expectantly. Without any more hesitation, Mel reached out and slapped Sophie's face.

"Ouch!" Sophie gasped. "That hurt!"

"You told me to slap you," Mel said defensively.

"Yeah, but did you have to do it so hard? Not to mention that you seemed to enjoy that way too much." Sophie touched her tender cheek.

"Well, your face is *annoyingly* perfect. I'm not gonna lie, I have thought about it a few times." Mel threw her hands on her hips.

"*Mel*." Sophie rolled her eyes. Sophie looked in the mirror. Her left cheek was now bright red. "Great," she mumbled. "You're gonna have to do the other side so I match for the photos."

"I told him that you have been completely miserable," Mel admitted quickly. "That you spoke to Lucinda and you two were friends now. The past is the past and you were ready to dive into his hotness and hold on forever…and I told him that if he didn't come back I was going to get some of the bouncers from the strip club to make you forget about him."

"What!" Sophie gasped before Mel reached up slapped Sophie across the other cheek. "*Ouch!*" Sophie reached up to cover the sting of her cheek.

"Charles has a huge dick. I can guarantee a few minutes with him and you'll forget everything else."

There was a knock on the door. "Sophie, hun? Are you all right in there?"

"Yes, Mom. We'll be right out," Sophie said in a controlled voice as she eyed Mel harshly.

"Call him," Mel instructed before she pulled open the door. "She'll be right out, Rachael. She's just going to call Ashton first." Mel looked back at Sophie as she walked out the door. Sophie's mother stayed in the doorway with her hand on the door.

"It's about time." Her mother gave her a knowing smile. "Take your time. I have a few minutes before I have to get in my dress." She pulled the door closed, leaving Sophie alone in the washroom.

Sophie let out the breath she was holding. When she finally got her feet to cooperate she reached for her phone with shaking fingers. She held her breath and listened to the ring. She was met with his answering machine. His beautiful voice made a sob escape her throat. She hung up without leaving a message, turned her phone off, and tucked it away in her purse.

***

"You look so beautiful, Mom." Sophie said with teary eyes as she fastened her mother's dress in front of a full length mirror.

"My favorite person in this whole world made this dress for me."

"I'm really trying not to cry until after the photos. Don't push me or you will have to live with a mascara-streaked maid of honor in your pictures."

Sophie took a deep breath.

"You would still be the most beautiful girl in the world." Her mother gave her a hug.

"I love you, Mom."

"I love you too, baby girl, more than you will ever know." Her mother swept her up in a hug.

"Look at the two of you." They both turned to see the other bridesmaids in the doorway, wearing their matching black dresses. "Hold on. I need a picture." They were surrounded by flashes as Sophie helped her mother with all of the final touches.

***

Sophie took a deep breath as she walked through the two large wooden doors. The aisle was carpeted beneath their feet and covered with red rose petals as she slowly made her way toward the altar. Sophie smiled at all the familiar faces. When she reached the front of the church she turned around to watch her mother make her appearance. The church was full of people who had come today to watch her marry the man who owned her heart.

Rachael walked down the aisle by herself. Her father was not there to give her away. She believed that since she had to find her way in life without her parents' help, she would give herself away. Her mother was a source of strength and love that Sophie would always cherish. She loved her mother beyond words. Peter had tears in his eyes as he watched his bride walk toward him. His love for her mother was written all over him, it was beautiful.

The ceremony was wonderful and everyone was brought to tears as Rachael and Peter exchanged the vows they'd written for each other. The reception followed immediately after the photographs were taken. Sophie sat with Mel and Dustin at their table and watched her mother and Peter dance to their first song as husband and wife. The room was beautifully decorated with black and white accents around. White twinkling lights were suspended from the ceiling. It looked like a starry night, the effect was magical. Red roses were the only color that was incorporated into the decorations, placed on tables and around the room.

"They really are a beautiful couple." Sophie watched them with a warm heart.

"They sure are." Mel reached over, took Sophie's hand, and squeezed it tight.

When the song came to a close an announcement called for Sophie to come to the dance floor over the speakers. Sophie stood up when Peter and her mother waved her over. "Peter would like to share a dance with you."

"Of course. I would love to." Sophie smiled. Peter stretched out his hand in an exaggerated display of formality. Sophie laughed as she accepted his request. Peter swept her around the dance floor, causing both of them to laugh and enjoy the moment.

"I promise you, Sophie, I will take care of your mother every day for the rest of my life," Peter said as they settled into the rhythm of the music.

"You are a good man, Peter. I have no doubt that my mother is in good hands," Sophie said with true belief in his words.

"I know that I'll never be your father, but I want you to know I'm here for you." He leaned in and kissed Sophie's forehead. Sophie hugged him tight. He returned the gesture by wrapping his arms around her in a warm embrace.

"That means a lot."

Before they knew it the song faded into the next and the dance floor became flooded with people moving to the music. Her mother returned and Sophie left the happy couple to enjoy each other while she found Mel and Dustin who were among the bodies dancing.

Sophie lost track of time while dancing as one song flowed into the next. It wasn't until an announcement was made that the band was going to take a break that she stopped to take a breath and get a drink. Sophie collapsed in her chair and sipped on her wine. Mel and Dustin sat down beside her with their drinks in hand, laughing as they carried on. Sophie's face was beginning to hurt from laughing so much. It was nice to let go and enjoy the evening.

Mel elbowed Sophie in the side. "Ouch. What was that for?" She glared at Mel and noticed her attention was elsewhere.

Sophie turned to see what had Mel so captivated. Ashton stood in the middle of the dance floor, his piercing blue eyes trained on her. The entire room faded away.

Sophie stood up immediately, walking toward him. The dance floor had thinned to only a few people as she approached him.

Time apart did not lesson the pull that she felt toward Ashton. It was still so strong and undeniable. Every part of her body wanted to be closer to him. Every part of her craved him. He was the center of her world and she was falling into the depths of his beautiful eyes and this time she was all in. There was no more holding back. He was her heart and she was taking it back. Sophie knew the entire room was watching them but the only thing she could focus on was the gorgeous man in front of her that only had eyes for her.

He looked nervous as he looked down at her. Sophie stood only inches away—she only had to reach out and she could touch the one thing she wanted the most in the whole world. He was standing before her in his impossible perfection with his stormy eyes searching hers.

"Sorry I missed your call. I was on a plane." Ashton smiled tentatively.

"You came back."

"For you." Ashton brushed her hair from her face, letting his fingers trail across her cheek.

"I love you, Ashton King," Sophie confessed in a rush.

"You don't know how much I wanted to hear that." His face broke into the most beautiful smile that Sophie had ever seen. "Did you hear that, everyone? Sophie Rogers loves me!" The room erupted into cheers as Ashton grabbed Sophie in his arms, squeezing her tight before he set her down and looked into her eyes. He cupped her face before bringing his lips to hers, soft and slow, savoring the kiss that was too long denied them.

"I'm so sorry for…" Sophie began but Ashton cut her off.

"Just tell me that you love me. I want to hear you say it again," he whispered as he held her close.

"I love you."

"That is the most beautiful thing I have ever heard." He brought her hand up to his mouth to kiss it.

"I'm glad you like it because I'll be saying it a lot." Sophie beamed.

"You guys are so disgustingly cheesy!" Mel screamed across the room and everyone erupted into laughter.

Epilogue

Mr. Walters,
I am pleased to say I have been proven wrong after all.
Sophie Rogers

"Who has you so captivated with your phone this evening?" Ashton asked as he slipped his arm around Sophie's waist.

"I just had to send an email to one of my professors, unfinished business," Sophie explained as she hit send.

"Is that so? I have some unfinished business that I would like to take care of." Ashton smiled wickedly as he leaned in and kissed Sophie's lips.

"If you guys keep this up I'm gonna lose my supper," Mel huffed.

"It's not so bad. It's nice to know someone's getting lucky." Lucinda looked uncomfortable in her dress that was visibly too tight around her stomach, now round with child. Lucinda still refused to modify her wardrobe to accommodate her pregnancy, insisting that maternity clothes were too frumpy. Sophie knew it was a battle that Lucinda would soon lose.

Things were not always smooth sailing when it came to Mel and Lucinda. With both having strong personalities, they managed to butt heads more often than not, but Sophie loved knowing that they were making an effort. She could tell they were slowly growing on each other, especially now with the news that Corbin had recently been arrested under drug trafficking charges and would now be spending time behind bars. Mel had been on cloud nine lately.

Lucinda's pregnancy was progressing as well as could be expected. Though she did tend to panic with every pound that she gained but it never stopped her from showing up at the cookie shop and eating a dozen cookies in one sitting. She hadn't spoken to her family since she decided to keep the baby but Ashton and Sophie were committed to filling the role of her much needed support system. She was extremely grateful for their support and Sophie was glad she could be there to help. Sophie was amazed at how her relationship with Lucinda had turned full circle. Lucinda was still cynical and tended to complain about everything but Sophie loved their new dynamic of mutual respect. She was going to make a great mother.

The grand opening at their cookie café was a huge success. Sophie and Mel were thrilled that they were so well received in the area. They had a growing list of regulars and their name was spreading to the point that they had to hire additional help to keep up with demand.

"Well, it looks like you got a little *too* lucky," Mel mumbled.

"*Watch it*," Lucinda warned.

"Okay, ladies," Sophie interjected lightly. "Let's at least pretend we're civilized." Sophie leaned into Ashton. She would never get used to how his touch affected her.

Sophie looked at her paintings displayed in the same gallery as some very well-known artists in the city. Falon's art gallery was a huge warehouse with a modern polished industrial feel that gave a perfect backdrop for the range of art displayed. A maze of walls were constructed to hold all the pieces. The building itself was a piece of art.

Sophie only sipped her wine but felt giddy from the excitement that bubbled within her. She was nervous how her work would be received among all the other beautiful pieces. When sold stickers began marking her paintings, the worries faded away.

"I tried to buy the portrait of me but I was told that you refuse to sell it." Ashton raised his brow.

"Nope. That one I want to keep hanging on my wall," Sophie said, looking at the painting Ashton referred to. She would never part with it, like she would never part with the man himself.

"Well then, maybe I have to make your walls mine as well." Ashton pulled her closer against his side. "Truth or Dare?"

"What are you up to? Dare." Sophie smiled suspiciously, not sure where Ashton was going with this.

"Move in with me."

"You want that picture so much that you want me to move in so you can have it?" Sophie narrowed her eyes.

"It does look incredibly hot," Ashton teased. "But no, I want *you* that much." He kissed her lips. "You and only you. So will you make me a very happy man and move in with me?"

"I never turn down a dare," Sophie offered playfully.

"Good to know."

"Sophie dear, you must be so pleased." Margaret approached them with her mom and Peter close behind. All of them offered warm, welcoming smiles.

"I am. This is a perfect evening," Sophie gushed.

"I'm so proud of you, honey." Sophie's mother wrapped her arm around Sophie's shoulder.

"Yes, it seems you're making quite the name for yourself," Margaret commented excitedly.

"Thanks to you."

"Heavens no, don't give me any credit." Margaret waved off her comment. "It was all you."

"Oh, before I forget, since everyone is here I want to say thank you for coming tonight. It means a lot that you're here to support me." Sophie looked at all the people standing around her that she held close to her heart. "I love you guys."

"We love you too, Sophie."

"Since this party is winding down, why don't we move this love fest to our cookie shop and eat some treats?" Mel broke in. "I made something special for tonight to celebrate."

"Sounds good to me," Sophie said excitedly.

"Me too." Lucinda suddenly brightened with the comment of food. "I'm starving."

Ashton wrapped his arm around Sophie's shoulders and leaned in close before he presented her with a bouquet of flowers. "Ah…thank you!" Sophie took the flowers and looked at the card.

Love is not being with someone because you think you can be happy with that person, but because without that person you know you can never be.

"It's a new quote for you about love. I didn't like your old one. Besides, it no longer fit your outlook since you are now a believer." Ashton grinned. "It was either that or say how much I want to rip your clothes off because you look so fucking hot in the dress."

"It's perfect."

"You're perfect, Sophie. I love you."

"And I love you."

Acknowledgements

A huge thank you to:

Ryan McNeil, my husband,
for his unwavering support.
My parents, who are always my biggest fans.
My children, for inspiring me.
Limitless Publishing, for giving me the
opportunity to share this book with the world.
These were only words upon the pages,
until you brought them to life.
Thank you.

About the Author

Aimee McNeil was born and raised in Nova Scotia, Canada, where she continues to live today with her husband and three children. She is a stay-at-home mother that loves every colorful moment with her family.

Aimee spends most of her free time indulging in her love of writing. You can also find her lost in the pages of a good book, or making a mess with her paints. Aimee loves to explore anything that promotes creativity. It is one of the many reason she enjoys writing.

Facebook:
https://www.facebook.com/aimeemcneilswriting

Twitter:
https://twitter.com/aimeeswriting

Website:
http://aimeemcneilswriting.blogspot.ca/